Child *of the* Mist

Child
of the
Mist

Kathleen Morgan

These Highland Hills
Book 1

Published by Fleming H. Revell
a division of Baker Publishing Group
P.O. Box 6287, Grand Rapids, MI 49516-6287

Printed in the United States of America

Library of Congress Cataloging-in-Publication Data
Morgan, Kathleen, 1950–
Child of the mist / Kathleen Morgan.
p. cm. — (These highland hills ; bk. 1)
ISBN 0-8007-5963-X (pbk.)
1. Scotland—History—16th century—Fiction. 2. Highlands (Scotland)—Fiction.
I. Title. II. Series.
PS3563.O8647C484 2004
813'.54—dc22 2004020704

To my sister Susan.
A beautiful, loving, and very special person.
I'm honored—and humbled—to be your big sister.

Prologue

March, 1563

Kilchurn Castle, Argyllshire, Scotland

"N-Niall!"

The weak but insistent cry rose above the muffled sobbings, carrying across the large, stone-walled bedchamber to the fireplace. A man, tall and powerful, jerked upright. With a resolute straightening of his shoulders, he released his white-knuckled grasp on the mantel and was at the bed in a few quick strides. Waving aside the midwife and maidservants, he lowered himself onto the soft down comforter. Gently, he grasped his wife's hand.

"Aye, lassie?" Try as he might, Niall couldn't hide the catch in the dark register of his voice.

Her slender fingers squeezed his. "Och, my braw, sweet Campbell." She smiled wearily up at him. "I'm so verra sad, I am . . . to leave ye. I'd never willingly cause ye such pain . . ."

He gathered her to him. "Wheesht, lassie. Save yer strength for what matters. Ye . . . yer healing."

"N-nay," she said, her voice quavering. "It isn't time . . . for false hopes. I pray only that our babe lives—" A sharp hiss of pain escaped as yet another contraction shuddered through her.

Niall swallowed hard against his angry, helpless anguish. *Dear God, why must she suffer so? Give* me *the pain. Let* me *bear it.*

His grasp on her tightened, and he willed all the strength of his heart, his body, into hers. God forgive him, but he'd sacrifice the babe if only he could keep his bonny wife. How would he go on without her? She *must* live. She must . . .

"Ye m-must go on. Take another wife." Her eyes, bright with understanding, stared up at him from a waxen yet still hauntingly lovely countenance. "A wife . . . who'll give ye . . . a son. A wife . . . to love . . . as ye've loved me."

"Love again?" Niall's bitter laugh pierced the air. "And how can that be, when ye're the only one for me? Nay." Vehemently, he shook his head. "There'll be no other—now or ever!"

"P-promise me! Promise—"

Her words were lost in a strangled scream. Her eyes widened in sudden comprehension. "The babe. Och, sweet husband. At last . . . our babe comes!"

For one final, exquisitely tender instant they clung to each other. Love, deep and bittersweet in this moment of truth, arced between them. Then there were hands, pushing them apart, drawing Niall away.

"Yer pardon, m'lord," came an anxious voice. "It's time. It's women's work now. Step aside."

The tortured sounds followed Niall as he stumbled back to the hearth. Muted cries, choking sobs, mingled with the snapping, crackling clamor of the hungry fire. Time passed with lumbering slowness as Niall stared into the agitated flames, hearing it all from some place far away, even as the night's horror charred its memory into his soul. Never had he hurt so, not from any wound in battle, not from . . .

He paused. The sounds had ceased. His ears strained for some word, a babe's first cry—anything. There was nothing.

Niall turned. His anguished gaze sought the form in the bed. She was still now, her beloved features relaxed, peaceful. A tight, smothering sensation constricted his chest. He wrenched his attention to the women surrounding her.

All but one averted their eyes. Niall's glance riveted on her.

Old Agnes, his wife's loyal maidservant, returned his gaze, the answer to his question flickering despondently in her eyes. A shudder wracked Niall's big, hard-muscled frame. He shook his head, his black mane of hair grazing his shoulders in a movement of tortured disbelief.

A cry rose in his throat, tearing past the strict control, the years of well-schooled discipline. His glance moved back to the frail, lifeless form in the bed, oblivious to the small bundle of white lying in her arms.

"Nay!"

The shout echoed across the room, reverberating off the walls to carry far beyond the chamber's thick wooden door. With staggering, stumbling strides, Niall returned to the bed, throwing himself down to gather his wife into his arms. Soundless spasms shook his body as he rocked the limp form to and fro, murmuring her name.

✦

Quietly, the servants drew back to afford the grieving husband a semblance of privacy. They stood there, huddled in the shadows, uncertain what to do. All, that is, but one.

An ebony-haired maid slipped from the room. As she closed the chamber door, her glance swept the dim, torch-lit corridor. A beckoning movement from a dark corner caught her eye. With a knowing smile, she scurried over.

"She's dead then?" a deep voice demanded.

The girl nodded.

"And the bairn?"

"Stillborn, m'lord."

A mirthless sound rose from the shadows. "Good. Then there's still time for the misfortunes of *my* family to be righted. Still time for the clan chieftainship to pass from Niall Campbell to me." He chuckled, an icy rim of triumph sharpening his voice. "Aye. Time enough indeed . . ."

I

April, 1564

Castle Gregor, Western Perthshire, Scotland

Anne MacGregor paused on the castle parapet walk, gathering her long, woman's plaid about her. Swirling vapors blanketed the winter-browned land, filling the low hollows and rills, curling restlessly about the trees to spread ever onward in an eerie sea of fog. She smiled and turned to the man beside her.

"Fortunately, the mists are heavy this day. It'll cover our going and, hopefully, my return as well." Anne motioned toward the stout rope dangling over the side. "Come, Donald. Lead on."

Wordlessly, the young, shabbily clad Scotsman scrambled over and down the wall, then held the rope taut as Anne nimbly followed. They hurried into the enshrouding whiteness. Until they were well out of earshot of the clansmen walking guard on the fortress battlements, their journey was swift and silent.

Grasping his long, gnarled walking stick, Donald plowed through the dense mists as if he saw through them, his steps sure and bold from years of traversing the beloved terrain. Anne, not quite so certain, kept close company, her large leather bag of herb powders, potions, and salves clutched tightly at her side. Clan MacGregor might be nicknamed the "Children of the Mist," but one false step in the frequently impenetrable whiteness could still be dangerous, if not actually fatal.

Her thoughts raced ahead, planning the childbirth preparations. It was Fiona's first, and Donald's young wife was frightened half to death. Only the promise Anne would attend her had calmed the girl's fears.

Though barely eighteen, Anne MacGregor was already renowned for her skills in the healing arts. Both noble and poor alike called for her in their hour of need and, unstintingly, she gave to one and all. *Aye, one and all,* Anne mused with a fleeting twinge of pain, *and still the cruel tales about me persist.*

"I'm grateful, ma'am." Donald slowed his steps to hers. "I know yer father forbade ye to leave the castle. If it wasn't my Fiona's time, I'd have never asked . . ."

A pang of guilt shot through Anne. Alastair MacGregor, clan chief and doting sire, had always given her free rein. Still, though she well understood his motives for now forbidding her to leave the castle, it couldn't be helped. At least not this time.

She had made a vow to Fiona long before the cattle raids had started up again, and was honor bound to keep it. The word of a MacGregor was sacred. Marauding Campbell reivers or no, she'd see it through. Her father would understand, if there were ever need to tell him.

Anne smiled up at her companion. "Dinna fash yerself, my friend. It isn't yer fault the savage Campbells roam our lands. Life must go on in spite of them, though I fear they'll never let up until they've stolen every bit of MacGregor holdings—the thieving, heartless knaves!"

"Knaves?" Donald's lips twitched. "Och, that's too kind a word for the likes of them. And most especially for that young Campbell heir." He shot her a worried glance. "I only wish ye'd worn yer short sword. A bodice knife is nigh useless against an armed warrior. And they don't call him the Wolf of Cruachan without reason. Why, he's the most bloodthirsty, murderous—"

"Don't speak of him!" A sudden chill coursed through Anne. Instinctively, she touched the small, sheathed dagger nestled between her breasts. It was enough to be out, virtually defenseless in such dangerous times, without having Donald dwell on the most feared Campbell of all.

Her pace quickened. "Time's short and Fiona needs us. We've more important things to concern us than some churlish Campbells. Besides, they haven't raided MacGregor lands in over a fortnight. Surely we've naught to fear on such an early morn."

"Aye, ma'am." Her sturdy companion glanced uneasily about him. "As ye say. There's naught to fear."

✦

"That's it. That's my girl," Anne said, gripping Fiona's hand in hers. "Ye're a braw, braw lassie and will soon have yer sweet babe. Are the pains still strong? Then take a breath and push again."

Fiona glanced up, a weak, trusting smile lighting her face. "Aye. A sweet babe," she whispered. Then, tensing, she bore down with all her might. The contractions soon passed and she fell back, exhausted.

Anne lifted a cup to the girl's lips. "Drink a bit more, lassie. The raspberry leaf tea will hasten yer birthing."

The brew was obediently sipped before Fiona fell into a deep slumber. It wouldn't be long before the next pains came, Anne knew, but until then rest was the best thing for a laboring mother.

She looked about her. It was long past darkness, the day having come and gone. She hunched her shoulders in an effort to ease the ache of hours spent crouched beside Fiona, then tucked an errant strand of russet-colored hair behind her ear. Glancing down at the young peasant woman, she sighed. Dear, frightened, trusting Fiona.

Wearily, she scanned the shabby little croft house. Despite Fiona's untiring efforts, the thatch-and-clay dwelling was little more than a hovel. *What a life to bring a wee babe into. The only bed a mound of peat covered with a coarse blanket, the air so smoke-laden one can hardly draw a breath without choking.*

If only there were more we could do for our people. The thought stirred anew the old, angry frustration. Her father tried, but the years of endless feuding had worn him down. The MacGregors were no match for the cursed Campbells—never had been—and still their enemies persisted.

Her hands balled into tight little fists. Would they never cease until they had stolen all her clan possessed? If there were but a way to stop them . . .

Fiona stirred, a sleepy grimace twisting her face. *The pains*, Anne thought. *They come again.*

A damp blast of air swirled through the tiny cottage. She glanced up. Donald walked in, his arms laden with squares of dried peat to stoke the small hearth fire. At that instant Fiona moaned, her eyes snapping open in sudden anguish.

"Blessed Saints! I . . . I . . . The babe!"

Anne scooted down to check her, then looked up at Donald. "It's time. Come. Help me."

She motioned toward Fiona's head. "Hold her, talk to her while I—"

A scream of terror, followed immediately by others, pierced the night air. Rough, angry voices mingled with frantic cries. The staccato rhythm of hoofbeats pounded through the village. A hoarse shout of "Cruachan!" rose from the tumult of noise, slicing through the thin walls to the three people within.

At the dreaded war cry, Anne and Donald's gazes met. The Campbells were back and raiding the village.

Donald rose. "I must help defend our people."

"And what good would it do?" Anne bluntly demanded. "If they mean to murder us, we've no chance. Mayhap they'll be satisfied with the animals. Stay, Donald. No matter what happens, ye're more use here than outside."

Indecision flickered in the young peasant's eyes, then he sighed his acquiescence. "Ye're right. If I'm to die, I first want to see my wee one."

The minutes passed as they worked, Donald encouraging his wife while Anne struggled with the slowly emerging infant. Her heart leaped to her throat when the head appeared, the cord tight about the neck. It was vital the babe be free of the choking noose as quickly as possible, but nothing Anne did hastened the emergence of the shoulders, which suddenly seemed too large for easy passage.

Sweat beaded her brow as she struggled with the difficult birth, praying to God to help her as she encouraged the straining mother. At last the shoulders slipped free. The babe was born.

The tiny girl child lay there, unmoving, her body blue and lifeless. Frantically, Anne worked to tie and cut the cord, then gently rubbed the infant dry. The babe remained silent.

Anne's gaze lifted to the two anxious parents. "I . . . I can't . . ." She stopped, mesmerized by their pleading expressions. She was all they had.

In an instant slowed in time Anne harked back to the day Fiona had first revealed her pregnancy, of the look of joy and anticipation on the young woman's face, of her eager plans. They had so little, Fiona and Donald, but they were rich in generosity and love. Of that, they had an abundance, for each other and for their babe.

She had to do something.

Anne turned back to the limp little form. Her gaze scanned the tiny, perfectly shaped girl. *Dear Lord Jesus,* she silently implored. *Help me. I beg Ye. Show me what to do.*

Anne leaned closer, her own breath wafting over the babe. A sudden impulse filled her. Dared she share the life-sustaining air from her own body? Dare she even try? Yet, dare she not?

She lifted the little girl and, as if compelled by some force beyond her, settled her mouth over that of the baby. Tentatively at first, then more confidently when she saw the tiny chest rise with each breath, she blew small puffs into the infant. At first nothing happened, the only sound her own panting breaths mingling with the ragged rasps of the two parents. Then, after what seemed an eternity, the babe gasped, then choked, uttering a strangled cry.

The sound, weak at first, grew in strength until it filled the small croft house. And with each shuddering, indignant little breath, the joy, the immense satisfaction, grew within Anne. She lifted her gaze to Fiona and Donald, eager to share their happiness. But their glances, bright with terror, were no longer directed at her.

Anne whirled, steeling herself for the sight she knew must lie behind her. She could never have prepared herself, however, for the look of unmitigated revulsion on the face of the tartan-clad man standing in the doorway. Gleaming with a half-mad light, he riveted the full force of his stare upon her.

"Witch! Vile, devil-worshiping witch!"

The man with the crazed eyes shoved Anne forward, sending her sprawling in the dirt outside the croft house. She tried climbing to her feet but, with her hands now bound behind her and the hindrance of her long skirt, she slipped and fell again. Her thick hair tumbled loose, falling about her face and into her eyes.

Anne fought to catch her breath. The nightmare dogging all her waking moments had finally come to pass. The vicious rumors, the unkind tales about her healing skills, had found her at last.

She was to die—condemned as a witch.

Flinging back her hair, she stared up into a dozen hostile, torch-lit faces. Campbell men. Anne's breath caught in her throat. In their eyes gleamed superstitious fear—and an absolute certainty of death.

The injustice of it all welled up within her, mingling with her fierce MacGregor pride. From somewhere, from some place buried deep within, a blazing anger burst forth.

Anne glared at them, and for an instant she thought she saw the raiders quail. Good. If they feared her for the powers they imagined she possessed, so be it. She had naught to lose.

"Be gone, ye cowardly, thieving knaves!"

She climbed to her feet, noting, from the corner of her eye, a large form—another Campbell?—edge into her line of vision. It was of little concern, one man more or less. She turned the full force of her gaze on the clansmen already facing her.

Anne threw back her shoulders and stood there, defiantly proud. "Ye trespass at yer risk, for this village is mine. Do ye imagine binding my hands will save ye? Think again, Campbells, fools and cowards that ye be!"

A low, angry growl rumbled through the men. Anne knew she had stung their fierce Highland pride by questioning their courage. She also knew she was playing a dangerous game threatening them with powers she didn't possess. Their affronted dignity might yet override their fear of witches, inciting them to attack her in a mindless rage. Yet if the man with the crazed eyes was their leader, she was already as good as dead.

"Come forward, any who dare face me," she cried. "I grow impatient with yer girlish fears." Slowly, she surveyed each man. "Och now, my wee laddies, won't even one of ye step forward?"

The Campbell with the strange look in his eyes made a hesitant movement in her direction. He withdrew his sword from its scabbard. All gazes, Anne's included, turned to him.

"Aye?" Her hands clenched until her nails scored her palms, but she managed to maintain her air of feigned indifference. "And what does this wee bairn think he can do against me?" She laughed. "Is he the best of ye then?"

The man leaped forward, his eyes blazing with an insane rage. Before Anne could dodge him, he was upon her, roughly grabbing her by the hair to force her to her knees, his sword hand arcing high above his head.

Och, sweet Jesus, I'm going to die! Anguish squeezed her heart.

Nevermore to see the beloved heath bloom on the hills. Nevermore to gaze upon the snow-capped peaks of MacGregor land. Nevermore to feel the warmth of her father's arms . . .

"Enough, Hugh!" a deep-timbred voice cut through the air.

The man hesitated, his hand twisting painfully in Anne's hair. For an instant, she thought he'd strike her anyway. Then slowly, blessedly, his grip loosened. With one last, vicious kick that sent her sprawling into the dirt, he stepped away. She heard the rasp of metal as he resheathed his sword, then the tread of another's footsteps moving toward her.

Anne struggled to rise, but the sharp pain in her side kept her gasping on her knees. Tossing the hair from her eyes, she satisfied herself with gazing up at the two men now standing before her.

His hand still gripping his sword hilt, Hugh glared at another tall Campbell, also wrapped in a belted plaid. The bulk of the fabric, forming both kilt and mantle, only added to the other man's imposing size and aura of power. As Anne's glance scathingly raked him, a realization flashed through her. *He* was the raiding party's leader.

He looked to be in his early thirties, with thick, gleaming black hair that just grazed his shoulders. His nose was straight, his jaw square and stubborn, and his full, firm lips had a cynical twist as he quietly listened to his compatriot's rantings. His eyes, when his glance briefly followed Hugh's gesture in her direction, flashed tawny-brown, intense, and coldly assessing.

Once more, anger filled her. The villain, the rogue! How dare he look at her as if she were some piece of vermin, because he was Campbell and she MacGregor! She opened her mouth to berate him, then thought better of it.

"My orders haven't changed," he was calmly saying. "No MacGregor will suffer unless they raise a hand against us. We came for their livestock and naught more."

"And ye're a fool if ye let this witch live," Hugh spat, drawing near so none but the three of them could hear. "Ye know the law demands her death. Will ye go against it?"

✝✝

"Hold yer tongue, man!" His leader's voice slashed through the air. "Ye cut close in calling me a fool. Cousin or no, if ye utter one word more—"

At the ominous tone, the color drained from Hugh's face. "I-I meant no offense." He began to back away. "Do what ye want with the witch. It's on yer soul, not mine."

The dark-haired leader watched him go, then turned to where Anne was still kneeling on the ground. He pulled her to her feet.

For a long moment they faced each other. His cool gaze seemed not to miss anything, from her tousled hair and defiant stare, to the torn and dirty dress. A strange, indefinable light flickered momentarily in the brown depths, then died.

His hand moved to her breasts. For the space of a sharply inhaled breath, Anne thought he meant to ravish her right there before his men. Then he withdrew her bodice knife.

"Turn. Give me yer hands."

The order was brusque, emotionless. Anne obeyed. It wasn't the time to argue or curse him for being a Campbell. She had barely escaped death, and the tone of his voice warned that his patience had worn thin. Cold metal touched her as he cut through her bonds. Then she was free.

Anne glanced down to rub her hands. "I'll not be thanking the likes of ye, for it'll never make up for what ye've done here." She looked up at him. "Nonetheless, I owe ye a debt."

His mouth quirked. "A debt? Between Campbell and MacGregor? I think not, lassie. There can never be aught between us but the deepest enmity."

He flipped the knife in his hand and offered it back to her, handle first. Wordlessly, she accepted it, then watched him turn and walk away. His long, muscular legs, bare beneath his kilt, swiftly carried him to the black stallion waiting nearby. In one agile leap he mounted, then reined his horse about to look at her.

"Though I admire yer spirit, ye're an impertinent, foolish wench to taunt my men. Mark me well. I didn't spare ye because I feared ye, for I don't believe in witches. But if our paths ever cross again, think twice before opening yer mouth. We Campbells don't take kindly to disrespect—especially from MacGregors."

With a wave of his hand, he signaled his men forward. Out of the village they rode, driving the stolen MacGregor stock before them.

Her knife still clasped in her hand, Anne watched them go, filled with such a powerful yet helpless rage that she momentarily forgot everything she had ever learned at her mother's knees of Christian love and forgiveness. *Curse ye foul Campbells! Curse yer thieving, heartless ways!* she silently screamed at their retreating backs. *And, most of all, curse the dark, arrogant man who leads ye!*

✦

Alastair MacGregor reread the missive one last time, then crushed it in his fist and threw it onto the fire. Recalling the scribbled words, a fierce emotion flared in his breast. Was it possible? Dare he hope for a way to end the feud before MacGregor pride was irretrievably broken, ground into dust beneath Campbell heels?

Yet as dearly as he yearned for peace, dared he believe, dared he trust, the man whom he awaited even now—a hated Campbell, assured, just this once, safe passage through Castle Gregor? How could anyone trust a clan that so blithely instigated a vicious feud during the happy occasion of a marriage feast, refusing to see any side but their own?

He shook his head despairingly. Nay, it wasn't likely any good would come of this night's meeting, yet what else—

A fist rapped at the door. MacGregor wheeled about, paused to stare at the portal, then, squaring his shoulders, strode resolutely toward it. A man, shrouded in a rain-soaked MacGregor tartan, was shown in.

Alastair shut the door and bolted it behind him. He walked to a small table that held a whiskey decanter and several cups, then glanced over his shoulder. "Do ye fancy a dram of the potents to chase the chill from yer bones?"

"Aye, that I do."

He poured a liberal dose into two cups, then as an afterthought sweetened his with a splash more. Tonight of all nights, he'd need every bit of courage he could muster.

The two men sipped their drinks silently, allowing Alastair a moment more to assess his visitor. The MacGregor tartan had been his idea. He wanted no one to suspect what was afoot. His guest's face, however, was difficult to make out. Despite the fire's warmth, the man seemed reluctant to remove the plaid from his head and shoulders.

He doesn't wish his identity known.

The realization sent an inexplicable chill down Alastair's spine. He was a cool one, and no mistake. Whatever he was up to, the man didn't care to be implicated.

Suddenly, MacGregor wanted this night's meeting done with as quickly as possible. He cleared his throat. "Yer letter spoke of an offer. A plan to end the feuding between Clan Campbell and the Children of the Mist. What exactly might that be?"

"The Campbell's ailing and won't last the summer. With a new chief comes new policies—and an end to the feud."

"And do I look that big a fool? Niall Campbell will never end a feud his father began. If ye've come to offer me hope the Wolf will go against his sire, ye can leave the way ye came and be making it quick!"

"And who was saying Niall Campbell will be the next chief?"

Alastair tilted his head to study the man before him. "He's tanist and the chosen successor. Short of an untimely death . . ."

Teeth gleamed in the mantle's shadow. "Aye, an untimely death. Niall leads many raids on yer lands. If ye were to know in advance when and where he'd strike, ye could set yer own men there. Niall's band is always small. Outnumber them and ye could kill them all—Niall included. Then the Campbell would be forced to choose a new tanist."

"And who might that be?"

"Someone sure to see my way of things."

There was a finality in the man's voice that brooked no further discussion. Alastair decided not to pursue it. It didn't matter anyway. Any choice but the Wolf of Cruachan was bound to be an improvement. But what if the offer led MacGregors into a trap?

"Why should I trust ye?" He strode back to the whiskey table and poured them both another dram. "What assurance do I have ye'll not betray me and mine?" He returned and handed the visitor his cup.

The man shrugged. "My word. The word of a Campbell, to be sure, but then, what's there to lose? If I fail ye, are ye any worse than ye were before? Take it or leave it."

MacGregor emptied his cup. The fiery liquid seared a hot trail down his throat, spreading rippling fingers of warmth throughout his chest. It calmed him a bit, allowing him the opportunity to sort through his jumbled thoughts.

Take it or leave it. Had it come to this then, when a MacGregor was forced to accept whatever leavings a Campbell threw his way? Ah, what a bitter draught to swallow! Yet swallow it he must if his clan were to survive. *One thing is for certain,* Alastair vowed with a fierce determination. *Before I'm done with him, Niall Campbell will rue his birthing day.*

He sighed. "Tell me when the Wolf plans his next raid. As ye said, any chief would be better than he. Help me capture him, and yer troubles will be over."

"I want him dead, MacGregor."

Alastair's bitter laugh cut through the air. "Och, he'll die, and no mistake. Just how and when I leave to my own pleasure."

2

Through a red haze of pain, Niall Campbell gazed out upon the castle's outer bailey. The early morning sun stained the sky with lavender. Save for the MacGregor sentries guarding the parapets, no one was about. He clenched and unclenched his fingers to ease the numbness in his hands, which was the only movement allowed by the tight ropes binding his limbs in a spread-eagle position to the wooden cross posts.

Had it been but two days since his capture? It seemed an eternity. He licked his dry, cracked lips, thirst raging through him like wildfire. His battle wounds ached fiercely, yet none were severe enough to kill him before lack of water did. But then, wasn't that the MacGregor's plan—a slow, agonizing death?

With a weary sigh, Niall leaned his head against the stone wall supporting the cross posts. If only he had fallen with his men, brave lads one and all. That fate, however, had never been meant for him.

It had been a trap from the start; that was more than evident. He and his small band had no sooner ridden into the narrow draw leading to one of the MacGregor villages than the attack had begun. Once the Campbells were surrounded on all sides, MacGregor crossbows quickly thinned their ranks. Then the hand-to-hand combat began.

Though they had fought with all the courage and ferocity of Highlanders, one by one his men fell. Eventually, the MacGregors managed to separate him from his remaining warriors, and a heavy net dropped on him from the cliff above. Pinned to the ground, his sword useless in the stout rope snare, he had turned to his dirk with desperate effect.

At the memory, a grim smile touched Niall's lips. Before they had finally beaten him senseless, he had hamstrung more than a few MacGregors.

In the end, though, it had all been for naught. To a man, his lads were dead, and he was now a MacGregor prisoner. Not for long, though. Niall didn't delude himself as to his eventual fate. After all these years, the animosity between the clans ran deep and bitter. And he of all Campbells, clan tanist and leader of the debilitating raids in recent months, was hated most of all.

Nay, his death was a foregone conclusion. Niall could accept that with a certain equanimity. What he couldn't accept was the galling realization he had been betrayed—and by one of his own.

A foul, blackhearted traitor in their midst! But who and why? The question had tormented him all the long hours of his capture, nibbling away at his strength as inexorably as had the lack of sleep and water. A traitor, and naught he could do, neither discover who he was nor warn his clan. Naught left to do but die with the terrible knowledge unspoken, unshared.

Once again a frustrated rage grew within him. Curse the man, whoever he was! Niall twisted futilely in his bonds, accomplishing little more than abrading the bloody sores of his wrists and ankles further. The pain only fueled his anger, and he fought all the harder. Finally, his rapidly draining strength exhausted, Niall fell back, his wounds and tormenting thirst beckoning him toward a blessed oblivion.

Anne hurried across the outer bailey. The thought of her own bed, covered with its plump down comforter, had never seemed so attractive. But then, never had she felt so exhausted.

✣ ✣

It was early morn and she had been up all night nursing a feverish servant, not to mention all the clansmen who still needed tending after the skirmish with the Campbells two days past. Though the victory had ultimately been MacGregors', the outnumbered raiders had sold their lives dearly.

Aye, the victory had been dearly won, but perhaps it would finally bring an end to the raids. After all, didn't they now hold prisoner the Wolf of Cruachan himself? His death, her father had assured her, would make the Campbells think twice about venturing onto MacGregor lands.

Though the man in the castle's outer courtyard had never shown MacGregors any mercy, dooming him to a slow, thirst-maddened death didn't sit well with Anne. Enemy though he was, even the thought of watching him succumb, inch by agonizing inch, made her stomach churn. It was brutally cruel and un-Christian. It was also, despite her attempts to convince her father otherwise, out of her hands.

Her steps quickened. Perhaps all the years of trying to save life made it so hard now to look at him, but in the two days since he had been tied in the bailey, she hadn't once glanced in the prisoner's direction, nor ventured past him unless absolutely necessary. In some way, not seeing him spared her the harsh reminder of his presence—and ultimate fate.

A low groan floated across the bailey. Reluctantly, Anne's gaze lifted toward the prisoner. His head was down, his full weight hanging from his hands. Perhaps the sound had been her imagination, but then as she turned away, he moved. Anne halted, then took a hesitant step toward him. There was something familiar about him . . .

He stirred again, attempting to lift his head, but couldn't seem to muster the strength. The slight movement, however, sent a premonitory shiver through her. She *had* seen him before, but where?

She inched her way over. As she studied the bent head, dread insinuated its oppressive tendrils about her heart. His form was powerful, awesome in size and inherent strength, even half-dead and trussed, awaiting execution like the criminal he was. The mane of unruly black hair hid his features, and the Campbell plaid and torn, bloodied shirt gave no hint as to why she should recognize him. Yet, for some inexplicable reason, she felt compelled to know more.

Laying aside her leather herb bag, Anne raised trembling hands to cup his face. It would take but an instant, she assured herself, and he'd never know. Slowly, ever so carefully, she lifted his head and brushed aside the dark hair.

At the sight of the finely hewn features, Anne gasped. Her fingers tightened into his flesh. His eyes flickered open, tawny-brown and pain-glazed, then slid shut.

Bruised and bloodied though his face was, his cheeks darkly shaded by a heavy growth of beard, Anne could no longer deny recognition. It was the Campbell leader who had rescued her from his crazed cousin. The Campbell leader, Niall Campbell . . . the Wolf of Cruachan!

With a shudder, Anne released his head and stumbled backward. Gathering up her bag, she hurried away. Holy saints in heaven! Not him, anyone but him!

Anne scrambled up the steps of the keep and into its dark stone coolness. She climbed the winding staircase, never pausing until she was safely in her own little room, the door bolted behind her. Then, flinging herself onto the bed, Anne buried her face in her hands.

Long minutes passed as she struggled to still her pounding heart. It was he, the greatly feared and despised Wolf of Cruachan—the MacGregors' fiercest enemy—and the man who had saved her life. Never had she dreamed the day would arrive when he'd be in need, and it would be in her power to save him. Yet, in but a few weeks' time, that day had indeed come.

Now, the debt was hers to repay. But at what cost? To spare his life now, to set him free, would most certainly lead to dire retribution.

Still, Anne reluctantly admitted, she owed him a debt, a life for a life. To turn from him now would be a dishonorable act. Yet, if she didn't, she might well jeopardize her people's welfare.

Och, dear Lord, what to do, what to do? she inwardly cried. Still, as the hours passed in agonizing indecision and unanswered prayers, the answer was always the same. At long last, when day had faded to early eve, Anne rose from her bed and went to seek her father.

✦

"Ye did what? Ye owe him what?"

Anne cringed at the explosive force of her father's anger. Never, in all her years, had he so much as raised his voice to her. Now to see his pain and rage and know she was the cause . . . She stifled an uncharacteristic urge to flee and faced the man standing across the room.

"As I said." She swallowed hard, then continued. "The Wolf spared my life, and now I owe him a debt of honor. Ye can't kill him, Father."

"Can't? Can't kill him, ye say?" Alastair MacGregor covered the distance between him and his eldest daughter in a few quick strides. Grasping her by the arms, he jerked her to him. "Do ye know what ye're saying, lass? If I let the Wolf go, do ye think he'll not try to avenge his men? Until now his raids have lost us our cattle, a few horses from time to time, but no lives. But now—now Campbell blood's been shed. Do ye think he'll stop until MacGregor blood flows as freely? Most likely even *more* freely," he muttered, "knowing that blackhearted fiend!"

Anne hung her head. "I-I'm sorry, Father. I didn't want to go against yer orders, but I'd promised—"

"Promised? Promised?" The MacGregor's face turned a mottled red. "I ordered ye to stay within the castle for yer own safety, and still ye wouldn't listen! And now ye've done it, for well ye know yer honor's MacGregor honor. To deny a debt such as this shames not only ye, but the entire clan. Och, lass, lass. Ye've gone and muddled things now!"

He began to drag her toward the door. Anne dug in her heels. "Where are ye taking me?"

"To the Wolf," her father growled. "I'll hear the truth from his own lips."

Through the keep he led her, and Anne's embarrassment grew with each pair of questioning eyes and raised brows encountered along the way. Out into the early evening sunshine they went, toward the lone, shadowed form tied in the outer bailey.

The Wolf must have heard them, for he lifted his head at their approach. "Time for another . . . gloating visit, is it?" the prisoner croaked, his voice raw and rasping. "Sorry to disappoint ye . . . MacGregor. I'm still . . . verra much alive."

Alastair shoved Anne in front of him, pushing her almost into the prisoner's face. "Do ye know her, Campbell? Tell me true!"

Reddened eyes, one purpled and nearly swollen shut, quietly studied her. Anne saw the recognition flare then purposely flicker out. For an instant, she thought he might deny he knew her. But why? Did he think her in danger if he spoke true? Did he hope to protect her by lying? Fleetingly, she almost wished he'd mistake the situation, even if it meant his death. It would solve everything.

"The truth," she forced herself to whisper. "Yer life hangs in the balance. Tell him the truth. No harm'll come to me."

His suffering eyes knifed into hers, probing deeply until Anne felt an unwilling compassion flow through her. Then his dense black lashes lowered. He sighed, the sound one of utter weariness.

"Aye, I know the lass. What's it to ye, MacGregor?"

"What's it to me?" Alastair nearly choked in frustrated rage. "Rather, ask what's it to ye? She's my daughter, man! Ye saved her life. Her debt's my debt. As much as I yearn for it, I cannot kill ye now. MacGregors have little else left, thanks to ye and yers, but we still have our honor. That'll never die, until ye wipe the last of us from the Highlands."

"Then . . . ye'll let me go?"

The MacGregor shook his head. "I haven't decided. Content

yerself with the fact ye'll live. Debt or not, ye're no guest here. Ye're merely trading the cross posts for the dungeon." He turned to Anne. "And ye, lass. I haven't decided what to do with ye yet, either. In the meantime, I task ye with tending our prisoner. Yer need to nurse every beggar who crosses yer path led to this. See how ye enjoy nursing him!"

Her father shot the man one final, contemptuous look, then stalked off, shouting orders at two guards to take the Campbell prisoner to the dungeon and clasp him in chains. As Anne watched him stomp away, tears stung her eyes. She had heard the pain, the deep concern in his voice beneath his anger, as he had spoken to Niall Campbell. She had backed him into a corner. And, indeed, what choices *were* left? He seemed doomed if he freed the Wolf, and just as doomed if he didn't.

"I wouldn't cause ye trouble, lass."

At the sound of the deep voice, Anne turned to him. "And why should one MacGregor more or less matter to the likes of ye? Don't waste yer pity on me. My debt's paid. It's my only comfort, and little will it be, in the coming days of caring for ye!"

Anne strode away. Soon Niall Campbell would take his rest in the damp, fetid depths of MacGregor dungeons. He'd need food, water, and his wounds tended, and he was now her responsibility.

Even the thought of touching him sickened her, vile, vicious beast that he was. But touch him she would, nurse him in the best way she knew how. Until her father decided the proper course of action, Niall Campbell's welfare was now of utmost concern. For her people's sake, if need be, Anne would care for the devil himself.

"More," Niall gasped, thinking he'd never get enough to slake his thirst. "Give me more!"

Before he could reach them with his chained hands, Anne pulled back with the cup and water pitcher. "Nay, that's enough for now.

Ye'll only make yerself sick if ye drink too much too soon. Give yer belly time."

Niall wiped his mouth with the back of a grimy hand. "Och, and aren't ye the heartless wench? Is this but another MacGregor torture? Tormenting me with a sip or two, not enough to slake my thirst but only to tease it?"

"Call it what ye will." Anne set the pitcher and cup aside. She took up her herb bag and a box filled with bandages and bowls. "One way or another, ye'll get no more to drink until I deem fit."

She paused to eye him closely, her glance moving down his body with a coolly detached air. "Yer leg looks the worst. I'll tend it first. Raise yer kilt."

Dark brows arched in weary amusement. "Are ye certain ye want me revealing that much of myself? Ye're a maid, aren't ye?"

She expelled an exasperated breath. "And sure, don't ye suppose I've seen a man's body or two in my years of healing? Besides, it's only yer leg I'm wanting to tend. Do ye wish yer wounds seen to or not?"

Niall shrugged, then lifted his kilt and tucked it high to present nearly the full length of his leg. "I only thought to spare yer sensibilities." He gestured toward the jagged cut. "Have at it, lass."

As Anne worked in the flickering torchlight, silence hung heavily over the dank chamber. She could feel his eyes upon her, sense them slide over her as she carefully labored on his leg. It angered her, though she knew it for the normal masculine act it was.

Gritting her teeth, she forced her attention back to the task at hand. The wound was long but shallow. Apart from some redness at the edges, it appeared it would heal well enough.

Her gaze moved outward from the cut, noting his powerful thigh. He was in superb physical condition, the muscles and sinews bulging under tautly stretched, hair-roughened skin. *A terrible, lethal enemy in battle,* Anne mused, *and the murderer of many a fine MacGregor lad.* The thought once more stirred her anger. Her touch, as she applied her herbal healing salve, was brisk.

"Why are ye so furious with me, lass?"

The unexpected query startled Anne. Her head jerked up. Her gaze careened into his. Calm brown eyes, flecked with gold, stared back at her. For a moment, no words would come.

Was he daft? What did he expect, Campbell that he was? Anne shook her head, perversely refusing to give him the satisfaction of admitting he was right.

The faintest glimmer of a smile touched his lips. "Ye nearly bit off my head earlier, when I told ye I was sorry to cause trouble between ye and yer father. And now ye're tending me with less than a gentle hand. I haven't said a word since ye began, so how have I suddenly angered ye?"

Anne opened her mouth then clamped it shut. She didn't owe him an explanation. Inhaling a calming breath, she turned back to the bandaging of his leg. "I'm not here to be yer companion, only to see to yer wounds and nourishment. Ye needn't make nice talk with me."

"Mayhap not, but I'd like to nonetheless." The chains binding him to the wall clanked as his hand moved to raise her chin gently. Silver eyes flashed at him, but Niall persisted. "It isn't yer fault, lass, no matter what yer father's told ye. My death would've set far worse on MacGregors than my living ever will. Yer father'll see that, once his anger cools."

"Will he now?" She wrenched her chin from his grasp. "And will yer living end the feuding? Tell me that, Niall Campbell!"

Aye, he thought, *it might well if I can discover who the traitor is, if yer father willingly reveals his name.*

A sudden, horrible thought assailed him. The traitor. How long had he been behind this? Since the very start of the feud? It was too terrible even to think such a thing, for the feud between Campbell and MacGregor had burned hot and bloody for more than eight years.

Niall shrugged. "It's possible, lass. It depends on yer father."

"Ha! Lay it all on my father's back, will ye? That's so like a

Campbell to stoke the pot, then claim he was nowhere about when it boils over!" Anne stepped back, her hands settling on her hips. "And why should ye even want the feuding to end? The sanctity of a wedding wasn't enough to keep ye from starting it. And it's well known how ye like the raiding, the bloodshed. Ye're slowly wearing us down with yer greater numbers. Why should ye want to stop until ye've stolen all we possess—including the land itself?"

His mouth tightened. It wasn't her fault she had been led astray as to the true cause of the feud. "We don't want yer land, lass." He sighed wearily. "It's but a matter of clan honor. If the MacGregors would stop, then so would we. And I think ye've been misled as to who actually caused the feud."

Anne arched a brow. "Indeed? And how would ye know?"

"I was there. It was my wedding day. While all were feasting after the ceremony—MacGregor as well as several other neighboring clans—one of our villages was raided, the people murdered to a man, woman, and child, and the livestock taken."

"Aye, I know the tale." Anne gave an impatient wave of her hand. "And the only clue to the raiders' identities was a scrap of MacGregor plaid. More than sufficient evidence that we'd been the reivers, despite my father's protests to the contrary. Thank the holy saints my people were safely back on MacGregor lands before ye discovered the village. No doubt ye'd have murdered us all, right there at yer wedding feast."

"What would ye have done, if the crime had been against *yer* clan?" Niall asked softly. "Wagged yer finger and asked them not to do it again?"

"I'd have waited a bit, investigated more thoroughly, before beginning a blood feud. A scrap of plaid's hardly a fair piece of evidence."

"And how thoroughly did the MacGregors investigate their own?" Niall countered. "Have ye no renegades who might've done such a thing? But, nay, we never heard of any MacGregors brought to trial, or ever received one word of apology."

“Apology for what? For a crime we didn’t commit? Highland honor would never permit such a thing!”

Niall shrugged. “Aye, that’s true enough. But, one way or another, the feud is set and there seems little either of us can do about it. For my part, I had yet to be named clan tanist and wasn’t privy to the rest of the evidence, nor was I part of the final decision. I accepted the council’s decision, though, as any good Highlander would.

“As far as yer other accusation that I like raiding and the shedding of blood, well, I do admit to enjoying the thrill of occasionally lifting a few cattle—what Highlander doesn’t?—but I don’t like bloodshed. Feud or no, neither I nor my men have ever killed any of yers save in retribution for the death of one of ours, or in self-defense.”

“And I say ye lie!” The words slipped out before Anne could stop them.

Niall struggled to his feet, then sank back to the stone bench, his face pale with the sudden exertion. “Don’t ever, ever call me a liar!” he growled, his sweat-damp features taut with anger. “I’ve never lied and I’ll certainly not begin now just to please ye. Think of me what ye will, but don’t justify yer clan’s shortcomings with false accusations!”

Eyes wide, she stared down at the man before her. She had been a fool to taunt him. Grudgingly, Anne had to admit Niall Campbell seemed to place great store on his word. His reaction had been too immediate, too violent, not to have sprung from the heart. And if he hadn’t been privy to the decisions surrounding the beginning of the feud, he might truly feel justified in accepting the Campbell view of things. Yet how could she believe him? To do so could perhaps place blame, at least some of it, on her own people.

Confused emotions whirled in her head. Sweet Jesus, what was she about, that a hated enemy could stand here and make her doubt her own kind? He was clever, that was all.

Tread lightly with him, Annie, she warned herself. *It isn’t important what he says. Humor him and then be gone.*

“I-I beg pardon,” she forced herself to say. “My tongue’s too sharp at times and forges ahead of my good sense. My purpose here isn't to upset ye or relive the feud but to see to yer needs." She motioned toward his battered face. "Allow me to finish tending yer wounds. Ye must be sore weary. I'll bring ye some food before ye take yer rest."

The anger left Niall with a rush. In its place flowed heavy exhaustion. With a sigh, he leaned back against the stone wall. "Aye, that I am, lass." He grinned up at her. "Mayhap it's also why my anger boils so near the surface."

Anne picked up a clean cloth and wet it in a bowl of water. She studied him for a moment then began to wash the gash over his left brow. "This cut's deep and won't cease its oozing. I'll apply witch hazel to stop the bleeding, then some of my marigold ointment. It's excellent in mending wounds."

Niall grunted his assent, well aware she didn't wish to discuss the subject of their families further. Instead, he occupied himself watching her. For the first time, he took his leisure in closely studying the woman before him.

Her hair, now pulled into a long, thick braid down her back, was a rich, glowing color. Its dark red hue set off the ivory radiance of her flawless skin to perfection. Her nose was straight, short and charming, her lips full and delightfully pink as she bit into them in her intense concentration.

His glance slid from her arresting face, moving down her small, slender body. The plain woolen dress wasn't meant to entice, but its simplicity flattered her curving figure better than the stiff, exaggerated outlines of courtly gowns ever could.

She was a beautiful woman. When engaged in something she loved, as Niall sensed she loved her healing, she radiated a serenity and strength that made her seem almost ethereal. The lass was different, and no mistake. In his younger days before he had wed, Niall knew he'd have found her attractive. Aye, most attractive, but not now, and perhaps never—

He quickly shook aside that painful memory. There was naught wrong with him. Mayhap all he needed was a lovely witch's potion.

She had certainly been bewitching that eve of the raid. Standing there before his men, her hair wild and tousled, defiantly taunting them. Niall couldn't help but admire her spirit and courage. He had easily guessed her ruse, her intention of using the prevailing witch panic to turn them away and protect the village. And it would've worked on a sane man. But Hugh wasn't quite sane, not all the time. She had nearly lost her life because of it.

"That night we raided the village." He took her hand to stop her ministrations. "Why did my cousin think ye a witch?"

Surprise flickered in her silver eyes. "He thought I'd used witchcraft to bring a wee babe back to life."

"And why would he have thought that?"

Anne hesitated. *If I tell him, he may think the same of me.*

For some inexplicable reason, she didn't want him to, though she knew his opinion of her shouldn't matter. In the past she had never let the whisperings or clacking tongues give her pause. Yet, gazing down at him, into the measureless depths of the big Highlander's rich brown eyes, she felt herself falter.

"A misunderstanding, as are most claims of witchcraft." Anne gave a small shrug and averted her gaze to dig into her bag.

"Aye." Niall chuckled. "Misunderstandings . . . rumors . . . I can well understand how they grow until the tales faint resemble the person." He dragged in a sudden, sharp breath. "I know ye. Ye're the one they call the Witch of Glenstrae."

Intent on applying the healing salve to his brow, Anne only nodded. "I've been called that. Does it disturb ye?"

"Nay. I told ye before. I don't believe in witchcraft. Besides, I've been called a wolf, yet I feel no more one than I imagine ye feel a witch."

In spite of herself, a smile sprang to Anne's lips. She put aside her ointment and looked at him. "Rumors, I fear, move faster and last longer than truth ever can. And with far more damage."

"Yet ye persist in yer healings, knowing full well the danger of the tales spread about ye."

"And would ye have me stop my work? Cower in a dark corner because of idle gossip and the mouthings of ignorant minds?" Anne vehemently shook her head. "Nay, I've a God-given gift to help others. Just because my talents lie in paths different from most women, I cannot serve the Lord by hanging back in fear."

Laughter rumbled deep in his chest.

"And pray, what's so amusing?"

"Och, naught, lass." Niall grinned. "I was but wondering how yer future husband will look upon all this."

She tossed her head. "What does it matter? I'll never wed, for I'll not be constrained by the rules of some blustering, narrow-minded fool. And besides, I've no worry. With my reputation, none will have me. My poor father, though he hated to shame me as his eldest, was finally even forced to marry off my two younger sisters before me." Anne laughed. "Not that I cared. What was one more broken custom among so many I'd already tossed by the way?"

Admiration mingled with bemusement in Niall's eyes. "Och, ye'll run some man a good race before he's tamed ye, and no mistake. Never fear, though, lassie. There are lads aplenty who'll not turn from the task. After all, a spirited filly, if gentled well, is of greater value than a plodding nag."

"So, now I'm compared to a horse! Yer opinion of women is sorry indeed, Niall Campbell."

He threw back his head and shouted with laughter, then stopped, clutching his side. A grimace of pain twisted his handsome features. "Och, I forgot my bruises. Have a heart, lass, and don't make me laugh again." He cocked his head. "Tell me yer name. We've never been properly introduced, ye know."

An unaccustomed warmth surged through Anne, followed quickly by a flash of irritation. She shouldn't feel so . . . so friendly, so flattered by his interest. No matter how pleasant he could be, he was still her enemy. Her lips tightened, and she forced down her natural affability.

"I can't fathom the import, ye knowing my name. It changes

naught. All that matters is ye're a Campbell and I, a MacGregor. But since ye asked, I'm called Anne."

The color drained from Niall's face. His expression hardened. Anne thought she saw a flash of pain in his eyes, but it passed so swiftly she could've been mistaken. There was no mistaking, however, the physical distance he meant to put between them as he leaned away.

"Ye're right, of course," he said, his voice deepening to a growl. "I was wrong to ask. It changes naught. Naught at all."

3

Anne hurried up the dungeon steps, thankful her task of caring for Niall Campbell was over. His wounds had been tended, a light meal served, and he was now resting, a thick fur provided him against the room's chill. Later, after he'd had time to sleep, she'd return with some wash water and a fresh shirt to replace his dirty, tattered one.

But, from the haggard look of exhaustion on his face, later was hours away. For the time being she was free of him, free of the disconcerting emotions he so easily stirred. She meant to spend that free time outside, breathing the fresh Highland air.

The day was nearly spent. Savory smells of roasting meats and yeasty breads filled the air. Anne sighed contentedly. How she loved this time, when the dying sun cast its mellow glow upon the land, when the day's struggle and strife were over and the only labor left was the satisfying contemplation of one's accomplishments.

As she strode into the main hall and toward the huge open doorway, a loud commotion reached her. From the outer bailey came the sound of men's shouts, the clang of weapons, and the stamping and snorting of nervous horses. She stepped into the keep's inner courtyard. No one was about. Anne's pace quickened.

She was out the gate and halfway across the outer bailey before a servant scurried by. Anne grabbed her arm. "What's amiss? Why is everyone rushing about?"

"Rushing about?" the little maidservant panted. "Didn't ye know, ma'am? It's the Campbells! They're at our gates, a whole army of them! Och, it'll go bad for us now, verra bad!"

Anne turned to the parapets where, even now, MacGregor clansmen were massing, the stiff wind flapping their red tartans about their legs like crimson flames. The stout form of her father paced the walkway. She headed toward him.

He was staring out over the hills, his features grim. Anne followed his glance and gasped. There, in what seemed an endless array of tartan hues, was a vast army. Though Campbells were most prevalent, Anne could also make out the colors of several other clans. *Campbell allies, one and all,* she thought bitterly, *and armed to the teeth for war.*

"Give him to us, MacGregor!"

Three Campbell men rode forward. From her vantage point, Anne recognized one of them as Niall's mad cousin, Hugh.

"Give us our tanist or ye'll rue the day ye so foully took him!" the oldest of the trio, a tall, bearded blond man, shouted.

"And who are ye to threaten me?" Alastair MacGregor boomed back at him. "I'll keep yer man as long as I please, and no amount of threats will make me give him up before I'm ready. Ye'll not menace me from my own castle!"

"Och, and will we not?" The sandy-haired Campbell gestured about him. "Think long and hard, man. On the morrow, at dawn's first light, we'll ask ye again."

Before her father could reply, the leaders turned their horses and galloped away, their army following swiftly behind. On a distant hillock they halted. As Anne and her father watched, the warriors began to set up camp.

"What will ye do, Father?"

"And what do ye suppose?" he snapped, his eyes burning with a mixture of rage and frustration. "They'll lay siege if we don't give him up, and how long could we last?" Alastair gripped the stone wall, his shoulders hunched in despair. "Och, curse the day I ever laid eyes on that man," he muttered half to himself. "Curse the day I ever entrapped Niall Campbell! I should've known a traitor helps neither side."

"What are ye saying? How did ye entrap Niall Campbell?" Anne's nails sank deep into the flesh of his arm. "And what do ye mean, 'a traitor'?"

He shook her hand away. "Leave me be, lass! I've got to think! Got to find a way out of this that'll save both our hides *and* our honor." Her father stalked off, his head bent in thought.

Anne turned back to the scene outside the castle walls. Lovingly, her gaze swept the wooded glens, the bracken-strewn hills and meadows, the rocky crags. MacGregor land.

For eight years now they had borne the periodic raids, the dreaded attack of intruders. Today, however, was the culmination of their deepest fears. The nightmare had at last become reality in an army standing ready to destroy them. And there was naught they could do about it.

✦

"What do ye want of me?"

Niall stood before Alastair MacGregor, groggy from being dragged from a deep slumber, his hands and feet in shackles. His glance strayed to the deep, stone-cut window across the chief's room. It was pitch black outside. What time was it? Midnight or past?

Alastair watched the guards shut the door behind them before answering. "We've a problem."

Niall's attention riveted on the older man. "*We* do? And what might that be?"

MacGregor cursed silently. Even in chains the arrogant young whelp refused to make it easy. Something inside him hardened. *Well, he'll not best me in this. I've naught left to lose . . .*

"Yer clan camps outside the castle," Alastair said. "They demand yer return."

Niall shrugged. "Then it's simple. Give me to them."

"Nay, it isn't simple at all. MacGregor honor couldn't bear such disgrace."

Tawny-brown eyes studied him. Alastair saw understanding flare in their depths.

"As ye say," Niall admitted at last. "Highland honor's never a simple matter. I ask again. What do ye want of me?"

MacGregor's hands clenched. His heart quickened in excitement. "An end to the feud."

"And how do ye propose we do that?"

Alastair shrugged. "How else but in the age-old custom of joining the clans? Ye'll take my Annie as wife."

Niall stared at him for a long moment, then shook his head. "Nay, it cannot be. I'm honored by yer offer, but I cannot wed yer daughter."

"And why not?" Alastair eyed him calmly. To find offense at the refusal would only weaken his plan. "It's a marriage made in heaven. My Annie's a beautiful, kindhearted lass, if a wee bit headstrong. Still, from what I've seen of ye, ye're just the man to tame her. She's well built, healthy, and will bear ye fine sons. What more can a man ask? It'll join our two clans and put an end to the feud."

"Indeed, she seems all ye've said and more." Niall ran a hand through his hair. "The problem lies not with her, but with me. I still mourn my wife."

Alastair nodded sympathetically. "I can well understand yer hesitation. I, too, lost a beloved wife. But it's been a year, a fair time for mourning. Ye're the chief's son and clan tanist. Ye, of all men, recognize that the people's welfare comes before yer own desires, however justifiable they may be. None will condemn ye for ending yer mourning, not when it'll also end the feuding."

"And I don't care what anyone thinks!" Niall's tall frame tensed in anger. "Who's to say a year's long enough? I'll not shame the memory of my wife for anyone! Do ye hear me, MacGregor? Not anyone!"

Alastair's jaw clenched. This was proving more difficult than he had anticipated. He hadn't counted on the man's deep emotions for his wife clouding his judgment. "And I say, think again. Ye're hardly in a position to refuse. Though ye managed to escape death once, I've naught to lose now—and ye've everything."

Niall laughed. "And do ye think I believe ye'd kill me with a Campbell army outside yer gates? Yer castle would be overrun, every man, woman, and child put to the sword. It's the Highland code."

"Who said I'd kill ye?" MacGregor shook his head, a grim, deadly smile twisting his mouth. "I'm not fool enough to make a martyr of ye, to return ye clothed in the glory of death. Nay, I thought rather to send ye back a little less a man than when ye came." One of his bushy gray brows lifted. "Even if the act was the end of me, as long as ye *lived*, there'd be no further retribution against my people. If ye get my meaning?"

Niall stiffened. The man must be addled even to suggest such a thing! He shuddered at the thought then, regaining his composure, looked deep into the MacGregor's eyes. His enemy's gaze was as firm as his own.

He's backed to the wall. All that's left is his honor. And that, Niall well knew, was a life-or-death matter.

But where was the honor in shaming his beloved's memory? Though he was far from wanting another wife, the MacGregor lass was comely, and many marriages had been made for less than romantic reasons. He never hoped to have again what he'd had anyway. Surely that kind of love came only once in a lifetime. But to wed before he had mourned as he saw fit . . .

"If ye did such a thing, what good would I be to yer daughter then, man?" Niall inquired coolly, determined not to give the MacGregor an inch in this battle of wills..

The look of surprise on the man's face salved some of Niall's wounded pride. He made his decision. All issues of love and honor aside, if for no other reason than to discover the traitor, he knew he had to survive.

"Ye're a hard one, MacGregor." He sighed. "I'll give ye what ye want, but ye must meet me halfway. After all, I've my pride to consider, too."

Alastair smiled, sensing the victory within his grasp. He had won. Why not be generous? "Ask, and if it's within reason, it's yers."

"I'll need another year before my mourning's done. I'll handfast with yer daughter for that time, then wed her."

Handfast, Alastair thought. Annie would balk at that unwed state worse than at marrying a Campbell. To live together as man and wife without a church-sanctioned ceremony might be acceptable to many, a "trial marriage" so to speak where both could go their way if things didn't work out, but he knew his daughter. For all her flaunting of a woman's customary strictures, she'd never go against the proper religious morals her mother had instilled in her. Yet, noting the determined set to his prisoner's jaw, he also knew Niall Campbell wouldn't budge from his offer. Annie would just have to understand.

A huge grin on his face, Alastair extended his hand. "We've a bargain. My Annie's yers." As Niall clasped his hand, a sudden thought struck him. "I'd be obliged if ye treated her kindly. It's not her fault, whatever bitterness ye may feel toward me because of this. Don't take it out on her."

"Dinna fash yerself, man. I'll not harm her."

Yet, even as he spoke, Niall remembered the Reformed preacher who had just a year ago returned from Edinburgh to take up residence once more on Campbell lands. Malcolm Campbell, one of his father's sisters's illegitimate sons, was a narrow-minded witch fanatic who had already managed to stir the clan to the edge of panic. Niall wondered what the man's reaction would be to Anne.

He turned to Alastair. "It'll go hard for her, nonetheless. Her witch's reputation has spread far and wide."

A wild fear sprung to the MacGregor's eyes. "Ye'll protect her, won't ye? She's not a witch. It's just her great healing skills and her strange gray eyes that give some folk pause. But she's not a witch."

"I know that, man. I'll do what I can." Niall paused. "One thing more. As we're soon to be family, I can expect yer full measure of loyalty, can't I?"

The older man's gaze narrowed. "Ye already know the answer to that. What's it ye want?"

"My capture. It was too easy, ye knowing when and where we were to attack. Who told ye, MacGregor?"

"I-I don't know what ye—"

"No games, man! Don't protect a Campbell from one of his own. Besides, he may have been the one responsible for the feud. Stranger things have happened. Tell me his name. Ye owe loyalty to me now, not him."

Alastair shook his head. "I can't tell ye that. I don't know the man. He came to me alone and kept his face covered. He was a crafty one and full of hatred for ye, but why, I don't know. He was careful to say little. I fear I can't help ye."

Frustration swelled in Niall, nearly choking him. Save for having his suspicions confirmed, he was no closer to discovering the traitor than before. His only advantage lay in the fact the man didn't yet know that Niall suspected anything amiss. It was small indeed, but it was all he had. But not for long. He'd see to that.

"No one must know, MacGregor. Ye mustn't reveal the fact ye told me this to anyone. Do ye understand?"

"Aye. Ye've my word on it."

"Good. Now, how soon can the handfasting be done?" Niall skewered Alastair with a sharp glance. "I've a need to return home as quickly as possible."

The MacGregor's brow knit in thought. "I must tell Annie, give her time to accept it. And her possessions need packing. Do ye desire an elaborate ceremony?"

“Nay. We’ll save that for the wedding.”

“Then why not have it at midday? It’ll give ye time to rest and me time to break it to my daughter.”

“As ye wish, but we must depart immediately thereafter. Also, I’ll need one of my own as witness.”

“Yer clan will return at dawn’s first light. Ye can come with me to the walls and call one inside. But no tricks. I’ll not have ye shame my daughter by telling her I forced her on ye. Yer word on it, Campbell.”

Och, man, Niall thought. *Suddenly ye’re caring for yer daughter’s feelings, after all but trading her off like some prize cow?* With only the greatest effort, he controlled the sneer that threatened the corner of his mouth.

“Ye’ve my word on it, not that it’ll matter. Yer daughter’s too clever not to guess the truth.” Niall laughed. “I don’t envy ye the task of convincing her. I may yet get out of this. Then what’ll ye do?”

The MacGregor’s face reddened. “For all her spunk, my Annie’s an obedient lass. She’ll obey her father, and no mistake.”

Niall’s dark brows arched in challenge. “Then call her, man. Now. Let’s get this settled once and for all.”

Anne awoke to her serving maid shaking her. “Ma’am? Please, ma’am, yer father’s calling for ye.”

“What?” Anne sat up, brushed the hair from her eyes. “Father? Did he say what he wanted?”

The little maid shook her head. “Nay. I was only told to dress ye, fix yer hair, and send ye on yer way as quickly as possible.”

“Then let’s get on with it.” Anne sprang from bed. “At this hour, I fear it must be important.”

It had to have something to do with the Campbells, perhaps even Niall Campbell himself, Anne mused ten minutes later as she hurried down the chill stone corridor toward her father’s chambers. But what would her father need her for? How could she be of any help? Well, no matter. She paused to smooth her dress and hastily braided hair before knocking on the door. One way or another, she'd discover the answer soon enough.

"Come in, lass," her father's voice beckoned at her first knock.

Hesitantly, Anne pushed open the door. Her father and Niall Campbell stood together, warming themselves at the hearth. She walked in.

"Close the door and come here, lass."

Anne quickly did as she was told. "Aye, Father?" She searched his face in concern. "Ye called me. What troubles ye?"

Alastair gestured toward Niall. "We've come to an agreement that'll end the feuding."

Her gaze swung to meet Niall Campbell's. "Is it true? Ye've agreed to end the feud?"

He nodded.

"But how? What common ground could ye two possibly find? What honorable recourse to ease the wounded pride of both sides?"

A strange light flared in Niall's eyes. "I've no talent for smooth words, and I won't lie. Ask yer father. It'll come better from him." He looked at Alastair. "I'll wait at the window, give ye a moment of privacy together."

Alastair nodded. Both he and Anne watched as Niall took a seat across the room. Then Anne turned to her father.

"What did he mean? Why should an end to the feud cause me pain?"

"Och, lass." He sighed. "Hear me out before ye fly into a rage. It was, after all, the best, the only thing, I could do." He took her by the arms. "I've given ye to him."

Shock warred with anger until Anne could barely speak a coherent word. "What? Y-ye did what?"

"Ye heard me, lass. I gave ye to Niall Campbell."

"Ye *gave* me to . . . to *him*?" Anne's voice rose on a thread of hysteria. "But why? He doesn't want me!"

Niall winced at the naked anguish in her words, knowing full well their truth. Pity slashed through him. Though it was evident she was just as adamantly against their union as he, Anne would suffer far greater consequences. She'd be the one to leave her home and adjust her life to his. She'd be the one to lose the freedom she so dearly cherished, not to mention the opportunity to heal, for it would be far too dangerous for her to roam about ministering to his more superstitious clan.

Perhaps she didn't realize that yet. Niall prayed so, for the knowledge might be more than she could bear. Better to break it to her later, after she'd had time . . .

"Nay!"

The cry wrenched free of the muted speech coming from across the room. Niall jerked around. At that moment Anne turned to him. Their gazes met, his eyes locking with tear-bright silver.

"Nay," she whispered, the entreaty so direct and personal it sliced right to his heart.

He quashed the unexpected impulse to go to her, gather her into his arms and comfort her. Instead, he forced his glance back out the window. *It'd do no good,* Niall told himself.

What could he promise her anyway? He didn't know if his people would ever accept her or if she'd find happiness at Kilchurn. And he had no hope of love to offer. Better she seek what comfort she could from her father.

"How can ye do this?" Anne demanded of Alastair, the tears now coursing unchecked down her cheeks. "How can ye give me to a man such as ye know Niall Campbell to be? He's ruthless, cruel, and will probably ill treat me solely out of hatred for MacGregors. Ye forced him into this. I know ye did!"

Alastair gently wiped her tears away. "It's for the good of both our peoples, lass. He saw the wisdom, as ye must. Don't fear him. He's an honorable man. I know that now. He'll not mistreat ye."

"But I don't need a husband!" she wailed. "I don't want to wed!"

“Er, it isn’t exactly a marriage,” her father mumbled, coloring fiercely. “Or, leastwise, not for a time. Ye’re to be handfasted to him for a year and a day, until his mourning for his wife’s over.”

Anne jerked away, her tears staunched in her scorching anger and disbelief. “Handfasted? Ye’re handfasting me? I don’t believe it! Why not just give me to him as his mistress? As far as I’m concerned, it’s one and the same!”

“Now, lass.” Alastair moved toward her, his voice low with warning. “Calm yerself. It isn’t the same at all. Handfasting’s an ancient, honored custom. There’s no shame in it. Besides, he’s agreed to wed ye when the year’s up. Ye can’t blame him for wanting to mourn his wife, can ye?”

“Let him mourn the rest of his life for all I care!” Anne hotly replied. “It doesn’t matter to me! It’s my right as a Scotswoman to refuse this. I will not handfast or anything else with him!”

“And I say ye will!” her father roared, apparently at the end of his patience. “Ye’re still my child, my firstborn and heir. Our clan’s welfare, nay, its verra survival, is now in yer hands. Ye know where yer duty lies.”

He pointed toward the door. “Now go, and not another word from ye. The ceremony will commence at midday. The Wolf wishes to depart immediately thereafter, so see to yer preparations. I don’t wish to discuss this further!”

Anne opened her mouth to protest then, noting the tense, rigid expression on her father’s face, thought better of it. It was no use anyway. Her time was better spent attempting to make Niall Campbell see the sense of things.

She glanced to where the big Highlander stood staring out the window. “I need a few minutes, then, to speak with him,” she said, looking back to her father. “Before I’ll agree to this mockery of a union, we’ve some details to work out.”

Alastair’s gaze narrowed. “What are ye about, lass? If ye think to get him to reconsider . . .”

“And is that possible?” She managed a brittle laugh. “Well, we’ll see, won’t we?”

Muttering the whole way, her father walked to the door and exited. Anne wasted no time joining Niall Campbell. “What did my father promise ye?” she asked.

He half-turned, the vestige of a smile hovering about his full, firm lips. “My life and freedom. Can ye better that offer, lass?”

She couldn’t, and she knew he knew it. “Then yer mind’s made, is it?”

“It’d seem so. And what of yers? Are ye finally willing to yield and do yer father’s bidding?”

Anne sniffed in disdain. “Hardly. To my mind, handfasting’s naught more than an excuse for—”

When she caught herself in mid-sentence, Niall cocked his head. “For what? Fornication?”

Heat flooded her face. “Well, aye.” She forced herself to meet his amused gaze. “And I won’t do that, leastwise, not outside the bonds of holy matrimony. I love my father. I love my clan. But I love the Lord Jesus above even them. I won’t sin.”

“And have I asked ye to, lass?”

His softly couched question gave her pause. “Nay, not in so many words, but everyone who handfasts—”

“I’m not everyone,” Niall said. “I meant what I told yer father earlier. I need more time to mourn my wife. Mourn her in every way. I’ve no taste for fornicating with anyone.”

“Aye, ye say that now. But a year’s a long time. What if, in that time, ye change yer mind?”

“Then that’ll be my dilemma, not yers.”

She didn’t know what she had hoped for, but she wasn’t prepared for such a response. “So, ye’ll give me yer word our handfasting will be a chaste one?”

“Aye. Ye have it.”

“And what if, at the end of the year, I wish to return to my clan? Will ye allow me to sever the vows we’ve made?”

"Aye. I also think it only fair that I've the same option."

Anne laughed then. "Och, that's fair and more." She held out her hand. "Then we're agreed?"

Niall looked down at her outstretched hand and, after a moment's hesitation, took it in his. "Aye, we're agreed."

✦

The ensuing hours until midday flew by in a flurry of activity. From a place far removed, Anne watched the preparations for her departure. Her gowns were carefully folded, her slippers and small collection of jewelry wrapped in soft cloths, her beloved clarsach safely tucked among them all.

A heavy pain settled around her heart. Despite the pact she and Niall Campbell had made, her situation had barely changed. Would there ever be reason to strum the curved wooden harp in Kilchurn Castle?

Soon, nothing remained save the traveling gown of deep emerald velvet and a heavy woolen cape to ward against the blustering spring winds. Her entire life, Anne mused sadly, had quickly condensed into a few bulky parcels.

One last time, she visited the keep's private garden. The sturdier plants that had overwintered were beginning to sprout fresh shoots of green. Her beloved herbs. Life-giving, heart-and-body soothing. Would there be a place for them in her new life?

A sob rose in Anne's throat. In but the span of a few hours, her life had completely changed. She had become a pawn to be manipulated at the whim of others. The freedom and control she had once had were now lovely illusions.

Aye, illusions indeed, Anne thought, *for they were never more than that in anyone's mind but my own. I've never had any power over my life, save what was permitted me.*

She knelt to brush a bit of dirt from a chamomile plant. *Soon their delicate, daisy-like flowers will bloom, and I'll not be here to see them.*

The realization stirred something, firing her resolve, feeding her wounded spirit. She rose to her feet, her hands clenched at her sides. She'd not let this defeat her! Though her circumstances may have changed, the Lord still called her to this work. The censure of others had never stopped her before. Why should it do so now?

She had risked death for a long while now. Even in Campbell lands, there was nothing more they could threaten her with.

Anne hurried away, soon returning with a trowel and an empty wooden box. A grim smile on her lips, she carefully dug up a sampling of every herb in her garden and placed them in the container. Somehow, she'd find a spot to transplant and grow her precious friends at Kilchurn Castle. She had to. Symbolically, their rebirth would also assure hers.

An hour later Anne stood alone in her father's chambers, awaiting his and Niall Campbell's return from fetching one of his men to witness the ceremony. Dressed in a green gown with fitted bodice and tight sleeves with their trailing edges, her hair gathered in a pearl-studded snood and topped with a small green velvet cap, her only jewelry, in deference to the journey ahead, was a long pearl necklace, knotted just below the high-collared neckline.

She jumped when the heavy tread of footsteps echoed suddenly in the hallway. Before Anne could compose herself, the door swung open. In walked her father, followed closely by Niall Campbell and another man. She swallowed hard and forced her gaze to meet that of the tall, dark-haired warrior who strode over to stand before her.

"Lass," Niall's deep voice rumbled, "allow me to introduce another of my cousins, Iain Campbell. Iain, this is Anne MacGregor."

At mention of her name, the equally tall, dark-blond-haired man jerked his admiring gaze from her to Niall. "Anne?"

"Aye," he replied tersely. "Pay yer respects."

Iain, who appeared several years younger than Niall, looked back at Anne. He accepted her proffered hand. A pair of intensely blue eyes studied her for a moment, then his head bowed to kiss her hand.

"It's my greatest pleasure to make yer acquaintance, ma'am. Truly, ye're one of the loveliest women I've ever laid eyes upon."

"And ye're as gallant as any court gentleman to say so," Anne murmured stiffly. "I hope we can be friends."

A reckless grin split Iain's handsome face. "If Niall hadn't claimed ye first, I'd have liked to be more than friends. Still, fate being what it is, I suppose I'll be pleased to settle for a friendship."

At his blunt, forthright manner, Anne couldn't help but smile. Here was one Campbell, at least, who seemed willing to accept her. Perhaps there was hope.

Niall cleared his throat. "Now that my cousin's finished charming this gathering, let's get on with the handfasting. We've several hours' journey ahead, and I wish to be home before dark."

Iain merely quirked an eyebrow in amusement, but Anne, irritated by Niall's rudeness, shot him an icy glance. "Aye, by all means. I've no wish to deter ye from more important matters."

He opened his mouth to snap something back at her, then thought better of it. *It isn't her fault,* Niall reminded himself for the tenth time. *Be gentle. It's even worse for her.*

Instead, he addressed the MacGregor. "The ceremony, if ye please."

Alastair's gaze skittered anxiously from his daughter to Niall, then he opened the small book he held. After a prolonged bout of throat clearing, he began to read. "We gather here for the time-honored ritual of handfasting. An ancient custom, it is, meant to prepare a man and woman for the lifelong partnership of marriage, binding them hand in fist for a year and a day. If any children be born of this union, custody and care are the father's responsibility. If the couple parts at the end of the year, the mither's reputation will not in the least be held in question."

He paused to inhale a shaky breath. "Now, let them be brought before us." He raised his eyes to Anne and Niall. "Take each other's hand and step forward."

A large, heavily calloused palm extended toward Anne. After a moment's hesitation, she placed her trembling hand in Niall's. There was a momentary squeeze, as if he were trying to reassure her. Then, as one, they moved to stand before the MacGregor. Out of the corner of her eye, Anne saw Iain take his place beside his cousin.

Alastair directed his gaze to Niall. "Repeat after me. I, Niall Campbell, do come here of my own free will, to seek the partnership of Anne MacGregor. I come with all love, honor—"

"I'm not a hypocrite, MacGregor!" Niall cut in harshly. "Leave love out of this or I'll not make the vows."

"A-as ye wish," the older man stammered, apparently unnerved by the vehemence in Niall's voice. "I meant no offense. It's but the customary rite."

"And I care not what the custom is," Niall hissed through clenched teeth. "Now, get on with it."

"I come with all . . . honor and sincerity, wishing only to become one with her whom I . . . er . . . I honor."

He paused as Niall repeated the words. "Always," Alastair then continued, "will I strive for Anne's happiness and welfare. Her life will I defend before my own. All this I swear, on my word as a Scotsman and Highlander."

Niall spoke the words after him. Then Alastair turned to Anne, guiding her in her pledge. Once she had finished, he withdrew two rings from his pocket. Made of plain gold workings, the pair gleamed with the patina of age and loving use.

"These were yer mither's and mine." His eyes misted as he smiled down at his daughter. "I know rings aren't called for with a handfasting, but I'd still be pleased if ye'd wear yer mither's."

"Aye, Father." Tears welled in her eyes. Though he was trying, in his own way, to make something more of this ceremony than it was, she hadn't the heart to disparage it. "If it'd please ye."

He handed the ring to Niall. "Place it upon her finger."

Niall slid the golden circlet onto the third finger of Anne's left hand. Then his gaze returned to Alastair's.

"Would ye consider wearing my ring?" the older man asked. "Once before, it was part of a long and happy union. Mayhap it'll bring the same fortune again."

Niall gritted his teeth, a muscle twitching furiously in his jaw. *It's a farce, all of this,* he inwardly raged, *yet the old man persists in trying to force some romantic symbolism into it. Well, this goes too far! I won't compromise my honor.*

A gentle squeeze of his hand halted him. Turning, Niall found himself captured by a mesmerizing pair of silver eyes. Warm with silent entreaty, they pulled at him. He knew, for Anne's sake at least, he couldn't refuse.

"I-I'd be honored, MacGregor," Niall mumbled, still ensnared by the strange feelings roiling within. He watched as the man presented his daughter with the ring and she placed it on his finger.

"As the tall grass and mighty trees bow beneath the force of the wind," Alastair once more intoned, "so too must ye both bend when the storms of life blow strong. But know as swiftly as the storm comes, so equally swiftly may it depart. Stand strong always in each other's strength. Together ye are one; apart ye are naught."

He looked up at them. "Be faithful, one to the other. Ever honor each other. Help each other—and know now that ye're truly one." A broad smile lit his face. "It's over, the handfasting ceremony, I mean. Ye may kiss her."

Kiss her, Niall thought. *Ah, well, she's mine now and if it'll put an end to this odious ceremony . . .* He pulled her to him, his powerful arms encircling her, and lowered his head.

4

Strong, hard lips slanted over hers, forcing Anne back against the unyielding grip of Niall's hand. For a brief moment she fought him, her fingers digging into his broad, linen-covered chest, before finally surrendering to his overwhelming power—and the cruel reality of her fate.

She was a fool to fight him; perhaps she had even been a fool to trust him at his word. Anger filled her. Whether she liked it or not, Niall Campbell owned her now in body and life. To resist would only shame her before the clan. There was nothing left but acceptance, but that acceptance would be as cold and unyielding as she could make it. Anne relaxed in his arms, neither pulling away nor returning his kiss.

The change in her response startled Niall. He drew back to scan her face. Silver eyes, devoid of expression, stared up at him.

So, this is how it's to be. Disappointment shot through him, then Niall reminded himself of the true purpose of the handfasting. Even if she *had* been willing—which she wasn't—he had neither the time nor inclination to woo her. Issues of far greater import demanded his attention . . . like the identity of a certain traitor.

The realization, hovering at the edge of his consciousness, rushed back with disconcerting force. With a low, angry curse, Niall released Anne.

His frowning glance found the MacGregor. "It's done then, the vows said and sealed." He nodded to his cousin. "Let's be gone."

Iain grinned. "Not so fast, cousin. Custom, not ye, dictates the pace. As clan witness to this handfasting, I'm required to give yer lady a kiss. Would ye have her feeling unwelcome to the family?"

Niall's gaze narrowed. He gestured toward Anne with an impatient sweep of his hand. "Make it quick, then."

As she stood there in stunned surprise, Iain took her into his arms. His intense blue gaze, deep and fathomless as the waters of mighty Loch Awe, swept over her. Then his lips touched hers, gently covering her mouth.

It was too much. First the cold ownership of Niall's kiss, and now Iain's expert assault. She had never kissed a grown man, aside from her father's affectionate caresses, and now to have two in one day! Anne groaned in dismay, moving to push Iain away.

"Enough, cousin."

Stirred by the unexpected surge of possessiveness Anne's small sound evoked in him, Niall stepped forward to grasp Iain's arm.

With a reluctant grin, Iain released Anne. "Welcome, lass. Ye'll make a fine Campbell, and no mistake."

Anne shook her head. "Nay. That'll never be. Though I journey far from home and hearth, I'll always be a MacGregor."

"And journey ye shall," Niall's steel-timbred voice intruded. "Yer belongings are packed; the horses await. Let's be gone."

Anne glanced toward her father, unable to hide a look of silent supplication. He paled. Remorse surged through her at the expression of pain and regret that crossed his face.

With a determined thrust of her shoulders, she faced Niall. *It'll do no good to bemoan yer fate,* she told herself firmly. *Ye're handfasted, and that's that. It's in the Lord's hands now.*

"Aye." She returned Niall Campbell's glittering stare with a resolute one of her own. "Let us be gone. Naught's served lingering over things that cannot be changed." She extended her hand to him.

"Better to face bravely what God gives, to forget the past and forge on—for the good of all, MacGregor and Campbell alike."

The lowering sky, heavy with dark, moisture-laden clouds, precluded overlong farewells. For that, at least, Anne was thankful. If she had lingered a moment longer, she'd have surely burst into tears in front of them all, mortifying both herself and her father, and no doubt adding to Niall Campbell's rising exasperation. But the thought of several hours' ride, in what rapidly threatened to turn into a typical Highland downpour, was enough to put a damper on leave-takings between travelers and well-wishers alike.

They mounted quickly. The huge castle doors swung open. For a moment, Anne stared out upon an assemblage of tartan-clad warriors. Then Niall urged his mount forward. As he cleared the fortress's portals, a cheer rose from the army outside the gate.

"The Wolf! The Wolf of Cruachan lives!" At the outcry Niall rose in his saddle, his right hand lifting in a close-fisted salute. "Cruachan!" he shouted, the harsh Campbell battle cry echoing across the hills.

Urging his horse onward and followed closely by Anne and Iain, Niall rode to the head of his forces. With a motion of his hand, he signaled the journey to begin.

Anne never looked back. She didn't dare or the tears would've surely flowed. Riveting her gaze on Niall, riding ahead with his cousin, Hugh, and the older man who had been the spokesman for his return, she steeled herself to the sight of the beloved land she was leaving behind.

The road turned south along the River Strae. This time of year, the river's current was turbulent with melted winter snow, and a fine mist rose from the water-battered stones. Anne inhaled deeply of the scent of rich, damp earth.

The meadows were alive with springtide flowers, gallant little daffodils, delicate snowdrops, and yellow primroses. The milk-white petals of the delicate Star of Bethlehem gleamed among the rank growth of ivy and fern in the nearby woods. Everywhere she looked she saw the heartbreaking beauty of her land. A lump rose in Anne's throat.

"Don't fret so, lassie," Iain Campbell said as he rode up alongside her. "It isn't as if ye'll never see yer home again. In time, when the feuding cools, ye can coax Niall into bringing ye back for a wee visit. We're nearly neighbors, after all."

She gave him a misty-eyed smile. "My thanks for yer kindness. I don't think yer tanist will have much time for humoring the likes of me, though."

Her glance turned to rest again on Niall, who was now deeply immersed in conversation with Hugh and the sandy-haired man. "He seems to find Campbell concerns of far greater import. I wonder what clan he's planning to raid, now that MacGregors can no longer be his enemies?"

Iain's mouth quirked. "Och, lassie, don't be so hard on him. With his father ailing, Niall's had a heavy burden laid on him these past few years. Give him a chance. He's not a cruel man, just a wee bit harder since his wife's death."

"Aye," she muttered, "I know how deeply he mourns his wife. Too bad he didn't mourn her enough to prevent our handfasting."

"Well, I'll not speak of what I know naught about." He turned toward her. "Would ye like to learn a bit about our clan, before we reach Kilchurn Castle? Mayhap it'd ease yer way."

Anne nodded. It was hard to stay glum with a man as handsome and charming as Iain Campbell at her side. "Aye, that'd be nice."

She pointed to the older man riding on Niall's right. "And who might he be? Surely someone of power, for he spoke for yer clan in demanding Niall's return."

A bitter smile touched Iain's lips. "Och, a man of power, and no mistake. He's Duncan, laird of Balloch Castle on Loch Tay and the Campbell's younger brother. He's also my father."

Anne shot him a sideways glance. *He doesn't get on with his father,* she thought, noting the tight expression on Iain's face. She quickly stilled the impulse to ask him more. It wasn't her concern. She had problems enough without seeking more.

"And Hugh, the witch hater." Anne gestured to the brown-haired man riding on Niall's other side. "Where exactly does he hang on the Campbell family tree?"

"Mad cousin Hugh? His mother's Lydia Campbell, younger sister to the Campbell and my father."

"Is he really mad?" Anne asked, recalling the crazed look in Hugh's eyes the day of the raid.

"In some ways, aye. And yet, there are times when I wonder if there's not a method to his madness . . ." Iain paused. "At any rate, when he commits himself to a cause, he can be quite fanatical, going on for hours, even days, on the same subject. He bears a heavy grudge that his mother was born female, for it puts him fourth, after Niall, my father, and me, in line for the chieftainship. As ye can imagine, it's one of his favorite topics. We tend to ignore him when he starts up about it."

"Poor man."

"Niall told me Hugh tried to kill ye." Iain shook his head in wonder. "Yet ye can still say that, after what he almost did to ye? Och, ye're a rare one."

She glanced at him. "Not only am I a Christian, but I'm a healer, Iain. We're all God's children. My heart goes out to those in distress, whether of the body or mind."

"Well, don't concern yerself with Hugh. He'd not appreciate yer efforts. On the contrary, it'd be verra dangerous for ye. He hates witches above all else."

"And why's that?"

Iain shook his head. "I don't know all the details, lass. Something to do with a lost love who was killed, but I was away at the time, and no one cared to talk about it. At any rate, it makes about as much sense as most things Hugh takes a disliking to, but for yer own sake, stay clear of him."

"Aye," Anne muttered uneasily. Movement up ahead distracted

them into silence. They watched as Niall, with a wave of his hand, sent a rider galloping off down the road.

Stretching tall in his stirrups, Niall stared after the man until he disappeared from view. Then, with a dark frown, he settled back onto his horse.

A plan. He must have a plan for discovering the traitor. He glanced behind at the ruddy, good-hearted faces of his warriors. To question the motives of even one of them sickened him, but he must. More was at stake than just his personal safety.

His clan was in grave danger. If the traitor had truly stirred the feud all these years, ambition was evidently a higher priority than Campbell welfare. And he, as tanist, seemed to be all that stood in the way of that ambition.

But who'd want him dead? There were several lairds to consider, ones he'd had, as tanist, dealt with severely in the past. And he didn't dare discount someone holding a secret grudge, one he had no way of knowing about. Yet, as thoroughly as Niall tried to sift through every possible motive, the specter of the chieftainship rose above them all.

His own family. Could one of them possibly covet it enough to eliminate him as rightful heir, to turn traitor? There were several males in direct line for the eagle feathers of clan chief—his uncle and two cousins closest of all. To add their names to the list, much less actually consider them, gouged like a dagger in Niall's gut. But consider them he did and, gradually, one name rose above the rest.

Iain.

Who else would have better cause than Iain to see him dead? When his father had first turned ill, Niall, thanks to a faction in favor of Iain, had not so easily been chosen tanist, a position which all but guaranteed an eventual succession to the chieftainship. In the end, though, the position—which should've, as firstborn son of the current chief, been automatically his—*had* finally fallen to him. He had thought Iain had accepted it, but now he wondered. Perhaps, even after all these years, Iain was biding his time.

But his boyhood friend, gallant, courageous Iain? Niall flung aside the gnawing suspicions with a violent shake of his head.

Proof. He had no proof, and there were others. He mustn't forget the others, like Hugh and Uncle Duncan.

But Hugh, though it was well known he coveted the chieftainship, was far too unstable to be accepted by the clan. He was also not blessed with the cleverness of wits to mastermind anything. And Duncan, though his father's brother, a strong advisor and, after him, technically next in line for the chieftainship, might be considered too old to bring much long-term stability. But Iain . . . Iain was young, strong, and very capable.

Suddenly, proof or not, Niall couldn't stand the thought of Iain near anything that was his, and that included Anne MacGregor. He growled a brief word of explanation to Duncan, then wheeled his mount around and rode back to join the pair.

He pulled up alongside Anne. Niall's keen glance scanned both of them before finally settling on his cousin. "Yer father wishes to speak with ye. Ride ahead."

Iain laughed. "Have a need to be with yer lady, have ye? Och, cousin, why not just come out and say it? Ye've never couched words so gently before."

"Ride ahead, and no more of it!"

"M'lady." Iain nodded to Anne then urged his mount forward.

When her blond companion was out of earshot, she turned to Niall. "Was it necessary to be so rude? He only tried to keep me company, to distract me from my sorrow."

Niall gave a disdainful snort. "And did he now? I think, instead, he sniffs a wee too closely at what's not his."

Indignation surged through Anne. "Why, ye crude, churlish knave! We may be handfasted, but I'm not some piece of chattel. And I won't abide ye telling me who I may and may not take as friend. There'll be few of those at Kilchurn as it is."

"Fear not, sweet lass." Niall chuckled grimly. "I've already taken steps to remedy that wee shortcoming. The rider I sent ahead will notify the castle of our arrival. And I've ordered a feast this eve to welcome ye to the clan. So ye see, ye'll soon have more friends than ye'll know what to do with."

"A . . . a feast?" Anne swallowed hard. *He thinks to unsettle me.* She shook her head firmly. "Pray, don't go to such trouble for my sake. There's no need to make pretenses ye don't feel. It'll fool no one, at any rate."

Niall scowled over at her. "And I say ye mistake yerself, madam. All pretense aside, the only way ye'll ever gain acceptance is if I first accept ye. The feast is but my way of showing that. So don't turn up that haughty little nose of yers. It won't endear ye at Kilchurn."

"I don't care—"

"And I say, don't let fly what ye can't call back. For better or worse, Kilchurn's yer home, the Campbells yer people, for the next year at least. Besides," he continued in a gentler tone, "I don't wish ye ill. Ye saved my life, after all, and at great expense to yerself."

"And I don't need yer pity," she snapped back. "It was but a point of honor that saved yer life and naught else."

"Then attend the feast as a point of honor, for to hide in yer room would only confirm what my clan already thinks of MacGregors."

Anne's hands tightened about her horse's reins. "And what might that be?"

Niall's glance moved casually to scan the countryside. "Och, naught really. Just that MacGregors are all cowards."

"Why, ye big, arrogant—"

"Calm yerself, lassie." Her dark companion laughed. "Those weren't my thoughts. I've certainly never doubted yer courage. I was thinking of what others might say, if ye failed to show yer face this eve."

"I'll be there," Anne muttered, at last admitting defeat. "And are there any other surprises ye've planned tonight? If so, tell me now."

Niall returned her glare. "Nay, no others. I'd imagine ye've already envisioned far worse than I could ever surprise ye with. Now, if ye'll permit me, I'll remove what must surely be my unpleasant presence. Will ye mind riding alone, or shall I send back one of my men?"

Anne shot Niall a contemptuous look. "Don't concern yerself about me. Considering the choice of company, riding alone is far more to my liking."

He grinned then signaled his mount forward. Anne watched him ride away, relief flooding her at being free of Niall Campbell's loathsome presence. She knew she shouldn't have spoken so harshly to him, that it was neither kind nor loving, but there was just something about him that set her teeth on edge. Something that both stirred as well as angered her . . .

To distract herself from her increasingly unsettling thoughts, Anne sought out the form of his golden-haired cousin riding up ahead. *Och,* she silently mourned, *if only Iain had been my father's choice.* He, she could've come to care for. He, she could even imagine wedding at the end of this odious term of handfasting. But not so with the likes of Niall Campbell. All she could envision with him was pain and heartache. What else, indeed, could any woman expect at the hands of the legendary Wolf of Cruachan?

The rain that had held off all day began to fall. Anne pulled her cloak tightly around her to ward off the encroaching dampness, shivering even as she did. Up ahead, through the mist rising from the land, she could make out the white-capped, twin peaks of Ben Cruachan. Soon, they'd clear the last of the hills. Soon, the deep waters of Loch Awe would come into view.

Loch Awe and Castle Kilchurn, that great stone fortress of Clan Campbell. Soon it would imprison her as mercilessly as it held others out. And soon, all too soon, she must, on a daily basis, face Niall Campbell and his clan. A year suddenly seemed like an eternity.

✦

"Here, lassie," Old Agnes murmured soothingly as she stepped away from the tub of steaming water and bustled over to Anne, "let's get those wet clothes off and ye into this nice warm bath. Ye don't want to catch the ague, do ye?"

The ague, Anne thought humorlessly. Folk sometimes died if its fever and lung sickness couldn't be controlled. It would be the answer to all her problems. She'd escape this unfriendly place and not be forced to face Niall Campbell or endure his most unwelcome presence. Aye, for once the ague seemed a welcome fate.

Numbly, Anne felt hands touch her as the old maidservant worked free the fastenings of her gown. The air of the bedchamber, though warm from a roaring hearth fire, still made her tremble when the sodden clothes finally fell away.

Agnes wrapped an arm around Anne's shoulders, firmly guiding her to the large wooden tub. "That's my lass," she crooned. "Just step into this nice warm water and ye'll soon feel better. We've enough time before the feast even to soap yer hair then dry it before the fire. Ye'll look glorious when I'm through with ye, and no mistake."

Anne obediently climbed in and sank beneath the water. As the heat gradually replaced the shuddering spasms, her eyes closed and she sighed.

A gnarled hand stroked her head. "See, lassie? Didn't I tell ye? It'll be all right soon enough. Now, let me wash yer hair with some of this fine soap. Doesn't it smell heavenly?"

Anne inhaled deeply of the sweet lavender scent. The gentle, kneading motion of the maid's fingers lulled her into a deeper and deeper state of relaxation. She sank lower into the water. It was so blissful, so comforting, Anne thought dreamily, after the tense, uncomfortable journey and arrival at Kilchurn.

The rain had continued for hours, and their party had arrived miserably soaked to the skin. Though Niall immediately hustled her upstairs to her room, insisting she get out of her clothes before she took a chill, Anne couldn't help but notice the sullen stares and raised brows that followed them through the keep. *News travels fast,* she thought grimly, *and bad news fastest of all.*

Hostility pervaded the Great Hall as they walked across it, hounding her down the cool stone corridors, tailing her to the very door of her chamber. Only now, safely inside, the cold finally seeping from her in the gently lapping water, did Anne at last allow herself to relax. If only she didn't ever have to leave this room . . .

All too soon, it seemed, Agnes was urging Anne from the rapidly cooling water. "Come along, lassie." The old woman wrapped a bath sheet about Anne's water-slick body. "Come, sit before the fire and I'll comb out yer hair. It'll be so lovely when it's dried, as thick and wavy as it is. How would ye like me to dress it for the feasting?"

Anne lowered herself to the cushioned stool before the fire. She shrugged. "It's of no import. Do with it what ye will."

Agnes frowned. "Now, lassie, don't talk like that. Of course it matters. Ye want to be looking as pretty as ye can for the young lord, don't ye? It's past time he found happiness again, and no—"

A cool gust of air halted the maidservant's good-hearted ramblings. Both turned to the door now standing ajar. In its opening stood the tall, slim figure of a girl of about fourteen, her long, black hair wafting gently about her shoulders in the back draft of the hallway. Even from across the room, Anne could see the flashing brilliance of her turquoise eyes.

"Lady Caitlin," Old Agnes gasped in surprise. "What brings ye here so near the feasting? Why haven't ye dressed . . ."

The old servant's words died as Caitlin strode across the room. She eyed Anne then sniffed disdainfully. "So, this is the wench Niall brought back from MacGregor lands. Ye're comely enough, I'll warrant, at least for warming my brother's bed, but I can't understand why he'd willingly bind himself to a MacGregor."

As the maidservant gave a horrified "M'lady Caitlin!" Anne went rigid. Clasping the sheet to her, she rose and moved the few feet to stand before Niall's sister. Though the girl was taller by half a head, Anne stared steadfastly up at her, returning the hostile glare with a calm one of her own.

So it begins, and I must be the one to swallow my pride and offer my hand in peace. Well, it's no more than the Lord expects of me. Besides, she's little more than a child.

"Aye," Anne admitted quietly, "I'm MacGregor, and no mistake. I'll thank ye to remember that. Otherwise, we can never be friends."

Caitlin's lips curled in ill-disguised contempt. "Friends? Ha!"

"Aye, friends. It's past time for the feuding to end. Can't it begin with us? It would set an example for all to heed."

Surprise widened the girl's striking blue-green eyes. For a moment, Anne thought she saw hesitation flicker there. Then something passed across them, a memory perhaps. Caitlin's lips tightened with renewed resolve.

"Nay, it can never be. Though ye saved my brother's life, too much has been ruined by this handfasting." The ebony-haired girl vehemently shook her head. "Nay, I cannot be yer friend. It's impossible!"

In a flurry of skirts and whirling tresses, Caitlin hurried from the chamber. Silence hung heavy for a time, until a fire-eaten log fell to the hearth in an explosion of wood and glowing sparks. With a deep sigh, Agnes went to shut the door, then moved to the curtained bed. She returned with a blue velvet dressing gown.

"Here, lassie," she said as she held it open for Anne to put on, "cover yerself before ye take a chill. It's cold enough in this castle without ye enduring the stone damp on top of it all."

Aye, Anne mused, wrapping the dressing gown about her, *the castle's dwellers are a chill lot indeed. And each, for his own reasons, resents my presence here.* Expelling a deep breath, Anne turned back to the fire's warmth, fearing it was the last comfort she'd find in the night ahead.

A firm knock at the door interrupted Agnes. Quickly brushing the long mass of dark red curls to cascade down her mistress's back, the old servant finished fastening the clasp of the heavy pendant necklace around Anne's neck. Then she hurried to the door.

Anne continued to stare into the hand mirror, her pensive gaze riveted on the twinkling blue stone surrounded by its ornate silver setting. It had once been her mother's, but that gentle lady was now dead five years past. Anne wished she was here with her now, to offer comfort and advice. Ah, how she needed both, if she was to survive this next year, and especially this most arrogant and frustrating of men!

The creak of iron hinges intruded on her musings, and Anne laid down the mirror.

"M'lord. Yer lady's ready just this moment."

Anne's gaze jerked around. Tall and broad-shouldered, Niall Campbell's powerful form filled the doorway. He now wore doublet, skintight trews that, save where the bandage bulged, molded to his hard-muscled legs, and a plaid draped across his body and over his left shoulder. A high-collared white shirt peeked from beneath the close-fitting, long-sleeved jacket. Stockings and soft heelless brogues covered his feet.

Niall moved toward her, his leg wound barely seeming to hamper him, his stride one of a lithe, confident Highland warrior. Anne swallowed hard, a strange, languid warmth flowing through her.

His eyes, though still bruised and swollen from his beating at MacGregor hands, glittered in the firelight. A curious half-smile lifted the corners of his mouth. At his bold perusal, heat flushed Anne's cheeks. It angered her, this continued, uncharacteristic response to him.

"Are ye quite done staring at me, m'lord? If I haven't dressed to yer satisfaction, there's yet time to change."

A chuckle rumbled deep within Niall's chest. "For such a wee wisp of a lass, ye're certainly always looking for a fight. But ye won't get one from me." He glanced admiringly down the length of her body. "That particular shade of pale blue does special things to yer eyes. Ye've dressed to my satisfaction and more."

Warily, Anne eyed his proffered arm. "What are ye about? It isn't time for the meal."

"My father wishes to meet ye. He's confined to his bed and won't join us for the feast. We'll visit him in his chambers."

Anne's heart gave a small flutter of trepidation. The Campbell. She was going to see the Campbell—the man, in the end, responsible for the long, bitter feud. The man who cold-bloodedly sent his son out to wreak terror and havoc upon MacGregor lands. With a rush of renewed anger, Anne realized she despised the Campbell chief even more than she did his son. It was at his command that the feud had been allowed to continue. Niall Campbell, as ruthlessly competent as he was, was only obeying orders.

Her father's words came back to her. *"The clan's welfare . . . its verra survival . . . now in yer hands."*

No matter her true feelings for the despicable Campbell leader, Anne knew she must mask them with courtesy and goodwill. She accepted Niall's arm. What did one more compromise in a day beset with compromises matter?

"As ye wish, m'lord."

The journey down the long stone corridors, their dank walls decorated with tapestries and weaponry, passed all too quickly. Before Anne knew it, Niall pushed open the door of a brightly lit room. The chamber was graced with a large hearth filled with briskly burning logs and a red brocade-curtained bed piled high with fluffy pillows and a comforter. The frail form of a man seemed lost among the bedclothes.

He waved them over. "Niall? Is that ye, laddie? Come closer and bring the lass with ye."

Faded blue-green eyes peered up at her as Anne neared the bed. Blond hair, heavily streaked with gray, graced a weather-beaten, deeply furrowed face. Yet though the hair coloring and eyes were different, Anne noted the strong resemblance between father and son. She managed a tentative smile.

"Come closer, lassie," the Campbell urged kindly. He glanced at his son. "Niall, don't stand there. Pull up a chair for yer lady."

Once Anne was settled, the older man leaned over to take her hand. "My son told me how ye saved his life, lassie. I'm forever in yer debt."

"It was naught," Anne began stiffly before a sound from Niall stopped her.

She glanced back at him. He was standing behind her chair, a warning light gleaming in his eyes. Anne knew he half expected her to brush aside his father's gratitude as "a point of honor."

With a small smile, she turned to the Campbell. "It's kind of ye to say that, but it was the least I could do. After all, yer son first saved my life."

The Campbell lay back on his pillows, a wry grimace on his lips. "Aye, Niall told me how Hugh thought ye a witch. He's a troubled lad, my nephew. I hope ye can find it in yer heart to forgive and forget."

"I'll do my best, m'lord."

He cocked his head. "And aren't ye the sweet one? My son did well in handfasting ye. Beauty and goodness, all rolled into one delightful bundle. But then, he always was lucky with the lassies. Weren't ye, laddie?"

"Aye, Father," was Niall's dispassionate reply.

The Campbell's gaze returned to Anne. "I'm glad the feud has ended with yer joining. It went on far too long, no matter who was first to blame. It was a wise idea, yer father's. I only wish I'd thought of it." He paused, a troubled look darkening his features. "It'll solve a lot of things."

For a long moment the Campbell was silent, then, as if a sudden thought had assailed him, he grinned. He looked up at his son. "It'll solve yer problems, too, laddie. It's past time ye put off yer mourning and gave me a grandson. Aye, a wee bairn is just what this castle—"

A hard, wracking cough cut short his words. He gestured to a nearby table. "W-water!"

Before Niall could react, Anne was at the table pouring out a cup. Her emotions churned. How could a man so bent on another clan's destruction be so kind? He hardly seemed the sort.

Her hand clenched the cup of water. The Campbell, it was rumored, had been ill for several years now. He had been forced to delegate more and more responsibility to his son, finally naming him tanist a year ago. Had Niall Campbell taken it upon himself to step up the raids, in the hope of finally ending the feud?

Anger filled Anne. The bloody knave! Of course, that would explain everything. And the Campbell probably didn't even know . . . poor old man.

She returned to the bed and gently lifted his head. "Drink, but slowly, and in small sips," she instructed, struggling to contain the rage that shook her voice. "That's the best way to soothe the catarrh."

He swallowed half the cup's contents before falling wearily back onto the bed. "Thank ye, lassie."

Anne plumped the pillows behind his head and pulled up the comforter. "I've done naught. Tomorrow, if ye'll allow me, I'll brew ye a tea of lavender flowers. It's wonderful for the catarrh."

He smiled weakly up at her. "Och, and won't that be a pleasant change from my physician? He gives me no relief with his endless purgatives . . . and bloodlettings. I get so verra . . . verra . . . tired . . ."

The Campbell's eyes slid shut. Soon the deep, even breathing of slumber filled the room.

Niall's hand settled on Anne's shoulder. "Come, lass. It's time we were leaving."

Carefully, so as not to disturb him, Anne disengaged her fingers from the old man's clasp. They left the room. Before she could turn to walk down the hallway, Niall gripped her arm.

Anne halted. "Aye?"

✝ ✝

"It was kind of ye to treat my father so gently. Especially since I know ye must hate him as much as ye hate me."

Anne stared up at him, aware he had yet to make his point.

"My father's dying."

The brutal truth of his words startled her. "Aye, that's apparent."

"He spits up blood most times now. There's naught ye can do."

"I can ease his sufferings, make his last days less painful."

Niall inhaled a shuddering breath. How could he make her see the danger of using her healing skills in Kilchurn? His father would die no matter what she did, but none would remember that. In the end, all that would be recalled is that he died of her ministrations.

He shook his head. "Nay, ye can't, lass. I want ye to stay away from my father with yer potions." His grip tightened painfully on her arm. "Do ye hear me? Do ye understand?"

Anne wrenched free, both hurt and angered by his words. Did he think she'd harm his father? That because of the years of bitter feuding she'd stoop to using her skills for revenge? Her hands clenched into tight little fists. Well, what did she expect?

She glared up at Niall with burning, reproachful eyes. "Have it yer way, m'lord. Yer unfair suspicions will only make yer father suffer and hasten his death, but then, mayhap ye cannot wait to claim yer chieftainship. And what should it matter to me? One Campbell is as bad as another!"

With a flounce of her hair, Anne turned to go. Before she had taken her first step, however, Niall's ice-rimed voice halted her in her tracks.

"Don't walk away from me, madam," he growled. "I haven't finished with ye yet."

5

Anne turned, every muscle tensed for battle. Her cheeks flushed with fury. "Not finished with me?" she slowly ground out the words. "Surely ye jest, m'lord. Ye've all but named me a despicable murderer, completely unworthy of yer trust. What more is there to say?"

Niall's own anger rose to meet Anne's. His dark eyes slammed into hers. By mountain and sea, he had neither the time nor patience for this! He had more pressing problems. Why couldn't she see beyond . . .

He paused. There, flickering behind her thin veneer of rage, Niall found her pain. *Unfeeling swine!* he mentally cursed himself. Once again he had hurt her, viciously clawing away the few consolations she had left like some Highland wildcat, without warning, without mercy. All his good intentions to the contrary, he seemed to wound her at nearly every turn.

Niall ran a hand through his hair in exasperation. "I don't despise ye, lass, nor think ye a murderer. But as far as trust goes, I don't give that easily to any man, friend or foe."

His reply nonplussed Anne. What was she to do with his abrupt changes in mood? One moment he was the cruel, ruthless enemy she expected him to be, and the next . . .

"Then why did ye forbid me to help yer father? I told ye. I've a calling to heal, and it's sacred to me. I'd never turn from anyone in need, no matter—"

"Och, so there ye are, nephew."

✢✢✢✢✢✢✢✢✢✢✢✢✢✢✢✢✢✢✢✢✢✢✢✢✢✢✢✢✢✢✢✢✢✢✢✢✢

Duncan Campbell's voice intruded from the shadowed hallway. He strode into view and halted before them. "The folk are gathered, the tables laden with food and drink. We await only ye and yer lady for the feast to begin."

"Aye." A small frown darkened Niall's brow. "We were just now on our way."

Frustration and relief warred within Niall. He hadn't expected the matter of forbidding Anne's healing in Kilchurn to come up quite so soon. He had hoped for time to ease her into life here, then break the news. If it hadn't been for his uncle's timely intrusion . . .

Niall cast aside his confusing clash of emotions. The confrontation wasn't over, just delayed. He offered Anne his arm. After a moment's hesitation, she accepted it.

Duncan eyed them. "Er, I've never had the pleasure of an introduction."

The tension of the past few moments drained from Niall. He chuckled. "True enough and entirely my fault, I'm sorry to say. But what with all the confusion surrounding our departure from Castle Gregor and then during our arrival here . . ."

Niall dragged in a deep breath. "Lass, this is my uncle, Duncan Campbell." He nodded toward the older man. "Duncan, Lady Anne MacGregor."

Duncan bowed. "Welcome, lady. Ye're long overdue in my nephew's life. It's my pleasure at last to make yer acquaintance."

As she extended her hand, Anne studied Niall's uncle covertly. He was tall, as were all the Campbell nobility and, though not as powerfully built as his nephew, an imposing, substantial man. His sandy-colored hair was pale with a generous scattering of gray. His full beard was even paler, nearly white-gold. He possessed the same strong, ruggedly attractive features as his son, Iain. If not for his eyes, Anne would've found Duncan Campbell a most compelling man.

But dark as the depths of an angry, storm-tossed loch, they were cold, their expression flat and unreadable. And the smile that touched his lips as he bent to kiss her hand, though correct in every way, never passed his mouth.

A small tremor coursed through her. *So, yet another Campbell unhappy with my presence. Is there no end to the enemies I'll discover in Kilchurn?*

Niall noted the shiver and mistook it for the chill of the corridor. "Come, lass. It's warmer in the Great Hall. Time enough to talk further once we're there.

This time Anne was in a more receptive frame of mind to examine the Great Hall. It was a large, impressive room, in size as well as in luxurious appointments. The walls were wainscoted with carved fir, the upper portion of bare stone lavishly hung with intricately woven tapestries to brighten the room and absorb its chill.

Rushes covered the floor. The fragrant scent of the sweet woodruff scattered among them mingled with the tangy wood smoke wafting from the great hearth on the far wall. A group of men and women stood before the blazing fire, laughing and talking in happy animation.

Anne found Iain there. Like a beacon in the night he drew her, the only person in the crowded room whom she knew to be friend.

At that moment, Iain looked up. He smiled and strode over to her.

When he noted the direction of his cousin's path, Niall tightened his grip on Anne's arm. Then, aware of the almost reflexive response, he forced his muscles to unclench, his breathing to even.

Iain. Can it really be Iain? he asked himself for the hundredth time. *I can't believe it. I won't believe it, not yet, not without proof. Besides, it isn't yet the time to reveal yer suspicions to Iain or any man. Play the fool awhile longer. Lure the traitor into the trap. The victory, when it comes, will be all the sweeter for the waiting.*

Despite the calming words of reason, at Anne's welcoming smile for his cousin, a cold anger stirred in Niall. All his iron control couldn't contain the muscle that twitched in his jaw as a sudden thought assailed him. Could his cousin's flirtatious attentions toward

Anne have a more sinister purpose than the lighthearted teasing it appeared? Could Iain somehow plan to use her against him? It would be the way of a traitor.

Still, it was too soon to focus all his suspicions on Iain. There were others just as suspect. He must remember that. He *must* remain clearheaded and in control. It was the only way to ferret out the traitor.

Niall inhaled a rasping breath. Curse it, but the doubts, the constant questions, were eating him alive!

"Lady." Iain's deep voice intruded on Niall's tormented thoughts. His cousin rendered Anne a customary nod. "I'm pleased to see ye're no worse for the journey's wear." His eyes gleamed in open admiration. "The blue of that dress becomes ye greatly."

Anne flushed. Grimly, Niall recalled she hadn't reacted half so strongly when *he* had complimented her earlier. He glared at the younger man. Iain seemed not to notice.

"It's time to be seated," Niall said.

Until he could ascertain Iain's true intentions, every effort must be made to keep Anne from his cousin. It was the safest course. Niall turned to her, eliminating Iain from the conversation.

Anne wrenched her gaze from Iain's smiling countenance. "Aye, as ye wish, m'lord."

The hard glitter in Niall's eyes startled her. Whatever was the matter now? She glanced at Iain. "It'd please me greatly if ye'd sit by me at table. A familiar face, among so many strangers—"

"Iain will sit elsewhere."

"But it's a simple matter to move one person. Please, m'lord—"

"My mind's made. Now, no more of it." Niall led Anne toward the table.

She considered protesting his high-handed manner, but a glance at Iain quashed that idea. His deep blue eyes had narrowed to slits. Were they always so at odds with each other?

The main table was raised above the others on a dais, situated perpendicularly to two other long tables. Though the lower tables were comfortably provided with padded benches, the chief's had English chairs covered in bright green damask. As Niall held out a chair for Anne, Iain took his place down at the far end of the main table. It seemed too great an insult to one of the Campbell's immediate family, when she knew Iain's rightful place must surely be at center table. Her heart went out to the young man.

"How can ye be so cruel to yer cousin?" she demanded softly when Niall finally seated himself beside her. "He means ye no discourtesy in his kindness to me."

"I've my reasons," he muttered. "Now, no more of it."

Anne's lips tightened, but she withheld comment. Rebellious, uncomplimentary imprecations, nonetheless, roiled in her head. *If I were ye, ye pigheaded dolt,* she raged at Niall silently, *I'd withhold my goodwill from the father, not the son. He's the one to beware, with those dead eyes of his.*

Out of the corner of her eye, Anne noted Duncan Campbell seating himself on Niall's other side. At the memory of the older man's inscrutable expression, a chill prickled down her spine. Mad cousin Hugh, cold-eyed Uncle Duncan. The disparity between the Campbell's personality and his reputed conduct toward her clan. The strange circumstances surrounding the Wolf's capture. What had her father said that day about the Campbell army's arrival? Something about entrapping Niall . . . and a traitor?

Aye, there was indeed something dangerously amiss in this castle, but what, she had yet to fathom. And now, vowed to the Campbell tanist as she was, Anne sensed she risked full involvement—even to the endangerment of her life.

Niall signaled for the feast to begin. Anne found little interest in the sumptuous fare, though, at any other time, the fresh, fried Loch Awe trout, succulent slices of cured mutton, and stoved chicken surrounded by onions, potatoes, and carrots would easily have tempted her appetite. There was scant energy left for eating at any rate. All her efforts were needed in maintaining a calm, proud front for the hostile-eyed Campbells.

Her lack of interest in the fare wasn't lost on Niall. He noted how she moved the food around on her plate to feign eating it, her refusal of the dessert of sugar rolls and honey cakes sprinkled with ground almonds, the pale, taut look on her face. The coolly restrained reception of his people didn't help, he knew, nor did Caitlin's glaring animosity on Anne's other side.

Curse it all, Niall thought in exasperation. Though he knew a MacGregor wouldn't be readily accepted after years of bitter feuding, he had hoped for a more pleasant evening. A sense of the long, difficult road ahead for Anne filled him. He made a silent vow to aid her as best he could.

Guilt at the memory of the look on her face earlier plucked at him. Perhaps he had been too harsh with her. He knew she had been upset over his refusal to allow Iain to sit with them.

Niall sighed. If only he dared trust her with his cousin. But he didn't dare trust anyone right now, not even his own family. Och, curse that scheming, blackhearted traitor!

The meal ended, and the minstrels with pipes and harps arrived to entertain the gathering. Niall sat through the singing, becoming more tense by the moment. Finally, when the fiddlers entered to take their seats and the rushes were moved aside for the dancing, he could bear it no longer.

His wounded leg notwithstanding, perhaps a turn at a reel would ease the unpleasant churning in his gut.

He offered Anne his hand. "It's time for the dancing to begin."

She stared down at his large, calloused palm, well aware tradition dictated the lord and his lady lead the first dance. But to go down to the dance floor, to stand there and subject herself to the full examination of all . . .

Anne rose in a rustle of skirt and petticoats, her expression inscrutable save for the resolute look she gave him. "As ye wish, m'lord."

She allowed him to escort her onto the dance floor. Together with Iain, Duncan, Hugh, Niall's sister, Caitlin, and two other women of the clan nobility, they formed lines, the men opposite the women, for the reel. As the music began, Anne turned to face Niall. Standing in place, they executed the intricate *pas de basque* steps recently popularized by Queen Mary's court. Then, moving in unison, the two of them crossed behind Iain and his partner to meet in the center with the third couple in line, Duncan and the dark-haired Caitlin. Joining hands above their heads in the middle, they moved in a circle to the music.

As they danced, Caitlin's seething animosity, barely restrained during the meal, flared into overt hostility. It grew until Anne thought, at any moment, the girl would halt and, in the presence of all, attack her. Fortunately, the dance just then required partners to be exchanged. Niall whisked his glaring sister away.

"Ye must be patient with our little Caitlin," Duncan murmured as he moved with Anne down the center of the line behind his niece and nephew. "She doesn't take kindly to a MacGregor in our midst, and hasn't the maturity of years to hide it."

Anne shot him an assessing glance. "Indeed. It's a trait in short shrift this eve. But don't lay the blame too heavily on Caitlin's shoulders. She, at least, has the excuse of youth."

Duncan's mouth tightened. "That may be, lady, but ye'll not win our hearts with an arrogant air. If compromise is needed, mayhap it should come—"

Once more they met in the middle with Niall and Caitlin. Anne met Niall's searching gaze, then looked away.

With a frown, he noted the anger burning in her eyes. Had Duncan said something untoward?

Niall shot a glance at his uncle before the two couples separated once more to dance away. The older man's features were calm, a slight smile on his lips. Niall relaxed and turned back to his sister. It seemed there was no need to look further than her for the source of Anne's discomfiture.

"Ye've played the role of hostess poorly this eve, lassie."

Turquoise eyes glared up at him. "Och, and how so?"

“Ye know the answer as well as I.” Steadily, Niall returned her gaze. “It isn’t proper to treat Lady Anne so inhospitably. I expect ye to set the example. No good’ll come of continuing the feud at her expense.”

“Easy words, when ye’re the only Campbell here who stands to profit from her presence.” Caitlin’s rosy lips curved disdainfully. “Couldn’t ye have found a bedmate closer to home, brother dear?”

Niall’s eyes narrowed, but he withheld comment. He swung his sister about and headed up the outside of the line to rejoin Anne and Duncan.

“She saved my life!” he finally growled. “I’d have thought that alone would’ve endeared her to ye. But no matter. Ye’ve only to obey me in this. Do ye understand?”

“Och, and all too clearly.” Caitlin’s eyes filled with tears. “I’ll obey ye, but, though I love ye with all my heart, I can never be her friend. Her presence here has ruined my life!”

She danced off to rejoin Duncan, effectively ending the conversation.

Caitlin’s parting words echoed in Niall’s head. More unsettled than before, he rejoined Anne to begin the same dance routine with the next couple, Hugh and his partner.

That set, though no words were exchanged, was equally disconcerting. Hugh never ceased his furious glaring at Anne. Only Niall’s quelling presence, hovering nearby, prevented outright rudeness on his cousin’s part.

To Anne, the dance seemed to drag on interminably. One by one, she was forced to meet and deal with a gamut of hostile gazes from the other dancers. *And what did ye expect,* she asked herself wryly time and again, *open arms and Highland jigs?*

The music finally faded, signaling the end to the dance. Niall glanced down at Anne. “Ye’re tired, lass,” he murmured, leaning close. “It’s been a hard day. It’s past time ye were abed.”

“Aye,” she whispered, wearily meeting his gaze. “It’d seem so.”

They left the hall, the lilting tunes and happy laughter following them like so many mocking specters. Yet as eager as she had been to leave the prying, unfriendly eyes in the Great Hall, the nearer they drew to the bedchambers, the faster her heart began to pound. Would Niall hold to his word? Tonight would be the first test.

Niall paused in the corridor outside Anne's bedchamber. He turned to her, searching for words to express his regret at the night's unpleasantness. In spite of himself, all he could think of was how lovely the interplay of shadow and light was upon her face. Had he ever truly realized how beautiful she was?

Her hair fell like curling silk about her shoulders before cascading down her back. The sight of it filled Niall with a sudden yearning to touch it. Her soft, moist lips were slightly parted, her mouth lush and ripe. Yet it was the sweep of her long, sooty lashes, lowering to rest gently against the curve of her high cheekbones, that was his true undoing.

Anne's flowerlike scent wafted up to him. Niall inhaled deeply. Desire, unwanted, unexpected, swept through him, igniting a roaring conflagration like flame through dry tinder. His breath caught in his throat. His hand brushed her cheek.

She tensed, and the effort to restrain herself from stepping away was evident. It shattered the mesmerizing fascination that held Niall entranced.

This is madness, he raged at himself. *I gave her my word. Besides, I haven't desired a woman since . . .*

The admission was painful, yet at the same time, oddly exciting. And it would explain the sudden, strange yearning Anne's presence had stirred in him just now. Aye, it would explain but never justify it.

His hand cupped her chin. Apprehension flared in Anne's luminous eyes.

Niall shook his head, his voice ragged. "Ye've naught to fear from me, lass. Truly, I mean no harm."

"I-I don't fear ye."

His mouth quirked. "Och, and don't ye now?"

She didn't answer.

"Well, no matter." His hand fell from her face. "If it's concern I'll go back on my word and force myself on ye this night, ye've naught to fear. That isn't my way." His gaze lowered. "I'm not ready to commit to a woman, or sire another bairn, no matter how dearly my father desires it. I spoke true in my reasons for our handfasting. The loss of my wife and wee son pains me still."

Anne stared up at him, deeply stirred by the undercurrent of intense sorrow, by his plea for understanding. How quickly he could change from an arrogant, self-possessed warrior to a vulnerable, tormented man! Och, it was too much to fathom, especially tonight of all nights.

She managed a small, tentative smile. "Dinna fash yerself, m'lord. It's enough ye mean to keep yer word." She scanned him thoughtfully. He, too, looked weary. The past days had been just as hard for him, with his capture and wounding. She suddenly remembered she hadn't tended to his injuries since yesterday.

"Yer leg, m'lord," Anne began hesitantly. "How does its healing go? I should cleanse it and apply more of my marigold ointment."

Niall tensed. Though, in truth, he preferred her skills to the castle physician's, he knew he couldn't allow her to care for him then forbid her to do so with everyone else.

He shook his head. "My leg fares well, lass. Our physician saw to it when I bathed. Ye needn't concern yerself."

There was a momentary prick of hurt, which Anne quickly quashed. Niall Campbell had no reason to trust her abilities over that of some physician, even if most physicians were little more than purveyors of purgatives and bloodletting as treatment for every illness. It would take time to win his confidence, that was all.

Anne smiled. "Then it's good night, m'lord."

"Aye. Good night, lass." For an instant longer Niall stared down at her, the torchlight sending glinting shards of gold to dance in his eyes. Then, turning on his heel, he walked down the hall to his own bedchamber.

✦

Late the next morning as they unpacked the rest of Anne's possessions, the maidservant discovered the box of plants.

"What would ye have me do with these, lassie?" Agnes held up the container.

Anne turned from the lace-trimmed nightgown she was folding to glance at the old woman. Her face brightened. Her herbs! How could she have forgotten them?

She laid aside the nightgown and hurried to Agnes. Tenderly, her fingers caressed the delicate leaves, examining one, then the other. They all looked well, if a bit wilted, and needed replanting soon.

Taking possession of the box, Anne carried it to the sunlit window. She watered the herbs carefully. Only when her ministrations were complete did Anne turn back to the servant. "Is there some patch in the castle garden where I might plant these?"

"Aye, lassie." A distinctly uncomfortable look spread across the old woman's face. "But it isn't my place to grant ye leave. Sir Niall instructed me to send ye to him with any requests."

So, Anne thought in exasperation, *and must I also ask him permission to breathe?* She smoothed the wrinkles from her skirt and tucked an errant strand of hair in place. "Then so be it. Where might I find him?"

"Mayhap in the inner bailey, near the walled garden. He and his warriors always meet in swordplay at this time of day. Shall I take ye there?"

Anne nodded. "Aye. It'll be a while before I've grasped the intricacies of this castle."

As soon as they left the keep's imposing bulk and stepped outside, the sound of clanging swords reached their ears. They passed quickly around the building's corner buttress to find eight men engaged in energetic sword practice. Anne easily singled out Niall's broad-shouldered form from the rest.

All were stripped to the waist, the excess of their belted plaids wrapped around and tucked into their belts. Their upper torsos and arms glistened with sweat. Anne swallowed hard and moved closer, Agnes following.

Niall's hands gripped the leather-wrapped handle of a claymore; the giant sword was as long as its owner was tall and a weapon only of the strongest men. His arms moved in large, seemingly effortless arcs as he deftly parried the blows of his companions. A grim smile touched his lips and a fierce light gleamed in his eyes, the love of battle settling about him in a heated aura.

Only when his men began to falter then cease their swordplay did Niall at last pause to look about him. His searching glance found Anne's. A wrinkle of puzzlement formed between his brows.

Laying aside his claymore, Niall strode to a nearby water trough. After immersing his head, he straightened, the fluid sluicing down his chest and shoulders. Then he flung back his sodden mane, scattering water everywhere. With a grin, he then approached her.

"I-I wish a word with ye, m'lord," she murmured, forcing the words past the strange tightness in her throat. Distractedly, she motioned to the walled garden. "Away from the others, if ye please."

Niall shrugged. "As ye wish." He grabbed up his shirt and pulled it on as they walked along.

They strolled in silence until the garden's wooden gate was shut behind them. Then Anne turned, gathering all the tact she possessed. "It's a fine garden," she began, gesturing about her. "The soil rich, the sun shining full upon it for most of the day. By yer leave, I would plant my herbs here."

"And what purpose would that serve?"

Anne glanced up in surprise. At the set look to Niall's face, a sense of unease stirred. "Why, to use for my healing potions, of course. Did ye think I'd refuse to help yer people because they were Campbells? Didn't I make my position clear last eve?"

“It was quite evident what yer feelings were. Nonetheless, it cannot be.” He shook his head. “Ye’ll not plant, nor harvest, nor treat anyone with yer herbs at Kilchurn. Do ye understand?”

“But why—” Her voice broke as she struggled with the frustration that roiled within. Och, to ask him for anything and then have it refused! And this, her precious herbs, her beloved healing, above all else!

Anne stared up at him, confused. “Why? Why would ye refuse me such a simple request?”

“I’ve no heart to refuse ye aught, lass,” Niall replied, his voice rough with regret. “But in this matter I can do no less. Ye’re well aware how strong the witch panic burns since the law passed. Have ye already forgotten yer admission that even some of yer own clan imagine ye a witch? What do ye suppose *my* clan will think if ye resume yer healing?”

“I don’t care! I’m good at what I do. There’s no taint of evil in it. In time they’ll see that and accept me.”

Niall hesitated. He wanted to grant her this one request but knew it was unwise. Since the law enacted just a year ago making witchcraft punishable by death, the Reformed Kirk had been zealous in its persecution. When a hapless person, and it was almost always a woman, was accused, she’d be deprived of rest, food, and water, and finally tortured to extract a confession. And, though confession meant certain death by burning or drowning, most eventually confessed. The instruments of torture were that effective.

He shuddered, harking back to the one victim he had seen burnt at the stake. It had been Dora, his cousin Hugh’s one and only love. Malcolm Campbell was responsible for that, one of his first acts upon resuming control of the village kirk. Poor, unstable Hugh had been easily swayed to the preacher’s side, especially after finding Dora in the arms of another man.

She was dead before Niall could reach her, though the flames had yet to consume her body. That day he had made a vow never to allow another burning on Campbell lands. Up until now, he had been successful in keeping that promise.

"Nay, lass." Niall sighed, steeling himself for the task at hand. "I fear that'll never be. My people are too superstitious, for good or bad, too easily led when it comes to matters of religion. A priest of the Reformed Kirk, yet another of my cousins, lives among us. His hatred of witches runs deep. As deep as Hugh's, I fear. He may well stir the people against ye."

"And what of ye?" Anne demanded, her voice now taut with rising anger. "Are ye not clan tanist, soon to be chief? Can't ye control yer own people? Why, oh why, do ye persist in being so . . . so pigheaded?"

Niall struggled to keep the irritation from his voice. "A wise chief knows when and where to interfere in the lives of his clan. Matters of religion aren't one of them. I won't allow witch burnings on Campbell lands, but that doesn't lessen the danger to ye all the same."

Anne made a move to protest. Niall held up a silencing hand. "I've enough problems to deal with at present. As hard-hearted as it may seem, I don't need ye adding to them."

She could feel her cheeks flame as she fought to contain herself, to find some small thread of hope to cling to. As harsh as his refusal was, she also heard the sincere regret in his voice. And she knew he had many problems and responsibilities. But not to plant her herbs . . .

Well, he couldn't worry about the existence of something he knew naught about, Anne consoled herself. She exhaled an acquiescent breath. "I don't wish to become a hindrance or an embarrassment to ye."

His stern mouth relaxed a bit. "Then ye'll obey me in this?"

"Aye, m'lord. I won't plant my herbs in Kilchurn." Though guilt surged through her at the near lie, Anne tilted her head in feigned consideration, eager to change the subject before he prodded her further. "But if I cannot heal, what can I do? I've little talent at sewing or most of the other womanly arts."

A relieved grin spread across Niall's face. He had feared a much more emotional and protracted battle over the issue of her healing. Not that she didn't bear watching, for a time longer at least.

"Why not go riding? Ye've free access to the stables, and Kilchurn and its lands. I ask only if ye ride from sight of the castle ye take one of my men with ye. As powerful as we are, the Campbells are as prime a target for reivers as any other clan. I wouldn't wish ye to fall into unfriendly hands."

Aye, Anne thought, her rebellion growing anew as she left the garden and walked back to rejoin Agnes. *It would surely add to the difficulties if ye're forced to ransom me. But then, why should I care one way or another? I warned ye before I'd not be constrained by the rules of others. And that, my arrogant rogue, includes ye, no matter how beset with difficulties or how tormented ye may be.*

At the memory of those moments with him outside her bedchamber last night, a small, regretful smile touched Anne's lips. *Though perhaps I should, I cannot wish ye ill, Niall Campbell. Truly I can't, for ye've been more than gentle with me. But my life's work won't be denied, not for ye or any man. It cannot be denied—even to the sacrifice of my life. Perhaps someday ye'll see that and understand.*

Anne found a sunny clearing in the midst of a forest of fir, oak, and alder that covered the hills a short walk from Kilchurn. There she planted her herbs.

I do this for the good of all, and someday he'll see this, she reassured herself as a renewed pang of guilt swept through her. *But, truly, how can one reason with such a pigheaded man? I must be daft to care what he thinks, or how he'd feel if he knew, but I do.*

She paused in her thoughts to pound the earth around a fragile feverfew plant. *Well, I won't let it matter. I warned him, that I did, that no one . . .*

"Och, ye'll surely kill those wee plants if ye force them into the ground so cruelly."

Eyes wide, Anne swung about to find an old, shabbily dressed lady standing there. On her arm the woman carried a large basket filled with plants. Wispy, snow-white hair peeked from beneath a red linen kerchief, and the small face was weathered and lined. The eyes studying her, though, were bright and alive, belying the age that bowed the woman's shoulders.

"I . . . I . . . Who are ye?" Anne rose to her feet.

The old woman chuckled. "I'm known as Ena. I live in the village over the hill from Kilchurn. I've birthed the babes and tended the hurts and ills of Clan Campbell all my life." Her gaze narrowed as she examined the neat rows of herbs Anne had already planted. "Do ye know the healing art, then?"

Joy flooded Anne. Here was a kindred spirit, someone to understand and be understood by. "Aye." A happy smile lifted her mouth. "Before I left home, I was healer to Clan MacGregor."

"Och, so ye're the one our young lord took in handfasting." Ena moved closer. "And what are ye called, lassie?"

"Anne." She motioned toward her plantings. "Would ye see what I have, tell me what else grows well here and where I might find it? I'd be grateful for aught ye'd share with me."

Ena squatted to examine the plants. "Hmmm, I see ye've the Saint-John's-wort, agrimony, colt's foot, as well as the soothing chamomile, yarrow, and meadowsweet. All fine herbs for healing." She cocked her head. "Do ye know of the leaf of the fairy fingers? It's a powerful remedy for the dropsy but must be used with caution or it can kill."

Anne shook her head. "I've heard of it, but never grown the plant."

The old woman smiled. "It's also called bloody fingers, or gloves, or foxglove, but I prefer its ancient name. Ye dry the leaves and grind them into a powder. It's bitter and sickening to the taste, so best ye cover it with a strong drink. Too much, even a single leaf chewed and swallowed, can cause seizing of the limbs and the heart to stop. Yet for those cursed with the swollen limbs of the dropsy, it's truly a wondrous plant. Come to my hut in the village and visit me someday. I'll teach ye of it and more."

"I'd like that verra much." Anne helped Ena to her feet. "How will I find ye?"

"It won't be hard, lassie. Folk for miles know where Ena lives." She began to walk away, then glanced over her shoulder. "Ye're a bonnie lass, and no mistake. Don't be afraid of the young lord. He's a braw, good man."

With a wave, Ena disappeared into the forest. Anne stared after her. A friend . . . another friend. It seemed for every obstacle Niall Campbell put in her way, someone came forward to lead her around it.

The realization heartened her as she bent to finish the transplanting of her herbs. Gradually, however, a feeling of coldness wafted over her. Anne shrugged the unpleasant feeling aside. It was naught, she assured herself, but a chill wind blowing through the trees.

Yet as she continued to work the emotion grew, burgeoning into a full-fledged sensation of being watched. Watched by someone, something, evil and full of hatred. A hatred that encircled her, cloaking her in a smothering cloud of malevolence.

Anne rose. *Surely it's my imagination,* she thought. *My mind's but overstimulated, strung too—*

She heard a rustling behind her and froze. Her hand moved to the small dagger nestled at her bosom. Withdrawing it, she turned. There was nothing but the windblown leaves of the large, ferny bracken. She moved closer, her knife clenched in her fist, yet found nothing.

Anne sagged in relief. Just then, a flash of lighter color among the forest-dark shrubbery caught her eye. She inched closer.

The shades took form in the colors of a tartan. A chill, black silence enveloped her. Within it reverberated the sudden pounding of her heart.

There, floating on a gentle breeze, was a scrap of Campbell plaid.

6

"M'lady?"

A few steps from her bedchamber door, Anne jerked to a halt. The familiar voice beckoned her from the morose thoughts dogging her since she had found that piece of Campbell cloth. And, as cowardly as she felt in the act, Anne turned and flung herself into Iain's strong arms.

He gathered her to him, pulling her against the hard-muscled wall of his body. Tenderly, he stroked her hair. "What is it, lass? What's frightened ye so?"

She started to reply, to tell him of the forest's evil intruder, then hesitated. If he knew, he might want her to take him there. Then he'd see her garden, and she couldn't risk Niall finding out about the forbidden plants, at least not for a time.

"Och, it's naught." Anne met his gaze. "Ye startled me, that's all." She glanced down at the arms that held her. "Please let me go. I'm fine now."

His gaze met hers. A flush crept up Iain's neck and face. He released Anne and took a step backward. "Aye, it'd help, I'd wager."

Anne felt the warmth rise in her own cheeks. What must Iain think?

"I-I'm sorry for throwing myself at ye."

The tension eased from Iain's face. He chuckled. "Aye, and I immediately flung ye from me, didn't I? Nay, I fear the blame for our extended embrace must be shared."

"Then so be it. I don't wish . . ." Her voice faded at the tenderness in his expression. Heavy silence settled between them. In the emptiness, Anne could hear the blood rushing through her body.

He cares for me! The realization filled her with panic. She could never be his and, because of that, didn't dare examine the depth of her feelings for him. Nay, for then she'd also be forced to face her true feelings for Niall Campbell. And that was the most frightening consideration of all.

"I-I must go." Anne stepped back.

"Wait!" Iain grasped her arm. "I came to ask if ye'd like to ride with me, see the loch."

"A ride?" In the happy anticipation of going riding, the tension of the past few moments drained from Anne. "Aye. I'd dearly love a ride. When can we leave?"

Iain grinned at her eagerness. "Just as soon as ye're ready. Shall I meet ye at the stables?"

"Aye." She glanced down at her soiled skirt. "It'll take me but a few minutes to prepare myself."

Anne hurried into her room.

Iain is so good, so kind, she thought as she quickly stripped down to her petticoats. At every turn he attempted to think of her happiness. And now, it seemed he saw her as more than just a friend.

The warm glow in his eyes a few moments ago confused Anne. How was it possible he cared for her after such a short time? Was he, mayhap, as lonely as she?

She sighed. If it were true, she must tread carefully with his heart. There could never be anything between them. She was vowed to another, whether she wished it or not.

It'll do no good to curse the fate that bound ye to him *instead of Iain,* Anne chided herself as she donned a simple, forest green woolen dress. Yet, even as the sense of futility filled her, Niall's darkly handsome face rose in her mind's eye. She remembered how the sorrow, as he talked of his lost love, had deepened his eyes to an intense shade of brown and had turned his voice husky with barely suppressed emotion.

In that moment he had opened his heart to her, shared a deeply personal part she sensed he revealed to few others. And, in that moment, Anne had felt herself irresistibly drawn to him. Aye, she admitted, drawn to him as woman to man.

That realization, most of all, disturbed her. She didn't want to care for the enigmatic, ruthless man known as the Wolf of Cruachan. He stirred emotions in her better left unexamined, the kind that sent a woman's heart to pounding and turned her brain to mush. And no man was ever going to do that.

Anne moved to close the chest when her glance snagged on the MacGregor plaid neatly folded within. After an instant's hesitation, she pulled it out and draped it around her shoulders, fastening the cloth with a silver brooch adorned with the form of her clan's beloved Scots pine.

Though she knew it wasn't wise to wear her clan crest and colors in Kilchurn, Anne suddenly didn't care. She wasn't ashamed of her heritage. Let them all, Niall Campbell included, know they must accept her for herself, and part of that identity was MacGregor. Why must all the adjustment be hers? *Aye, why indeed?* Anne angrily asked herself as she finished dressing and left her room.

Iain awaited her at the stables, garbed in a loose, snow-white shirt, snug-fitting tartan trews, and a sturdier, ankle-high laced pair of cuarans. At his side hung the ever-present dirk, and across his back, his claymore. His dark blue gaze skimmed Anne as she walked up, but he made no comment about the plaid slung around her shoulders. He helped her mount, and they were soon galloping out of the castle and along the shore of Loch Awe.

The day was cool, the sky a clear, delicately cloud-strewn blue. The loch's aquamarine waters were placid. Long-necked swans floated serenely upon its mirrored surface, passing near the imposing stone castle.

‡ ‡

Kilchurn, Anne thought as they rode away. *Guardian of Loch Awe, standing lonely sentinel on its narrow outcropping of land. Tales were that when first built it had stood apart on an island.*

Looking at it now, she wondered if the fortress might not someday break free once again, to float like some massive warship down the length of darkling water. It was indeed a beautiful land, this seat of Campbell power, of mighty, snowcapped mountains, forested hills, and heather-clad meadows, reminding her so much of Glenstrae . . . and home.

Anne shook aside the painful memory. She turned her glance to the blond man riding beside her. "And where are ye taking me, Sir Iain? Do ye plan to abduct me and hold me for ransom?"

Iain shot her a rueful smile and shook his head. "If ye were still a MacGregor lass, aye, the idea would be foremost in my mind. Not that I'd ever give ye up for any amount of money."

His smile broadened into a grin. "It'd be an easy thing to hide ye in these mountains. When we were boys, Niall, Hugh, and I used to explore Ben Cruachan, spending the summer days roaming its rocky heights and the nights sleeping beneath the stars, wrapped only in our plaids.

"Once we came upon an ancient, deserted tower high in the mountains. Surprisingly, it was still quite sturdy. All it needed were new floors and doors to make it habitable. Each summer, for several years, we'd journey up to it, to work on its repairs."

"Did ye ever finish it?"

Iain laughed. "Aye, as a matter of fact. But that was over ten years ago. I haven't been there since."

"And is that where ye plan to take me?" Anne asked, a twinkle in her eyes.

He reined in his horse. "Nay, not this time." Iain gestured toward a small burn that emptied into the loch. Huge oaks, their gnarled arms outstretched across the coldly gleaming torrent of water, grew nearby. Below, the grass was starry with wild anemones in vivid purples, reds, lavenders, and whites.

✢ ✢

Anne gasped in pleasure. "Och, it's heavenly!" A radiant smile touched her face. "Thank ye for sharing this with me."

He dismounted, then moved to take her hand. "I'm pleased ye like it. It's little to leave ye with, but I wanted ye to have this special place to come to, to be yer haven, when I'm gone."

She frowned in puzzlement. "Gone? Are ye leaving, Iain?"

"Aye, lass. It's time to return home, to Balloch Castle."

Anne lowered her head, her thick curls tumbling forward to hide her suddenly downcast face. Her only friend in Kilchurn besides Agnes, and now he was to be taken from her.

"When?" she whispered.

"On the morrow."

Her hand covered his. "Och, nay, Iain. Must ye leave so soon?"

He sighed. "Aye, I must go. My father'll stay a time more, awaiting a response from the Crown related to some enterprise he and the Campbell have been working on all these months. But there's too much to be done at Balloch now that summer draws nigh. One of us, at least, must be there to oversee things."

"But I've only been here a day . . ." Anne shook her head. "Och, I'm selfish to think only of myself. I beg pardon."

Iain pulled her gently down from her horse but didn't let her go. Instead, he gathered her to him, wrapping his arms about her. Anne knew she shouldn't let him, but at this sweet moment of parting she no longer cared.

"Ye can't keep yer hands off what's mine, can ye, cousin?" a deep voice intruded.

Iain paled. His arms fell away.

Awash in a sea of grim foreboding, Anne turned. Niall's dark eyes were cold, glittering with suspicion. She took a hesitant step toward him. "M'lord—"

A movement of his hand silenced her, for his glance had returned to Iain. "Well, cousin? I await yer reply."

The younger man glowered back, uncowed. "I care for her, if that's what ye're getting at, but I'm not low enough to sneak behind yer back and cuckold ye. It wasn't what ye thought, at any rate. Anne was but sad to hear of my departure, and I—"

"Was but comforting her?" Niall supplied dryly. "Then it's well ye're leaving, for if ye ever touch her again—"

"And what will ye do?" Iain demanded. "Have me thrown in the dungeon or mayhap flogged? Or would ye prefer to just beat me to a pulp right here and now?"

He moved into a fighting stance, his hands fisted before him. "I tire of yer foul mood of late. Why not put it to rest once and for all? I'm not afraid of ye. Answer me, Niall. Why not here and now?"

Anne turned to Niall. His hands had clenched, and his face was rigid with glacial anger. They were about to come to blows, and all because of a simple misunderstanding!

Instinctively, she ran to her blond companion, knowing she'd have a better chance of reasoning with him. "Iain, don't fight yer cousin," she pleaded. "If there's any fault, it's mine. I foolishly keep running to yer arms, and I've no right. The sin's mine, not yers—"

"A wee hug for comfort's hardly a sin," Iain muttered. "I won't leave ye here to suffer his wrath. I'm not afraid of him."

"He won't harm me. Ye know that. It'll be all right." Her hand gripped his arm. "Please, Iain."

Iain hesitated, indecision wavering in his eyes, but at last he lowered his fists. Taking her hand, he raised it to his lips. "Farewell, lass. If ever ye need me . . ."

Anne smiled. "Aye, well I know. Fare ye well, my friend."

After Iain had mounted and rode away, Anne faced Niall. He, too, had relaxed his fighter's stance, but the look in his eyes remained hard and unforgiving. Slowly, like a person going to her doom, Anne walked up to him.

Her small chin lifted a defiant notch. Perhaps she was partly in the wrong, but she was past weary of his suspicions. "Well, m'lord? What have I done wrong now? Since it seems I'm not fated *ever* to please ye?"

"Don't mock me!"

"Then what would ye have me say? I doubt ye'd believe me at any rate!" Anne threw up her hands. "Och, why do ye treat us like this? I've done naught, and neither has Iain. Are ye trying to destroy our friendship? Is that it? Do ye hate me so much ye wish me friendless?"

"I don't hate ye!" Niall growled. "Don't put words into my mouth, nor lay deeds at my feet not of my doing." He ran a hand through his hair. "Why is it every time we're together we fight? It isn't my intent. I swear it."

"Then why such anger toward Iain?"

"I'm not at liberty to say, save that Iain may not be all he seems." Niall stepped closer, and crooked a finger beneath her chin. "I'm sorry if that's not enough, but it's the best I can offer."

Anne wrenched away. "Ye insult me with yer suspicions, all but do battle with Iain, and then offer that most sorry of explanations? Nay, it can never be enough! Despite what ye may think, I'll not shirk my vows, no matter how odious they be. And don't worry about my fidelity to ye, not with Iain or any other man. I can bear aught for a year—and that includes the likes of ye!"

He cocked an amused brow. "Och, and can ye? And exactly what've I done that's so unforgivable? Ravished ye, beat ye, locked ye in yer room? I've the right to do all that and more, yet all I've asked is ye stay away from Iain—"

"Is that the truth of it, now? Yer truth, mayhap, but not mine. I say ye've tried to take away my only friend, not to mention refused me my greatest joy in life, my healing. Why, ye've really done naught but attempt to destroy my freedom and identity!"

His glance strayed to the plaid she wore. "Aye, yer verra identity. MacGregor identity, and the source of all our problems."

His hands moved to the silver brooch upon her shoulder, and he began to unfasten it. "Ye talk about having no friends, then ye flaunt this plaid in everyone's faces."

Anne's hands halted his. "What are ye about?"

"Isn't it obvious? I don't want ye wearing this in Kilchurn."

She stared at him for a moment and read his hard resolve. What was the use? And she *had* been a fool.

Her hands fell to her sides. "As ye wish, m'lord."

The cold irony in her voice vibrated along Niall's tautly strung nerves. With a force that surprised him, his fingers tightened in the plaid, and he pulled her to him. "Curse ye, woman! Why do ye fight me every step of the way? Why must all the effort be mine? Ye say ye want friends, then don't wear this for a time. Appear to them not as a MacGregor, but as a woman—my woman. And as for Iain," he added, anger beginning to thread his voice, "why do ye constantly run to him and shut me out? Ye're vowed to me, yet have ye ever made one gesture of friendship?"

Anne's anger evaporated, leaving only confusion. Friendship? Was it possible? Could he truly want her friendship? Her mind whirled back to the events of the past few days.

The memory of his anger and arrogance immediately flooded her, but, when the roiling emotions settled, she admitted many were the times he had also been gentle with her, apologized for his earlier harshness. And last eve, when he had lowered his defenses to explain why he had no inclination to bed her . . .

"I-I don't know what to say," she murmured, "or how to answer ye."

Anne grasped his forearms. How warm he felt beneath his linen shirt. She ran her fingers along the corded length, marveling at the crisp texture of hair where the rolled-up sleeves met bare skin. Awesome power lay coiled beneath the rippling surface, yet he had never so much as threatened her. True, he had tried to control her—and that was harm enough—raised his voice a time or two, but he had never, ever, lifted a hand to her.

Her eyelids, weighted with growing languor by the heady nearness of him, reluctantly lifted. Compelling, gold-flecked brown eyes stared down at her, kindling a deep, aching fire. Niall's lips were clenched, his jaw rigid, but his erratic breathing belied his outward semblance of control. Strong fingers dug into Anne's arms, but the pain was fiercely sweet in the spiraling current of excitement that engulfed her.

"Say naught, lass." Niall's head lowered, his voice rough velvet. "It's past time for talking. Show me what ye feel."

His mouth descended, capturing hers in a hard, hungry kiss. For a moment Anne struggled; then she yielded to him. Her arms entwined about his neck, and she leaned into him.

At her eager response Niall shuddered then crushed her to him. His lips moved to trace the soft fullness of her mouth, and he kissed her slowly, thoroughly, the long-repressed desire rising to surround him in a red-hot mist.

She trembled but didn't pull away, shyly meeting his kiss. A harsh spasm wracked Niall. He groaned, then pushed Anne away.

No matter how fiercely he suddenly desired her, it was still too soon. And he didn't know her, had yet even fully to give her his trust. He willed his breathing to slow, his body to relax, and avoided Anne's glance until he could handle the excitement that stirred anew at the sight of her ripe, kiss-swollen mouth.

"I . . . I beg pardon," he muttered at long last, his voice still husky with desire. "It's not right. I'm not ready."

Anne stepped back, wrapping her plaid protectively about her. "Aye, ye said that, though yer actions just now spoke far differently. But fear not, m'lord. I'll respect yer request. I'll not force myself on ye."

Wheeling about, Anne strode toward her horse. *Och, curse the man!* she thought through her rising sense of shame and frustration. *He kisses me, and when I respond, he acts as if I was too eager to throw myself at him.*

She stopped short. Well, mayhap she was. And that after her vow to the Lord not to sin in accepting this handfasting, and her agreement with Niall that there'd be no carnal rights taken.

Tears, maddeningly unwelcome, filled Anne's eyes. *I hate him!*

He toys with my heart at every turn. God forgive me, but how I hate him!

A hand gripped her shoulder and jerked her around. Brown eyes blazed down at her.

"I didn't mean it was yer fault, lass," Niall rasped, his expression one of bewildered remorse. "I—I'm not angry at ye, but at myself. Aye, angry and totally confused." A sheepish grin twisted his rugged face. "And, truly, can ye blame me? One moment we're talking about friendship and the next . . . well, we're well past all talk of friendship."

Anne shook off his hand. He was right. What had just happened was indeed confusing, and that was the very least of the problem.

"It was a mistake on both our parts. Enough said."

"Aye, so it was." A soft smile grazed his lips as he moved to help her onto her horse. "Mistake or not, enough said . . . until the need arises to speak of it again."

✦

The hissing and popping of pine sap splattering onto hungry flames drew Niall's attention from the letter. He glanced up from the massive oak desk that commanded an entire corner of the library, his bleary gaze moving in the direction of the stone hearth on the opposite wall. Outside, a heavy, late-spring rain slanted past the window, pelting the castle with wind-driven sheets of water.

A fine day to be indoors attending to clan business, Niall thought. *Warm and dry, with a cup of fragrant mulled cider to chase away the ever-present dampness.* Yet the feathery script on the parchment spread before him seemed as illegible as some foreign language. Too many impressions, too many memories, bombarded him until he found himself reading and rereading the page in an unseeing daze. Finally, after a futile hour of little progress, Niall put away the letter.

With a sigh, he leaned back in his chair and picked up his cup. He swirled the amber liquid, watching the interplay of firelight and shadow in the backdrop of fine crystal. It sparkled and shimmered in the hearth's fiery glow like tongues of flame. Like the auburn glints in Anne's hair. Like the inner fire that flared in her eyes when she was angry.

Anne. When had he begun to think of her as Anne? A small, wondering frown puckered Niall's brow. The mention of her name—his beloved wife's name—no longer chafed the raw, festering wound of his loss. Yet when had that happened? He had met Anne MacGregor barely three weeks ago, when she, a glorious, defiant beauty, had stood before all his men. Since then he had spent but a few days with her, and most of those filled with constant conflict.

Already he looked at her in a different light. She stirred him like no other since the death of his first Anne. Stirred him deeply, yet what did he really know of her?

Until a few days ago, she had been his enemy. In her heart, she might be his enemy still. What did he really know of her true feelings? What if, somehow, she was involved with the traitor?

What if Anne was conspiring with Iain to bring about his downfall? Had yesterday at the loch been the opportunity they had awaited? Had their embrace been arranged to goad him into a fight?

The thought of Iain willingly challenging him to fight sickened him. True, they had sparred many times as boys and young men, but always in fun, solely to improve their skills.

But not so yesterday. Yesterday the blood lust flared brightly in Iain's eyes, so brightly Niall wondered if any mercy would've been given if he had fallen victim to the younger man. At the very least, Iain had greatly desired a vicious brawl. And at the worst . . . ? Niall preferred not to even consider what darker motives might have lain beneath his cousin's challenge.

It would also explain the seeming devotion that had so quickly grown between Anne and his cousin. Mayhap there was more there than affection, however platonic Anne claimed it to be. For that matter, his and Anne's handfasting could've also been part of a greater plan. After all, he had only Alastair MacGregor's word on the true circumstances of his betrayal. What if it had all been lies, twisted to manipulate him to the ultimate MacGregor revenge?

Niall lowered his head to rest it in his hands. By mountain and sea, how he wished he had someone to talk all this over with, to help him sift through the questions until he found the answers! His father would listen and understand, but he dared not burden him with this. Robert Campbell already clung to life by the most tenuous of threads. And, though he respected his uncle Duncan's wisdom, for some reason—call it instinct—Niall knew he dared trust no one with any possible claim to the chieftainship.

It was past time to put a plan into effect. On the morrow, he'd summon several of his most trusted warriors to a secret mission. He'd send them out across Campbell lands to visit secretly all the higher lairds, instructing them to keep their eyes and ears open for any sign of suspicious activity. He'd ask for the first report in a month's time. Time enough for his men to uncover any plots outside Kilchurn, if that indeed was where the treachery lay.

In the meanwhile, Niall would continue to center his efforts on his immediate family. Besides Iain, that had to include Hugh, Duncan, and even Malcolm. Preacher though he was, he too was a possible traitor. Niall dared leave no stone unturned, no person unexamined. Now, all were suspect, including a certain lovely, silver-eyed woman.

Of its own accord, Anne's pale, delicate face insinuated itself into his mind. A fierce anger swelled at the thought of her possible deception, an anger that, upon closer examination, more accurately resembled pain. How could he misjudge her? She seemed so brave and kind and good.

Mayhap his mourning heart had betrayed him. Mayhap he was so needful and she had happened along at the right moment. And mayhap, just mayhap, she saw him for the fool he was.

His head bent under the weight of such a possibility. His fist unconsciously clenched around the curved bowl of his cup until it shattered in his hand. The cider ran between his fingers to mingle with his blood, but Niall was oblivious. With an angry motion, he swept the crystal shards from the desk.

Curse it all, he was no one's fool! Not his ambitious cousins' or any of his relatives' or lairds', and certainly no woman's! There wasn't time to cloud his mind with a beguiling lass, no matter how well-rounded and tempting. His clan needed him; his father depended on him.

He must harden himself to her, no matter how difficult or how cruel he might seem. Though Anne MacGregor might not be a traitor, he couldn't allow himself to forget the danger she presented from a less obvious side—his hungry, wounded, needing heart.

Save at the supper meal, Anne barely saw Niall for the next two weeks. Even then he seemed reserved, remotely polite as he inquired after her activities, offered her an additional portion or tempting dessert. After that tumultuous day at the loch, she didn't know whether to be relieved or concerned over his behavior. Finally, she let the matter cease to bother her. Even in Iain's absence, there were more pleasant, less disturbing, matters at hand. Like learning more of the healing art from Ena.

Brushing back a stray tendril that had escaped the snug braid hanging down her back, Anne returned her attention to the little hut and the decoction of comfrey tea Ena was carefully pouring into a small, earthenware cup. Her gaze followed the gnarled hands as the old woman offered the brew to the young child held in her mother's arms. The little girl had fallen from a tree several hours ago, breaking her right wrist. She now looked at the liquid offered her with youthful suspicion.

"Drink it, lassie," Ena urged. "It's the knit bone tea. It'll hasten yer healing." Her eyes twinkled with warmth and humor. "Ye wouldn't want all yer friends to call ye a wee bairn, would ye?"

The girl grimaced then swallowed the tea. Ena gave the mother a few more instructions. Both she and Anne then assisted the pair out to the oxcart where the father waited.

After seeing them off, Ena turned to Anne. "Will ye share a spot of tea before ye leave for the castle?"

Anne smiled. "Aye, but I can't tarry long. It'll soon be sunset, and I must return to Kilchurn."

"Ye don't wish to miss the evening's meal with yer lord, do ye, lassie?"

A teasing light gleamed in the old woman's eyes. Anne started to deny it, then thought better of it. It was true enough at any rate. The more she was with Niall Campbell, the more she enjoyed him.

She gave a rueful nod. "Aye, he's certainly not the evil man the tales would have him be." They halted at the hut, and Anne allowed Ena to enter first.

"The tales of the evil, murdering Wolf of Cruachan?" Ena sat and began filling two cups with rose hips. "Och, lassie, that's all one warrior's silly boasting to another, until the man scarce resembles the legend. Not that Niall Campbell isn't a braw man."

She paused to pour a pot of simmering water over the rose hips. "He's just not a self-serving whiner, like some of the Campbells these days."

Anne's brow puckered. Perhaps she could learn a bit about Niall's problems from Ena. "There's trouble in Castle Kilchurn then?"

"Something's afoot." Ena paused to allow the tea to steep before handing her a cupful. "I'm not certain exactly what, but I don't like the feel of things these days. The portents don't bode well—"

"Are ye a witch then," Anne interrupted uneasily, "to speak so of portents?"

"Nay." Ena shook her head. "I'm no witch, just a watchful old woman with a bit of wisdom after all these years." She shrugged. "Mayhap it's but something in the air or the scraps of talk I hear now and then. I don't know. What I do know, for I can feel it in my bones, is that the young lord's in danger. Ye mustn't cease in yer prayers for him, and, in every way, ye must help him."

Anne stared at her. "In danger? But how and from whom? And how, aside from commending him to God's care, can I possibly help him?"

Ena sipped her tea. "I don't know from whence the danger comes, lassie. It isn't something of the head but of the heart. I feel it, that's all. And as far as helping him, why, keep yer eyes and ears open, give him all yer loyalty and devotion. Ye never know when ye might see or hear something, have some bit of information cross yer path that could be of use."

"He won't trust me or what I say over his kin." Anne sighed. "I mean naught to him. He doesn't want or need my help."

"Doesn't he?" Ena's brows lifted. "I wonder. Ye've already won over the heart of the Campbell. I hear ye visit him every day. How far behind can his son's heart be?"

"The Campbell's a sick and lonely old man," Anne said by way of protest. "Few will stay near him long for fear of catching the consumption. I but try and bring a little cheer to his days. Why, I don't think Niall even knows I visit him. If he did, he'd most likely forbid it."

"Mayhap, and then mayhap not." Ena eyed her intently. "Does it bother ye then, the fact Sir Niall might find ye appealing?"

At the sudden turn in the conversation, Anne felt the heat flare in her cheeks. "Nay, of course not. I don't care what he thinks of me. Our handfasting's but an act of convenience—clan convenience. I fully plan to return home as soon as the year's over."

"Och, and that'd be a sad day for Campbell and MacGregor alike! He needs ye, lassie. Can't ye see that yet?"

"Nay." Anne vehemently shook her head. "That's not true. He needs no one, and certainly not—"

A firm knock sounded at the door. Anne glanced at it, then back to Ena. The old woman climbed to her feet and hobbled over. At the sight of the person who stood there, she dipped in an awkward curtsey. "M'lord. I'm honored—"

"Is the Lady Anne here, Ena?"

‡ ‡

At the sound of Niall's deep voice, Anne rose. Had she violated yet another one of his strictures by coming to visit the old healer? She moved to stand behind Ena. "I'm here, m'lord. What do ye wish?"

Niall's dark glance swept over her. "Come away, lass. I've a need to talk with ye."

Anne smiled at Ena. "Thank ye for the tea. I'll return soon."

They were hardly out the door when a strong hand gripped Anne's arm. She turned to Niall. "Aye, m'lord?"

He began to lead her away. "Ye're determined to thwart me every way ye can, aren't ye?"

"How, m'lord?" At his grim tone, her anxiety rose. "What do ye mean?"

Niall halted, pulling her around to face him. "I asked ye not to do yer healing among my people, explaining all the while my reasons for it, my concerns over yer actions being misconstrued as witchcraft. And still ye keep company with old Ena. Don't ye know she's thought by some a witch? What do ye think the village considers yer visits here to be? What do ye think they consider ye? Curse it, lass. Are ye bent on yer own destruction?"

"She's not a witch!"

"It doesn't matter what ye or I think." An undercurrent of exasperation threaded Niall's voice. "I've discussed this with ye before. Why won't ye heed my words? I grow weary of talking."

"I don't mean to disregard yer request, truly, m'lord, but it seems we're fated always to be at odds." Anne tried to temper her reply with reason, knowing, in his own way, Niall meant well. "I think it better ye not try to control my life. Let it take its natural course. That's best for the both of us."

"Is it now?" Wearily, Niall shook his head. "Do ye think I could stand by and watch ye go to the—" He paused and inhaled an unsteady breath. "Ye're my responsibility now. I promised yer father—"

Anne wrenched her arm from his grip. "I'm no one's responsibility but my own! When, oh when, will ye see that? I never asked for, or desired, yer protection." She forced her voice to soften. "When will ye allow me my freedom, m'lord? I can't live without it."

His brown eyes darkened in pain. "I'll give ye all the freedom within my power, lass, but I won't, I can't, allow ye to endanger yer life." He paused, noting the crowd of interested bystanders beginning to gather. "Now, no more of this. I'll not allow ye to entertain the people at my expense. Will ye come willingly?"

She stared up at him, confused by the strange mixture of frustration and compassion whirling inside her. Frustration at having her life so strongly held in check. Compassion for him in his sincere belief that he was right in doing so. Yet what else could she do but continue to fight him?

With a deep sigh, Anne turned from Niall. Her brisk strides carried her quickly across the village commons, and the acute sense of being watched followed her once again. The feeling grew until it became one of almost tangible discomfort. Full of malevolent intent, it hung heavy on the air, filling Anne with the memory of another unsettling day—of that day in the forest.

She whirled to confront the sender of such evil thoughts. Her glance careened into those of three men glowering at her beside the village well. There, dressed in bright plaids, were Duncan and Hugh Campbell. Beside them was yet another man, hostility burning in his eyes. He was dressed in the robes of a Reformed preacher.

7

As Anne's nimble fingers plucked its strings, soft, lilting notes rose from the clarsach. The resultant melody, however, fell on unheeding ears. Her thoughts were far away, flitting over rain-drenched loch and mountains to a place called Glenstrae. She stared out at the leaden landscape, her somber gaze following the torrents of water relentlessly pelting the earth. Was it raining just as long and hard on MacGregor lands?

Anne sighed and laid down her harp. It had been well over a month now since she had left her home. Relegated to a life among a hostile people, she found that little had happened to change her initial expectations. True, she had found friends, but Iain was gone and the Campbell was dying. And her relationship with Niall Campbell, what little had developed from their mutual debt of each other's lives, seemed slowly to be deteriorating.

They hardly saw each other of late. The Campbell tanist rarely found time even to make it to the evening meal and, for the past week, had been far from the castle itself. From this very window Anne had, on that mist-shrouded morn seven days ago, watched Niall and his warriors depart in pursuit of a band of reivers who had burned several Campbell crofts and murdered the inhabitants. Seven long, lonely days without even the consolation of knowing that somewhere on the castle grounds was a tall, dark, unsettling man.

A mocking grimace twisted Anne's lips. *Dear Lord, help me,* she thought, lifting her heart heavenward. *The solitude's beginning to turn me into some love-besotted fool! Is it possible? Is this the man You've finally chosen for me?*

She shook her head in disbelief. This couldn't be love. True, Niall Campbell was brave, strong, and revered by his men, but those weren't reasons enough for the small, needing ache she felt whenever she thought of him. Why, they hardly knew each other!

Anne paused. Aye, she hardly knew him. Still, the brief glimpses of his deeper side, those times he had revealed a bit of that raw wound of his wife's loss, filled her with an inexplicable yearning to know more about him. Niall Campbell was a man like any other, and yet he was like no man she had ever met.

With a snort of disgust, she rose from the window seat and grabbed up her heavy cloak. It was boredom—and naught more—driving her to such romantically melancholy thoughts. There was still much about the man she didn't know. She must stop placing so much value on the little she did know of him. And she must never forget all the damage Niall Campbell had wreaked on the MacGregors in the fearsome guise of the Wolf of Cruachan.

What she needed was a change of scenery. Old Ena would be in her hut, huddled before her fire for comfort from the bone-chilling dampness. There was sure to be a welcome there.

A timid knock halted her. Anne's glance swung to her bedchamber's thick oaken door. Who could it be? If it was Agnes, the servant woman wouldn't sway her from her determination to visit Ena. Squaring her shoulders, she headed toward the door.

Instead of her maidservant, a small lad stood there. It was Davie, one of the Campbell's personal servants.

"Aye, laddie." Anne smiled down at him. "What is it?"

He swallowed a nervous laugh. "Th-the Campbell, ma'am. He wishes yer presence."

Anne tossed her cloak onto a nearby bench. "Then lead on, Davie."

The boy hesitated, his gaze scanning the room. "Er, m'lord wishes ye to bring yer clarsach. He's a need for some music to lighten the day."

"Och, and does he now?" As she walked back to the window for her harp, a soft smile lit Anne's face. Despite her intentions to the contrary, she and the Campbell had grown close of late. Her initial impression had indeed been accurate. Unlike his enigmatic son, the father was open, warm, and sincerely seemed to enjoy her company.

In the social isolation of the past month, Anne had been surprised to discover how deep ran her need to be of service, to interact with others. She was well aware of her calling to heal, but the strength of that drive, the spiraling ache deep in her gut when she found her natural instincts to be with others so stymied by Niall Campbell's well-intentioned if misguided constraints, was disconcerting. There were times she feared she might go mad from the pain. A slow death, indeed, and far worse than any fate the Campbell tanist might imagine for her.

With a determined shake of her head, Anne flung the disquieting thoughts aside. Her mind had been made a long while ago; it was only guilt at her deception that pulled her back, time and again, to the same pointless reflections. Pointless, as were her tumultuous feelings for Niall Campbell.

"Come, lad." Anne paused before Davie. "Yer master awaits."

The Campbell sat in a huge English chair, his feet propped on a stool, his arms comfortably padded with pillows. His pensive gaze was riveted out the window. At the sound of Anne's entry, he turned. A smile brightened his pale face.

He motioned to her. "Come, lass. An old man requires a bit of cheer on such a gloomy day."

Anne smiled as she lowered herself into the chair Davie pulled over for her. "On such a day, what cheers ye cheers me, m'lord."

✝ ✝

She positioned the clarsach on her lap. "And what ballad would ye hear? Yer favorite—the Douglas tragedy?"

"Aye, lassie, but wait a bit. I want to talk." The Campbell's eyes strayed to where Davie sat on his stool by the door. "Fetch me a bowl of Maudie's cock-a-leekie soup from the kitchen, laddie. And a goblet of claret."

He glanced at Anne. "And ye, lass? Have ye eaten yer midday meal?"

Anne shook her head. "Nay, m'lord, but I'll see to my hunger later. I much prefer visiting with ye."

He grinned, then waved Davie from the room. His smile faded. "The old woman . . . Ena's her name, is it not? Niall told me ye visit her often."

Uneasiness rippled through Anne. "Aye, that I do, m'lord. She's harmless enough."

The Campbell frowned. "She's thought by some to be a witch. It isn't wise to be seen associating with her, lassie."

Anne stared at him for a long moment. "I find no harm in Ena. She's a good, gentle, God-fearing woman. Are ye ordering me to stay away?"

"Nay, lassie." He took her hand. "I've no wish to deny ye yer friends." The Campbell eyed her closely. "It isn't Niall's desire to make ye unhappy, either. He has spoken to me about his decision to forbid yer healing arts in Kilchurn. As hard as it may seem, his choice is wise. Mayhap someday, when things are more stable, but not now. My clan's superstitious, and the witch law . . ."

Anne laughed wryly. "Och, well I know about that. Yer son constantly reminds me of the witch panic. But I'm a healer. And I've already learned much from Ena that can help all."

He arched a graying brow. "Have ye, now? Is a cure for the consumption mayhap part of that knowledge?"

"Nay, m'lord." She smiled sadly. "But if ye ever have the dropsy . . ."

The Campbell chuckled. "Och, lassie, ye brighten my lonely

days. My children love me, but I see them so little of late. With Niall forced to take over the chieftainship in all but name—as well he should—and my Caitlin spending most of her time visiting the MacArthurs and the rest of it mooning over the MacArthur heir, well, it seems life itself is slowly stealing them from me."

He paused to shift to a more comfortable position in his chair. "Aye, they're both good and faithful children, but life must go on, and a sickroom's a gloomy place." Robert squeezed her hand. "But ye, lass, ye come here every day and spend hours with me."

"I don't mind, m'lord. I value yer friendship—"

"And ye've found few friends in Kilchurn," he finished for her. Bright blue eyes studied her closely. "What of Niall? Have ye two grown close? I'd hoped for a grandson before I died."

Anne flushed. "M'lord . . ."

"Och, lassie, I'm sorry." He engulfed her hand between two of his own. "Forgive an old man's meddling. It's naught but an honest concern for yer happiness—and that of my son."

"I doubt our handfasting brings yer son much happiness, m'lord. It seems all we ever do is fight. And there are even times when I think he must despise me, for he never calls me by my given name." She shook her head and frowned. "Truly, I don't understand it."

"There's a simple enough explanation, lassie." The Campbell released her hand to lean back in his chair. "Niall's first wife was named Anne. Mayhap it's still too painful for him to speak her name."

Anne straightened in surprise. "I didn't know, m'lord." At every turn, despite her determination to view Niall Campbell as a hard, heartless villain, he instead proved himself a man of deeply felt emotions.

In spite of her resolve to keep her perspective regarding Niall Campbell, Anne couldn't help wanting to hear more. "He told me little of his wife. If I knew more of her, mayhap it'd ease my understanding."

A faraway light shone in the old man's eyes. "She was a Stewart lass. Niall loved her from the first time he set sight upon her. It was at a ceilidh one winter's evening. The Stewart chief had come for a meeting and brought his family. To honor him, I'd ordered the traditional gathering of singers and musicians. Och, what a fine evening it was, with the storytelling, rousing music, and dancing."

He glanced at Anne. "But I ramble in my tale. She was a bonnie lass, Annie Stewart was, her hair of palest gold, her form as sweet and lush as a summer-ripened peach, her nature of the gentlest kind. Niall was devoted to her, and she to him. Yet their love, it seemed, was not sufficient to overcome the cruel fate that dogged Annie's childbearing. In the eight years they were wed, she miscarried three bairns, finally dying in the bearing of the fourth, a stillborn son. Her death almost destroyed Niall."

"And I, because my name's the same, constantly remind him of his beloved wife." An unexpectedly savage pain slashed through Anne. Niall's first wife was everything she wasn't—meek, gentle, delicately feminine—and Niall had loved her madly.

"I didn't tell this to discourage ye, lassie."

The Campbell's deep voice intruded on Anne's pensive musings. Startled, she turned back to him. "Wh-what did ye say, m'lord?"

"Ye must have patience with him. Someday Niall will allow himself to love again, and that lass will be the most fortunate woman in the world. It could well be ye, Annie."

"Nay, that'll never be!" She shook her head vehemently. "We've naught in common save the battleground of our opposite opinions. He never even wanted to handfast with me. He only tolerates my presence as a clan necessity."

"Nonetheless, there's something growing between ye. Even I can see it."

Struggling to contain her sudden swell of hope, Anne could only stare at him. "Nay, it's not true," she finally managed to say. "Yer affection for me only clouds yer perception of the situation. Ye see what ye want, not what is."

He wagged a silencing finger, an affectionate smile on his lips.

"Wheesht, lassie. I know my son. And, one way or another, time will tell. I only hope to live long enough to see that happy day." Once again, Robert shifted in his chair. "Now, I've a need for a song. Play the one ye spoke of. Play for me, lassie, and have patience."

For a long moment Anne fought the impulse to deny once more the content of Robert Campbell's words, as if in the doing she could bury the persistent hope his words had stirred. Her gaze turned toward the narrow slash of window across the room.

The rain had ceased sometime during their talk. A furtive ray of light escaped the clouds to find entry through the window. Like some happy portent after the long days of gloom, it illuminated the chamber, bathing it in golden radiance. Like the promise of happiness at the end of a terrible sorrow, Anne thought in rising joy, if only one could first weather the storm. If only one had the patience, the love, to persevere . . .

She picked up the clarsach and strummed the opening chords, a smile on her lips. "Patience ye say, m'lord? That I have aplenty."

The Campbell sighed, a look of peace on his face, as Anne began to sing.

Rise up, rise up, now, Lord Douglas, she says
And put on yer armor so bright;
Let it never be said, that a daughter of thine
Was married to a lord under night.
Rise up, rise up, my seven bold sons,
And put on yer armor so bright,
And take better care of yer youngest sister,
For yer eldest's away the last night . . .

Niall strode down the long corridor leading to his father's room. He had only just now returned from a week's pursuit of the reivers, and he was wet, cold, and hungry.

For a fleeting moment, he allowed himself the fantasy of sinking into a hot bath and cleansing the filth from his body, of imbibing a glass or two of a fine claret. He could almost taste the dry red wine, imagine how the liquid would course down his throat to spread its sweet, mellow warmth throughout his body. Then he sighed. No matter how pressing his own needs, his first duty was to his father, who'd be awaiting a report of the expedition.

To a man, the reivers had been caught and hanged, but the effort had cost him two good lads, not to mention a varied assortment of wounds on several others. His hand rose to the ragged slash winding its way from his left temple to his jaw line. The outlaw leader, a huge bear of a man, had left his mark just before Niall had run him through with his claymore.

A grim smile twisted his lips. The slight movement tugged painfully at his wound. Niall ignored it. Another scar was small payment for the safety of the clan and far less than the life price he had exacted from his opponent. He'd have to take care, though, or he'd soon be so marred of feature Anne wouldn't be able to stand the sight of him.

Anne. Unbidden, her silver eyes flashed through his mind, followed swiftly by the vision of her finely sculpted features and slimly rounded form. How many times in the past week had his thoughts turned to her? And how many times had he jerked himself from the recollection only to find his breathing heavy and labored?

The restless yearnings had been with him almost constantly in the past few days. Aye, it had finally come to this. With a force that amazed him still, his need for a woman had returned—and the woman he needed was Anne MacGregor.

A sweet voice, accompanied by a harp, floated down the hall. Niall halted. It was Anne, singing to his father.

The melody flowed over him like a soothing balm. Once again, Niall grew warm with desire. With a low oath, he shook the languid feeling from him. By mountain and sea, the woman could stir him with but the sound of her voice!

A lad rounded the corner. Niall halted in the shadowed hallway. As he watched, Davie knocked on the door to Robert Campbell's room.

The singing ceased, and a minute later the door swung open. Anne's flame-dark head peeked through. When she saw the boy, she smiled.

"Aye, laddie? Do ye wish to see yer master?"

Davie shook his head and shyly held up his right hand. "Nay, m'lady. It's my hand. I spilled hot soup on it. Cook said ye've knowledge of healing and asked if ye'd tend it."

Anne stepped into the hall and closed the door behind her. She took Davie's small hand in hers. The skin on the back was reddened and beginning to blister. A simple poultice of nettle tea would alleviate the pain of the burn, and then . . .

She stopped. Niall had forbidden her to treat anyone in the castle. Up until this moment, she had obeyed him in that at least. Of course, until Davie, no one had asked for her assistance. That didn't lessen her obligation, however, to obey in thought if not in deed. It was just so hard to turn from someone in need.

"Please, m'lady." Davie's voice was taut with pain. "It hurts so. Isn't there aught ye can do?"

Anne chewed on her lower lip. Why was the act of healing, that she knew to be good and right, suddenly so hard to carry out? Because Niall Campbell had asked her not to? Because she didn't want to hurt him, or cause him further trouble? Well, it wasn't reason enough to ignore Davie's plight.

She released the boy's hand. "Come to my room in five minute's time. I'll see to yer hand as soon as I take my leave of yer master. And, laddie—" Anne stayed Davie as he turned to go—"for yer sake as well as mine, no one's ever to know. Do I have yer word on it?"

"Aye, m'lady."

"Good." Anne stepped back into the room and closed the door.

Niall watched until the boy once more rounded the corner and disappeared from view. The long-dreamt-of sight of Anne, bent over Davie's small hand, her beautiful features glowing with kindness and concern, filled him with a possessive pride. He could almost imagine her in the same role, examining the hand of one of their own children.

He caught himself. It didn't matter what his dreams were for the future. Reality was too harsh, too potentially dangerous to ignore. Anne had lied when she had said she'd not heal in Kilchurn.

A spiraling rage grew inside him. Despite his requests to the contrary, she stubbornly refused to listen. Still, he hadn't the heart to deny the wee lad his healing, no matter how long Anne had been disobeying him in this.

Niall ran a hand across his jaw, stirring anew the raw, burning pain of his wound—and the memory of his concern over how its appearance would affect Anne. *Fool!* he derided himself fiercely. *While ye waste precious time mooning over her, she's been going about her business of scorning yer requests and flaunting them in yer face. Not only does the woman have no feelings for ye, but she actively seeks to undermine all ye've tried to build toward peace between Campbell and MacGregor.*

As he stood there, impotently fuming, the door opened once more and Anne slipped through. Niall watched her walk away, well aware her destination was her own room, her purpose the healing of little Davie. With the greatest of efforts, he stilled the impulse to go after her. He couldn't risk his father hearing them. This issue was Anne's and his alone.

A sudden thought assailed him. Did the Campbell know? Despite the discussion he'd had with his father, had Anne managed to extract permission all the same? The possibility angered Niall, but at the same time it offered him hope that she hadn't completely disregarded his requests, only chose to obey a higher authority.

But, no, it wasn't possible. Anne had been far too quick to step outside his father's chamber when Davie had shown her his hand, closing the door carefully behind her. Those were not the actions of a person with the Campbell's permission.

All thoughts of a pleasant interlude with Anne after the meeting with his father fled. He was far too angry to face her. If he saw her now, if she even dared give him one of those defiant little smiles, Niall feared he might lose control. And, when it came to a beguiling MacGregor liar, self-control was about all he had left.

"A flagon! Bring me another flagon and be quick about it!" Niall shouted to the servant standing watch nearby.

The man scurried in the direction of the kitchen. Niall turned back to his glass. With an exaggerated flourish, he emptied the last dregs of claret into his goblet, then threw the empty metal flagon aside. He stared at the glass, swirling the ruby liquid so hard it sloshed over the sides to course down his hand.

Blood, Niall thought, his bleary gaze following the sticky rivulets until they mingled with the hairy expanse of his arm. It might as well be his own blood he was spilling, for all that MacGregor wench cared. One way or another, she was slowly tearing him apart.

The servant hurried over with a fresh flagon. With a low growl, Niall snatched it from him. He downed the remainder of claret in his glass, then refilled it from the new vessel. He had been drinking for hours. Why couldn't he drown the painful memories? It had always worked before.

But now the liquor coursing through his veins only stirred him until he felt aflame with desire. Desire for a woman who flagrantly disobeyed him, who mocked his every attempt at friendship . . . at tenderness.

Niall emptied his goblet in one long swallow, heedless of the wine dribbling from the sides of his mouth to spatter onto his white linen shirt. *She doesn't care.* The thought was like a knife twisting in his gut, but instead of blood, rage poured out.

She didn't care that he had tried every way he knew to be kind, to ease her way with his clan. She didn't care that she tempted him, set his blood afire. He sat here, drinking himself into oblivion, and she felt nothing.

The fury within him burgeoned to explosive proportions, stirring him from his drunken lethargy. He staggered to his feet. Why should he be the only one who suffered? Let Anne experience some of the gut-wrenching torment of unfulfilled passion. It wouldn't change anything, but at least it would ease his pain. And she'd never again be safe in her self-absorbed little world.

The servants slunk away as Niall staggered across the hall. He saw nothing, all his powers of concentration centered on the corridor at the head of the stairs. A corridor that led to a bedchamber wherein waited a beauteous, heartless witch.

Anne lifted her gaze from the intricate flowers she was attempting to embroider on the hem of the crimson silk gown. She glanced at Agnes, who was intently working a smaller version of the same pattern at the gown's neckline. Since her return from the Campbell's room, how many hours had they been sewing now? Surely it must be close to time for the evening meal.

The evening meal. At the contemplation of seeing Niall this eve, a warm glow suffused her. Agnes had lost no time in informing Anne of his arrival late this afternoon, though he had yet to visit her.

For a fleeting instant Anne wondered why he hadn't taken even a brief moment to stop by and greet her, but then she banished the thought as unreasonable. Niall was tanist. After a week's absence, he had many responsibilities demanding his immediate attention. The evening meal would be time enough to see him.

With a sigh, Anne shrugged her shoulders to ease the stiffness brought on by hunching over the small pattern of flowers, then critically surveyed the results of her work. The satin stitch of the leaves and petals was lumpy, the running line of the stem unevenly spaced, but the flowers' colors were a bright contrast against the crimson fabric. If one didn't look closely, the embroidery didn't appear too badly done. *Not bad at all,* Anne mused dryly, *if one was cross-eyed, half-blind, and besotted with drink.*

"It'll get easier with practice, lassie," Agnes offered, apparently noting Anne's disgusted scowl. "And the Lady Caitlin isn't too handy with the needle, either. I doubt she'll see past the fine color and fabric of the dress herself."

Anne laid aside her portion of the gown and rose. With a small yawn, she lifted her arms in a stretch. "I hope so, Agnes. I want this gown to be a token of peace between us. I'm at wit's end in trying to make friends with Caitlin." She shook her head in dismay. "Why, I've never seen a more stubborn, unfriendly child in all my life!"

"Give her time, lassie. Little Caitlin's fast growing into a young woman and has her own cares of the heart." Agnes frowned. "The young lord seems sore beset with cares of late, as well. I haven't seen him turn so oft to the bottle. Why, no sooner had he returned this afternoon than he was downing one glass of wine after another."

At the worried look Anne shot her, the old servant nodded solemnly. "Aye, lass. I passed him in the Great Hall only an hour ago, and he was still in his cups, glaring so fiercely none dared approach him." Agnes chuckled. "Well, no matter. He'll pay the price for his foolishness on the morrow."

Agnes cocked an inquiring brow. "If ye'll forgive an old woman's curiosity, how do things go with ye and the young lord? I know I overstep myself in asking, but I care for ye both and—"

"We're barely friends." A bright flush spread across Anne's cheeks. Holy saints and martyrs, first Robert Campbell and now Agnes! Why did everyone seem so interested in her and Niall's relationship today? Were her own thoughts so transparent?

She walked over to gaze out the window. "Ye see better than most how little time he spends with me, the conflict between us. There's naught worth discussing about Niall Campbell and me."

"Aye, yer words are true, but even so I see that old fire, that fire he had for his first wife, flaring to life again." The maidservant came up behind Anne and laid a gentle hand on her shoulder. "And it's ye, lassie, ye and no other, who've stirred that fire anew. Does that please ye?"

"Please me?" Anne caught a glimpse of the first star twinkling in the night's dark expanse. "What woman wouldn't find the attention of a man such as Niall Campbell pleasing? For all his blustering male bravado, he can be as kind and gentle as—"

The bedchamber door swung open, slamming with a loud thud against the stone wall. Anne and Agnes jumped then whirled around. There, striding into the room, his face flushed and eyes over-bright, was Niall.

He was dressed in snug-fitting trews, and his wine-stained linen shirt hung loosely open to expose a glimpse of his strong chest and muscled abdomen. His dark mane was disheveled and, when he moved toward them, his gait was just the slightest bit unsteady.

That he was besotted was evident to Anne. When his piercing gaze found her, a small tremor shuddered through her. The light that burned in his eyes was feral and cold.

Niall beckoned her forward. "So, there ye are, my rebellious little MacGregor. Don't hide so in the shadows. It won't help yer plight or lessen yer well-deserved punishment. Come here, I say."

Anne glanced at Agnes, searching for some sign of how to deal with this new aspect of Niall Campbell. Eyes wide in apprehension, Agnes stared blankly back.

"I grow tired of waiting, madam." His ominous voice cut through the air. "Yer disobedience only adds fuel to my anger. Don't make me come to ye."

Strange that the wine didn't slur his voice, Anne thought for a brief, disjointed moment. He was still completely in command, his tone unyielding and imperative. To prolong the confrontation would be worse than unwise. It would be foolhardy.

Anne gave Agnes's arm a parting squeeze. "Go now. It isn't fitting ye be witness to our personal differences."

Agnes hesitated. "But, lassie . . ."

"Nay, no more of it. "Anne gently pushed her toward the door. "I'll be all right."

With one last, uncertain look, the old woman made her way across the room and out the main door.

‡ ‡

Anne watched her go, then turned to face Niall. "We're quite alone now, m'lord." She met his furious glare with a steady one of her own. "Pray, what's my crime to warrant such churlish behavior?"

A fierce oath on his lips, Niall reached her side in two swift strides. He grasped Anne by the waist, pulling her to him. A glittering fire lit his eyes to darkest gold, but Anne's glance barely lingered there.

Her gaze riveted on the wound traversing the left side of his face. Who had dared hurt him so? Her hand moved toward the jagged cut. Niall jerked his head away. He grabbed her arm and wrenched it behind her back.

"Ye've mocked me one time too many," he snarled, his wine-scented breath engulfing her in a warm, heady cloud. "Yer punishment's long overdue. But before I lock ye in the tower, I plan first to have my rightful taste of ye."

8

Anne's hand shot out, meeting the wounded side of Niall's face with a resounding slap. He staggered back, his own hand rising to the reddening imprint of her fingers across his cheek. Surprise, mixed with pain, flickered briefly in his eyes. Then the hard, shuttered expression returned.

With a low growl, Niall pulled her to him. He entwined a hand in her hair, anchoring her head. His lips crushed down on hers. Anger at his brutish treatment surged through Anne. She caught his lip between her teeth and bit hard. He jerked in pain.

"Am I too gentle with ye?" Niall demanded softly. "Do ye mayhap like it rougher? I would've thought not, but the way ye bite and slap at me . . ."

"There's naught I like about ye!" Anne cried. "Ye're a crude, rutting beast to treat me so! Let me go, I say!"

A grim smile touched Niall's lips. "I've every right to do whatever I wish with ye, lady. Do ye deny it? Have ye forgotten yer vows?"

The reality of her situation became painfully clear. Anne inhaled a tremulous breath. Why was he punishing her? What had she done to deserve this?

Hot tears filled her eyes. It didn't matter. He'd never have treated the Lady Anne Stewart in such a manner. The pain of that realization was suddenly more than she could bear.

With a harsh sob, she shook her head. "Nay, I haven't forgotten my vows. Have ye? The ones we made to each other even before we handfasted?" She raised tearful eyes to him. "What've I done to deserve such harsh treatment? Tell me, and I'll do all in my power to make amends."

Niall stared down at her, the sweetness of her entreaty piercing the thick fog of his drunkenness. For the first time since he had entered her room, he saw her as the beautifully stirring woman she was rather than an object of his enraged frustration. His glance moved to her lips, a streak of his own blood upon them. She was his, and he had treated her brutishly. No matter what she had done, she didn't deserve such handling.

Shame flooded him. Though he wanted her still, Niall found he could no longer touch her. He stepped back. "Ye can never make amends. All ye care for is yer own wants and needs, and I'm tired of it. Do ye hear me? Verra, *verra* tired."

He strode from the room, leaving the door wide open and Anne staring speechlessly after him. She stood there for a long while, her limbs frozen, her heart twisting within her chest. She had hurt him, but in what manner she still had yet to fathom.

One thing was crystal clear. She was the cause of this eve's drunkenness, the source of an anger so great he had almost resorted to violence. The realization tore through her, and Anne floundered in a maelstrom of emotion. Then reason returned.

No matter what the cause, he had no right to treat her this way. Yet, as reprehensible as his conduct had been, Anne felt compelled to go after him. Once and for all, they'd settle the bitter differences between them.

He wasn't in the Great Hall, though all were engrossed in the evening meal. He had passed this way, however, for none would've begun eating without him giving leave. Anne paused at the top of the stairs leading down from the sleeping chambers. Once more, her eyes scanned the room for Niall. He was nowhere to be seen.

✣✣✣

She hesitated, gathering the courage to cross the Great Hall. The kitchen, storerooms, and stairs to the lower level were on the other side. Though Anne doubted Niall would have gone there, she had to make certain before searching elsewhere.

At Anne's approach, the conversations at the dining tables lowered dramatically. She pretended not to notice. Head held high, she crossed before the outright stares and whispered comments, nodding her greeting at the occasional passing servant who acknowledged her presence. She pushed open the kitchen door. The servants immediately ceased their work.

Anne motioned to Maudie, the head cook, who straight away headed in her direction. The rotund little woman curtsied nervously before her, the wooden spoon she had been using to stir a pot of soup still clutched in one hand.

"Aye, m'lady? What is it ye wish?"

"Er, Sir Niall." Anne lowered her voice for Maudie's ears alone. "I've a need to talk with him. Has he passed this way?"

A distinctly uncomfortable expression settled over the cook's face. "Aye, m'lady. He was here a few moments ago but soon departed."

"Do ye know which way he went?" Anne persisted, irritated at the woman's reluctance to volunteer further information.

"Aye, m'lady."

Anne's annoyance grew. "Well, then pray tell me!"

Maudie pointed to the door across the kitchen. It led downstairs to the servant's quarters. "He went that way, m'lady."

"Thank ye, Maudie." Anne gathered her skirts to head across the kitchen when the cook stayed her.

"M'lady," Maudie began, anxiously searching Anne's face. "H-he wasn't alone."

"And, pray, who was with him?"

The other woman couldn't quite seem to meet her gaze. "He took that girl, Nelly, with him."

The admission sent a frisson of unease through Anne. Though she hardly knew most of the servants, she hadn't failed to notice the striking, flirtatious Nelly. How could one not be aware of her seductive looks and swaying hips, or of the lusty appraisals and ribald comments from the men every time she was in the vicinity?

But what business could Niall have with the serving maid? Before the question fully formed in her mind, Anne knew the answer. In his besotted state, it could be anything—even the bedding of the woman.

Anne's mouth went dry. "Thank ye, Maudie." She backed away. "Ye may return to yer—"

"She's a tart, that one is." The cook's features softened in concern. "And she's always cozying up to her betters, the Campbell men in particular. Why, I know for a fact she's bedded Hugh Campbell many a time, and it's even said Sir Duncan—"

Anne held up a silencing hand. "It doesn't matter, Maudie."

"But if ye'd seen the way she came up to Sir Niall and all but rubbed her body against his, and he so befuddled with drink," the woman protested, "ye wouldn't be so quick to blame him. He's just a man, with a man's natural appetites, after all."

"It's no excuse, Maudie."

The little cook fell silent. Woman-to-woman, she met Anne's gaze, then nodded. She curtsied and hurried back to the hearth.

The woman stirred the kettle of soup simmering over the fire, her mouth moving silently. Anne dragged her glance from the hearth to see how much the other kitchen staff had overheard. All eyes were carefully averted, all hands busily engaged.

They know. The realization motivated her to action. With a whirl of skirt and petticoats, Anne was gone, her destination the stairway to the servant's quarters. She'd not allow foolish gossip or speculation to influence her. There could be some reasonable explanation for Niall's departure with Nelly. And she still needed to talk with him.

Yet as her hand traveled along the rough stone wall leading downward, Anne's resolve faltered. The dank mustiness of the ancient corridors wafted up to her on a chill current of air. In the pitifully inadequate light from the flickering torches, a pervasive feeling of dread grew.

She halted and inhaled a fortifying breath. What was she afraid of? Whatever she discovered, it would be the truth. As difficult as it might be to face, it was far better than allowing the doubts to nibble away at her.

Anne forced herself onward, her footsteps soundless on the hard dirt floor. The corridor seemed to go on forever. She suddenly realized she had no idea which room was Nelly's, for she had never been below stairs. Perhaps it was better if she turned back now.

A low, husky laugh floated from the darkness. Anne halted. It came again, followed by the murmur of a feminine voice. Anne forced herself to move in the direction of the sound, down the next corridor that crisscrossed the main one.

A door stood open, a dim red-gold light spilling out to puddle on the hallway floor. The woman's voice came again, this time loud enough to reach Anne's ears.

"Och, m'lord," the woman purred. "I've wanted ye for such a long, long time and now, at last—"

"Hush, lass," ordered a deep masculine voice, rough with desire. "No talk. Just let me look at ye, kiss ye . . ."

Anne drew up at the door. A man and woman stood in the room's opposite corner. It was Niall, his dark mane tumbling down to hide his face as he lowered his head to Nelly's lips.

A light sheen of sweat glistened on his unclothed upper torso, glinting off the powerful play of muscles in his shoulders and back. Anne could hear the ragged rasp of his breath as Nelly pressed herself eagerly to him.

Anne's nails scored her tightly fisted palms. She felt as if she were drowning, the horror of what she was witnessing driving the breath from her body. She backed away, whirling in one direction then the other, attempting to recall which way she had come.

"Ah, Nelly!" Niall exclaimed on a shuddering, blissful breath, and Anne cared no more.

She fled down the shadowed corridors, toward what, she didn't know. It didn't matter. The anguish of Niall's betrayal followed swiftly on her heels, mocking her even as she went.

✦

The woman's sweetly intoxicating scent wafted up to Niall. The softness of her, snuggling close to him, felt so good. It had been so long—too long—since he had been with a woman, and he realized now how much he had missed it. Ah, but it felt good. So very, *very* good!

Nelly drew back, lifting her dark, dancing eyes to his. "M'lord?"

Niall's hands moved languidly over her shoulders and upper arms. "Aye, lass?" His voice was but a thick rasp in the stone-muffled silence.

"Do I please ye, m'lord?"

"Aye . . ." Niall next stroked the side of her face. "That ye do, Nelly lass."

"Then ye'll take me as yer mistress?" The maidservant's arm entwined about his neck. "I'm as lusty as any man and will warm ye through many a cold winter's night. And I'm not jealous that ye're bound to another. I'm more than a match for that whey-faced MacGregor wench."

At the mention of Anne, Niall halted. The liquor coursing through his veins had worked its mind-drugging magic for a long while now. Long enough to allow Nelly's earthy sensuality to seduce him down here, long enough to relax his strict personal code against sexually involving himself with the servants.

But now its effects had waned, helped along by the memory of Anne MacGregor striking his conscience like a cold dash of water.

With a low curse, Niall pushed aside Nelly's hands and stepped away. He eyed her voluptuous form for one last, lingering moment, then shook his head.

"Nay, lass. That can never be." Averting his gaze, he shrugged back into his shirt.

She made a move toward him and laid a hand upon his chest. "But, m'lord. What have I done to offend ye? Just say the word and I'll make amends."

Another voice, murmuring almost the same phrases, slipped forward from a distant corner of Niall's mind. *Anne.* She had been just as confused, just as pleading this eve when he had stormed into her room and all but ravished her. Yet the look in her eyes had been different, sweetly concerned despite his brutal treatment of her, not at all like the sharp, calculating gleam sparkling in Nelly's dark eyes.

Nausea surged through him. Suddenly, Niall had to get out of a room that seemed to whirl about his head. He backed away.

"There's no need to make amends. I erred in coming down here. I beg yer pardon."

"But, m'lord—"

Niall held up a hand. "It's over, Nelly."

A look of disbelief contorted the woman's face. "I can't believe ye prefer her to me. Why, it's—it's impossible! She's bewitched ye, she has. Aye, that's the answer. She's a witch!"

Niall strode from the chamber, refusing to listen a moment longer to the edge of hysteria that sharpened Nelly's words to a strident pitch. The voice, however, endlessly calling Anne a witch, followed him down the corridor, grating on his tautly strung nerves until it made his head pound.

By mountain and sea, he thought dolefully as his steps carried him toward the stairs, he'd have one excruciating—but well-deserved—hangover in the morn.

✦

Anne thought the dawn would never come. She lay in her bed, tossing and turning in a futile attempt to escape the memories of the evening past. The recollection of Niall, his powerful form bared as Nelly's mouth rose to meet his, came back time and again to haunt her. She didn't know what hurt worse—the fact he had so quickly sought out another woman, or the fact that his act was blatant proof he cared naught for her.

It was a common enough practice among the married nobility for husbands to take mistresses. She had thought—or mayhap just hoped—Niall was a better, more honorable man than that. He had said, after all, he still mourned his dead wife. And to say that he was totally disinterested in her, Anne added, was not altogether true, either.

When he had come to her chamber last night, he had admitted she stirred his desires, that he wanted her. True, his actions had left a lot to be wished for in a romantic sense. For a few moments, though, he *had* wanted her. Then Niall had stopped, suddenly angry.

He had accused her of thinking only of herself, of being incapable of making amends. Then he had left, finding eventual solace with that—that woman! Anne rubbed her throbbing temples. Och, what was she to think? What was she to do?

She laughed derisively. What was she to do, indeed? She was his, vowed for at least the span of a year, and there was naught she *could* do. Niall Campbell could have all the women he wished, flaunting them in her face if he so desired, and there was nothing she could do but bear the humiliation with dignity and pretend it didn't matter.

He had told her he wasn't ready. That it was too soon after his wife's death for him to desire another woman. And he had told her he never lied.

White-hot anger swelled in Anne. Curse him! He had the soul of a dog! He was a liar and heartless brute! She hated him. How she hated him!

Fury moved her like no amount of pain ever could. Anne leaped from bed and dressed. She'd not lie about like some weak, love-besotted girl, helpless save to weep her heart out into her pillow.

Her glance moved to the window. The first rays of dawn streaked the sky with a lavender-rose light.

She needed to get away. Go for a ride in the brisk morning air. Sweep clean the clinging tendrils of her romantic dreams and sear harsh reality back into her brain. Anne grabbed her cloak and headed toward the door.

Agnes met her halfway down the steps to the Great Hall. The old woman's gaze swept over Anne, her eyes narrowing in suspicion. "And where are ye off to, so early in the morn?"

Anne stiffened, sensing a battle. "I mean to go riding." She made a move to skirt the other woman.

The maid servant stepped in her way. "And who do ye plan to take with ye? It's too dangerous to ride alone."

She glared down at the old woman. "I'll go anywhere I please, and I'll not be accounting to ye for my every move. Now, pray, get out of the way."

Agnes refused to budge. "Does Sir Niall know of yer plans? If he doesn't—"

"Ye'll run and tell him?" All the old bitterness welled in Anne's throat like some acrid, spoiled wine. "Well, go ahead. I don't care. I know ye spy on me for Niall. So run. Go and tell him! But if it's the last thing I ever do, I'm riding this morn!"

With that, Anne pushed past Agnes and all but ran down the stairs.

✦

From the shadowed doorway of the keep, a man watched Anne mount her horse. His cold gaze followed as she rode away, the stable man shouting after her to wait while he found an escort to ride along.

A thin smile touched the man's lips. "Ride alone, will ye, lass? And hasn't Niall warned ye of the dangers outside the castle walls? Mayhap I'll have to teach ye a wee lesson, a lesson, most unfortunately, that'll be the last one ye ever learn."

He stepped from the doorway, fastening his short sword to his hip. With long, ground-eating strides, he headed toward the stable.

✦

Loch Awe passed in a blur. Though she didn't consciously plan it, Anne's direction led her toward the small burn where Iain had taken her the day before his departure.

Like some bittersweet note from her clarsach, the memory of him plucked at her heart. How she missed him! It seemed like years since he had left. But then after the agony of last night, everything seemed so very long ago.

How could she bear the shame of handfasting to a man who cared so little for her feelings that he wasted no time seeking out the servants? Yet even as she cursed him, Anne knew if Niall had treated her with the same tenderness he had showered on Nelly, she'd have welcomed him with open arms. Not to share his bed outside of marriage, of course, for she'd never do that. Yet mayhap, just mayhap, in time even marriage, too, might have become a reality. And that wild and now apparently unattainable dream was the most painful realization of all.

She desired Niall Campbell. Though she knew she shouldn't let her thoughts carry her to such forbidden places, even now the memory of him, of his tall, powerful body, of the dark hair swirling across his hard-muscled chest and rippling abdomen, of his strongly chiseled, heartbreakingly handsome face couldn't help but stir her anew.

Anne swallowed hard. Och, never before to have thought of a man in such a way, and now to have it squandered on one such as he!

As if the action could outdistance her thoughts, with a nudge, she urged her mount to a run. The towering oaks came into view. The noise of rushing water filled her ears. Anne reined in her horse and slid from its back.

‡ ‡

The scene was as before. The gnarled limbs of the ancient trees reached across the gurgling burn. Since she had last been here the flowers had faded, replaced by a lush, emerald carpet of grass. The oaks had leafed out as well and would now provide ample shade from the afternoon sun. Mayhap she'd stay here the whole day, Anne mused, seeking respite beneath their sheltering arms.

Head lowered in dejection, she walked toward the giant trees. Ah, to hide away from the world for a time, she sighed to herself, to find solace and healing among friends who had seen far greater tribulations than hers . . .

She sat beneath the trees for a long while, unable to still the restlessness, the sense of unease that had begun to swirl through her. Finally she stood, following the burn down to the lake. Anne's gaze traveled across Loch Awe, past the narrow outcropping of land where she caught a glimpse of one of Kilchurn's towers, toward the snowy peaks of Ben Cruachan.

Cruachan. The Wolf of Cruachan. The name the people had given to Niall, that brave and fearsome warrior.

Though her feelings for Niall Campbell were unrequited, Anne struggled to assure herself there was still some solace to be found. One month had already passed in the year of handfasting. She had only eleven more to endure. Eleven long months to be sure, but not an eternity.

Anne paused at the lake's edge. Her gaze lowered to the gently lapping waves. She knelt and leaned over to cup a handful of the sparkling liquid, her long hair skimming the water. The movement of a wave caught a lock and carried it on its bobbing surface, to and fro as the current changed directions.

Fascinated, Anne watched her shimmering image reflect in the deep blue water, calling to mind her father's voice many years past. She remembered that day well, a time when she had first entered womanhood.

He had found her swimming unchaperoned in a spring-fed pond and had reprimanded her severely for her unladylike behavior. He had smiled, though, when he had called her his bonnie water kelpie, certain to lure men to their deaths in the water's depths if ever they saw her swimming there. Anne had returned to the pond many times more, but always when her father was away or early in the morn before he arose. She couldn't help it; she loved the water so.

A sudden breeze whipped the lake's surface, sending agitated ripples through her image. Anne watched the wind-churned water as it momentarily obliterated her reflection then again calmed to a mirrorlike surface. In it, she once more saw herself. This time, however, she wasn't alone.

The form of a Campbell warrior loomed behind her, his identity blurred by the gently undulating water. For a wild, joyous moment she thought it was Niall, here to set things right between them.

"Come to the loch to cast yer spell over it, have ye?" Hugh Campbell snarled. "To poison the water that we drink, mayhap? Well, no matter. I've caught ye in time. Ye shan't escape justice again."

Anne whirled, losing her balance to fall backward into the muddy shallows. She stared up into Hugh's twisted features. A smile of pure malevolence lifted his lips.

Dread ensnared her. She had indeed been a fool to ride here alone. She should've remembered there were those in Kilchurn who wished her dead. And now, in her angry confusion over Niall, she had played right into one of their hands.

"I-I cast no spell over the loch," Anne said, desperately striving to soothe the madness from Hugh's eyes. "I but watch the water, full of my own thoughts and dreams. Have ye never done the same, Hugh?"

For an instant, the brown-haired man's face softened. A faraway light gleamed in his dark eyes. "Aye, that I have, lassie. Long ago, with a girl named Dora." Then, as fast as it had appeared, the light faded. A cold, furious expression transformed his face. "But Dora wasn't what she seemed, the conniving, heartless wench. She tried to steal my soul, and I was forced to expose her for what she was—a witch."

Hugh moved closer. He towered over Anne, his shadow blocking the sun. "She roasted at the stake and I made myself watch. I had to, ye see, if I was to purge the taint of her from my heart."

He leaned down and jerked Anne to her feet, his strong fingers gouging the soft flesh of her arm. "It's a blessing for ye I haven't the time to turn ye over to the authorities. Ye'll die this day, but at least yer suffering won't be that of my Dora's."

With a cruel turn of his hand, Hugh began to drag Anne into the water. She fought him every step of the way. She beat at him. She kicked at his legs as best she could.

Hugh seemed oblivious to the pain. His crazed, fixed smile never wavered as he drew her deeper and deeper into the water.

Anne screamed. At the cry, Hugh grabbed her about the neck, throttling her.

A sob rose in her throat, a mixture of hopelessness and abject terror. Yet still she fought him as the lake rose now to her waist. There was so little time left before he turned and pushed her beneath the water. So little time and nothing—absolutely nothing—she could do against his far greater strength.

As he choked the breath from her, Anne's hands gradually relaxed. Then Hugh shoved her into the cold, dark lake. From a place far removed, she screamed at herself to fight on, not to give up.

With one last, superhuman effort, Anne twisted and bucked against him. Breaking the water's surface, she gasped for a precious breath and grabbed at his shirt to pull herself upward.

A fist slammed into the side of her face.

Pain exploded in Anne's jaw. Blackness engulfed her.

9

"Curse the woman!" Niall groaned as he swung up onto his mount. He urged the horse out of the stable yard, clearing the castle gate at a dead run. *Of all the morns to have to ride off after Anne,* he thought in groggy disgust. His head pounded, his eyes were gritty and blurred, and his stomach churned unpleasantly. But then, when had she ever made things easy for him?

He turned his mount in the direction of the only place, besides Ena's hut, he knew Anne might go—the little burn where he had found her and Iain that day. The movement of his horse's legs, striking the earth in relentless rhythm, gradually intensified the thrumming in Niall's skull. He thought he'd go mad. He lowered his head in an attempt to ease the throbbing agony, the nausea welling inside him. How, in this sorry condition, would he be able to confront Anne when and if he finally found her? He could barely stay astride his horse!

With a supreme effort, Niall straightened. It didn't matter how he felt. He had borne worse; battle was a pitiless arbitrator when it came to one's injuries. The rules were simple. Ignore the pain and continue fighting—or die. He just fervently hoped that, this day, there'd be no fighting or dying required.

Niall cleared the top of the hill overlooking the burn, to find her horse grazing peacefully nearby. There was, however, no sign of

Anne. His irritated gaze swept the area, finally following the little brook down to Loch Awe itself. There, not far from the shore, was a man bent over someone. As Niall watched, the man shoved the limp form beneath the water.

"Cruachan!" Niall roared.

The man in the lake stiffened then turned. An icy chill spread through Niall. It was Hugh, his hands clenched around Anne's neck. In the next instant he dropped her and began to move toward the shore. Anne slowly sank below the water. Rage exploded within Niall.

He reached the water's edge just as Hugh gained the shore. With a powerful swipe of his arm, Niall knocked his cousin to the ground, then leaped from his horse and flung himself into the lake. He plowed through the water, his progress an eternity, but at last he reached Anne.

Niall pulled her into his arms. She was waxy pale, limp. "Annie," he cried, "can ye hear me? Ah, open yer eyes, lass!" Niall turned, his long strides carrying them swiftly back to shore.

He laid her on the ground, tenderly brushing the wet, tangled hair from her face. A hollow, hopeless feeling swelled inside him, calling forth a memory of another time, another loss.

"Nay, not ye, too, lassie," he whispered. Niall gathered her to him, pressing her tightly to his chest. "Not ye, too."

"Move away, cousin."

Niall lifted his head. Hugh stood before him, sword drawn, the familiar crazed light gleaming in his eyes.

"Go to the devil!" Niall clasped Anne protectively to him. "I won't give her to ye!"

The tip of Hugh's sword came to rest against the side of Niall's neck. "She's a witch and I must be sure she's dead. It's for the best, cousin. Unhand her."

Masking his rising anger behind a shuttered expression, Niall lowered Anne to the ground then rose. He forced a casual motion in her direction. "Ye're right, of course. Have at it, then."

✦✦✦

As he stepped toward Anne, Hugh's eagerness betrayed him. With a swift movement, Niall slammed into his cousin, knocking both of them to the ground. Hugh brought up his sword hilt, striking a blow to the side of Niall's head. Niall's grip loosened. Hugh rolled away.

Shaking the scattering of stars from his eyes, Niall sprang to his feet. His grip on his own sword was none too soon. With a wild cry, Hugh was upon him. Metal met metal. Hugh's madness lent him a power beyond that of most men. Niall backed off from his cousin's nearly overwhelming strength.

✦

An irritatingly incessant clanging pierced the fog surrounding Anne. Consciousness returned. She inhaled a painful, shuddering breath, then coughed. A choking spasm shook her. For a long, terror-filled moment, she thought she'd never breathe again. Then the air began to fill her lungs.

She rolled over onto her stomach and expelled a weak groan. How it hurt to breathe! And her throat . . . At the realization of what had happened, of the danger she still might be in, Anne struggled to rise.

The effort proved fruitless. She had to content herself with lifting her head. For a moment, confusion mingled with a nauseating weakness. Her world whirled before her. Then it righted.

The sight of Niall, engaged in combat with Hugh, filled her with renewed strength. She pulled herself up to rest upon her elbows. He had come! Niall had come to save her!

Hugh was tiring. Niall, however, though the sweat beaded his brow, appeared as fresh and strong as if he had only begun to fight. His claymore moved with effortless ease, parrying each of Hugh's more awkward thrusts with battle-honed skill.

Relentlessly, Niall drove the other man backward, his face set in grim determination. Hugh, scrambling away from the increasingly damaging blows, finally lost his footing. He fell, the sword still clasped in his hand.

Niall's blade found his throat. "Yield, cousin."

Hugh shook his head. "Nay. I won't yield to one who defends a witch. Kill her first. Then I'll surrender."

"Ye're mad." Frustration threaded Niall's voice. "Yer unreasoning hatred has twisted yer mind until ye can no longer divine truth from fantasy." He sheathed his sword. "Be gone from me. Until ye can find it in yer heart to accept Anne, ye're banished from Kilchurn."

Hugh struggled to his feet. "Ye cannot! Ye haven't the authority."

Niall arched a dark brow. "Haven't I? Do ye think my father would fail to back me in this?"

"She . . . she has bewitched ye both!" As if to add further emphasis to his accusation, Hugh turned his head and spat on the ground. "Ye'll see. The Campbell will soon die, no doubt helped along by her spells. But there's still ye, then, isn't there? And ye aren't fit to be chieftain, with that devilish witch at yer side. Something will still have to be done about ye."

"And ye're the one to do it, mayhap? Do ye conceal yer treachery behind a mask of false madness?"

Even as he spoke, Niall regretted his words. He knew Hugh wasn't the traitor. He couldn't be certain, though, that his cousin wasn't in league with him. Hugh, even as a lad, had always been easily led by others more clever than him. And that issue of succession had always stuck in his cousin's throat. Unfortunately, for all his lack of intelligence and common sense, Hugh *could* be fiercely loyal when he put his mind to it. Niall knew he'd never wring a willing confession from his cousin.

Niall sighed, suddenly weary to the point of exhaustion. "Anne's no witch. It's but yer madness that makes ye see that." He motioned toward Hugh's horse. "Now, no more of it. Yer banishment stands. It's death if I set sight upon ye before ye come to yer senses."

His cousin glared at him. "This isn't the end of this, Niall. I'll be back to finish what I began this day, and no mistake!"

"Well, it'll be the end of *ye* if *ye* return. Be grateful ye've yer life. It's likely more than ye deserve."

Hugh sheathed his sword and stomped off to his horse. With a despairing eye, Niall followed his cousin's progress until Hugh rode from sight. One by one, his family was splitting apart. First Iain and now Hugh, both now at odds with him—and both because of Anne.

Nay, Niall quickly corrected himself, the main cause of his falling out with Iain was because he suspected him traitor. And Hugh simply because he had tried to kill Anne.

Anne! Niall wheeled about to find her sitting there, quite alive. For a fleeting moment he was overcome with the impulse to run to her, gather her into his arms, and tell her how thankful, how happy he was she had survived. But only for a moment.

The look in Anne's eyes was bitter. It rekindled the original emotions that had sent Niall out after her. The wench had the audacity to be angry with him, after all she had just put him through? Well, two could play this game.

He strode over, refusing to be moved by her sodden, bedraggled appearance or by the purpling bruises on her neck and jaw. He surveyed her indifferently. "Well, madam? What have ye to say? Ye seem determined to get yerself killed."

"And what do ye care?" she was barely able to croak. "I'd have thought it would've solved all the problems our handfasting has caused ye. Mayhap, for yer own good, ye were a bit too quick to arrive."

Something exploded in Niall. He pulled her up to him. "Little fool! Why do ye say such things? Why do—"

Ensnared in her tear-filled silver eyes, Niall couldn't continue. He saw nothing but her delicately carved features, her soft, slightly parted lips.

Their glances locked. Something intense flared between them.

Anne's tearful defiance evaporated like the morning mists. Niall's overpoweringly masculine presence, towering above her, banished the memory of last night. Nothing mattered but this moment and the sweet reality of being in his arms. With a small moan, she laid her head upon his chest, her hands entwining about his neck.

Niall stiffened. His hands dropped. Afraid he'd push her away, Anne clung all the more fiercely to him.

After a time weighted slowly on the passing wind, he groaned and wrapped his arms about her. "Och, Annie, Annie," he whispered, "why do ye persist in tormenting me? Do ye know the terror I felt this morn when Agnes burst into my chamber and told me ye'd gone riding alone? And then when I saw Hugh drowning ye, I almost went mad!"

Anne stood there, not quite sure she was understanding all she was hearing. Niall had been worried, even frantic over her leaving the castle alone? Was it possible? Did she actually mean something to him? If only it were so!

Then what about Nelly? a small voice persisted in asking, squelching the rising joy. *Ask him about Nelly.*

Inhaling a deep breath, Anne released her grip. She leaned back to stare up at Niall. "There's no need to say things ye don't mean, m'lord. I'm quite aware yer tastes don't run to women like me."

A furrow wrinkled Niall's brow. "What are ye talking about? What've I ever done or said to make ye believe I don't find ye appealing? As crude as my behavior was last night in yer chamber, I'd hardly call it the act of a man who didn't want ye."

"Then why did ye turn to Nelly?" Anne blurted the question in a painful rush of words, then immediately regretted them. Why, oh why, had she asked? Now he'd only smile smugly and inform her it was none of her concern, that he'd do whatever he wanted with whomever.

"Turn to Nelly?" For a long moment Niall couldn't fathom what Anne was talking about. Then a sickening realization flooded him. Anne knew about his tryst with Nelly. But how?

“Who told ye? Who—”

“I saw ye with her below stairs!” Now that the truth was out, Anne couldn’t seem to curb her words. “Ye were holding each other . . . and kissing . . . and . . . and then I couldn’t bear to watch a moment longer and I ran away.”

Niall gave her a small shake. “Enough, Annie. I believe ye were there. But if ye were, ye must also know that was as far as it went. I couldn’t go on.”

She lowered her head. “I didn’t see aught after that. I told ye. I didn’t stay.”

A gentle hand lifted her chin. Warm brown eyes met hers, and Niall’s mouth curved up in the beginning of a beautiful smile. “Och, Annie, I didn’t bed her. I swear it. She made the mistake of calling yer memory back to me, and by then the liquor had begun to wear off. I realized it wasn’t her I wanted. It was ye.”

He searched her face. Anne’s expression was carefully blank, betraying nothing of what she was feeling. Niall sighed. “I know ye’ve no reason to believe me, but I’ve never before done that with a servant. It doesn’t excuse my behavior, but I wanted ye to know.”

“Truly.”

Her flat response stirred Niall’s growing exasperation. “Ye’re determined not to make this easy for me, are ye?” A wry grin touched his lips. “Well, I suppose I deserve it. I hurt ye, and now ye’re exacting a fair measure of pain from me in return.”

“I am not!” The denial was quick and hot. “I-I haven’t a care one way or another what ye do!”

“And I say ye lie, Annie lass.”

A spark of deviltry danced in his eyes, melting the last bit of Anne’s resistance. She wanted to reach up and kiss him. At the thought, a sweet tremor shook her slender form.

Niall noticed the small shudder. “What a dolt I’ve been to keep ye standing here in this breeze, soaked to the skin as ye are. If ye don’t get out of those wet clothes soon, ye’ll surely catch the ague.”

Before Anne could protest that it wasn’t the cold that had her trembling, Niall swung her up into his arms and strode to his horse. He placed her atop the animal. In the next instant, he leaped up behind her.

The failed opportunity for a kiss momentarily disappointed her, then she decided all wasn't lost. As Niall guided his horse to where her own mount waited, Anne comforted herself with the realization that, at long last, she had managed to extract some admission of affection from the Campbell tanist. And, though a kiss would've been heavenly, riding back to Kilchurn in the strong embrace of his arms wasn't so bad either.

✦

After a hot bath and bracing toddy, Anne slept well into the afternoon. Then, quite refreshed, she rose and dressed. Deciding to catch a breath of air before seeking the company of the Campbell as was their late-afternoon habit, she headed up to the tower walk.

The wind on the open roof area was strong. The flag bearing the Campbell arms of a fierce boar's head snapped briskly. Anne was soon forced to seek the shelter of the tower wall near the stairs.

She had just settled on the rough wooden bench positioned to afford an impressive view of the rolling, tree-covered hills surrounding Loch Awe, when Caitlin exited the tower stairway. The girl's gaze met hers. Caitlin hesitated, then resolutely gathered her skirts and approached.

"Well, are ye quite happy with yerself?" the black-haired girl demanded with a sneer. "Ye knew of Hugh's hatred for ye, and yet ye insisted on riding out alone, luring him into what he'd no control over. Now he's banished, and all because of ye!"

"Because of me?" Anne wasn't prepared for an argument over Hugh. "I nearly drowned because of *him.* I'd hardly say that was much of a plot to lure Hugh to his destruction. If it hadn't been for Niall's timely—"

"Exactly!" Caitlin swept Anne's protest aside with an imperious wave of her hand. "Ye knew he'd come to yer aid. Why, ever since yer arrival, my brother acts as if he has a ring in his nose and all ye've to do is tug on his rope and—"

"Och, Caitlin!" Anne laughed. "If ye think I've such influence over yer brother, ye've been sadly misled. Niall's his own man and beset with far more important matters than when and how high to jump at my behest." Her smile faded. "It was never my intent to get Niall to banish Hugh. Hugh needs help, not punishment."

Caitlin faltered momentarily, then gathered new ammunition and forged on. "It all comes down to the same thing. Ye're not wanted here. Even if my brother *is* temporarily entranced with ye, he'll soon lose interest. Ye'll never be half the woman the Lady Anne Stewart was. Niall will eventually realize that."

Though the girl's words stung, Anne refused to show it. "Only time will tell, won't it?"

"Och, aye." Caitlin sniffed. "In the meanwhile, though, ye could well destroy him. Every day the rumors grow that ye've bewitched Niall, that ye have him under yer spell. By the time he assumes the chieftainship, no one will want to follow him."

"And are ye one of those who believe I'm a witch?"

The softly couched question gave the girl pause. "I . . . I'm not sure I believe in witches." She tossed her head in defiance. "It doesn't matter what I think, anyway. The rumors are beginning to undermine my brother's position. If ye care even a fig for him, ye'd leave, and be quick about it!"

"And if ye cared even a fig for me, ye'd have made more of an attempt at hospitality toward Anne," a deep voice dryly interjected.

Both women turned to find Niall standing in the tower doorway, a grim expression on his face.

"Now, brother, this isn't what it seems," Caitlin began, hurrying to him.

"On the contrary. It's more than evident what's going on here." Niall held up a hand to halt her. "And I won't have it, do ye hear me, Caitlin? Wed or not, Anne's now the lady of this castle. She'll be treated as such."

“Ye’re not chief yet, though ye seem more than eager to forget that of late. I need only obey Father’s orders, not yers.”

Niall grabbed his sister’s arm. “Then why not pay him a visit? Let him decide Anne’s proper treatment in this castle.”

“Nay.” Caitlin jerked away. “I don’t want him upset. Besides, she’s won him over too.”

“Och, and has she now? Then more the reason for ye to treat Anne well. It’s past time ye gave up this foolish nonsense.”

“Nay.” Anne moved toward Niall. It was time to end this battle between brother and sister. “I’ll not force my presence where it isn’t wanted. I know ye mean well, m’lord, but it’d be too humiliating, having others coerced into including me when they’d no wish to.” She could feel her cheeks warm as she held his strangely piercing gaze. “Let it be, m’lord. Ye can’t force friendship or respect. It has to be earned.”

“Aye, that it does, lass.” Niall’s calloused palm caressed the silken line of Anne’s jaw. “And ye’ve certainly earned mine.”

Caitlin glared at Niall, an expression of youthful distaste contorting her pretty mouth. “Och, if ye could only hear yerself! Ye’re so besotted—”

“Enough!” Niall roared. “I care not for yer opinion, only for yer compliance. I asked ye before and I ask ye one time more. If ye cannot find it in ye to obey, mayhap ye need opportunity to think upon it more closely. Say, while visiting a few months with the Lady Mathilda in Edinburgh?”

His sister blanched. “But that’s so far away, and ye know what a puss Iain’s mother is about chaperones. Why, I’d hardly ever be able to see Rory, and I’d never have any time alone.”

“It’s yer choice.”

She stamped her foot. “Och, and ye’re a hard one, Niall Campbell!” Then, noting the unrelenting glint in her brother’s eyes, Caitlin’s slender shoulders slumped. “But what choice have I? It’ll be as ye ask. Yer lady’ll suffer no further slights from me.”

“Good. Now leave us. I’ve a wish to speak with Anne alone.”

✢ ✢

They watched Caitlin depart then turned to face each other. Anne wet her lips, wondering how to put her next words. She decided no matter how she said it, it would probably sound like a rebuke. "I thank ye for yer kindness, m'lord," she murmured finally, "but the difficulty between yer sister and me is too insignificant to concern yerself over. Ye've problems of greater import—"

Niall took her into his arms. His head lowered until his warm breath wafted across her face. "Wheesht, lass. What I choose to do in regard to ye is my decision, not yers." Slowly, he surveyed her. "Ye look well rested. Have ye recovered from this morn's swim, then?"

She grinned. "Och, aye, except for a tender jaw and sore throat." Anne touched her neck. "I fear I'll wear this circlet of marks for a few weeks, though."

Niall's gaze dipped to the blue-tinged impressions of Hugh's fingers. He bent and gently kissed Anne's bruised neck.

At the soft brush of his lips, Anne gasped. Her eyelids slid shut in pleasure. "M'lord!" she breathed then gave herself up to the welcoming haven of his arms.

But only for a moment. Then Anne pulled back. Brushing a windswept lock from her eyes, she stared up at him.

At the perplexed look on Niall's face, a small smile touched her lips. There was one matter more between them, which until now had been overshadowed by last eve's scene with Nelly. One matter more, and then mayhap they could begin anew.

"I've a question weighing on me, m'lord," she began. "It was the reason I followed ye below stairs last eve."

"Did ye mayhap desire the reason for my behavior in yer chamber?"

"Aye, m'lord."

He sighed and motioned for her to sit beside him on the bench. "It was a combination of many things, lass. Lust . . . anger . . . hurt."

"Hurt?" At the startling admission, Anne's heart skipped a beat.

Earlier, he had admitted to his lust, and she could understand how she angered him; he spared no words in reminding her of that quite often. But to have distressed him in some way!

She searched his face. "Pray, how have I hurt ye, m'lord?"

Niall turned from her. Leaning his head back against the tower wall, he appeared to study the scene beyond the castle. Finally he spoke, his voice low and controlled. "I was a fool to have thought this, but I'd hoped to forget about last night and the reason for my confused feelings. But it cannot be. It still stands between us."

He turned to her, anguish burning in his eyes. "It's but part of our ongoing battle over yer healing, lass. I came upon ye and Davie yester eve in the hall outside my father's chamber. I heard ye tell him to meet ye later, so ye could treat his hand."

At the sadness in his voice, Anne's heart twisted in her chest. Och, the one and only time she had tried to heal someone in Kilchurn, and Niall had been privy to it! She had indeed helped little Davie, all the while feeling so guilty she had made a vow never to do it again—at least not until she had Niall's permission. And now to have the painful sacrifice been for naught!

"I didn't want to go against ye in this. Truly, I didn't," Anne said, placing a hand upon his arm, "but he was such a wee lad and in so much pain. How could I, or anyone, turn from him? Could ye?"

Niall shook his head. "Nay, I couldn't. I suppose I was unfair to expect ye to. But I meant well, lass. Surely ye can see that. Already the rumors about ye are spreading. Caitlin's words just a few moments ago must convince ye of that. And now I've banished Hugh . . . Well, tongues are sure to wag. Yer healing skills would only add to the talk."

"I know that, m'lord. I try, truly I do. But it hurts to see folk in need and know I've the skills to aid them, yet not be able to do aught." Anne bit her lip to keep the sob from her voice, but her words trembled nonetheless. "It fair tears out my heart!"

"Och, lassie." Niall took her into his arms. "I'm sorry. Ye know

I wouldn't cause ye pain." He paused to stroke her cheek tenderly. "Ye do know that, don't ye?"

She managed a tremulous smile. "Aye, m'lord, I think I do."

"Then will ye trust me in this for a while longer? Give my people time? Things'll die down. Then we'll see about yer healing."

"Aye, m'lord. I'll try."

Niall frowned. "One thing more."

Anne's eyes widened. "Aye?"

"Could ye possibly call me Niall, rather than m'lord all the time? I know it's quite proper, but it strikes me as rather distant." He crooked her chin with his finger. "And, if it's acceptable, from now on I'd rather things not be so cold between us."

Anne's heart sang with delight. "Aye, that's quite acceptable, m'lord—Niall." She grinned.

Niall stared into her eyes, the look smoldering there igniting an answering flame in her. His lips, firm and sensually molded, moved toward her. He was going to kiss her!

The harsh sound of a throat clearing interrupted their heated reverie.

"Er, m'lord," the tartan-clad man began when Niall and Anne turned to meet him. "The Campbell requests yer immediate presence in his chambers."

Unconsciously, Niall gripped Anne's hand. "Is there aught wrong with my father? Has his condition worsened?"

The man shook his head. "Nay, m'lord. A messenger arrived with an important document from the queen. Sir Duncan's already with yer father, and it requires only yer presence as tanist to break the royal seal."

"As ye wish." Niall looked at Anne. "This should take but a short time. We'll finish where we left off when I return. Will ye wait for me here?"

Anne smiled, her whole heart in the act. "Aye. I'll wait."

✦

✠ ✠

Niall never returned. Instead, he sent Davie to tell her he'd be detained longer than he had originally anticipated and that he'd meet her at the evening meal. Anne was disappointed, but she consoled herself with the thought that it was only two hours to supper time. They'd have the rest of the eve together.

The rest of the eve to talk and laugh and mayhap even take a walk together, she thought dreamily as she dressed. Anne hardly noticed when Agnes slipped the pale blue silk gown with the square, lace-trimmed neckline over her head, or when she fastened the sapphire pendant necklace about her throat. Her thoughts were far away as the maidservant plaited her hair then tucked it beneath a matching blue silk cap. All Anne could remember was the touch of Niall's lips on her neck, of the fire burning in his dark eyes.

"There, all done." Agnes dabbed lavender scent at the base of Anne's throat. Her brow wrinkled as she glanced once more at her mistress's bruises. "I wish ye'd allow me to hide those marks with a bit of tinted lead powder. It's all the fashion at court nowadays."

Anne firmly shook her head. "Nay, Agnes. I won't cover the bruises Hugh gave me. It would make it seem as if I've something to be ashamed of. Besides, if I'd a need to hide aught, it'd be with one of my own concoctions, not with that foul lead powder."

Agnes shrugged. "Have it yer way, lass." She gave Anne a small shove. "Now, get on with ye. It's time for the meal to begin, and ye don't want to keep Sir Niall waiting."

No, she certainly didn't want to keep Niall waiting, Anne thought in anticipation as she hurried down the corridor. Even the occasional glares and whispered comments as she strode into the Great Hall failed to dampen her rising excitement. Indeed, only when Duncan appeared at her side and offered his arm did Anne's happy bubble finally burst.

She eyed his proffered arm. "Thank ye, Sir Duncan, but I'd prefer to wait until Niall can escort me to table."

"And it's at Niall's express request that I'm here, lady." A flatly courteous smile touched Duncan's lips. "He's still in conference with my brother, and said to tell ye he didn't know when he'd be done. I'm to lead ye to table and commence the meal."

Anne's heart sank. What could possibly be so important that Niall would miss the meal? The hope of a pleasant evening with him vanished before her eyes. It seemed there was always something, some duty, arising to thwart their budding relationship.

With a deep sigh, she accepted Duncan's arm and followed him to the main table, trying mightily to hide the dejection that had suddenly engulfed her. She barely tasted the sumptuously prepared food or noticed the boisterous laughter and talk from the lower tables, so immersed was she in her disappointment. Little by little, though, as her natural optimism slowly resurfaced, Anne dragged herself from her misery.

For the first time she paid note to the elegant dress at the main table and the larger than normal amounts of wine being served. With a puzzled frown, Anne turned to Duncan. "Have I imagined it, or are the people more merry than usual this eve?"

A slow grin twisted Duncan's mouth. "Och, it isn't yer imagination, lady. There's indeed cause for celebration."

"And, pray, what's the cause?"

Duncan's brows drew up in surprise. "Hasn't Niall informed ye of the queen's charter, delivered just this day?"

Anne fought a surge of annoyance. Why must he persist in making her drag the news out of him? She shook her head. "Nay, I haven't seen him since the arrival of the messenger. If ye'd be so kind as to enlighten me . . ."

He stroked his beard thoughtfully. "It'd be best if ye first heard it from my nephew. The news might well upset ye. Mayhap he could find some way to soften it."

"Please, Sir Duncan!" An uneasy premonition stirred within her. "He isn't here and I'd prefer not to wait all night. Tell me and be done with it."

The older man shrugged. "As ye will, lady. The queen has finally given us a land grant, one we've sought for many years. If ye recall, ye MacGregors have never had legal title to the lands ye've claimed, holding them only on the clan principle. Tradition, however, never carries the same power as a sheepskin grant."

As rising comprehension, then horror, filled Anne, Duncan gave a harsh laugh. "Aye, it's as ye suppose. Yer lands, m'lady, are now ours."

10

"Why, Father?" Niall demanded, his voice hoarse with frustration. "Why did ye do such a thing?"

Robert Campbell straightened in his chair and sighed. "Why obtain legal ownership over MacGregor lands?" He shrugged wearily. "Because I finally tired of their senseless raids, their burning of our crofts and theft of our livestock. It was the work of fools, this incessant picking at us when they never had any hope of winning. Duncan convinced me it was the only way to end the feud. They'd either come to heel or be driven off. It was the best course for all, even if the MacGregors were too blind to see it."

"But they've held those lands for centuries, legally or not. It's their heart's blood. They won't give them up, not until the last one of them is dead. Our feud will now escalate to all-out war!"

"Even the MacGregors can't prevail against a royal charter. They'd risk banishment, if not proscribement."

Niall shuddered at the word. Proscribement required the clan name be struck from existence, the lands forfeit, and the men hunted like animals with a price on their heads. Yet what other choice would the MacGregors have? Clan honor would never permit them to give up their land, to become little more than tenants to the Campbells.

"The feuding had to stop!" Robert said defensively, apparently noting his son's gloomy countenance. "We, too, have our honor, and that honor requires we do all within our power to protect our own. And I meant to be gracious with the MacGregors. Only their chief would've known the full extent of the grant. It was my bargaining piece." His face brightened. "But now it doesn't matter. Our clans will be joined when ye and Anne wed. Ye can sign the grant over to her as a wedding gift. MacGregor lands will stay MacGregor."

"Somehow," Niall muttered, "I don't think Anne will see it quite so benignly. I wish ye hadn't given Duncan leave to tell everyone. I could've used some time to break it to her in a gentler fashion."

His father frowned. "Aye, mayhap that wasn't wise. But Duncan was so happy, so eager to share the news, and now that the feuding's ended . . ."

Niall clamped down on his anger at his uncle's cruel thoughtlessness. In the past, he knew his father would've never been so easily manipulated, but the sickness ravaging his body had also weakened his mind. There was naught to be done about it. Naught save get to Anne as quickly as possible and try to explain.

He gripped his father's shoulder in a parting gesture. "It'll all work out in the end. Anne and I'll work it out. By yer leave, I would see to that now."

Robert waved him away. "Aye, do that, laddie. I've no wish for the lass to suffer needlessly. Go to her. Tell her the truth of the matter."

Niall strode from the room. *Tell her the truth of the matter.* He wondered if the truth might not come far too late to assuage the pride of a beautiful, russet-haired MacGregor.

His pace down the corridor quickened to a dead run. The evening meal was sure to have started by now. Anne may have already heard the news about the land grant. He needed to get to her, to explain, to soothe away her fears, or yet another wall would come up between them.

Curse it all! Why, when they finally seemed to be coming to some sort of understanding, did this have to happen?

✝✝

He reached the head of the stairs overlooking the Great Hall and paused, scanning the room for sight of her. Though the meal was over, Anne was still seated at the main table. Even from the other side of the room, Niall could see her pale, drawn expression, the rigid set of her slender shoulders. *She knows,* he thought with a sinking feeling, *yet is too proud to leave, seeing it as an admission of her pain.*

His clan, however, seemed oblivious to her. There she sat in the midst of the jubilant toasts and joyful revelry, alone and suffering, as beautiful in defeat as in defiance. An overwhelming impulse to go to her rose in Niall.

Anne sensed his presence even before she felt his touch. She tensed, barely controlling the impulse to jerk away. Ever so slowly, she turned to look up at him, making no attempt to hide her contempt.

He smiled thinly, flashing her a gentle but firm warning. "Not here, Annie." He offered her his hand. "Pray, come with me."

She rose, refusing his assistance. "Aye, m'lord. Ye're right. What I've to say is best heard in private, or this verra eve the feud will start anew."

In silence, they made their way to the library. As soon as Niall closed the door behind them, she rounded on him. "Of all the greedy, thieving—"

"Are ye going to judge and hang me before I've even had a chance to defend myself?" Niall eyed the little spitfire standing before him. He had never seen her so mad or so exquisitely beautiful. All he wanted was to take her in his arms and kiss away her anger, but he knew the act would never soothe the pain lying beneath her rage. The only way to do that was first to win back her trust.

Her fists clenched at her sides, Anne glared up at him. "There's naught ye can say that speaks more clearly than what ye've done, Niall Campbell! Ye've finally succeeded in destroying us. Ye must feel so verra, verra proud!"

“I’d naught to do with this, Annie. Today’s the first time I knew about the grant.”

“And I say ye lie!”

He grabbed her arms and pulled her to him. “Woman, I told ye once before—I never lie! Are ye so blinded by emotion ye can’t listen to reason? Am I talking to a fool?”

“The only fool here is ye, if ye think I or my clan will accept this! We’ll fight ye to our last breath before giving up our land!” Her voice lowered to a calm flatness. “But then, mayhap that’s what ye wanted all along. With this royal grant, we now go against not only ye but the Crown as well. What better ruse to annihilate us completely?”

“By mountain and sea, Annie! Listen to me!” Niall gave her a small shake. “I’ll be chief soon. Do ye truly believe I’d do aught like that? What purpose would it serve? Ye’re firstborn of yer clan. There are no males with greater claim than ye. If we legalize our union at year’s end, in a sense we’ve joined our lands anyway. So ye see, there’s really no problem.”

“No problem? A year’s too late! Ye legally own our lands as of today. It’s no longer ours, don’t ye see? We’ll be the laughingstock of the Highlands! No wedding a year from now will change that. Ye’ve made us look the fool. It’s done, Niall Campbell, and naught—*naught*—will ever change that!”

She wrenched away, turning her back to him. “I beg leave to return to my people. I’ve more than served my purpose and cannot bear another day in this castle. If ye’ve even a shred of compassion, ye’ll not humiliate me further.”

“Don’t even think it!” Niall growled. “Ye’re upset and not reasoning clearly. We had something growing between us, Annie. Will ye let the schemes of others destroy it?”

She whirled to face him, her eyes blazing with silver fire. “And I say ye’re mistaken, m’lord. We’ve naught. Do ye hear me? Naught! Don’t think to placate me with soft-spoken words. Ye’re no better than the rest of them! Let me go, I say!”

At the disdainful finality in Anne's voice, Niall's patience faded. In its place rose a hard resolve. If she wasn't clearheaded enough to know her own heart, he'd have to take command. All Anne needed was time. Time to be convinced of his true motives, to find some way out of this quagmire of wounded honor.

He shook his head. "I won't free ye from yer vows. We're handfasted for a year. Willing or no, ye'll stay here for that time and not a moment less." He turned to walk toward the door when her tear-choked voice halted him, her bitter words slicing deep to lay open his heart.

"I hate ye, Niall Campbell," she cried. "Mark well my words. If it's the last thing I do, I'll make ye rue the day ye brought me here!"

✦

"W-water . . ."

Niall slipped his arm beneath his father's head. Lifting him, he offered the dying man a sip of water.

The Campbell shot him a grateful smile then, with a sigh, closed his eyes. Niall laid him down. For a long while he sat there, watching the bedcovers rise and fall with his father's labored breathing.

I'll be chief verra soon now. The thought gave him little comfort. The position held no joy or attraction for him. It was nothing but a heavy responsibility and burdensome worry. Of late, all it seemed to do was drive one wedge after another between him and Anne.

Anne. When had she begun to fill all his waking moments and become so important to him? Yet now, when he needed her most, she couldn't be further away.

"H-have ye talked to the l-lassie?"

Niall shook his head, gazing down at the pain-bright eyes staring once more up at him. "Nay, she refuses to see me. It's been well over a week now, and she hasn't budged from her room. My only comfort is that Agnes assures me she's alive and eating."

"It's my fault. My foolish scheme to end the feud caused this."

Robert sighed. "Och, why did I let Duncan talk me into this? Wh-what was I thinking?"

Niall laid a comforting hand on his father's shoulder. "Don't waste yer strength worrying over this, Father. I, of all people, realize how hard the choices are. Ye made the decision in good faith. Ye couldn't know what lay ahead. Anne and I'll work this out."

"She's a sweet lass."

"Aye, Father."

"Y-ye care for her, don't ye, laddie?"

He stared down into his father's bright blue eyes. "Aye."

"B-bring her to me. I must say my farewells."

Niall frowned. "She won't come. She holds ye as responsible as I for the land grant."

The Campbell's trembling hand grasped his son's shirt to pull him close. "I-I'm dying, lad! She'll come."

The effort took all his remaining strength. Robert fell back, a harsh cough wracking his body. He motioned for his handkerchief, but not fast enough to hide the bloody spittle that rose to his lips.

Niall winced at the sight. He stood. "I'll do what I can."

Without a word, he strode past his sister and uncle and left the room. Niall's resolve, however, ebbed with each step down the corridor. Anne wouldn't listen to him. He knew too well her stubbornness, her fierce pride. If it had been anyone but his father he'd have never approached her at this time, for he wasn't fool enough not to recognize a hopeless situation. Yet, somehow, some way, he must convince her. It was his father's last request. He couldn't fail him.

Agnes answered Niall's knock. Her eyes widened when she peeped through the door. "Aye, m'lord?"

"Let me in. I must talk with her."

The maidservant blanched. "Och, nay, m'lord. It'll only make things worse. Give her more time, I pray ye."

"There's no time left. Let me in." He held her gaze until she finally stepped aside. Niall strode in then turned to the old woman. "Leave us."

Agnes shot a hesitant glance across the room, then curtsied and hurried out.

Anne stood by the window. Her gaze, riveted on some faraway spot, never wavered, though he knew she must be aware of his presence.

"Get out."

Her flat command only reinforced Niall's earlier misgivings. He squared his shoulders and headed toward her, prepared for the battle to come.

The afternoon sun bathed her in a golden hue, setting off sparkling auburn highlights in her long, unbound hair, drenching her delicate features in glowing radiance. Until this moment Niall hadn't realized how much he had missed her. An intensely painful longing swelled in his chest.

If only she'd let him hold her, kiss away all the cares that separated them. He knew, if only he could take her into his arms, he could ease the agonizing barriers between them. It had worked before. Dare he try again?

"Don't even think about touching me!" The words escaped Anne's lips in a low snarl. "I swear I'll scratch yer eyes out if ye do."

Niall inhaled a shuddering breath. Had his feelings been that strong, that palpable, that she sensed them with such ease?

"I believe ye, Annie," he finally replied, his voice low. "I wouldn't be here at all if it weren't for my father." He paused for some reaction. There was none. "He's near death."

"I know."

Her voice remained flat, her gaze unwavering in its direction out the window. Niall moved a step closer. "He wants to see ye."

"Nay."

It was the answer he had dreaded. Niall inhaled another ragged breath. "Please, Annie."

The catch in his deep voice sent a frisson through Anne. She wrapped her arms protectively about her. Even now, after all he had done to her, how could the sound of him so easily melt her resolve? *But not this time, not this time or ever again!*

The effort to deny him, though, brought tears to her eyes. She shook her head. "Nay, I said! I don't care if he's dying! I don't care what his last requests are! And I don't care that ye've a need to fulfill them. He's yer father, yer problem. Don't lay it upon me!"

"Don't lay it upon ye?" Niall's fists clenched at his sides. Och, but how he wanted to shake her! "And where else would one lay such cares but at the feet of a healer, especially one who claims to follow the Lord's call? Ye told me ye'd never turn from anyone in need. Doesn't yer sacred duty extend to the deathbed? If ye refuse him now, aren't ye gainsaying everything ye've devoted yer life to? And aren't ye also turning yer back on God?"

She glared at him then, her lips trembling. A wild hope flared.

"Hate me if ye will," Niall pressed on, sensing she was near her breaking point. "I'm alive and strong. Ye've many years to exact yer revenge upon me. But forgive my father and go to him. A healer's compassion shouldn't recognize clan loyalties."

All the anger, all the fight, fled Anne in one mighty rush, leaving only a hollow, aching void. What was the use? As powerful as her animosity toward Niall and his father was at this moment, her love for the Lord was yet stronger. And, if the truth be told, she hadn't the courage to see this through, anyway, or sever the emotional bonds that already tied her to the Campbells. Well, to at least one Campbell, at any rate. And he was dying.

Anne wiped her tears away. "Lead me to him then, but remember one thing, Niall Campbell."

"Aye, lass."

"This changes naught between ye and me."

Niall eyed her for a moment then nodded. He walked from the room.

Anne swept past him when he opened the door to his father's chamber, ignoring Caitlin's horrified gasp and Duncan's muttered oath. Only from a distance did she hear anything, as she leaned over Robert Campbell's bed.

He had worsened so rapidly in the past week. She studied his face, noting the almost translucent skin, the blue tinge to his lips, the sunken, haggard features. Niall had been right. His father was indeed close to death. In spite of Anne's intention to harden her heart to him, the pitiful sight of the Campbell, the memories of his kindness to her, erased her cold determination.

With a small sigh, Anne settled in the chair Niall provided. "Och, m'lord." She took the Campbell's thin, cool hand. "It's a sad thing to see ye like this. Is there aught I can do to ease yer suffering?"

A radiant smile spread across the old man's face. "Och, lassie, y-ye've already done it by coming to me." His glance moved to the tall man standing behind Anne. "I told my son ye would. D-didn't I, laddie?"

Niall's deep voice, so close behind, sent a curious thrill through Anne. "Aye, Father."

The Campbell's eyes crinkled with affection, then he slowly licked his lips. "I've a taste for a bit of broth, laddie. W-would ye send down to the kitchen for a cup of Maudie's soup?"

"Aye, Father."

The Campbell motioned toward Duncan and Caitlin standing near the window. "T-take them with ye. I've a wish for a private moment with the lass." He watched his son lead the others from the room before turning back to Anne.

She eyed him quizzically. "All of a sudden, ye've certainly regained yer strength and with it yer appetite."

The Campbell's smile was sad. "I've no hunger. Far from it. I but wanted a moment of privacy with ye, lassie. My son wouldn't like me interfering, but it's a d-dying man's prerogative, wouldn't ye say?"

"As if ye've ever needed anyone's permission for aught, m'lord."

He chuckled weakly then winced. "Och, lassie, my son has met his match in ye. His first wife was a sweet angel, b-but ye are as proud and brave as any warrior. Niall will need such a woman in the long, dark days ahead." A furrow of concern creased his forehead. "Y-ye'll stand by him, won't ye, lassie?"

Anne couldn't meet his gaze. "There are things between us, m'lord . . . things that cannot be breached."

"H-he needs ye, lassie!"

"Nay, m'lord. He has all he needs now, for he has MacGregor lands. He doesn't need me."

Robert clasped her hand between his. "It was never Niall's intent to take yer lands. If there be fault, it lies with Duncan and me. It was our plan, and our plan alone, to go to the queen. Niall never knew aught about it.

"In a moment of great a-anger against yer father," he continued, "I finally agreed with my brother th-that we should end the feud in any way we could. The land grant seemed the best, the only way."

The Campbell shook his head. "I was so tired of the endless years of fighting, the destruction on both sides. I only meant to gain control over yer clan, not destroy them. I might have been wrong"—he raised his eyes to hers—"but I made the best decision I could for the good of my clan."

Anne exhaled a long breath. "I understand, m'lord."

"Then ye'll forgive my son?"

"Ye said he knew naught about the grant. There's naught to forgive."

Robert leaned back and closed his eyes. "Good." He lay there a long while, his breathing labored, as if the talk had taken what little strength he had. Anne finally made a move to disengage her hand, thinking he had fallen asleep, but the action only caused his eyes to snap open.

He stared at her a moment longer, then smiled. "Ye'll stay with him, then? Be a good helpmate? Give him b-bairns?"

"M'lord . . ." Anne heard the door open and someone walk in.

"Yer word, lass!" Robert gasped. "I've no time left for—"

‡ ‡

He choked, the sound hard and gut-wracking. It increased in intensity until he seemed unable to catch his breath. Anne lifted his shoulders to aid his efforts, but it did little good. Robert Campbell's face turned red, then purpled as he struggled for breath.

Anne reached for the cup of water on the nearby table and held it to his lips. The old man took a sip and swallowed, and then a strange look crossed his face. A gurgling sound rose in his throat. As Anne watched in rising horror, bright red blood began to spew from his mouth.

Robert clutched at her. A glazed expression dulled his eyes. Anne turned. Her frantic gaze slammed into the serving maid standing there with a covered tray in her hands.

"Niall! Get Niall!"

Nelly dropped the tray and ran. Niall must have heard Anne's cry. Before the servant even reached the door, he rushed past her and was at the bed in a few quick strides.

"Father!"

Anne surrendered the limp form and stepped back. Through a mist of tears, she watched Niall clasp his father to him and murmur something into the old man's ear. Then there were hands pushing her aside, as Duncan and Caitlin hurried forward.

There was little more Anne could do. The lung hemorrhage was fatal. Caitlin's wails signaled the end. Gently, Niall laid his father down and pulled the comforter over his face. Then he took his sobbing sister into his arms, his tortured glance meeting Duncan's.

His uncle stood there, his shoulders stiff, his hands fisted. "Ye shouldn't have left him alone with her." He spat the words at Niall as if they had a foul taste. "She was looking for a chance to avenge the loss of her lands—and ye, ye fool, gave it to her."

A shuttered look darkened Niall's face. "Have a care, Uncle. It's yer grief that makes ye speak so."

Duncan grabbed Nelly. "Ye were here. Ye saw. Did she give my brother aught? Do aught untoward?"

The dark-haired maid shrunk back from the ferocity of Duncan's anger. "I-I saw the lady give him something to drink, m'lord. That was all."

"Was there something in the drink? Did she try to poison him?"

Nelly hesitated, then slowly wet her lips. "I can't be certain, but it looked as if she put something into the cup. What it was, though, I don't know."

With a low curse, Duncan released Nelly and stalked over to Anne. He grabbed her by the arm and jerked her to him. "What did ye give my brother, witch? Tell me now before I choke the life from ye!"

For an instant Anne stared up at him, too shocked to reply. Then she began to struggle. "I gave him naught but a sip of water. Now, pray unhand me."

"Do as she says, Uncle," Niall growled in an ominous tone. "I won't dishonor my father's deathbed by this ridiculous scene. Let her go."

Duncan dragged Anne toward Niall. "Ridiculous, ye say! Nelly just said—"

"And it'll take a lot more than Nelly's word to convince me Anne did aught untoward. Let her go!"

Niall stood before his uncle, his wide-legged stance emanating an unmistakable threat. Duncan glared back, his face a mottled red. Finally, he released Anne.

"I've tried mightily to ignore the rumors and gossip spreading through the clan about this woman," he said. "But no more, nephew. Does she now hold a greater power over ye than yer own family? If so, yer judgment's tainted, yer loyalty's suspect, and I don't know ye anymore. Don't know ye at all."

"Get out!"

In rising dismay, Anne watched as Niall motioned for his uncle to leave. The effort it took for him to control himself, from the furious workings of his jaw to the ragged rasp of his breath, filled her with pain.

Dear Lord, wasn't it enough his father had just died? Must he now be forced to endure the torment of fighting with his uncle? And why, once again, must she be so intricately entwined in it all?

"This isn't over, nephew!" Duncan cried, as he turned and walked away.

Niall expelled a weary sigh. "Nay, I'd imagine not. But as clan tanist I proclaim a truce between us until my father's buried. For the sake of our common love for him, can we have peace until then?"

"Aye," Duncan flung over his shoulder. "For the sake of our common love for him. But *only* until then."

Niall watched him depart then turned to Nelly and his sister. "Leave us. There's naught more to be done until the preacher has come and gone. Fetch him for me."

Caitlin opened her mouth, but the words were all but drowned in her tears. She nodded numbly and stumbled from the room, Nelly following closely behind.

"Niall?" Anne touched his arm. "I-I'm so sorry—"

He stared at her, his eyes burning pools of agony. "Not now, Annie. I can't bear much more. Please go to yer room and don't leave until I come for ye."

She took a step closer. "But I want to stay, be of help—"

"Please, Annie!"

"It'll be as ye ask, m'lord." Anne backed away, lowering her gaze as much to spare herself further sight of his pain as to hide the hurt misting her own eyes at his rejection. She gathered her skirts and fled the room, but not before the sound of Niall's voice, once more at his father's bed, reached her retreating ears.

"Father," he groaned. "Och, Lord . . . Father!"

✦

From her chamber window, Anne watched the endless procession of mourners arrive the next day. From dawn to dusk, the vibrant hue of various clan tartans, their lairds and warriors come to honor the memory of the powerful Campbell chief, blanketed the road leading to Kilchurn. All had journeyed to pay their respect and prepare for the funeral feast to be held in the Great Hall that eve. All said their good-byes, touching the corpse lying on its bier in the chapel to indicate they had done nothing to contribute to the death, and to gain immunity from future dreams about the deceased.

All, Anne mused sadly, *but I.* She, alone of the castle's inhabitants, hadn't been invited for the traditional visit. She, who had come to love the Campbell like a father, who had held him in her arms as he gasped out his last breaths, was relegated to the prison of her room—an outcast, a pariah. In the past day as the castle bustled with preparations, she had seen no one but Agnes.

It was from the old maidservant that Anne had gleaned what little information she could about Niall. He was holding up well, Agnes had said, but that look in his eyes . . .

The old woman had shivered when she said that, but Anne couldn't drag another word of explanation from her. All she could extract was a promise to ask Niall to come to her when he found a free moment. It was Anne's only comfort in the somber hours that dragged by—the anticipation of seeing Niall, of speaking with him.

He arrived just after dusk. For want of anything else to do, Anne was busy putting the finishing touches on Caitlin's gown, a gown she now doubted she'd ever be able to give the headstrong girl.

As she painstakingly stitched around the final neckline flower, Anne sighed. *Dear Lord, why is every overture of friendship I make twisted into some evil intent?* Out of Christian charity she had tried so hard to build a bridge, but it almost seemed as if someone was purposely thwarting her efforts.

"Who are ye making the gown for?" a deep voice inquired.

Anne jumped, stabbing herself with the sewing needle. She rose to her feet, sucking at the throbbing finger, and came face-to-face with Niall.

Dressed in formal doublet and belted plaid, he stared down at her. The pain in her finger vanished.

“The gown? It was meant for yer sister, though I wonder now if she’ll ever . . .” Her voice faded.

Exhaustion smudged the skin beneath Niall’s eyes. His face was drawn and haggard. She wondered if he’d even had time to sleep. Forgotten were the endless hours of worry and pain. An urge to comfort him filled her. Anne laid aside her sewing and took Niall by the arm.

“Come.” She pulled him over to a high-backed chair. “Ye look past weary. Seat yerself and have a cup of mulled cider.”

Niall allowed himself to be led to the chair and seated, but refused the drink. “The vigil begins at midnight, and I must keep it at my father’s side. As weary as I am, I fear even a cup of warm cider would put me fast to sleep. And that wouldn’t be conduct fitting the new clan chief.”

“Then they’ve already accepted ye?” Anne’s shoulders sagged with relief. “Despite Duncan’s threats, there was no problem?”

“There’s been no official confirmation or ceremony as yet. That must wait until after the funeral. But did ye doubt there’d be any difficulty?”

“All the talk about me, and now the rumors that I’d poisoned yer father . . .” Anne hesitated, not wishing to add to Niall’s already heavy burden. “Truly, I didn’t know what to think.”

“There’ll be no problem. I’ll see to that.” He took her hand and drew her to him. “But I didn’t come to speak of the chieftainship. I came to ask if ye wished to say yer farewells to my father.”

Anne nodded. “Aye. More than aught, I desire to pay him my respects.” In spite of herself, her voice trembled. “W-would it also be possible to attend his burial on the morrow? It’s my right and duty to be there.”

Niall frowned. “It might go hard for ye. Can ye bear it?”

“With ye at my side, I can bear aught.”

“Then, aye, ye may come. It’s past time ye left this room. To keep ye here any longer would only give credence to the foolish talk.”

Anne bowed her head to hide her happiness. Then, mastering

it, she met his gaze. "I've a confession to make. My words to ye, that night I learned of the queen's land grant, weren't the complete truth. I was angry, felt betrayed. I said things I didn't—"

A calloused finger touched her lips. "Wheesht, lass. It's of no import. Ye went to him when he needed ye. That's all that matters."

She knelt before him and placed her hand on his bare knee. "Then ye don't think I did aught to hurt him, do ye?" Though he had all but implied it, Anne still needed to hear him speak the words. "Truly, I've kept my word and treated no one since Davie. All I gave yer father was a sip of water. I swear it!"

Niall gazed down at her with tired, empty eyes. "I never doubted that for a moment, lass."

Relief washed through her, yet the lack of expression when he had answered plucked uneasily at Anne's heart. He was so exhausted he was driving himself on sheer will alone. It had to explain the dearth of emotion in his voice, the indifference that deadened his eyes. It had to, or else she'd be forced to believe he had finally admitted their problems were insurmountable. And that possibility—now, when they were both so vulnerable and needy—was more than she could bear.

She took the big, square hand lying listlessly on the chair's armrest. Raising it to her lips, Anne kissed it before pressing it to her cheek. "I wish there were more I could do for ye, now, in yer time of sorrow. I never meant to hide away in this room. It was only at yer express command that I did so. My place has always been at yer side." She kissed his hand once more. "I wanted ye to know."

Niall stared down at her, some deep emotion churning in his eyes. Then he sighed, the sound one of ineffable sadness. He took Anne's hand and rose, pulling her up with him. "Come, lass," he said. "It's past time we go to my father."

11

"How dare ye shame yer father's memory? How dare ye allow *her* in the funeral procession?" a woman shrieked as she leapt in front of Niall and Anne the next morning.

Her eyes were wild, her face tear-streaked and pale. Her hair beneath the plaid covering her head was tangled and tumbled down onto her face, but Anne still recognized the tormented features. It was Hugh's mother.

"Ye banish my son, then refuse to allow him to return for his uncle's funeral," Lydia Campbell cried, only half aware she had begun pounding on Niall's chest. "Yet ye permit this witch—"

Gently, Niall captured her hands and held her to him until two serving women hurried over. "Go with them, Aunt Lydia," he said, no trace of emotion in his voice. "Yer grief has befuddled yer reason. This isn't the time or place to question my decisions. We'll talk later."

He watched the women lead her away, his heart going out to the sobbing woman. Then, without another word, he took Anne's arm.

As they walked along, she shot him a hesitant glance but could detect no reaction beneath his stony mask. There were reactions aplenty, however, in the faces of those awaiting them.

Caitlin stood there, a horrified expression on her face. Duncan, a few feet away, had his head bent in heated discussion with the

Reformed preacher. Both men, as Anne neared, halted their talk to turn the full brunt of their hostile gazes upon her. She knew she had been the topic of their conversation.

Well aware of Duncan's feelings for her, she found it was all she could do to force a charitable smile. Then, to distract herself from Niall's unpleasant uncle, Anne next fixed her glance on the preacher in the hope of determining the extent of *his* animosity. She almost wished she hadn't.

Malcolm was a short man, with little of the Campbell look about him. His stern visage of dense black brows and beard fairly reeked of fanatical energy and inflexibility. The look in his penetrating brown eyes as he surveyed her was hard and unforgiving.

Anne shivered. One way or another, Duncan had turned another Campbell against her and gained a powerful ally in the bargain.

Concern for Niall filled her. Would his uncle somehow use the preacher and his religious influence over the people to turn the clan against their new chief? It'd be easy enough if the rumors of her involvement in the Campbell's death could be twisted into outright lies. Noting the look of malice curving Duncan's lips as he straightened and began to move toward them, Anne felt certain it was a distinct possibility.

Niall's grip on her elbow tightened. He gave Duncan a brief nod. "Aye, Uncle?"

"I've a wish to speak with ye." The older man's frigid gaze brushed over Anne before returning to his nephew. "Alone."

"Ye may say what ye wish in front of m'lady." A warning smoldered in his eyes. "I've no secrets from her."

The lines about Duncan's mouth tightened. "The matter concerns her. I thought only to spare her feelings."

Anne turned to Niall. "I've no wish to be cause for further discord. I can wait a ways—"

"Nay, lass," Niall growled. "Yer place is here, at my side. My uncle can speak his piece now and be done with it, or let it rot."

"Young fool!" Duncan took a step closer. "If ye continue on this path, ye're set on the course of yer own destruction! Yer loyalty to this woman's sadly misplaced. Will ye sacrifice family and clan for the likes of her?"

"And will ye fan the flames of this destructive feud by refusing to accept her?" Niall shot back, his voice a harsh whisper. "I didn't think ye capable of such petty conduct."

A challenging light flared in Duncan's eyes. "Would ye banish me, too, then? Ye've already driven Hugh and likely my son away too. Strange conduct, indeed, but mayhap all part of yer plan to assure that none of yer immediate male relatives are deemed acceptable for naming as chief over ye, not to mention as yer tanist. Is that it? Some insignificant laird as second in command would never present a challenge to yer chieftainship, would he?"

Niall ran a hand through his hair in exasperation. "I haven't time for such foolishness. Let it be, I say, until my father's buried. Ye gave yer word."

"Aye, that I did, and I'll keep it." Duncan sighed, the fight visibly ebbing from him. "Truly, nephew, I meant only to warn ye of what the people will think if ye insist on allowing yer lady to attend the funeral. Is that not my place, to keep ye attuned to the clan's mood?"

"Aye, Uncle." Niall's taut-muscled frame relaxed. "But I'll not bend to some whim that's false and unfair, either." He motioned toward the casket. "Now, enough of this. It's past time we buried my father."

He turned to Anne and once more offered her his arm. She hesitated, her glance skittering from one man to the other. Then she placed her hand on Niall's arm.

With each advancing step, Anne's feeling of apprehension grew. Niall may have been fooled by his uncle's apparent submission, but she knew better. Even as he had appeared to acquiesce, the hard, malicious light in the older man's eyes continued to burn. Niall's desire to make peace had blinded him to the evil fires smoldering beneath the surface of Duncan's smooth concern.

But Anne, freed of the ties of kinship, had seen the man's true intent. It frightened her. Duncan cared little for his nephew's welfare. And it began to appear he wished for yet further conflict to weaken Niall's standing as the new chief.

But why?

Ena's words shot through her mind. *"The young lord's in great danger. Ye must help him."*

Fear prickled down Anne's spine. Niall was indeed in grave danger—his position as chief yet unacknowledged, a dangerous enemy made in banishing his unstable cousin, and now there was also his uncle, who seemed bent on undermining him. *Dear Lord,* she prayed, *help him. Help me. We're beset by enemies, and only Ye can save us.*

She glanced up. Niall strode along beside her, tall and proud, his broad shoulders resolutely squared. Strong shoulders, aye, she mused, but increasingly weighted with new and more serious problems. Problems he had no one to share with as, one by one, his closest advisers and family slipped away—and all because of her.

For an instant, Anne's eyes burned with unshed tears. He hadn't even God to turn to, for he seemed a man bereft of God. Yet, in the end, who else could lead him where he truly needed to go?

A fierce determination swelled within her. They were innocent—she and Niall—of any wrongdoing, any fault, in this gathering storm of intrigue and betrayal. The time had come to fight. If Niall couldn't see the Lord beckoning, she did, and she'd be His voice, calling out over and over to him.

She was vowed to the new Campbell chief, the enigmatic and tormented warrior who had fought the battle for her heart and won. Aye, she'd stand by him to the end. Even if, ultimately, that end meant death.

✦

The funeral procession wound up the road to the cemetery, the preacher at its head periodically ringing his brass bell, followed by the six clansmen carrying the coffin. Behind them marched the chief's personal retinue—his bard and bodyguards who bore his sword and shield, the standard bearer, piper, then tatter or spokesman, and the two special men designated to carry the chief over running water. Niall came next, Anne at his side. The rest of the family followed. As the procession passed, the other mourners lining the road fell into place behind it.

The sun crept up from behind the hills, the cloud-shrouded sky dampening its light to a hazy glimmer. A misting of rain began to fall. One by one, the gathering pulled their plaids over their heads.

Thunder rolled in the distance. Anne winced at the sound. Wasn't the day miserable enough without the imminent threat of a downpour?

Gradually, a new sound intruded. The rhythmic thud of hoofbeats heading up the hill behind them must have caught Niall's attention as well. He turned. A dark scowl spread across his face. With a growing feeling of unease, Anne turned.

A man on a bay horse reined in at the back of the procession, then flung himself down and began to make his way through the crowd. Though his dismount was quick, Anne caught a glimpse of his face. It was Iain.

She glanced at Niall. His hands were clenched at his sides. A muscle ticked along his jaw. Considering the exhaustion that dogged his every movement and etched deep lines into his face, Anne knew the strain of dealing with Iain right now might be too much. But what could she do to ease the tension? How could she help him?

"A truce?" she whispered. "Until yer father's buried?"

Niall leveled his gaze upon her, his blazing anger fading to one of flat accusation. "Ye turn my words upon me."

She calmly returned his glance. "What's fair for the father's fair for the son. And, besides," she added, her eyes softening with concern, "it isn't the time or place to renew the battle between ye. It's no affront to ye that Iain attends his uncle's funeral. Let it be for now."

He eyed her for a moment longer then sighed. "Aye, lass, that I will—for now."

‡ ‡

Niall awaited his cousin, his stance still rigid, but Anne knew now there'd be no fight. She gave Iain a welcoming smile.

His mouth quirked in reply, then he riveted his attention on the dark-haired man standing before him. Iain's blond head lowered briefly in greeting. "I came as soon as I heard. I ask leave to attend the burying."

"It's yer right."

At Niall's emotionless reply, Iain exhaled a long breath. There was no forgiveness between them, he realized with a dull ache, only a brief peace for the sake of the dead Campbell chief.

He watched Niall stride on, his glance reuniting with Anne's for a fleeting moment before she turned and followed. Compassion warmed her silver eyes. Iain's gaze never left her as she walked away, a small, delicate contrast to his dark, fierce cousin. Far too kind and good for the likes of him.

Rage surged through him. Vainly, he fought against the destructive emotion, against the frustration following quickly on the heels of the admission of his anger. His hands opened and closed with the ferocity of his struggle.

Curse ye, cousin, he mentally flung the words at Niall's retreating back. *Ye don't deserve her, ye arrogant, power-crazed fool! Ye don't deserve her . . .*

Iain hesitated to knock on Anne's bedchamber door. Sound judgment cautioned against speaking with her, especially now, after being all but banished from Kilchurn. He had Niall to thank for that. No sooner was the funeral over and they returned to the castle, than his cousin summoned him into a private meeting room.

There, all pretenses had been flung aside. Niall had coldly informed him his continued presence was no longer desired. As soon as the meeting to confirm his chieftainship had met on the morrow, Iain was to return to his own lands.

Iain had considered swallowing his pride and, for the sake of kinship, attempting to make amends. But the hard, unyielding look in Niall's eyes had immediately squelched that. Iain refused to grovel or beg forgiveness for something that only existed in Niall's jealous imagination.

A large part of Niall's anger toward him had to be that. Jealousy over his innocent friendship with Anne. Not that Iain didn't want her. He was too honest to deny the truth. But, until this moment, he had never considered betraying his cousin, or tried to convince his woman to leave with him. Indeed, he had risked Niall's wrath in even bringing up the topic of Anne's continued safety at Kilchurn. For his efforts, Iain had received threats if he dared even think of seeing her again.

There was something seriously wrong with his cousin of late, but what it was remained a mystery. Surely the death of the Lady Anne Stewart hadn't addled Niall's brain. Iain had seen no sign of it before. But could jealousy, then, turn a man as levelheaded as Niall into an irrational, suspicious fool?

Well, whatever it was, Iain decided, his cousin's threats and unreasoning attitude had destroyed any lingering feelings of loyalty and affection. Though he wouldn't seek revenge, Iain no longer felt any commitment to support Niall.

Anne would be better off with him. *He'd* treat her kindly, would give her the love she deserved. And, besides removing her from Niall's cruel presence, he'd also be rescuing her from the storm of animosity and false rumors rising against her.

In the few hours since his return to Kilchurn, Iain had already heard enough foul tales about Anne to justify a burning at the stake. No, he thought with a small shudder. His plan to take Anne away had come none too soon.

With renewed resolve, Iain knocked at her door. Anne's sweet face greeted him a moment later. He smiled.

"Iain?" Her brow wrinkled in puzzlement. "Why are ye here?"

He glanced down the corridor then took a step closer. "I need to talk with ye. May I come in?"

She shook her head. "It wouldn't be seemly. Agnes isn't here."

"More the better. What I've to say is best said in private." When she hesitated, Iain grasped her arm. "Please, Anne. Ye know ye can trust me. I wouldn't ask if it weren't important."

She eyed him for a moment longer, then sighed. "I know, Iain." She stepped back. "Come in."

He waited until she closed the door, then motioned toward it. "Bolt the door. I don't want anyone walking in on us. I can always escape out the window."

Her eyes widened, but she complied. "What is it, Iain? What's wrong?"

"It isn't safe for ye here." He walked toward her and took her by both arms. "I want ye to come away with me."

"It isn't safe? Come away?" She shook her head. "Truly, Iain, ye make no sense."

"Don't I, lass? I haven't been back a day, and already I see naught has changed for ye. Niall still treats ye harshly, the people have yet to befriend ye, and the witch talk about ye grows to deadly proportions. Ye're in danger if ye stay here another moment."

"Och, Iain." Anne smiled and patted him on the cheek. "Always my friend and protector. But ye needn't worry yerself over me. True, I've made little progress where the Campbell clan's concerned, but it's only a matter of time. And, once they befriend me, I feel certain the rumors will die. So ye see, it isn't as bad as ye fear."

"And I say ye're blind to the truth!" He captured the hand that rested on his face and turned his lips to it. "Ye risk much in remaining here, and for what reason? Yer vows to Niall?" Iain lowered her hand to rest upon his chest. "Nay, Anne, ye owe him naught. He broke the handfasting long ago when he failed to treat ye kindly. Do ye forget I was there when he promised to strive for yer happiness and welfare?"

He paused when Anne's gaze moved from his. With a firm hand, he grasped her chin and turned her face back to his. "Ye know the truth as well as I, lass. Come with me. I'll love ye, care for ye as ye truly deserve."

Anne sighed. She had thought time and distance would ease that hunger burning in Iain's eyes. Did he realize how it tore at her heart to have to hurt him? But what choice had she now, even more than before?

"Nay, Iain," she whispered. "I can't go with ye. To do so would ruin yer life. Niall would come after us. He'd not give up until he killed ye. I wouldn't have that upon my conscience."

"And I don't care!" Iain cried. "I love ye, Anne! It'd kill me if I left ye here and something happened to ye. Would ye have *that* upon yer conscience?"

"Naught will happen." Her voice lowered in an attempt to soothe his anguish. "Niall will protect me."

"In a pig's eye, he will!"

"I know he would, and so do ye." Gently, Anne disengaged herself and stepped back. "There's more, Iain."

"He has bedded ye, hasn't he?"

She gave him a sad little smile. "Nay. We made vows to keep our handfasting chaste, and he's too honorable ever to go against them. It's why I love him."

A grimace of pain twisted his handsome features. "Nay, Anne! Don't say it!"

"Would my lying change what is?" she asked softly.

"But surely he doesn't love ye. I've seen no sign of it—in his actions or his words."

Anne lowered her head. "I think he feels something for me. It's enough for now."

"Yer goodness blinds ye to the truth!" Iain pulled her to him. "Ye'd see that in time. I should take ye away, with or without yer consent. Far from his presence, ye'd soon discover yer mistake."

"But ye won't." Steadily, she returned his gaze.

A fierce battle waged within him—Anne could see it in his eyes—but, finally, he released a deep breath. "Nay, I won't, for it'd destroy what's between us. But if aught happens to ye, I swear I'll come back and kill Niall. I'll never forgive him if he doesn't protect ye."

"He will. He's a good man."

"Is he now? I used to think so, but of late I'm not so certain." A bittersweet light in his eyes, Iain smiled down at her. "I think ye're mayhap blinded by yer love."

"Mayhap."

He sighed and released her. "Well, bemoaning what I can't have is pointless. Just swear that if Niall ever fails ye, ye'll send word to me. I must know ye'll do that at least."

"I know ye're my friend."

"Promise me, Anne!"

She grinned. "Och, but ye're the most persistent, pigheaded—"

"Promise me. Please, Anne."

"I promise."

The look in his eyes as his gaze swept over her sent a sad despair rippling through Anne. She had never meant to hurt him, but what else could she do? She had sealed her fate when she had admitted to loving Niall. There was no turning back.

Anne touched his arm. "Ye should go."

"Aye." He made no move.

"Now, Iain." She gave him a small push.

Iain forced himself backward, his gaze never leaving hers. When he reached the door, he paused. "Remember yer promise, Anne."

"I will."

He slid the bolt aside and opened the door. Not looking back, Iain slipped from the room.

Slumped in his bedchamber chair, Niall gazed at the tongues of fire lapping their greedy way through the pile of logs. In his hand, he clasped an untouched glass of claret.

It was nearly midnight. The castle folk had long ago been sent to bed, but still he sat there, painfully, acutely awake. Niall's eyes burned fiercely. His exhaustion weighted him so heavily that even the thought of getting up and walking to his bed required more effort than he was capable of. Yet still the blessed reprieve of sleep eluded him.

Disjointed thoughts whirled through his mind, mocking him with the futility of any possible solution. Duncan . . . Hugh . . . Iain.

Iain.

Thanks to Nelly, he knew his cousin had been up to see Anne earlier this evening. The dark-haired maidservant, whose primary duties were centered in the kitchen when she wasn't lustily warming someone's bed, seemed to be all over the castle of late. Niall knew he mayhap should've sent her away, after her lie about Anne having poisoned his father, but something had stayed him. Though her hatred for Anne may well have been the sole motive, there was yet another possibility for Nelly's falsehood. She might be in league with the traitor. If so, she bore close watching. If so, she might ultimately lead him to the man.

She had come to him a few hours ago, still hopefully seductive, informing him she had passed by just as Anne had let Iain into her bedchamber. Though Niall had thought to deflate her eager confidence with the comment that he knew all about the meeting, he sensed his ruse hadn't worked. Nelly hadn't looked convinced.

His grip about the wineglass tightened. Indeed, what *had* gone on between Anne and Iain? He had wanted to trust her, thought he had, but the news of this latest liaison strained even his newly admitted affection for her. What possible reason could she have for letting Iain visit her?

His cousin's motives were more than apparent. Iain wanted Anne.

But Anne—what did she want? With a mighty effort fueled by his anguish, Niall rose and walked to the hearth. Setting his glass on the mantel, he braced his hands on the wooden overhang and stared, unseeing, into the flames.

Did Anne love Iain? Had they lain together as lovers? He'd kill Iain if they had.

A rage, white-hot and searing, grew within Niall. He was surrounded on all sides by betrayal, and the one haven in which he imagined he'd find comfort had never been more than a sweet illusion.

Och, Annie, he thought with a bittersweet pang, *ye called to my heart. Yet, when I came, ye turned from me, leaving me more alone than I was before. I was a fool to have let myself trust ye . . . much less need ye.*

Music, soft and lilting, floated to his ears. Niall lifted his head, wondering at its source.

It was Anne, playing her clarsach.

He turned from the hearth. She was awake. Dare he go to her, as confused and exhausted as he was? He risked betraying too much. It would be wiser to avoid her.

Yet, even as he admitted the fact, Niall's legs were carrying him toward the door. Though he dare not trust his heart to her, the physical solace of her body was safe enough. Vows or no, she owed him that much.

Anne couldn't sleep. Exhausted from the emotionally draining day, she had gone to bed early but, once there, could only toss and turn. A jumble of thoughts and impressions assailed her. The haggard look of grief on Niall's face as they lowered his father into the grave. The strain of the supper meal, from which she had excused herself as soon as it was considered proper. And then, after everything else, the unexpected surprise of Iain's visit.

That, mayhap most of all, nibbled at Anne, driving all hope of rest from her mind. What was she to do about Iain? The chance of Niall hearing about Iain's visit was too great to ignore. There were too many in Kilchurn eager for her downfall for her not to consider the possibility. And if Niall should hear of this latest news from anyone but her, Anne feared it might drive the final wedge between them. More than aught else, Anne didn't want that to happen.

She never wanted to be a problem to Niall again. All she desired was to be close, to comfort and support him. To be everything to him, to the extent of his need. He might not ever love her, at least not like he had loved the Lady Anne Stewart, but what he was capable of giving she would accept and cherish.

Love was like that, she supposed, especially when it finally turned your brain to a pile of mush. With a sigh, Anne rose from her bed and donned her warm bed robe. She walked over to stare out the stone-cut window.

What time was it? At least midnight by her calculations. Far too late to speak to Niall tonight about Iain, no matter how desperately she needed to tell him. The admission would have to wait for the morrow.

Her clarsach lay beside the oaken bench beneath the window. Anne picked it up, nestling its curved frame in the crook of her arm. Her fingers strummed the taut strings, coaxing a hauntingly sweet melody from the vibrating strands. The music soothed her, easing the raw ache in her heart.

How she wanted to go to Niall, to feel the strength of his arms about her, to bury her face in the comforting warmth of his chest! But that was not to be. Niall's need for rest was of greater import than her petty desires.

She jumped at the sound of her bedchamber door opening, her fingers striking a discordant note. Anne turned, and her startled gaze met Niall's. He stood there, his stance wide-legged, still dressed in the garb he had worn all day. His chest heaved with some barely repressed emotion.

She laid down her clarsach and rose. "What is it, m'lord? Did my playing waken ye?"

A sudden surge of tenderness flooded him. She stood there

dressed in a simple white nightdress beneath her open bed robe, her curly mane cascading about her shoulders and down her back. She looked so beguiling, so sweetly girlish—and so innocent of any wrongdoing.

The anger ebbed, leaving only a curious, quivering ache in the middle of his chest. He was too weary for a battle tonight. Too overwhelmed with the events of the past few days to face the truth. The morrow was soon enough to deal with the unpleasant task of confronting her.

But now, now what he needed was rest. Perhaps Anne's songs would soothe him to it.

He sighed and shook his head. "Nay, lass, I was never asleep. I but heard yer music and thought to ask ye to play for me. Ye used to play for my father." His lips curved into a wistful smile. "Will ye do so as willingly for me?"

Anne nodded. "Aye, of course I will, and gladly."

Niall motioned to her clarsach. "Dress, then bring yer harp and meet me in the library."

Ten minutes later, she joined Niall in the library. The room was dark save for the small circle of light cast by the hearth fire. He pulled up a tall-backed chair to face his before the fireplace, then glanced at Anne.

"It's warmest here. Come, seat yerself."

Anne forced herself to move forward. She had thought she had until the morrow to tell Niall about Iain. Instead, the time was now upon her.

It was too late to turn back. That choice had been made when she revealed her love for Niall to Iain. She owed Niall at least the same honesty she had shown his cousin. And that honesty began with telling him about Iain's visit this eve. But how to begin? How to tell him without stirring afresh Niall's anger against his cousin? Anne settled herself in the chair, but the strings of her clarsach remained silent.

At the worried chewing of her lip, Niall cocked a questioning brow. He motioned toward her harp. "Have ye no song for me, lady?"

"Aye, but first I've something to speak of." Anne imagined he could hear the pounding of her heart from where he stood.

He waved her words aside with a movement of his hand. "In time, lass. But first, a song."

"What would ye like to hear, m'lord?" Both relieved and frustrated to put the matter aside, if only temporarily, Anne took her seat.

"A song of love," he replied finally, his voice a low growl as he seated himself opposite her. "About the enchantment of a beautiful woman."

Anne swallowed hard. The deeper meaning to his words sent a small shiver of excitement through her. Her fingers, seemingly of their own accord, strummed the opening notes. "Mayhap ye'd like the 'Vision of a Fair Woman' then? It's an ancient Celtic song."

Niall nodded. His eyes, burning with an inner intensity, so mesmerized Anne that the song flowed from her lips without conscious effort. Her voice rose and fell with the melody, breathless at first but growing stronger with each haunting phrase. And, all the while, Niall watched her.

> Tell us some of the charms of the stars:
> Close and well set were her ivory teeth;
> White as the canna upon the moor
> Was her bosom the tartan bright beneath.
> Her well-rounded forehead shone
> Soft and fair as the mountain snow;
> Her two breasts were heaving full;
> To them did the hearts of heroes flow . . .

Like some Highland cat he watched her, motionless, tense with waiting, but waiting for what? Anne felt like a doe, alone, poised for flight, sensing danger but not knowing from whence it came. And all the while Niall, the dark, powerful animal, sat there, watching . . . waiting.

> . . . her countenance looked like the gentle buds
> Unfolding their beauty in early spring;
> Her yellow locks like the gold-browed hills;
> And her eyes like the radiance the sunbeams bring . . .

The closing stanza ended in a breathless whisper as Anne's throat constricted. She had never seen eyes quite like his, smoldering golden-brown in the dim firelight. They glowed with some otherworldly fire. They beckoned her toward a heady oblivion she was helpless to resist. Her fingers fell from the strings.

"That night ye learned of the land charter," he said, his deep voice shattering the suddenly heavy silence, "ye begged me to free ye from our handfasting."

She barely had breath to reply. "Aye?"

Niall leaned forward. "Do ye still wish that?"

The question dissipated the dreamlike trance that had followed Anne into the room. Why was he asking this? Of all times, when she felt herself hanging on the abyss of surrendering everything to him, why was Niall asking such a question?

Did he need some pretense to free himself now that he was about to secure his position as chief? Mayhap he had finally admitted she was more hindrance than pleasure, that her unpopularity with his clan would never improve.

Or mayhap there was some other reason. Mayhap, just mayhap, Niall was attempting to plumb the depths of her commitment to him. Whatever the reason, it didn't matter. The truth remained the same.

"Nay, I don't wish to be freed from our handfasting." Anne laid her harp on the floor beside her chair, then squarely met his gaze. "My place is with ye, for as long as ye'll have me."

"And why do ye want to stay, lass?"

✦ ✦ ✦

Her grip tightened on the chair arm. "Because I love ye."

"Do ye?" he asked with a mocking smile. "As much as ye love Iain?"

"I don't understand." Unease spiraled through her. How could he be so calm, so casual, about her heart-wrenching admission? "What have my feelings for Iain to do with ye?"

Niall shrugged. "I was but attempting to determine the extent of yer loyalty. Whom do ye love more, Anne? Iain or me?"

She struggled to stand, tears glimmering in her eyes. "Ye mock me, mock the honest admission of my feelings for ye, to ask such a thing! Why would ye want to hurt me like that?"

"Hurt ye?" Niall leapt to his feet. "And can aught I say or do compare with what ye've wrought by yer liaison with Iain this eve? Answer me that!"

Anne blanched. *He knows, and because of my hesitation I've lost the chance to tell him myself. He'll never believe me now.*

"I was afraid of this." Anne sighed, lowering herself back to her chair. Her gaze slid to her hands clasped in her lap. "There are no secrets in this castle, however benign they may be."

"Allow me to be the judge of that," Niall said, his voice dangerously soft.

Anne met his fierce gaze. "There's little to tell at any rate. Iain was simply concerned for my welfare."

"And was it necessary to seek out the privacy of yer bedchamber to do so?" He paused. "Was Agnes with ye?"

"Nay." Even in the firelight, she could see the dark flush that suffused Niall's face. "Naught happened," Anne hastened to explain, panic rising within her. "I swear it!"

"Mayhap not." His voice was taut with barely contained fury. "It's difficult to judge without knowing the real reason for my cousin's visit. What was it, lass?"

She hesitated. The same dilemma confronted her as before. How was she to tell Niall the truth without betraying Iain?

"I await yer answer, madam."

The hard edge to his voice prodded her to action. She wet her lips, then hurried on. "I'll tell ye and gladly, if only ye'll swear Iain will come to no harm because of it."

"I'll make no oath on that! If ye think to protect his deceit—"

"There was no deceit!" Anne cried. "He but wanted to take me away with him, away from all the hatred here against me. He was concerned for my safety, that's all!"

"And I say ye lie! Ye're lovers, aren't ye?"

In one quick step Niall was before her, pulling Anne into the unyielding hardness of his body. She gazed up into eyes blazing with anger and, surprisingly, a tortured pain. For a moment, she couldn't find her breath. Then it came, expelled on a shuddering whisper.

"Och, nay. Nay, Niall. I don't love Iain, at least not in the way ye mean."

Niall's grip tightened painfully. Anne squirmed in his grasp. "Niall, please. Ye're hurting me."

He released her with a jerk and gave a shaky laugh. "Then we're even. But don't mistake my acceptance of this as trust. Too many times have yer path and Iain's crossed for me to ignore—or forgive!"

"Forgive?" Anne's temper finally got the best of her. "There's naught to forgive, ye suspicious, pigheaded dolt! Och, I don't know why I thought telling ye would've made a difference, if I ever had the chance! But, nay, no sooner was the deed done than yer people came running to tell ye everything. Do ye trust me so little ye must surround yerself with spies?"

Niall turned toward the hearth. "I can't afford to trust anyone just now. Ye know how precarious my position as chief is."

"Aye, and I suppose I should accept that I must also, of necessity, be considered a threat to yer precious chieftainship."

She paused, as an insight into the source of his continued mistrust suddenly struck her. "This isn't solely an issue of jealousy, is it? Of yer fears that Iain and I are lovers?" Anne took a deep, shuddering breath. "Nay, it's of far greater import. Like, mayhap, that Iain's yer traitor?"

12

The color drained from Niall's face. Then a studied mask replaced the fleeting look of surprise. "What are ye talking about? I never said aught of a traitor."

Anne wasn't about to let Niall's momentary lapse of control slip by. "It wasn't ye. It was my father who spoke of someone betraying ye to us."

"By mountain and sea! He swore he'd tell no one!"

"And he kept his word!" Anne hotly defended her father. "It was that day of yer clan's arrival at Castle Gregor. I followed my father to the parapets to hear them request yer return. He was so overwrought at the position he was in, he let slip the fact he'd entrapped ye and that there was a traitor. No one heard his words but me. He refused to tell me more, even when I prodded him. And that's the truth of it, Niall Campbell!"

"The truth as far as ye know it," Niall retorted. "But how many others know?"

"My father's a man of honor. If he gave ye his word, yer secret's safe. Besides, to betray ye would be to endanger me. He'd never do that."

Niall scowled. "Mayhap not intentionally, but what if he let it slip again?" His fist pounded the mantel in frustration. "Och, it was my only advantage over the traitor, and now I may have lost even that!"

"Ye don't know that. If I'm the only other one . . ." Anne's voice faded at the piercing look Niall shot her. "Aye." She sighed. "And once again I'm asking ye to trust me, aren't I? But if Iain's the traitor and I'm in league with him, then ye've lost even that advantage."

A sharp pain lanced through her. "It always comes back to that, doesn't it, Niall? Ye can't find it in yer heart to trust me—and never will."

He opened his mouth, then clamped it shut. He stared at her, his dark eyes capturing and holding hers until Anne thought she'd scream from the tension. Tears filled her eyes. She saw the dream of a life for them slowly disintegrate in the face of Niall's continued distrust. There was no hope, not anymore.

The tears rolled, unchecked, down her cheeks. "I said I loved ye, but it isn't enough, is it?" she asked in a choked whisper. "Well, I can't bear living with yer suspicions. Better for the both of us if ye let me go back to my people."

"Nay."

She swiped the tears away with the back of her hand. "But why? What good am I to ye, or to yer traitor, be it Iain or any other? Ye've discovered my complicity and now will guard against me. Ye can throw me into the dungeons, I suppose, but that, on top of the news that's sure to reach my father soon of the land grant, will only stir the feud anew. Far better to send me home, and be done with this mockery of a handfasting."

"Well, *I* don't see it as a mockery." Niall flung himself in the chair opposite her, his long legs stretched out before him. "If I did, I'd have ended it long ago. But I was lost from the first moment I saw ye in that little village, yer hands bound, proudly defying my men. Ye *are* a witch, Anne MacGregor," he groaned the admission, "but yer spells are of the heart, not the body. And I can't let ye go—not now, not ever!"

"Och, Niall!" Anne sobbed, kneeling before him.

He straightened in the chair, and his arms welcomed her, pulling her to him. She clung to him fiercely, her renewed surge of tears dampening his linen shirt.

"I've never wished to cause ye pain, truly, I haven't," Anne cried. "I know I've been foolish at times, concerned only with my needs and giving little thought to yers, but I swear I'll do better! I'll learn."

"Wheesht, lass." Niall stroked her hair. "I know, I know."

She raised her tear-streaked face to his, so close now his warm breath caressed her. "Truly?"

"Truly."

Anne sighed and laid her head back on Niall's chest. She knew there had been no admission of trust in his words, no avowal of love, but tonight it didn't matter. That he accepted the fact she was there and wanted him, that he seemed to want her too, was enough.

All her life, since the day Anne had realized the power men held over women, she had fought against surrendering even the smallest aspect of herself. She had fought against their control, flaunting customs and strictures of everyday life if they went against her own desires. She had paid the price in many ways, yet until this moment she had staunchly maintained her right to guide her own destiny.

But no longer. Now it was joined with that of the dark man holding her. Yet there was no loss, no sense of defeat in the realization. Quite the contrary.

Her love for this most magnificent of men had opened up the world to her, freeing her—empowering her. Her love only made her stronger. It revealed new mysteries, mysteries both wonderful and life-sustaining. There was no fear anymore, only an eagerness to delve further and, in the giving, receive.

Early the next afternoon, Anne awoke to bright sunlight streaming into her bedchamber. She shifted and stretched lazily, her thoughts turning immediately to Niall. Today was the meeting to determine Clan Campbell's next chief.

She leaped from bed, startling Agnes, who sat dozing by the fire. "Hurry!" Anne cried. "I must dress and find Niall!"

"So, after sleeping half the day away," the old maidservant grumbled, making her way over to Anne, "ye suddenly need everything done posthaste, do ye? Well, a wee bit of patience is in order. I'm not as spry as I once was, ye know."

Anne couldn't help but laugh at Agnes's scowling countenance. "Och, it's not as bad as all that, is it? If so, I beg yer pardon. I'm just so happy! I'm in love, Agnes," she cried, grabbing the other woman by both arms and twirling her around. "I'm in love with Niall!"

"Harrumph. Well, it's taken ye long enough to see it." She dug in her heels in an apparent effort to slow Anne's whirling about. "Now, stop this, I say. Ye're making me dizzy."

"Och, I'm sorry!" Anne instantly halted, released the maidservant, and stepped back. "It's just that I've never been in love before, and then to have fallen in love with a man like Niall . . ." She grinned sheepishly. "Ye must think me silly."

"Nay, m'lady." The old woman grinned back, exposing a few missing teeth. "On the contrary. I'm verra happy for ye and the young lord. I've helped raised him from a pup, I have, and when he lost his first Lady Anne, well, it nigh to broke my heart. But the good Lord saw fit to provide him with another fine mate, one as devout a Christian as the first Annie was, and equally strong enough to bear the difficult times ahead. I prayed to Jesus, I did, and, at long last, the Lord answered me."

"Well, I don't know if I'm truly the answer to yer prayers," Anne said with a chuckle, "or if my strength's sufficient to survive what might lie ahead, but I, too, love the Lord and strive always to do His will." She paused, then sighed. "I confess, though, that Duncan and Malcolm have been the verra hardest sorts to love or respond to in Christian charity. Sad to say, I've failed many a time to turn the other cheek when confronted by those two men."

"I don't think the Lord wants us never to fight back when we see injustice, m'lady. And besides, I've watched how hard ye've tried to make friends amongst so many who treated ye with such coldness and disdain. Even so, bit by bit ye're winning the hearts of the Kilchurn folk. Even"—she chuckled—"the heart of the wee Caitlin."

Anne rolled her eyes. "Och, if only that were true. I've seen little change in Caitlin save, when it comes to me, the grudging obedience she pays her brother. Still, I'm determined not to give up. The Lord Jesus expects more than that of me."

"Aye," Agnes said, nodding in ready agreement, "and His will matters more than the cruel, selfish machinations of some, and the petty jealousies and fears of the others."

Anne smiled. "Never let me forget that, Agnes. There are times, when things seem their darkest, that I'm wont to do that, ye know."

"Och, m'lady." The old woman patted her arm. "I won't. We're all called, after all, to help each other on the journey."

"That we are," Anne replied, heartened by the maidservant's good-heartedness. "That we are." She paused once more. "Now, it's past time I was dressing. I'd like a time with Niall, if I can, before he attends the chief's council."

"Right ye are." Agnes darted off toward the wardrobe, muttering to herself as she went. "Now, let's see. Should it be the sky blue gown, or mayhap the green one? But then the dark blue one flatters yer figure so . . ."

As she watched Agnes's head disappear into the depths of the huge clothes cupboard, the old woman's earlier words came back to Anne. *"The good Lord saw fit to provide him with another fine mate . . ."*

Ah, if only it were so, she thought, that God had, from the beginning, meant for her and Niall always to be together. Only time would tell, she supposed. Until the good Lord told her otherwise, though, Anne intended to work as hard as she could to that particular—and most gratifying—end.

✝ ✝

Anne found Niall in the library, staring out the window. At her entrance, he glanced over his shoulder, a thoughtful frown marring his brow. Her pleasure at seeing him, being with him, again slowly eked away. *Dear Lord,* Anne thought, *what is it now?*

"What's wrong, Niall? What makes ye scowl so?" she asked as she drew up beside him.

"Naught." He forced the words past taut lips. "It's naught."

"Nonetheless, I'd like to know. These days, most likely it has something to do with me."

He turned tormented eyes to her. "Aye, it has to do with ye, but only in my mind."

Her heart did a flip-flop. "Then even more the reason to speak of it."

Niall hesitated then sighed. "Last night, ye said ye loved me, that yer place was with me for as long as I'd have ye. Did ye truly mean it?"

Even in his strength Niall was vulnerable, vulnerable because he had let himself care for her. There was no other explanation for a question such as his. The knowledge sang through Anne with a fierce, exultant joy. She nodded, a soft smile curving her lips. "Aye, I meant it."

Niall's eyes smoldered. "Then I've one favor to ask, one last proof, let us say, of yer love."

Anne exhaled a long, unsteady breath. "And, pray, what is it?"

"I want yer promise ye won't speak to or be alone with Iain again."

Niall's request left her speechless. How could he ask such a cruel thing? It spoke more eloquently than words of his continued distrust. But was it just of Iain and his possible motives, or of her too? Bitter resentment warred with the knowledge that, where a traitor was concerned, trust was the rarest of luxuries.

Anne laughed, the sound ragged. "And what will that oath win me? Yer undying devotion?"

"Don't mock me!" Niall took her by the arm, his fingers digging into the soft flesh.

"Mock ye?" With a grimace of pain, Anne tried to pull away and, when that failed, turned back, her eyes blazing. "How can ye believe I still mean to betray ye? Do ye think I could tell ye I loved ye while in my heart I was plotting yer death? What kind of woman do ye think I am?"

He shrugged. "Women have always used sweet words and allurements to get what they wanted."

"Do ye seriously think I but said those things just to win yer confidence?" Anne cried in outrage. "To lull ye into thinking I'm not one of yer traitors? And all the while it was Iain's arms I wished to be in?"

Anne's words must have finally driven home. Niall flushed. "Nay, Annie, I didn't mean that. I only asked that ye not see nor talk with Iain." He sighed. "I didn't realize I was asking such a sacrifice. I withdraw my request."

"Nay." Anne moved until he, once more, was forced to look her in the eye. "Nay, Niall. Ye spoke the words, now explain them. Why don't ye want me talking with Iain?"

He shot her a hot, angry look. "Because I fear he'll try to use ye to get to me and, in the end, destroy us both!"

"Ye don't know yer cousin very well, do ye?"

"If ye mean to defend him—"

"Why are ye so certain it's Iain? What of Cousin Hugh and Uncle Duncan?"

"What of them?"

Incredulity widened her eyes. "Are ye saying ye've never considered either of them? Hugh's mad with ambition, not to mention just plain mad. And Duncan." Anne shivered. "Duncan's cold and heartless. There's something about him . . ."

"Why not add my bastard cousin Malcolm?" Niall offered. "Even if he is a man of the cloth, mayhap he, too, dreams of wearing the chief's feathers. Nay, Anne. Though all of them, as well, are suspects, just because they don't like ye is no reason to accuse them of treachery."

"Yet ye accuse one who does like me of it! I'm not so blind or emotional that I cannot set aside my personal differences and clearly see the truth of the matter," she countered, stung by his arrogant assumption to the contrary. "Ye accuse me of the same bias ye have against Iain."

"That isn't true."

Anne's hands fisted at her hips. "Isn't it? Ye've resented Iain's attentions to me from the start. Yet what, aside from that, has Iain done to deserve yer suspicion?"

"He has much to gain from my death. He could become clan chief."

"And what of Hugh and Duncan? Wouldn't they profit as well? They, too, stand in line for the chieftainship. And have ye ever considered others in yer clan—yer lairds, any outlaws ye may have banished? Only a fool closes himself to all possibilities."

"Are ye calling me a fool?" Fury flashed in Niall's dark eyes. "Next ye'll be calling me a liar, and ye know how I feel about that!"

He released her and moved a few steps away, his back to her. "And, aye, I have and am still considering others."

For an instant, Anne was suddenly so mad at him she couldn't think of another word to say. Instead, she closed the distance between them, grabbed him by the arm, and jerked him around. He glared down at her. She scowled back. Suddenly, in a long overdue rush of perspective, the total ridiculousness of their argument struck her. A giggle bubbled to her lips.

"What's so amusing?" Niall demanded with narrowed eyes.

"Why, that we're both fools!" In spite of her best intentions not to make Niall any angrier, a soft laugh escaped her. "Here we are, fighting each other, expending all our efforts in a battle royal, while the traitor stands back and watches. He has no need to do more than that. We'll gladly destroy each other for him."

Amusement tugged at the corners of Niall's mouth. The tenseness eased from his body. "We really should join forces."

Anne's expression sobered. "Are ye saying ye trust me?"

He smiled at her in gentle understanding. "Ye won't cease until ye've forced that admission from me, will ye, lass?"

"Nay, m'lord."

"Ye're a stubborn, defiant little wench."

"Aye, m'lord."

Niall sighed in exasperation. "My name's not m'lord."

She grinned. "Aye, Niall."

His arms opened. "Come here, lass."

With a giggle, Anne went to him. Niall lowered his head in an attempt to kiss her. Immediately, she leaned back.

He frowned. "And what's the matter now?"

A delicate brow arched in thoughtful consideration. "Well, let me think on it. Och, aye, now I remember. Ye still haven't answered my question."

"And what question was that?"

A hesitant little smile trembled on her lips. "Do ye trust me, Niall?"

"Aye, lass," he whispered. "I trust ye." Once again, he moved close to kiss her, and this time Anne rose on tiptoe to meet him.

The library door slammed open.

"Niall!" Oblivious to the fact her brother wasn't alone, Caitlin swept into the room. "A murrain! The cattle have a murrain!"

The girl halted, finally noticing Anne. Caitlin paled then colored bright red. Anger quickly replaced the shock. Her turquoise eyes flashed as she first looked at Anne, then Niall.

"So, brother dear." Caitlin ground out the words through clenched teeth. "Our father's barely cold in the grave, our cattle are dying of a pestilence, and ye hide here in the library, cavorting with the one woman responsible for it all!"

Niall strode past his sister to close the door, then turned to confront her. "Ye'll knock and await permission to enter from now on," he growled in a dangerously soft voice. "And ye may pack yer belongings posthaste. Ye're paying yer aunt a long overdue visit in Edinburgh."

The defiance in Caitlin's eyes crumbled. "Nay! How could ye? Haven't I endured enough of late, now to have ye all but banish me?" The girl sank to her knees, weeping as if her heart would break.

Anne ran to Niall's side. If it were within her power, she'd not permit him to send another member of his family away because of her. In time, Anne knew, he'd come to resent her for it. She couldn't live with that between them. She clasped his arm, diverting his scowling attention from his sister.

"Niall," she said, "don't do this. She's but a child and overwrought with all that's happened. And she speaks naught that others don't say. Caitlin has but the courage to say them to yer face, while others whisper behind their hands. Ye can't banish all yer people. We must face the problem head on. Any other way would be cowardly."

"Respect for ye must start somewhere, lass. And if I can't command it within my own family . . ."

She gave him a trembling smile. "I know, my love." Anne turned, walked to Caitlin, and gently touched her shoulder.

The girl jerked away and glared up at her.

Anne sighed. "I know ye hate me, but for love of yer brother can't ye support him in his decision to handfast with me? These past few days have been hard for ye, but they've been difficult for Niall as well. Ye're growing quickly to a woman. It's time ye begin to act like one."

Tear-filled turquoise eyes narrowed in anger. "Are ye calling me a child?"

"What do ye call yer actions a few moments ago?" was the gentle rejoinder.

Caitlin wiped away her tears and rose. She squared her slender shoulders. "I don't like nor trust ye."

"I know. But can't ye trust yer brother and his judgment?"

The black-haired girl shot Niall a pouting look. "I know enough of the power of women to think he doesn't know his own mind in this."

“Was Niall so besotted with the Lady Anne Stewart he didn’t know his own mind? Did his love for her weaken his judgment?”

“Nay.”

“Then why should he be any less able because he’s with me? If ye recall, I’m not half the woman she was,” Anne said, repeating Caitlin’s own words. “And ye don’t believe in witchcraft, so what other influence could I possibly have over him?”

Caitlin stepped back, her glance swinging from Anne to her brother. “Och, I don’t know. It just seems that everything’s turned sour since ye arrived. And the talk doesn’t help.”

“Have ye encouraged it?” Niall chose that moment to interject.

His sister’s head lowered. “Well, mayhap a little.”

“I need yer loyalty in this, Caitlin.” Niall walked over and grasped her by the arms. “I’m sore beset right now. If ye, too, turn against me . . .”

“Och, Niall, I won’t turn against ye. I swear. Ye’re my brother. We’re family.”

“Then ye’ll accept Anne?”

Caitlin’s glance slid to hers. “Aye, accept her, but that’s all. Don’t ask me to be her friend.”

“By mountain and sea!” Niall swore. “Why do ye persist—”

“It’s enough, Niall.” Anne laid a hand on his arm. “Let it be.”

His stormy countenance calmed. “Ever the peacemaker, aren’t ye, lass? Ye’ve had much to swallow since yer arrival here. My clan hasn’t met ye even halfway. But soon that’ll change. I swear it!”

She smiled up at him. “Aye, m’lord. That it will.”

“N-Niall?” Caitlin’s plaintive voice interrupted their warm glance.

Niall’s gaze returned to his sister. “Aye?”

“Must I still go to Edinburgh?”

A dark brow arched. “I don’t know. What do ye think, Anne?”

Caitlin stiffened, her fierce pride apparently stung at having her fate at Anne’s mercy.

Anne gave the girl a gentle smile. “I think Caitlin would be happier here, among family and friends.”

“Thank ye, m’lady.” Caitlin forced the words out through stiff lips, then bobbed a little curtsey.

As the remembrance of the original intent of his sister’s visit struck him anew, Niall frowned. “Ye said the cattle have a murrain. How do ye know this?”

“I was in the Great Hall when the head herdsman came rushing in. He was verra excited as he spoke to Duncan, and his voice carried throughout the hall. By now, I fear the news is all over the castle.”

“And the cause of it?”

Caitlin averted her gaze. “They say it’s witchcraft. Malcolm was there when the news was brought. He immediately raised a hue and cry, all but claiming it was Anne’s doing. There’s trouble afoot, brother.”

Niall’s face hardened with displeasure. “Aye, that there is.”

He waved his sister toward the door. “Ye may go. I’ve plans to make.”

They watched as Caitlin left the room, then Niall turned to Anne. “This couldn’t have come at a more inopportune time. The people will be stirred, fearful and angry.” He gave a cynical, self-mocking laugh. “And in but another hour I, in the midst of all the rising witch panic, must defend my right to the chieftainship.”

13

Forty-five minutes later, Anne's glance swept admiringly over Niall's tall, powerful form. She sighed. "I wish I could be there to stand at yer side. How many will there be at the chief's council?"

Niall shrugged into the plaid jacket she held out for him. "With my family and the clan's higher lairds, about twenty men."

"Twenty against one," Anne murmured in dismay.

He laughed and gave her an affectionate kiss before she slipped away to return with his plaid. "I'd prefer to think of this as a friendly reconfirmation of my father's wishes, rather than a battle of wills."

Anne busied herself draping the Campbell plaid over Niall's left shoulder, then fastened it to hang down his right side with a silver brooch engraved with the clan badge of wild myrtle. When finished with the task, she lifted her eyes to him. "Ye'll have enemies there, and no mistake. Be careful."

Niall's gaze was tender. "I'll be careful, lass. Though we Scots are a hardheaded lot, it'd still take severe misconduct on my part to negate my father's decision. And I think I'm man enough to handle a little dissension from my people."

"Aye, that ye are." Anne managed a smile. "Man enough and more."

A hot look flared in Niall's eyes. "Have a care, lass. If ye persist in talking like that, I'll have to take ye in my arms and kiss ye until ye swoon from the sheer joy of it."

"And ye know as well as I, it's time for ye to leave." Her glance swept over him one last time. Dressed in his doublet, trews, and white shirt beneath his plaid and jacket, Niall looked the consummate Highland warrior. The clothing clung to his powerful chest and shoulders, and molded tightly to his muscular legs and thighs.

Anne's heart swelled with pride. He had the physical presence to be clan chief as well as the maturity and intelligence. They'd be hard pressed to deny him his rightful position. Yet still she worried . . .

There was an aura of impending doom hovering over Niall, and it frightened her. No, terrified her, for the premonition of death and destruction seemed almost palpable. Anne opened her mouth to beg him not to go, then clamped it shut.

To ask Niall to turn his back on his people was to ask him to stop his heart from beating or his lungs from inhaling the fresh Highland air. As heiress to Clan MacGregor—for daughters, in the absence of any sons, could also lead the clan—she understood that better than most. Niall wouldn't be the brave, proud warrior she loved and respected if he didn't face the dangers. But how she wanted to be with him! Wanted it, with all her heart, though she knew it couldn't be.

Niall must face his clansmen alone. Her presence would only stir further resentment and speculation. But Anne's prayers and all the strength of her love would go with him. Mayhap, in some small way, it would even the odds.

He stepped toward her. "I go off to fight the dragons," he teased huskily. "Mayhap a kiss from a bonnie lassie would properly send me on my way."

"It's an honor and more, m'lord." Anne rendered him a small curtsey. Then, before he could respond, she moved close to cup his smooth-shaven jaw. Lifting on tiptoe, she planted a gentle kiss on his lips.

Niall gathered her to him, forcing her soft curves against the full length of his hard-muscled body. "I'd more than a genteel peck on the lips in mind," he growled and lowered his head toward her.

His kiss deepened, all but consuming her. Anne went limp in his arms, clinging to his jacket for support.

He raised his head, an arrogant smile on his lips. "I wanted ye to remember me, should I mayhap die in battle. Think ye I've left a lasting memory?"

"Aye," Anne breathed, barely able to force the words past her constricted throat. "That ye have, m'lord."

"Good." He released her and stepped back.

"Niall." Anne stayed him with a hand upon his chest.

"Aye, lass?"

"Yer request earlier—that I not speak to or be alone with Iain."

He went still. "Aye?"

"I give ye my promise."

An aching gentleness flared in his compelling eyes. "Thank ye, lass." His big hand covered hers. "I don't know anymore if I should've asked it, or if I even deserve yer sacrifice in this, but I accept yer offer nonetheless. It means a lot to me, especially at a time like this."

"It's all I can do, as little as it is."

A wry grin quirked his mouth. "It isn't a small thing, lass. Not small at all." He turned then, strode across the room and, without a backward glance, opened the door and disappeared down the hall.

Anne returned to her bedchamber to find Agnes tidying the room.

The maidservant bobbed a curtsey. "So, did ye find the young lord, m'lady?"

"Aye, Agnes," Anne replied. "I found him." She paused, a small frown puckering her brow.

"What is it, m'lady?" the old maidservant asked.

"Och, naught." Anne shook her head and sighed. "I'll just feel better when the chief's council is over. I'm the cause of such animosity here. I wouldn't want that to harm Niall's chances for the chieftainship."

"The young lord can well handle the fools in that room," Agnes staunchly defended him. "He'll win them over, and no mistake."

"Most likely." Anne sighed. "Still, I wish I could be there to know the charges they bring against me."

"They could be hard to hear, m'lady."

"Aye, but the knowledge might aid my efforts to win them over. I must know what's in their hearts if I've any hope of changing them."

"There *is* a way."

Anne's gaze riveted on her. "What are ye saying? Is there a chance I could overhear the council meeting?"

Agnes nodded. "It's a secret, a hidden tunnel that runs from the council chamber to the storerooms. From there, another tunnel leads to the outside. It was devised for escape in times of battle."

Anne could barely contain her excitement. "Would ye lead me to it? I swear I'd never reveal the secret, and it'd help in learning the charges against me. I only ask this in the hope of aiding Niall."

Hesitation flickered in the maidservant's eyes. Then she nodded. "Aye, lass. I'll help ye, but no one must learn of this."

"Then let us be gone." Anne gathered up her cloak. "There's not a moment to spare."

Few noticed their passage through the castle, for Kilchurn was abuzz with preparations for the evening feast to celebrate Niall's confirmation as chief. Anne knew Niall had ordered things to be carried out as if his new rank was a foregone conclusion, fully aware that any show of uncertainty would weaken him in the eyes of the council. He had planned for everything, from the feast to the magnificence of his dress, but the true battle had yet to begin.

The tunnel leading from the storeroom was musty, dark, and strewn with cobwebs. They stumbled along without a torch, for Agnes had said the approaching light might be discovered through the narrow vents on the secret panel separating the council chamber from the hidden corridor. Finally, Agnes gripped Anne's arm, pulling her to a halt.

"The chamber's just up ahead," she whispered. "The tunnel now narrows so only one may pass at a time. Go ahead. I'll await ye here."

Anne gave the old woman a quick hug. "Thank ye, Agnes."

"It's naught, lass. I'll do aught for ye and the young lord." She gave her a small push forward. "Now, get on with ye. The meeting starts even now."

From behind her, Anne could hear the scrape of chairs and the rise and fall of deep male voices. She turned and hurried down the tunnel toward the narrow strips of light in the panel wall. As she reached the secret door, the voices faded. Through the slits, Anne saw Niall stand and lean forward on the table, his solemn glance scanning the faces aligned down its oaken length.

She inhaled an admiring breath. The look Niall gave them was bold, penetrating, and self-assured. *Even now he begins,* she thought. Pride for the powerful, commanding man filled her. He was clan chief already, if only the others had the wisdom to see it. If only they had the courage to rise above their petty differences and groundless fears.

"As is our tradition," Niall began, his deep-timbred voice reverberating throughout the chamber, "I stand before ye, clan tanist and chieftain-elect, to accept yer sworn fealty to me as the Campbell. But first, custom allows the occasion to air questions or grievances that might preclude yer acceptance of me. I'll tolerate no doubts or lack of commitment once this council ends."

Niall lowered himself to his chair and leaned back with a demeanor of supreme confidence and lack of concern. "If there are any objections, speak them now or forever bury them in yer heart."

There was a heavy silence. Not a few uncomfortably averted their gazes from Niall's piercing stare. For several heart-stopping seconds, Anne thought Niall had managed to intimidate them with the power of his presence. Then one of the lairds cleared his throat.

"Ye've something to say, Andrew?" Niall demanded calmly of the man he had once mentioned was one of his most troublesome lairds.

Andrew glared at him. "This council's illegal!"

A dark brow raised. "And how so?"

The laird nervously scanned the others, searching for some sign of support. "There's one of yer family not present. One whose claim to the chieftainship is nearly as strong as yer own. Without his presence, how can the decisions made here be considered fair?"

Niall's eyes narrowed. "And are ye mayhap speaking of my cousin Hugh?"

Andrew swallowed convulsively and nodded. "Aye."

"And what was I to do with him," Niall inquired, his glance moving to encompass the entire gathering, "after he attempted to murder the Lady Anne MacGregor? Allow him to remain here and permit him the opportunity to try again?"

"He's mad, nephew," Duncan interjected. "Allowances must be made."

Niall's gaze swiveled to his uncle. "Allowances *have* been made for a long while now. But is Hugh worth endangering an alliance with Clan MacGregor, of stirring anew a feud we were finally managing to bring to an end? Or, leastwise we were until the land grant took away their lands and gave them to us." No one replied. "Well, be that as it may, I wouldn't deny my cousin his birthright. The welfare of the entire clan, however, comes before that of a single member," he said. "And Hugh forfeited that privilege when he threatened the peace between our clans."

"And what has Iain done?" Duncan demanded. "He isn't mad, nor has he threatened the lady's life, yet ye've banished him too."

Anne sucked in a startled gasp. *The attacks begin, and this one is as deadly as they come.* Niall dared not reveal his knowledge of a traitor, yet how could he justify what might otherwise seem an irrational vendetta against Iain? And what would Iain say to defend himself?

Niall shot Iain a thunderous look. The younger man had paled at his father's accusations and, for an instant, was speechless. "What's between Iain and me is personal," Niall ground out in the sudden silence. "It isn't a fit topic for this council."

Duncan turned to his son. "And what have ye to say, lad? Does or does this not bear on Niall's fitness to be chief?"

Iain's jaw hardened. Watching him, Anne realized he sensed he was but the pawn in some game being played out here.

He shook his head, as if refusing to be dragged in. "Niall's a hard-hearted, stubborn man," he said, "but that has never been reason to deny a chieftainship. I won't pretend my affection for him hasn't changed, but the rest of it, as he said, is between us."

Surprise mixed with anger flashed in his father's eyes. "Ye'd support his claim over yers then?"

"His claim was decided two years ago when the Campbell named him tanist. Why is there suddenly such doubt afoot?"

Pride swelled in Anne for her friend's honest heart, even in the face of Niall's continued animosity. Mayhap Niall would now realize Iain wasn't the sort of man to be a traitor. Mayhap, just mayhap, they could once again be friends.

"Hugh and Iain aren't the true issue here!" a smooth, articulate voice announced unexpectedly. "There's doubt afoot because Niall's immortal soul's in danger."

All eyes swung to Malcolm, who sat opposite Niall at the far end of the table. Anne's gaze followed the rest. She swallowed a panicked sob. *Och, Niall, here it comes now.* She glanced back to him and could have wept with pride.

Niall's face was an expressionless mask. "Matters of religion are also not a topic for this particular council," he coolly replied. "I govern Campbell hearts and bodies; ye govern their souls. I've no intention of interfering in yer domain, unless it endangers one of the clan."

A sly smile quirked the preacher's mouth. "And what say ye to a witch burning? There's now law to back me on that."

Niall smiled back, but the expression in his eyes was flat and hard. "I obey all laws, but those same laws will be applied in a fair and humane fashion. There'll be no witch panic on Campbell lands, or torture to extract confessions as the only means of evidence."

"And will ye just as fairly consider all accused of witchcraft," Malcolm persisted, "be they noble as well as peasant?"

"Aye," Niall countered smoothly, though even Anne could see the muscle jump in his jaw. "I haven't changed in my judgments or treatment of the people, *when* concrete evidence was truthfully given."

"Then," Malcolm said, triumph sharpening his voice, "in all fairness, ye're called to judge the Lady Anne MacGregor, named by her own people the Witch of Glenstrae."

A murmur of excited male voices swirled around the room as Niall sat there, staring stone-faced back at Malcolm.

"Curse ye, Niall!" Anne heard Iain mutter. "I warned ye of this."

Niall, however, seemed unaffected by the turmoil. He paused to pour himself a glass of claret from the flagon at his end of the table. Swirling the burgundy in the glass, he examined its sparkling hues as the others slowly calmed and silence once more fell upon the gathering.

At long last, he raised his glance to meet his cousin's. "And what has that to do with my fitness as chief? That the Lady Anne's called the Witch of Glenstrae are but words, naught more, as is my title of Wolf of Cruachan. Make no further accusations unless ye've proof."

"What about the Campbell's death?" the preacher shot at him. "It's said the wench was with him at the last, and gave him a cup of poison."

"She was with him little more than five minutes before the end came. And the word of a jealous serving maid is hardly a reliable witness. Not to mention," he added, "I later tasted the contents of the cup and found it was only water. Or would ye say my word is less than that of a serving maid, as well, since ye seem so determined to condemn Anne?"

"Then what of the murrain?" Andrew supplied. "It's strange our cattle have been untouched, while those from other clans have died, until the MacGregor woman arrived. It's said she put a curse on our cattle in revenge for the royal grant of their lands to us. What say ye to that, Niall?"

"Superstitious nonsense!" Niall snapped. "The pestilence most probably spread from diseased cattle brought here from other clans. The McCorquodales recently had a bout of murrain, and their lands border ours."

"What of her strange healing skills?" Duncan added quietly. "It was Hugh himself who saw her breathe life back into a stillborn babe. How do ye explain that, nephew?"

Niall's head turned to his uncle, the tension rising in his voice. "I'm no physician. I've no explanation for everything, but there's much in nature still unexplained. To attribute the unknown to witchcraft is the work of ignorant minds!"

"Then the Reformed Kirk, the religion of our land," Malcolm silkily offered, "is a Kirk of ignorant minds? Is that what ye meant to say?"

Niall froze. Though he might himself only pay lip service to this new but hugely popular religion, nowadays Anne knew it was the heart's blood of most Scotsmen. To ridicule or ignore its power would be folly indeed. For the first time since the council began, Niall suddenly looked unsure of its eventual outcome.

Anne saw the indecision flare in Niall's eyes. Her heart went out to him. Her greatest fear had been that, like a pack of wolves, they'd drag him down on this very issue. And now it seemed her worst fears were about to come to fruition.

Her nails scored her tightly fisted palms, but she made not a sound, expending her efforts in willing all her strength and support to Niall. *Help him, Lord! Och, help him!*

He finally expelled an exasperated breath and gave a mocking shake of his head, an action Anne knew instinctively was pure bluff.

"I intended naught of the kind, though all here will admit that ignorance grants little consideration to wealth or status in life. All I meant to say was, as clan chief, I must deal with all issues in a calm, informed manner. How else am I to govern wisely?"

Anne saw the doubts fade from some of the men's eyes. Several even leaned back in their chairs, their minds apparently made in Niall's favor. Hope flared in her breast. *Good. He's beginning to win them over.*

"Aye, govern wisely, indeed," Malcolm growled, apparently sensing he was losing support on this issue. "And how is that possible, when ye seem all but besotted with the MacGregor wench? Besotted so thoroughly," he added, "that some would say bewitched. It'd be an easy thing for her to have slipped a love potion into yer drink or sprinkled it on yer food."

"And it'd be an even easier thing to care for her because she's a kindhearted, beautiful woman," Niall countered. "If any of ye had taken the time or made the effort to get to know Anne, ye might understand that."

"We *have* tried, but there's something about her," Duncan said. "Those eyes . . ."

"They are eyes and naught more!" Niall snapped. "I find yer arguments dwindling to the ridiculous. If there are no further issues of import, mayhap it's time to end this council."

"Aye, nephew." Duncan sighed. "Mayhap ye're right. There's one issue more to discuss, though, before we swear our fealty."

"And what's that?"

"The naming of yer tanist. In times as unstable as these, a successor is vital."

Though he had the leave to name his tanist at his leisure and planned to wait until the traitor was discovered before doing so, the hearty agreement swelling around the table made Niall reconsider. Gaining the support of these men had been more difficult than he had anticipated. The tide could still turn if he miscalculated his real influence over them. Niall hated being forced into something he wasn't really prepared for, but a compromise in this case might well be the prudent course.

His gaze swept the gathering as he considered the merits and weaknesses of each man there. When his glance met Iain's, Niall stiffened. Though he had been surprised and more than relieved by Iain's support, Niall wondered what the true motives behind his cousin's actions had been. Iain could've guessed there'd be dissent and chosen the wiser course of appearing to be on Niall's side. A wiser course, indeed, if he had thought Niall was considering naming him tanist this day.

If it hadn't been for the issue of the traitor hanging over his head, Niall would have chosen Iain as tanist. But not now. He dared not place his cousin in such a position of power. But if not Iain, who?

His glance continued to skim the men, weighing, considering. None of his trusted warriors had returned as yet with any information regarding Hugh's activities or whereabouts, or of any possible traitorous actions on the part of his lairds. And now, more than ever, he desperately needed that knowledge.

Niall's eyes met those of his second cousin, Andrew. Traitor or not, that laird had never been a serious candidate. The man was far too concerned with his own needs. And, without further information, Niall dared not place his trust in any of the other lairds present, either. It would be too difficult to keep a close eye upon their activities, scattered as their holdings were on the huge expanse of Campbell lands. It was wiser to choose a tanist from those near by. It would be easier to watch him . . .

His gaze passed Duncan. As much as he hated to admit it, the reality was that even his uncle could be the traitor. There was something to be said, though, for keeping one's enemies close.

Anne certainly suspected him, but then those two hadn't really gotten on from the start. Still, though his uncle was a cold, controlled man, his advice in the past had always been directed toward the betterment of the clan. Yet, on the other hand, there was also the matter of his active involvement in securing the MacGregor land grant . . .

With a frustrated sigh, Niall rose from his chair. "The choice of clan tanist is a difficult one, for many issues must be taken into account. Youth and battle prowess must be weighed against the equally valuable attributes of maturity and wisdom. Sometimes, there's no one perfect individual for the task."

He leaned forward on the table, his next words low and carefully measured. "I possess the youth and battle prowess. Taking that into account, I've decided to draw on maturity in choosing my tanist."

In the anticipatory silence, Niall inhaled a deep breath and forged on. "As the first of my duties as yer new chief, I name my uncle Duncan tanist to Clan Campbell."

14

As the words fell from Niall's lips, Anne's horrified gaze sought out Duncan. A humble half smile lifted his mouth but, for a fleeting instant, she caught an exultant gleam. Was it the triumph of a traitor, or just an ambitious man?

The men rose from the table to congratulate the new tanist, then left for the chief's installation ceremony. Iain stood there, staring at Niall, who grimly returned the favor. Finally Duncan clapped his son on the back.

"Come, have ye no congratulations for yer father?" Duncan inquired jovially. "Allow an old man a few years of power. Then it'll be yer turn."

Iain wrenched his gaze from Niall to stare blankly at his father. "What? Och, aye, ye're to be complimented on attaining such a high position. May ye bring the wisdom of years Niall so dearly desires."

He wheeled about and strode from the chamber before his father could utter a reply. Duncan frowned at his son's retreating back, then turned to Niall. "The lad's disappointed, that's all," he said with an apologetic grin.

"I care not for Iain's feelings in this," Niall snapped. "As long as he swears fealty in the ceremony, I'll be content."

"Och, he will, and no mistake. The lad's as loyal as they come."

"So it'd appear," was Niall's sardonic reply. He motioned for his uncle to precede him. "The ceremony draws nigh. See to the final preparations. I'll meet ye in the Great Hall in ten minutes' time with the Lady Anne." He raised his hand to silence Duncan's attempted protest. "She's my wife in all but marriage vows and, as such, lady of this castle and our clan. We'll forget what was spoken in this chamber and start afresh. Agreed, Uncle?"

Duncan hesitated then reluctantly nodded his head. "Agreed, m'lord."

✦

Anne headed down the corridor to her bedchamber, grateful the feast wouldn't begin for another hour. The tension-fraught atmosphere of the council chamber, combined with the ordeal of the installation ceremony, had drained her energy. The past three days had been exhausting, full of pain as well as joy. Only now, at long last, was she finally able to relax.

Och, what I wouldn't give for a nice, hot bath, Anne thought with a wistful sigh. *If only there were time . . .*

Distracted, she rounded the corner and slammed into a hard male body. Sturdy hands grasped her arms to steady her. Anne stared up into dark eyes only a few inches higher than hers.

They were cold eyes. As they gazed down at her, a humorless smile touched the man's lips.

"So where are ye going, my wee witch?" Malcolm Campbell inquired. "To procure some potion to put into the Campbell's drink? Or mayhap to chant a few incantations over yer witch fires to hasten the death of our cattle?"

Anne jerked free. "I do no such thing! Yer unreasoning hatred blinds ye to the truth!"

A bushy brow lifted in amused tolerance. "Och, angry are ye now at being caught in yer devilish schemes?" Once more, Malcolm grabbed her by the arms, pulling her close. "Yer time's short, devil's spawn. Ye've bewitched the Campbell with yer seductive powers, but my powers are stronger still. Mine are the thumb and leg screws, and the fires of the stake. Think ye to prevail against them?"

At the fanatical gleam in Malcolm's eyes, fear shot through Anne. He meant to see her dead. She struggled wildly in his arms. "Let me go, I say!" she cried. "If Niall should hear—"

"He's not fit to rule us," the preacher hissed. "His soul's lost. Even when ye're gone, the spell can't be undone. He'll have to be tried and burned as the witch's consort that he is."

Niall. She had never thought of that horrifying consequence. But Niall had defended her and, in that defense, had come perilously close to insulting the Kirk and denigrating its fanatical witch persecutions. Men and women had been burned for far less.

Fear for him drove Anne to the edge of panic. "Ye mustn't blame him for his loyalty to me," she said in an anguished whisper. "He's a decent, God-fearing man. I beg ye. Don't punish him for whatever crimes ye think I may have committed."

"And what crimes are they, lassie?" Malcolm prodded smoothly, his dark eyes gleaming, mesmerizing in their sudden intensity. "Tell me now. Mayhap there's yet time to save the Campbell."

Dizziness swirled through Anne. The past days had drained her more than she realized. She couldn't seem to find the strength to fight back.

"That's enough, cousin!"

Iain's deep voice wrenched Anne from the hypnotic spell of Malcolm's gaze. In a stunned slow motion, she turned toward him. He looked angry, but why, Anne didn't know.

"Release her!" Iain demanded. "Now!"

Malcolm freed Anne abruptly. If not for Iain's quick leap to her side, she would've lost her balance and fallen.

"Ye tread where ye shouldn't go," the preacher warned. "Best ye leave while yer soul's yet untainted by this woman."

"Nay." Iain shook his head. "Best *ye* leave before I forget ye're family, and smite ye for yer cruel words to this lady."

✝ ✝

Malcolm's eyes narrowed in disbelief. "Ye wouldn't dare! I'm a man of the cloth."

"At this moment, ye're not fit to claim such protection. Now, get out of my sight!"

The preacher backed away, his face mottled in rage. "Young fool! Beware the witch or ye'll rue it to yer dying day!" He stalked away.

Anne inhaled a shuddering breath. "Ye shouldn't anger him, Iain. He has the power to be a deadly foe."

"The man's a fool," Iain muttered. "Did he hurt ye, lass?"

She shook her head. "Nay. But the threats he made against Niall . . . Och, Iain, what am I to do?"

"It's as I said before," he murmured, tenderly stroking her cheek. "Come away with me, Anne."

At his touch, the memory of her promise to Niall came to mind. Remorse surged through her, but she steeled herself to the difficult task. She had given her word and would support Niall in any way she could, even if it meant denying herself the harmless pleasure of Iain's company. Even if it meant hurting him.

With a resolute sigh, Anne stepped back. "Nay, Iain. It's as I said before. My place is with Niall." She gave him a gentle shove. "Now, get on with ye and don't attempt to speak with me again."

Iain frowned. "And why not? Has Niall forbidden that too?"

"I gave him my word." Anne's voice broke. "Please try to understand."

"Och, I understand," he ground out. "The man's jealousy has rotted more than his heart. It has now rotted his mind. This is beyond tolerance!"

Anne grabbed his arm as he turned to leave. "Ye're not going to see Niall, are ye?"

"Aye, that I am. I'll have it out with him, once and for all."

"Nay, Iain," she implored. "I beg ye—"

"Let him go, Anne."

At the flat command, Anne swung around. Niall stood there in the corridor leading from the Great Hall. In a few quick strides, he was upon them. Gently, he pried Anne's fingers loose and moved her aside. Then, in a quick move, Niall grabbed his cousin by the throat, slamming him against the wall.

"I've told ye time and again to stay away from her," he said, his voice low and savage. "What more will it take? A dirk between yer ribs?"

Anne grasped Niall's arm, tugging frantically. "Stop it! Stop it, I say! Don't do this, Niall!"

He shrugged her aside, his glance never leaving Iain's.

Iain's hand encircled Niall's wrist and clamped down tightly on it. "Release me now," he said in a soft voice, "or there'll be more than one dirk drawn this eve."

Panic rose in Anne. They meant to fight each other. Neither man's pride would allow him to back down. She glanced wildly around, searching for help, and found none. Then, in a flash of inspiration, she relieved Niall of the dirk that hung at his side before hurrying around to take Iain's.

Iain's hand stayed hers. Anne's gaze met his. "Let it go, Iain."

He eyed her for a long moment then released her hand. Anne withdrew his dirk.

Without warning, she turned and pressed Niall's own dagger against his ribs. He stiffened, going quiet and still, but maintained his grip on Iain.

"Do ye mean to kill me, lass?" He never shifted his gaze from that of his cousin's. "If ye do, make yer first thrust deep and sure. Otherwise, I swear I'll break his neck before I die."

"And ye're a great brute of a fool," Anne muttered in disgust, "if ye think I mean to kill ye. I only wanted to get that pigheaded attention of yers." She pressed the dirk a little deeper, until its tip pricked his skin. "Do I finally have it?"

"Aye," Niall said through gritted teeth. "Say what ye have to say, and be quick about it!"

"Ye're wrong to treat Iain thusly."

"I told him to stay away from ye!"

Anne smiled. "Aye, but I'm the one who gave my word, not Iain. Why aren't ye throttling me against that wall instead?"

Niall shot her a furious glance. "One thing at a time. I'll see to ye later."

"And will ye also see to Malcolm?" she persisted sweetly.

"Malcolm?" Niall scowled, puzzled. "What has my uncle to do with this?"

"He was threatening me, warning me of the dire consequences in store for not just me, but ye, if I continued with my witchcraft. Iain,"—she motioned toward the younger man—"rescued me from yer churlish cousin. And, just as ye arrived, I was informing him that I couldn't speak with him again. Let Iain go." Anne slid Niall's dirk back in its scabbard. "Ye've falsely accused him."

The request was uttered in a low voice, but the authority beneath it was commanding, nonetheless. Niall hesitated, then released Iain and stepped back. Neither man, however, relaxed his rigid stance nor extinguished the battle-ready look in his eyes.

"Ye owe Iain an apology," came the soft voice beside Niall.

His jaw hardened. "If it's truly as Anne says, I beg pardon."

Iain rubbed his bruised throat. "It changes naught, and ye know it. I don't want yer apology, nor will I accept it."

Anne touched him on the arm. "Iain, please."

He rounded on her. "Leave it be, lass. Ye've made yer choice, and that choice is for him. It's time ye start living with the consequences of his arrogance and mistrust. I only hope he doesn't destroy ye in the process of destroying himself.

"And ye," Iain said hotly, his glance swinging back to Niall. "I'm not so sure I made the wisest choice in the council. And that's a decision I may live to regret." Without another word, Iain strode away.

Tears filled Anne's eyes, but they were ones of fury. "How could ye treat him like that?"

Niall studied her impassively. "I apologized. What more do ye want?"

Her fists clenched at her sides. "And did ye convince Iain of yer sincerity? I think not! Ye could've tried harder, Niall Campbell!"

A look of utter weariness flooded Niall's eyes. "Aye, mayhap I could've. But this has been a trying day, and my patience is worn to its breaking point." He gathered Anne into his arms. "I'll seek Iain out and try again on the morrow. But only for yer sake," he hastened to add, seeing the joyous light flare in her eyes. "I still dare not trust him. Not him, nor any man."

She flung her arms about his neck. "Och, my love, ye'll not regret it. I swear it!"

He smiled down at her. "Mayhap. Now, where were ye going?"

"To my chamber for a short rest before the feast."

A dark brow arched in feigned consideration. "If things were different, if we hadn't made that cursed pact, I'd be joining ye there, ye know."

Excitement shot through her. Ah, but it was so good to be wanted by a man such as Niall Campbell! Still, as much as he tempted her, Anne knew she could never come to him in such a way.

Her arms fell from his neck. "But we *did* make the pact and are honor bound to keep it."

"Aye, honor bound," he repeated softly. "For a time more, I'm thinking. A verra short time more."

"Until God tells us otherwise."

Niall's mouth twitched. "Are ye saying I need to be talking all this over with the Lord, then?"

She grinned and tossed her head of russet curls. "It'd be an excellent place to start, m'lord. His wisdom far surpasses ours, ye know." Anne offered him her arm, and he took it. "Now, if ye will, pray accompany me to my bedchamber door. Though ye slew a passel of dragons at the chief's council, I fear there are yet a few more lurking about."

He threw back his head and laughed. "Well, then as a newly proven dragon slayer, I'm just the man to protect ye," he said and proceeded to escort her down the hall.

✦

Late the next morning, after a feast that lasted well into the night, Anne rose just in time to share a quick breakfast of porridge and cream with Niall before he headed off to his daily duties. At Anne's request, Agnes then had a bath drawn. Anne was soon lost in contemplation as she enjoyed the soothing water and her maid scrubbing her head.

Her thoughts harked back to last eve's encounter with Malcolm. Though Niall had discounted his cousin's threats, Anne was still worried. The man had the power of religion behind him, and that power wasn't easily discounted. Not when Niall's very life hung in the balance.

She'd do anything to protect him—anything. And that included giving up her healing. She had never thought she could ever compromise on such a vital issue, never imagined she'd be willing to sacrifice the good of many for just one. But Anne had never envisioned loving a man as deeply, as completely, as she loved Niall Campbell. And his life held precedent over everything else.

In time, the animosity toward her would cool. She'd be accepted. In the meanwhile, it was too dangerous to sit by and allow things to take their natural course. She had already given her word she'd not heal in Kilchurn, but Anne knew now there was yet more she must do.

If the clacking tongues were to be silenced, her visits to Ena must stop. Her store of potions and salves had to be discarded, or they could be used as evidence against her. And her secret garden in the forest must be destroyed. Every threat to Niall's safety must be eradicated. Her physical presence in Kilchurn was problem enough. She'd not knowingly add more.

When her bath was done, she dressed in a simple gown of deep blue wool, then hurried to the chest where she kept her herbal medicines. Not bothering to hide her actions from Agnes, she began to carry the jars to the privy, where she dumped their contents down the long chute. Her task, painful as it was, was carried out with fierce determination. Only when Anne reached the last of the jars did her resolve waver.

The container of dried foxglove caught her gaze. She had gathered the potent leaves under Ena's watchful eye. Under that same thorough tutelage, Anne had learned of the plant's curative, if sometimes deadly, powers. Holding the jar up now for a final, regretful appraisal, her heart skipped a beat.

She had put the container away full and had never had the opportunity to use any of the plant, yet the jar was now half empty. There was enough foxglove missing to kill twenty men!

Anne's throat went dry. She rose on unsteady legs and, the jar clasped in her hand, sought out Agnes.

The old maidservant was next door in Niall's bedchamber, sprinkling sweet woodruff on the freshly laid rushes. Anne crossed the room to shut the door, then returned to Agnes's side. She held up the jar of foxglove.

"Have ye taken any of this plant for some ailment, whether yers or some other's?" Anne demanded, her heart now pounding in her chest. "If so, tell me true, Agnes. There'll be no punishment."

Agnes's eyes widened. "Nay, m'lady. I've never been in that chest. I know naught of the healing art and would never presume to treat anyone from it."

"This jar's half empty. The last time I looked in my chest, it was full."

"Truly, m'lady. I haven't knowledge of such things."

Anne sighed. She trusted the old woman, yet someone had taken the leaves. But who? And why? "Have ye seen any looking in my chest, Agnes?"

"Nay, m'lady."

"Then who has access to this room? Who could come in here and not be found suspicious? I must discover who took these leaves."

Agnes pondered that for a moment. "Almost any of the female household staff. And even, on occasion, some of the male staff, as well. Like just now when they removed the old rushes and brought in fresh ones. We rarely lock the chambers in Kilchurn."

"Aye, that I know," Anne muttered, remembering Caitlin's unexpected, and most unappreciated, arrival yestermorn in the library.

Uneasiness crept through her as she headed to the privy with the jar. Mayhap it was just a well-intentioned servant bent on curing some relative of the dropsy. There were others who knew the healing art besides her and Ena. Mayhap the servant had come upon her chest one day by accident and had merely helped herself to some of the herbs there. Until she had reached the foxglove, Anne really hadn't paid much attention to the exact amounts left in the jars. Mayhap that servant had taken samples of most of the chest's contents.

But what if there were nothing missing but the foxglove? And what if the leaves had been stolen for more sinister purposes? There was no known antidote to the plant's heart-slowing and eventual heart-stopping effects. Only time and the body's own abilities to rid itself eventually of the drug could save a victim of overdose. And only if that overdose were discovered and halted in time.

Fear rippled through Anne. *Och, dear Lord, don't let my herbs become an instrument of someone's death! Not now, not when my position in Clan Campbell is yet so precarious. It'd be the end of everything. Everything.*

Anne quickly finished disposing of the remaining herbs. Then, grabbing up a trowel that she slipped into a fold of her skirt, she made her way back to Niall's room. Agnes glanced up from her sprinkling of the last of the sweet woodruff.

"Where are ye going, m'lady?"

Though she didn't wish to alarm the old woman, Anne knew it would be wise to let someone know where she was headed. "I go to my herb garden in the forest. I won't be there long."

Agnes frowned. "Ye shouldn't go alone. Let me accompany ye."

"Nay." Anne shook her head. "I'll be careful. If I'm not back within the hour, ye can tell Niall."

“An hour is time enough for harm to befall ye,” the maidservant muttered. “At least take the stable man. He won’t talk about what he sees. He and Maudie are too grateful for what ye did for their wee Davie.”

Anne sighed and nodded her acquiescence. “As ye wish. I’ll fetch Angus on my way out of the castle.” Agnes’s look of relief was enough to make her smile. “I’m a trial to ye at times, aren’t I? I’d imagine the other Anne never gave ye a moment’s trouble.”

The old woman grinned. “Well, she wasn’t as headstrong or impulsive. But then she didn’t have yer fire or fierce spirit, either. Ye’re a different woman, to be sure, but as perfect a mate for the Campbell as they come. So, don’t concern yerself with another woman’s ghost. The young lord loves ye for yer own self. There’s naught more that matters.”

Anne sighed. “He hasn’t said he loves me, Agnes. Not that I’m complaining,” she hastened to add. “What he does give me is wonderful. But I don’t know if he’ll ever love me. I think that emotion may have died with his first wife.”

“And I say ye’re mistaken, lassie. What the young lord truly feels and what he recognizes can be two different things. I’ve known him since he was a lad, and I tell ye true. He’s happier now, even in the midst of all these troubles, than he has been since the Lady Anne died. He loves ye, and no mistake. He’ll see it soon enough.”

At Agnes’s words, a fierce joy leaped within Anne. “I pray yer words come to pass. In the meanwhile, I can’t stand idly by and allow others to control our lives. I must do all within my power to help Niall. And the one thing more that needs tending to is my herb garden.”

In a determined flurry of skirt and petticoats, Anne headed for the door.

✦

Nelly saw Anne leave. A pleased smile twisted the corners of her darkly pretty face. The MacGregor wench was naively unaware that her every movement was being watched. Watched, weighed, and reported back to Nelly's master. He had paid her well, in and out of bed, to spy on Anne. And it had been money easily earned. As easy as was the theft of the foxglove leaves from the chest in her bedchamber.

Keeping to the shadows as best she could, Nelly followed Anne and the stable man from the castle and into the forest, until she was certain of the other woman's eventual destination. *The fool*, Nelly thought as she slipped away as unnoticed as she had come. The wench assumed everyone was unaware of that herb garden of hers.

Well, it had served her master's purpose to let her think so up until now. But when Nelly supplied him with the news Anne was there once again, mayhap this time her presence there could finally be used to her downfall. Mayhap she could at last convince her master to kill the MacGregor wench. A crossbow's quarrel straight through her heart would leave no witness or suspect.

Then Nelly could devote all her efforts to comforting the bereaved clan chief. Her pace quickened. *That* particular errand of mercy would be sweet. Very sweet, indeed!

Niall's first order of the day was to find Iain. Though he loathed attempting to apologize a second time, he had promised Anne and would see it through. Summoning up the right amount of enthusiasm would be another matter. Not that he wasn't sincerely grateful to Iain for rescuing Anne from Malcolm. The preacher would be seen to later and receive a stern warning, with dire consequences if it happened again.

But to feel any warmth for Iain or dare lower his guard was out of the question. Though Niall knew it was foolhardy to suspect his cousin to the exclusion of all others, it still served him best to have Iain gone from Kilchurn. If nothing else, he didn't need the added distraction of Iain panting after Anne.

✝✝

Aye, it was far wiser to send him away, Niall resolved. What went against his grain was having to thank his cousin in one breath, then in the next order him back to Balloch Castle. Unintended or not, of late he was beginning to feel the fool in nearly all his interactions with his family.

As he strode across the Great Hall, frustration roiled within him. *A fool indeed* . . . And he had the traitor to thank for that.

Iain was in the library, according to a passing servant Niall questioned. He took the steps to the first landing in several quick strides, then stalked down the hall.

The blond man glanced over his shoulder when Niall entered the room. A wary look in his deep blue eyes, he replaced a leather-bound volume on the shelf and turned to meet him.

Niall inhaled a steadying breath and approached his cousin. "My gratitude yestereve was lacking. I truly thank ye for helping Anne."

"She's in grave danger here," Iain said, dispensing with the amenities. "Ye should let her go. Now, before it's too late."

Niall stared at him, incredulous. "And who are ye to tell me what to do with her? If ye recall, *I'm* the one handfasted to Anne, not ye."

"Yet it seems *I'm* the one most concerned about her welfare," Iain shot back. "If ye weren't so stubborn, ye might see that. She isn't some prize to be held, no matter the cost. Anne's a living, breathing woman with a life to lose."

"And ye doubt my ability to keep her safe?"

Iain saw the anger darken Niall's eyes. He knew he trod on dangerous ground. For Anne's sake, though, Niall must be made to face the reality of her danger.

"Ye saw how difficult it was to win over the council, how many were willing, nay, eager, to attack ye. And the strongest argument of all was the allegation of Anne's witchcraft. Those aren't accusations ye can choose or not choose, like infidelity or barrenness, to deal with in yer woman. If she's convicted, she's in violation of the law—and ye know what the punishment is!"

“I don’t need ye telling me the obvious,” Niall ground out. “I told ye. I’ll take care of her!”

“And if ye fail, what then, Niall?”

“It won’t happen!”

Iain took a step closer and gazed into Niall’s eyes. “If it does, I swear I’ll kill ye.”

Niall returned the look of deadly earnestness. “Ye’ll never have that opportunity. I’ll be dead before I let anything happen to her.”

His cousin gave a mocking laugh. “Indeed, ye might be, but then what’ll become of Anne, alone and at the mercy of her enemies?” He gripped Niall’s arm. “Send her away before that happens, Niall. Swear to me ye’ll at least do that!”

Hesitation plucked at him. What if Iain’s dire predictions came to pass? If the traitor found some way to kill him, what *would* become of Anne?

Duncan would be chief, and Duncan, at the very least, disliked Anne. Would Malcolm’s fanatical ravings influence Duncan against her? And if Hugh was brought back from exile . . .

Of all his family, Iain was the only one who seemed truly to care for Anne. Niall knew that with a sudden certainty that startled him. Cared for her above and beyond whatever use he might have for her in his role as traitor. If something happened to him, Anne would be safe with Iain.

But even to consider giving Anne over to another! Niall knew Anne cared for Iain, if only in a sisterly fashion. But that could change, given time and his absence.

Iain was a handsome, charming man. The trail of broken hearts, however unintentional, his blond cousin always left in his wake was ample testimony to that. Aye, Anne could well come to love Iain. But to imagine her with another, whispering her love as she lay in his arms . . . It was like a knife gutting his insides!

Still, the time might well come when he’d have to let her go. To save her life, he’d do anything, even if it meant giving her up.

But that time had yet to arrive, Niall reminded himself, and he'd not give Iain the pleasure or any premature advantage over him by admitting that possibility.

He was now the Campbell. Now was not the time to show weakness or hesitation. Not to Iain, or anyone.

Niall shook his head. "I won't swear that or aught to ye, cousin. Though yer concern for Anne's commendable, if concern is truly what it is, it changes naught. She's mine, and mine she'll remain."

"And that's all ye have to say? All ye'll do?"

"Aye, for the time being."

"Ye're a fool, Niall Campbell!"

Niall took a step forward. "Nay, Iain," he said softly. "Ye're the fool, for ye've finally gone too far. Get ye to Balloch Castle this verra day or I'll send ye to the dungeon."

Iain opened his mouth to challenge Niall, then thought better of it. If he were drawn into a battle with the Campbell, a battle he might well lose even if it were but of words, Anne would be the one to suffer. And, in the end, this was all about her welfare.

Better to make a strategic retreat, lull Niall into a false sense of victory. It was a bitter pill to swallow, backing down from a man he felt the match of, but Iain knew where his priorities lay. Anne's life was of more import than his pride.

Free, he could still be of use to her. Clapped in chains in Kilchurn's dungeon, he was helpless. Iain forced a grim smile and bowed low. "It'll be as ye say, m'lord. This verra day I depart for Balloch Castle."

15

Niall's long legs quickly carried him through the corridors to Anne's bedchamber, his mood far from pleasant. Iain was right. He *should* send Anne away before it was too late. But how could he do so when he had just come to know her, and the knowing was so achingly sweet? From her gentle goodness to her fiery temper, Anne fascinated and challenged him. To let her go was painful past consideration.

He needed her. Only she could drive away the dark loneliness that had so long enshrouded his heart. Only she fulfilled him, like no other woman since his first Anne had. He couldn't, *wouldn't*, let her go. They'd work everything out. Niall had to believe that. Any other contemplation stirred anew the niggling fear that his own needs might be of more import than Anne's safety. The time might come when he'd be forced to face it, but not now. Now, there was still hope.

Save for Agnes, tidying the fresh rushes on the floor, her bedchamber was empty. Niall went to the old maidservant. "Where's the Lady Anne?"

Agnes whirled around. "S-she's seeing to some personal business, m'lord."

Niall's gaze narrowed. "And, pray," he drawled, "what's this personal business ye seem so hesitant to reveal? Yer loyalty's first to me, Agnes. I want a full accounting of where she's gone."

"Aye, m'lord." Agnes curtsied her obeisance. "She has an herb garden in the forest. She slips away to tend it whenever she can."

Niall's features tightened with disapproval.

"I saw no harm in it," Agnes hurried to explain. "The garden gave her pleasure. She never used any of the herbs for healing, only dried and stored them in that chest." She gestured to the carved box standing near Anne's bed.

With a low growl, Niall strode to the chest and flung back its lid. "It's empty. Where are these herbs ye speak of, woman?"

"Only this morn she tossed them all down the privy. I think she feared them being used against her, of their existence causing ye harm. It was a great sacrifice on her part, I think, m'lord."

"I've a calling to heal . . . It's sacred to me . . ."

Anne's words that night he had first taken her to see his father came back to haunt him. She had given up so much. So much, and now even to turn from all thought of healing . . .

Niall squared his shoulders. There was nothing to be done for it, leastwise not right now. Indeed, there was nothing that mattered more than Anne's safety.

He hurried to his own bedchamber and returned with a short sword. Fastening the scabbard belt about his hips, he motioned the old woman forward. "Lead me to her, Agnes. Now!"

Agnes nervously bobbed another curtsey. "Aye, m'lord."

It wasn't supposed to be this hard, Anne thought. Despite Angus's discreet presence nearby in the trees, the tears streamed unashamedly down her face. She dug up yet another feverfew plant, then tore it into tiny pieces before reburying it beneath the earth. Even dumping the jars hadn't tugged at her heart like this.

But these were living things, full of promise, brimming with hope. Hope for the future of her healing—and with their destruction that hope died. Still, she had to do it. Their death ensured the end of all evidence against her. For Niall, she'd do even that.

A weak breeze stirred the quiet forest, affording a brief respite from the unusually warm summer day. Anne paused in her vigorous efforts, lifting her damp, heavy mass of hair from the back of her neck. Sadly, she surveyed her garden.

Only half a row remained and all the plants would be gone, torn to shreds and buried beneath the dirt. In but a few weeks' time, the weeds and wild grasses would again take hold. Soon there'd be no sign a garden had ever grown here. Anne wondered if her life at Kilchurn would one day matter as little. No impression, no imprint left on anyone.

This time the tears were of self-pity, but Anne quickly wiped them away. Her life at Kilchurn *had* mattered, had made an impression. She had served the Lord there the best she could. And there was her friendship with Iain, with Ena and Agnes, all friends strong and true. There were glimmers of acceptance now from some of the other castle folk as well.

Maudie and Angus had definitely warmed to her after Anne's treatment of little Davie's burnt hand. And several of the serving maids had come to her for advice on feminine ailments, advice that required but a few quick words that any lady of the castle would be able to give. She had been more than happy to assist them, without a qualm that she was going against her promise to Niall.

Aye, Anne consoled herself, Campbell acceptance was indeed slow in coming, but coming it was. All it would take was time. All it would take was continuing faith in God. In the meanwhile, with Niall at her side, she'd forge ahead and face what life held bravely. Her love for him was that deep, that sure.

Perhaps the wind rustling through the trees covered the sound of their approach, or perhaps it was her self-absorbed thoughts, but Anne suddenly found Niall and Agnes standing before her. She climbed to her feet, the trowel still clasped in her hand.

"Niall, Agnes," she whispered, her gaze swinging from one to the other. "I—"

"Why are ye here?" Anger darkened his eyes. "Haven't I told ye time and again it's dangerous to venture outside the castle?" He paused, suddenly aware of his stable man's presence and that he was reprimanding her in front of servants. "Go Agnes, Angus," he growled, motioning them away. "Return to the castle."

The old maidservant glanced from her master to mistress, then hurried off with Angus.

Niall waited until the servants were out of earshot. "Well, madam? Why are ye here?"

A variety of responses swept through Anne's head, but she decided the truth was the best. "I felt the need to visit this garden one final time and destroy the last evidence against me."

"Evidence? Explain yerself. Ye speak in riddles."

"Evidence of my healing." Anne inhaled a deep breath and forged on. "I was there, behind a secret door, when ye met with yer council. I heard all the accusations brought against me to discredit yer claim to the chieftainship. I wouldn't have my conduct used against ye again."

"So ye disposed of all yer herbal medicines and are now destroying yer garden." Tenderness flared in his eyes. "Truly, lass, ye sacrifice too much for me."

The trowel dropped from Anne's hand. With a cry, she ran to him. They clung to each other for a long, soul-searing moment.

A soft smile curving her lips, Anne then lifted her eyes. "Do ye know how much I love ye? Don't ye know by now that I'll do aught for ye? Aught."

With a wild groan, Niall's mouth came down on hers, devouring her joyous offering until he teetered on the brink of control. Then, with a tremendous effort, he straightened, moved away.

Dazed, Anne staggered back a step. "What is it, Niall?"

His low, throaty chuckle echoed in the forest stillness. "Naught.

Ye said ye'd do aught for me, and I but need a moment to tell ye what I wish."

"And what is that?"

"A bairn. An heir." He stroked her cheek. "Yet though I desire that greatly, some part of me fears it as well. I don't want to lose ye in childbirth."

"And aren't we rushing things a bit, worrying about losing me in childbirth when we've both agreed to remain chaste until our year of handfasting's done?" Anne asked with a smile. "Not to mention I'll bear no bairns save for my legally wedded husband? But dinna fash yerself. I'm strong and healthy. And," she said, her face softening with a gentle, loving look, "I'd sooner have a few months in yer arms—God willing as yer wife, of course—even if it killed me, than a lifetime without ye."

Once more, Niall's arms tightened around her. "Don't say that! Don't ever speak of dying! I fear for yer safety enough as it is." His mouth lowered to the fragrant tumble of her hair. "Even now, I wonder if my selfishness in keeping ye here will be yer death. I should send ye away before it's too late."

Anne's arms entwined about Niall's neck. She clung to him, as if to prevent that terrible thought from becoming reality. "Nay. I beg of ye. Let me stay; let me fight at yer side. Though our enemies are many, we're not beaten. I'm not afraid. If the time comes when, because of me, I fear for yer life, then I'll leave and willingly. But not before. I won't desert ye!"

"Och, Annie," Niall groaned. "I don't want ye to go. I need ye. But—"

She pressed a gentle finger to his lips. "No more, my love. The time isn't right to speak further of this. God willing, it'll never be right. Don't ye agree—" She stopped, overcome with a sudden feeling of coldness, of lurking evil. It struck her so forcibly Anne knew it for what it was.

Niall noted the change, the shudder that wracked her slender frame. He grasped her arms. "What is it, lass? What frightens ye?"

Anne gazed up with fear-widened eyes. "Someone's here . . . watches us," she whispered.

Niall stiffened, bent close. "Where? Do ye see him?"

She shook her head. "Nay, but I know it all the same. I've felt it before. We're in danger."

"Stay behind me. If we're set upon, flee to the castle."

"But I can't—"

"I've my sword," he rasped in her ear. "I can hold them off until ye send help. Now, no more of it!"

Niall released her, then turned slowly, casually. Taking Anne by the hand, he began to lead her across the forest glade toward the castle. All the while, he scanned the area for sign of an intruder. Despite his vigilance, the warning came too late.

A movement, a flash of something metallic in the bushes off to his left, caught Niall's eye. He lunged to cover Anne. A crossbow quarrel plunged into his chest.

"Niall!"

"Stay back!" he cried, sinking to his knees. "Behind me!"

"Nay!" Anne gripped his short sword and wrenched it free. Evading Niall's attempt to stop her, she ran toward the spot where the quarrel had flown, the sword raised high.

Another crossbow bolt could come flying toward them at any moment. Her only hope was to take the offensive and pray their attacker was a coward, for to cower behind Niall could well be the death of them both. Many a Scotswoman, and she included, had been schooled in the defensive use of the short sword. She only prayed their mysterious intruder wouldn't choose to test her on it.

A glimpse of tartan—Campbell colors—was all Anne caught of the disappearing attacker. His plaid was pulled up to cover his head. She saw nothing more but a flash of bare, masculine legs and a body bulked beyond recognition by the belted plaid.

Anne halted and ran back to Niall. He was still kneeling on the ground, both hands about the quarrel's base where it protruded from high up in his chest. His breathing was ragged, his teeth clenched. Before she could reach him, he tore out the crossbow bolt.

With a low groan, he fell, the quarrel clenched in his hand. Anne ran to his side, flinging herself down beside him. She reached beneath her skirt to tear loose a large wad of petticoat. Gently, she turned Niall over, cradled his head in her lap, and opened his shirt to examine the wound. She breathed a sigh of relief. It had missed his lung.

From the trajectory of the quarrel and Niall's position just before he had lunged to cover her, Anne knew the quarrel had been aimed straight for his heart. Was it the work of the traitor, some disgruntled clansman, or one of her own people in Campbell disguise, at last seeking revenge for the land grant?

She quashed the speculations and shoved her petticoat inside Niall's shirt to cover his wound.

"Well, lass? Will I live?"

At the amusement in Niall's deep voice, Anne jerked her gaze to his face. He was pale, his brow damp, but a grin quirked his full, firm lips. She forced a trembling smile. "Aye, m'lord. It'll take more than a puny quarrel to fell a big lout such as ye."

He chuckled, and the movement brought a grimace of pain. "There ye go again, making me laugh when I'm wounded. Ye're a heartless wench, and no mistake."

"I'll show ye how heartless I can be, when I get ye back to the castle. Yer wound will need cauterizing, and I must send for Ena. I have no more salves or medicines, ye know."

A large hand clasped her arm. "Nay, lass. I'll allow Ena's ministrations because she's accepted by the clan, but not yers. And even hers I'll accept little of, for I must appear to respect the healer sanctioned by the Kirk. And that's Murdoch, our castle physician. I'd wish it otherwise, for I trust yer ministrations far more than his, but it's for yer own protection. If aught happened, if the wound festered and I died, I wouldn't have ye blamed."

"But he'll hurt ye," Anne protested. "Mayhap try to purge or bleed ye, as if those treatments would aid in the healing of a wound. How can ye expect me to stand by and watch that old fool—"

His grasp tightened, cutting off her protest. "Because I ask it, Annie lass. Ye said ye want to stay with me, to fight our enemies. Well, our battle must be waged in many ways and on many fronts. Some things must be compromised if we're to prevail. This is one such compromise. I'm willing to make it."

"But to ask me watch ye needlessly suffer!" Tears choked her voice.

"It's the way of war," he replied softly. "Haven't ye the courage for it?"

She studied him for a long moment. "I know not the depth of my courage, but my love for ye is more than sufficient to meet the task. Since ye ask it, I'll stand back and watch that simpleton of a physician treat ye. But hear me well, Niall Campbell. If ever the time comes when yer life's in danger because of his ministrations, I'll step in to save ye. Naught ye can ever say or do will keep me from that."

Something flared in the depths of his rich brown eyes. "Then let us pray that day never comes, sweet lass, for I fear it could well mean yer life."

Hard, angry eyes watched as Niall, supported by two clansmen, was assisted back into Kilchurn. Anne followed close behind, surrounded by an armed escort of six more men. The eyes, shining with a malevolent light, turned from the sight. Hands clenched knuckle-white at his sides.

Curse that insufferable, interfering witch! the man swore beneath his breath. If not for her quick response with the short sword, he'd have had the time to reload the crossbow and finish Niall. Taking care of her afterwards would've been easily seen to. But he had dared not linger to fight off some crazed female with only his dirk and crossbow for defense.

He had meant to kill her after Nelly had hurried to inform him of Anne's presence in the forest. But when he had seen Niall there and heard him ask her for a child, something had snapped. The memory of another time, another childbirth that had ended to his advantage, came to mind. And now, once again, his claim to the chieftainship was threatened from a similar quarter. Time was running out.

He didn't want peace between Clans Campbell and MacGregor. He didn't want a marriage alliance, an alliance that, if Niall and Anne's passionate response to each other in the forest was any indication, seemed to be rapidly becoming a reality. Niall's death was the only solution. With him gone, the witch would be helpless and easily seen to.

Things had taken a complicated turn with her arrival at Kilchurn. Plans, so carefully made, were suddenly going awry. It was past time to take a more subtle if even deadlier bent.

A cruel smile twisted the man's lips. Aye, it was indeed past time to seize a firmer hold on the situation. It was time to use the foxglove . . .

Anne stayed out of Niall's bedchamber whenever the physician was present, fearing she'd lose control if the man attempted some ignorant treatment that did little but hurt Niall. She was grateful for Ena's presence, for the wiry little physician seemed to respect her advice. Anne only hoped her old friend could successfully temper the man's more outlandish treatments.

Niall said little about what went on during the physician's visits and, though he appeared pale and exhausted afterwards, his wound still managed to mend. But thanks only to Ena's healing salves, Anne thought as she battled to maintain control of her frustration. Afterwards, she'd spend many hours in Niall's room, reading to him, talking with him, holding his hand while he slept.

At Niall's insistence, Anne was never alone with him—a trusted servant was always in attendance. Then there'd be no cause at a future date, he explained, ever to say she had slipped him a potion or poison if something untoward should happen. His concern for her worried Anne. Was he in more danger than he'd willingly admit, to now suspect attempts on his life from within his own castle?

Surreptitiously, Anne began to watch the preparation of Niall's food and drink. There seemed nothing out of the ordinary in the kitchen. And Nelly always brought him his meals. Knowing the maidservant's feelings for Niall, Anne doubted the woman would do anything to harm him. She wouldn't be surprised if Nelly attempted to poison *her* food—that would eliminate a rival—but Niall was another matter altogether.

By the third day of his confinement, Niall was climbing the walls from boredom. Against his physician's advice and Anne's concerns, he rose and dressed. Staring down at her from his imposing height, he laughed at her protestations.

"I feel quite well," Niall said with a maddening chuckle. "All I want is a short walk in the gardens. It won't require the use of my arm, and I swear to ye, my legs are quite up to the task." He encircled her shoulders with his good arm. "But, to assure my compliance, ye may accompany me."

Anne stared up into his handsome face. Her heart melted at his boyishly compelling smile. "Och, have it yer way. Ye always were a pigheaded dolt!"

"Sweet lass." He grinned down at her. "It warms my heart to hear such words of endearment fall from yer lips. Pray, what else is in that gentle, loving mind of yers?"

"Ye're a rogue and a knave, Niall Campbell," she declared in exasperation, "and well ye know it!"

"But ye'll come with me to the garden?"

"Aye."

A lazy smile teased his lips. "Good."

Kilchurn's gardens were spacious and well-tended. The air was scented with the lavender blooming from the many bushes scattered throughout the walled enclosure. Bright slashes of red and pink roses brightened the area, as did rhododendrons and fuchsias. It was a lovely, peaceful place. As Anne walked along with Niall, she was content.

A girlish giggle from the rose bower up ahead, followed by a low male voice, was the first hint they weren't alone. Niall halted. A dark frown marred his brow.

"Not a word, lass," he whispered. "I've a suspicion my sister's up to no good, and I can well guess who with."

He left her standing there and made his stealthy way to the bower. What Niall saw stirred his blood to a boil. Caitlin and Rory sat on a stone bench, locked in a heated embrace. As if they didn't know where to alight or what to do, Rory's hands roved over Caitlin's slender form.

Caitlin, however, seemed well aware what to do. Her hands were tightly entwined about Rory's neck, pulling him against her as they awkwardly but determinedly kissed. As Niall watched the scene of youthful ardor, his hands clenched at his sides. Didn't he have enough problems without worrying how much longer his headstrong, highly emotional sister would keep her maidenhood?

"That's enough, Caitlin."

With a gasp, his sister jumped away from Rory. The lad stared at Niall, transfixed with terror, while Caitlin frantically smoothed her gown and mussed hair. There was nothing she could do, however, about the becoming flush to her face, or that they'd quite obviously been kissing.

"H-how dare ye spy upon us?" she demanded, her surprise causing her to take the offense. "Ye could at least have made some noise to give us decent interval to compose ourselves!"

Niall cocked a sardonic brow. "Och, and is that the way of it? And should I have knocked first too?" His expression hardened with a glacial anger. "Nay, lass. Ye were raised better than this. If I hadn't happened upon ye, I can only wonder how much longer ye'd have kept yer maidenhood. Then who would've had ye as wife?"

Caitlin sprang to her feet. "How dare ye speak to me like that? Och, but ye're a crude, churlish knave to shame me so! And I care not for my maidenhood! I love Rory. I'd give it to him gladly!"

Niall's hand shot out to grab his sister's arm and jerk her to him. "Well, since *I'm* now responsible for yer conduct and marriageable state, and *I* don't wish to see ye wed to Rory MacArthur, it's past time I took firmer measures." He spared a brief, withering glance for the trembling young man standing there, rooted to the spot. "Get out of my sight and my castle. And don't come back!"

Rory fled, almost colliding with Anne, who had determined from the tone of the voices emanating from the bower that it was time she get involved. She paused to stare after the lad's rapidly retreating form, then once more gathered her skirts and forged on. The deadly grimness to Niall's voice filled her with rising apprehension.

"He isn't worthy of ye," Niall was saying in a low, furious voice. "Did ye hear him come to yer defense, or stand up to me for yer sake?" He gave her a small shake. "Well, did ye?"

Caitlin's mouth opened then closed, her eyes filling with tears.

"He's but a lad," Anne interjected. "For all his size, he was no match for ye."

Niall wheeled about, a thunderous look in his eyes. "And will ye, too, defend the little beggar? Well, I won't have it, Anne!"

Anne noted Caitlin's startled glance, swinging from her to her brother. In a flash of insight, Anne realized the only way to defuse the situation, before Niall took his pent-up frustration out on Caitlin, was to turn it upon herself.

Anne squared her shoulders and defiantly lifted her chin. "Ye won't have it, ye say?" she deliberately mocked him. "And what *would* ye have me do? Cower in some corner each time I see ye about to make a fool of yerself?"

He glared at her with cold displeasure. "A fool, am I? There's not a man alive I'll let call me that. Do ye imagine because ye're a woman ye can safely do so?"

"Safe or not," Anne shot back, "I'll do so, and gladly, if I think

I'm right." She deliberately turned from Niall to Caitlin. "Go to yer bedchamber, lass. It isn't fitting ye should see yer elders argue."

"Aye!" As if just remembering she was still standing there, Niall looked to his sister. "I'll see to ye later."

Caitlin fled without a moment's hesitation, most likely realizing this wasn't the time to attempt further defense. They watched her go, then Niall turned to Anne. "What do ye have to say for yerself, madam?"

She had never heard him use quite that silky, dangerous tone before. What if she had made him so angry he never forgave her? What if he turned his back on her forever?

Anne flung the foolish thought aside. Niall was proud, but he was also intelligent. He could be brought to see reason.

"I was wrong to call ye a fool, m'lord," she began, honest remorse in her voice and shining in her eyes. "I beg pardon. It was but a ploy to divert yer anger from Caitlin."

He subjected her to a cool appraisal, the taut look of rage already ebbing from his features. "And ye thought to turn it upon yerself, did ye?"

"Aye."

"Ye risked much. I won't be ridiculed before anyone."

Anne's head lowered. "I'm sorry, m'lord. Mayhap I chose poorly, but it was the best I could think of."

A long finger crooked beneath her chin to raise it. "Next time, ask to speak to me in private. If ye don't abuse that privilege, I'll know it's significant when ye use it. Agreed?"

She smiled, relief flooding her. "Agreed."

Niall took her by the elbow. "Come, lady." He led her into the bower, indicating for her to sit upon the stone bench. With a bone-weary sigh, he lowered himself beside her. "I fear my strength wasn't adequate for the emotions of the past few minutes," he said, his face suddenly drawn and haggard. "I've the strangest sense of fatigue, and my muscles feel so weak."

Alarm filled Anne. She slid close, slipping her arm about Niall's waist to steady him. "Mayhap yer wound has broken open. Should I send for help to get ye back to yer chamber?"

"Nay. Allow me a few minutes more and I'll make it under my own power. Though I may have erred in leaving my bed too soon, I'll never admit it to any, save ye." He lifted a halting hand to rub his eyes. "Och, but my head aches, and I can't see too clearly."

"How long have ye felt this way?"

Niall shrugged. "Off and on for the past two days."

"Then ye lied earlier when ye said ye felt well."

He gave her a mock scowl. "Do ye realize that, in the span of but a few minutes, ye've called me both a fool and a liar? What am I to do with ye?"

She returned his glare with a resolute one of her own. "Mayhap let yerself heal by staying abed as ye should?"

"Aye, mayhap ye're right." He smiled tiredly. "I thought my weakness was merely the effects of my wound. Yet I'm healing and these feelings worsen. Dinna fash yerself, lass," he said, noting Anne's look of concern. "It's most likely the result of some spoiled food. It has happened before. I'll get over it."

"Aye, m'lord," Anne murmured. "Ye're a strong, healthy man. Most certainly ye will."

16

Anne firmly tucked the comforter around Niall. "There," she scolded, "now stay abed! Though yer wound looks well, something has weakened ye."

He captured her hand before she could move away. "Why not climb in here with me? It'd do much to keep me abed."

She shook her head at the suggestive gleam in his eyes. "Och, and aren't ye the one who insisted on my never being alone with ye?"

"I've had a change of heart."

"Well, *I* haven't, Niall Campbell."

"Ye're a hard-hearted lass, Anne MacGregor." Niall laughed. "I'll be happy to be well again, so we'll have no further need of a chaperone."

"Rather, I think the need for a chaperone increases with each passing day, my love." She leaned over to give him a tender kiss.

A hot light flared in Niall's eyes. "Mayhap ye're right. One way or another, though, ye're in no danger from me at present. It's a hard thing when yer gut feels sick like mine does. I fear I've no appetite for aught, food or otherwise."

Anne touched his forehead with the back of her hand. She frowned. "Strange, but ye have no fever."

"It's spoiled food, as I said before. There isn't always fever with that."

"Mayhap."

Niall smiled at the doubt in Anne's voice. "There's naught to be done but endure. And I'd prefer to endure it in silence, rather than tell the physician. Murdoch would only make things worse."

Anne grinned. "Aye, that he would." Her expression grew solemn. "There's something we never finished in the garden."

"Caitlin?"

She nodded. "Would ye accept my assistance? This might be better dealt with woman to woman."

"Yer help would be greatly appreciated, lass. I can't seem to influence my sister anymore. She used to hang on my every word, scurry to do my every bidding. But no more." He shook his head, confusion in his eyes. "Truly, I don't know what to think or how to approach her."

"She's a young woman now. Though she loves ye still, other men will soon claim the special place that before she filled with a sisterly love. And she's proud, as proud as ye. Ye must begin to treat her as the woman she is."

"But Caitlin's barely fourteen!"

"Och, Niall," Anne chided gently. "And how many lasses are wed by that age? She's all but grown up."

"Mayhap," he admitted, his gaze lowering in frowning consideration, "but I can't say I like it. She was less a problem as a child."

"Grown women tend to be more of a challenge—to grown men."

He glanced up, subjecting her to an amused scrutiny. "Och, and well I know that, lass. Ye've been a handful since the first moment I saw ye."

"As well I will be to our dying days, m'lord."

A low chuckle rumbled in Niall's chest. "I wouldn't have it any other way."

Their eyes met, and something hot and sweet flowed between them. Anne felt vibrantly alive. Niall's gaze, as it slid down her body, ignited a melting warmth that set her afire. She swallowed hard, knowing she must get away from him before she was overcome with desire.

"By yer leave," she murmured, freeing her hand from his firm clasp, "I'd like to visit yer sister. She must be worried."

Niall's expression darkened. "She needs to stew a bit. The lass defied me, not to mention risked a scandal because of her behavior. I meant what I said before. She won't marry Rory MacArthur. I don't like the lad."

"Well, ye all but banished him from Kilchurn. There should be little problem where he's concerned for a time. Ye must speak with her when ye're feeling better—as one adult to another. Ye might be surprised to find she'll then respond to ye *as* an adult."

"Mayhap. But I've still a mind to send her to Edinburgh. I threaten her with it constantly of late, then back down. She's most likely laughing at me for my weakness in that."

"Ye must do what's fair, no matter the opinions of others. Yer compassion for yer sister shouldn't be viewed as a weakness. She's confused and lost right now, bewildered by her budding emotions and physical needs, hurting still from the loss of her father. Ye've been more than patient with me, who's defied ye far more than Caitlin has ever done. Can't ye spare the same patience for her?"

Niall sighed. "Go to her, Anne. Talk with her. I'll defer to yer judgment in her punishment, but punishment of some kind she must have. Agreed?"

"Agreed."

Reluctantly, she rose from the bed and left the room. As Anne walked through the long stone corridor to Caitlin's room, she considered and discarded several ways to approach the girl. A niggling worry ate at the confidence she had shown Niall just minutes before. What if Caitlin refused to talk with her or, worse yet, ridiculed the guidance she'd try to offer? Niall's anger, when he learned of it, would be more terrible than before.

Well, Anne thought as she raised her fist to knock upon Caitlin's door, *there's naught to be done for it.* All she could do was try. In the end, it was all for Niall.

A young serving maid answered the door.

"Jane, isn't it?" Anne asked. "Is yer mistress in?"

Jane bobbed a little curtsey. "Aye, ma'am. But she says she isn't receiving—"

"Who is it, Jane?" a tear-choked voice came from behind her.

The maid swung back the door to reveal Anne. Caitlin stared at her, a myriad of emotions playing across her expressive face. Then she sighed. "Bid her come in. And ye may leave, Jane."

"Aye, mistress." The girl slipped past Anne and closed the door behind her.

Squaring her shoulders, Anne walked to where Caitlin sat on a padded bench by the window. She gestured toward the seat. "May I sit with ye?"

The girl's glance moved to gaze out the stone-cut window. "Aye," she murmured dejectedly. "Do what ye wish."

Anne settled herself beside Niall's sister. For several minutes neither spoke, Caitlin staring out the window, Anne studying her. Finally, the girl wiped her tears away. Turquoise eyes proudly met Anne's.

"I thank ye for yer efforts on my behalf in the garden. At first, I was confused as to what was happening between ye and my brother. But later, when I'd a time to ponder it all, I realized ye deliberately picked a fight with him to divert his anger from me. That was a kind thing to do."

Anne remained silent.

"Thinking back," the girl continued, "ye've never once been less than kind, turning aside all my rudeness with gentle words and offers of friendship. I've been a stupid, selfish child."

"From the beginning, there was something gnawing at ye," Anne said. "Something that affected yer acceptance of me. What was it, Caitlin?"

Niall's sister's eyes widened in surprise. "It was so evident, was it?

Well, it was but a foolish dream, but I'll tell ye nonetheless. Rory's older sister, Sybil, was greatly desirous of a marriage to Niall. Rory promised it'd assure our eventual marriage, if our two clans joined in such a manner. I had hopes Niall might well consider Sybil, once his time of mourning was done. Then ye came to Kilchurn."

"It's only a handfasting, Caitlin. A trial marriage that could well end in a year."

Niall's sister smiled. "I saw how my brother looked at ye, even from the start. I knew there was no hope for Sybil after that. And even ye must now realize he loves ye."

Anne flushed. "I know he cares for me, but he's made no offers of marriage. Truly, I don't know how this handfasting will end."

"Well, I do," Caitlin said. "And I think I'll like having ye as a sister."

A lump rose in Anne's throat. "Will ye now? Then we can be friends?"

The girl took Anne's hand and gave it an affectionate squeeze. "Aye, if ye'll still have me." She paused to give a small, self-mocking laugh. "And if my brother doesn't yet banish me to Aunt Mathilda."

Anne smiled. "I think he can be made to see reason. He loves ye, Caitlin. He's just sore beset of late. Be patient with him."

"I-I'll try." The girl's eyes filled anew with tears. "But I love Rory, and now Niall has sent him away, mayhap forever. Och, Anne, what shall I do?"

"Be patient with Niall and with yerself. If it's true love between ye and Rory, it won't die. Even Niall will come to see that. He finds Rory too young to be a fit husband. But time may well alter that impression as well."

"But I'll wither on the vine, waiting that long!" Caitlin wailed.

"It seems so, when ye're but fourteen, but a woman must learn patience. It's a trait sorely in need when dealing with men, even the man ye love. Yer time of waiting won't be squandered if ye spend it learning patience. And the eventual reward will be all the sweeter because of it."

Admiration flared in Caitlin's eyes. "Och, ye're so wise. Would that I be, in the few years left until I reach yer age."

Anne laughed, warmed by the girl's compliment. "Ye'll be wiser by far, and no mistake."

"Aye, if ye teach me some of yer healing skills, that I will. As lady of Rory's house, I'll need to know how to aid his people."

Anne's expression grew serious. "Mayhap in time, but not now. It'd be too dangerous."

Understanding lit in Caitlin's eyes. "Aye, that I know. But in time . . ."

"Aye." Anne smiled. "In time."

Niall felt no better upon Anne's return, but listening to her account of her visit with Caitlin filled him with pleasure. He clasped her hand, raising it to his lips to kiss it tenderly.

"Ye see, lass?" he said in a husky voice. "We *will* prevail. Even now, ye've yet another ally in Kilchurn. One by one we'll wear them all down, show them the error of their ways."

"Aye, my love. That we will," she whispered, and watched as he lay back upon his pillow and quickly fell into a deep sleep.

Niall refused the evening meal, stating he had no appetite. Only with Anne's persistent coaxing did he finally take some stew. Then, despite her protestations that it wasn't proper, he insisted she stay near him.

"I don't care how it looks to Agnes," he growled in irritation. "I don't feel well, and yer presence gives me comfort."

There was nothing she could do or say after that, for Anne would never deny Niall in his time of need. She pulled up a chair beside his bed, took a seat, and began to play her harp for him. After a while, he dozed off once again.

Late in the night, Niall's agitated movements woke Anne. He mumbled in his sleep, tossing and turning until Anne was forced to take him into her arms to calm him. Concern for Niall's strange illness grew with each passing minute. Gradually, she became aware of his heart, thudding beneath her hand. It seemed slow, unnaturally so.

She lowered her ear to his chest. The heartbeat was indeed slower than usual.

The first tendril of real fear coiled in her stomach. This was no food poisoning or silent infection. Niall was drugged—and it was most likely the work of her stolen foxglove. She slipped away from him, gently pulling the comforter up to cover him. With pounding heart, she sat on the edge of the bed and struggled to think clearly, to devise a plan. Niall had become sick in the past three days, since he was wounded and brought to his bedchamber. He could've ingested the potent leaves in either food or drink—or in medicine!

Could the castle's physician be poisoning Niall? Anne leaped to her feet to pace the room. She knew the little man had made Niall drink a tonic every day, supposedly to strengthen him and aid in his healing. Could that have contained the foxglove? But if so, why? What would've been the man's motives? Surely he wasn't the traitor.

Nay, he couldn't be the traitor, Anne told herself, *but he might well be working for the traitor.* But how was she to fight him, forbidden as she was to interfere with the man's treatment of Niall? Well, she couldn't . . . but Ena could.

Anne slipped from Niall's bedchamber and into her own. From there she left. The keep was silent and deserted. None saw her sneak down to the storerooms, where she easily found the hidden tunnel leading to the secret passage from the castle.

A half hour later, she was beating on Ena's door. Finally, the old woman peered out. "What is it?" she croaked, her voice thick with sleep. "Is it a birthing, or someone—" She stopped, recognizing Anne. "Lass, what are ye about? It's the middle of the night!"

"Let me in, Ena."

The old healer quickly complied. "Well, lassie," she said once the door was shut behind them, "what is it? Is aught wrong with the young lord?"

"Aye, Ena. I fear ye left too soon. Niall's deathly ill."

"The wound festers?"

"Nay, it's more serious than that. Someone has fed him my foxglove."

"It's worse than I feared," Ena muttered. "The young lord . . ."

"Help me, I beg of ye!" Desperation threaded Anne's voice. "His heart has slowed. He's sick, has no appetite, and is terribly weak. He may die!"

Ena took Anne's hand. "Aye, that he well may if the source of the drug isn't halted. If he takes even one more dose . . ."

"I need ye to stop the physician from feeding him any more of his foul concoctions. He may be the one poisoning him."

"Nay, it isn't possible." Ena firmly shook her head. "I've known Murdoch for years. He'd never intentionally harm a body."

"Then who, Ena? Please come back with me. Help me discover the source. Help me stop them!"

The old woman nodded. "Aye, lass. I'll come back. Give me but a moment to gather my herbs. Though naught but time will ease the effects of the fairy fingers, I've some potions that might help strengthen the young lord in his battle against it."

"Thank ye, Ena." Anne breathed the words in a rush of gratitude. "Thank ye with all my heart."

Ena smiled. "We healers must help each other."

The journey back to the castle was slower by necessity, Ena's arthritic limbs stiff in the dampness before dawn. They took the secret tunnel into the castle and were soon back in Niall's room. After a quick but thorough examination, Ena glanced up at Anne.

"It's indeed the work of the fairy fingers," she said grimly. "Bring me a cup and some water. I'll make him a red clover tea. It's the best of blood cleansers and an excellent tonic."

She pulled an old pot from her bag and filled it with the water

Anne provided. A short time later, the simmering water was poured over the dried clover leaves to steep.

Finally, Ena motioned toward Niall. "Rouse him as best ye can and lift him. We must try to pour as much of this as possible down his throat."

Anne slipped behind Niall to prop him up. She gently shook him. "Niall? Niall, my love? It's time to wake. Ena's here. She has a tea for ye to drink."

He groaned and mumbled something incoherent, then tried to snuggle into her and go back to sleep. Anne shook him harder, her voice rising. "Wake up, I say. It's past time a lazy knave like ye were up and about." She grasped his jaw with one hand and squeezed painfully.

His lids fluttered open then, a confused, startled look in his eyes. "Lazy knave ye s-say?" He glanced around, noting the still-dark windows. "Why, it isn't even dawn. Ye're a heartless lass, Anne MacGregor."

Ena shoved the cup to his lips. "Here, m'lord. Drink this. It'll strengthen ye."

Niall drank deeply. Then, with an exhausted sigh, he fell back against Anne. The door to his bedchamber slammed open. Ena turned, the cup still in her hand.

In the doorway stood Duncan with Malcolm and several armed clansmen close behind. A scowl of rage twisted the tanist's face. "So," he snarled, "ye sneak back here in the dark of night to wreak yer witch's magic on our chief."

Duncan strode into the room, waving the others in behind him. "Seize the old woman. Ye're all witness to the fact she gave the Campbell some witch's potion."

"Nay," Anne cried, clinging tightly to Niall. "It was only clover tea, a tonic to strengthen Niall. He's so sick, can't ye see? Someone has poisoned him."

"Aye, poisoned him." Malcolm grabbed Anne by the arm. "And mayhap ye're as guilty as old Ena."

"It isn't Anne's fault," Ena was quick to intervene. "The Campbell instructed her to obey me in my healing of him. Ye all know that. She's innocent of wrongdoing."

Dark eyes, shaded by bushy brows, glared down at her. "She's a witch as much as ye. And soon enough ye'll both burn!"

"Enough, Malcolm!" Duncan snapped. "The truth will soon come out in Ena's confession." He motioned to the armed clansmen. "Take the old woman to the dungeon. We'll see to her later."

"Nay!" Anne screamed. She slid from beneath Niall and flung herself at the guards. Duncan pulled her away, capturing her arms to pin them at her sides.

"It isn't wise to align yerself with Ena," he whispered. "She's doomed. Malcolm will soon see to that."

"And why should ye suddenly care what happens to me?" she demanded. "Ye've been against me from the start. Why not throw me in the dungeon along with Ena?"

A cold smile touched his lips. "What need have I to condemn ye when others will soon do it for me? My hands will be clean no matter what happens. As well I should, I'll remain above all the tumult."

She stared up at him, struck speechless by the sheer malevolence of Duncan's reasoning. He, above everyone else, would come out as the man of pure motives, forced by law to condemn her and see her burn. And burn she would, while Niall lay helpless and near death. Anne knew they'd eventually extract the confession they wanted from Ena. No one could withstand the tortures for long, and Ena was a weak old woman.

Anne glared defiantly up at him. "We'll see how long ye remain above the rabble ye so slyly stir. Niall will yet recover, and when he does—"

"Och, I only pray that it's so, lady. No one wants for our chief to live more than me." Duncan smiled. "But if he doesn't, I'm tanist and must rule as I see fit. And no witch responsible for his death will live."

“Take her away,” he ordered the guards holding Ena. He released Anne only after Ena was led away. “And ye, lady, are refused further entrance to this room. I won’t have ye attempting to finish what Ena has begun.”

Anne stepped back from him. Incredulity widened her eyes. “Ye cannot—”

Duncan arched a graying brow. “Am I not Niall’s chosen successor, named before all? And, as ye see, he’s now incapacitated. In all but name, I’m the Campbell.” He motioned over Agnes, who had heard the noise and had entered Niall’s room. “Take yer mistress to her bedchamber and keep her there. If she dares step again into this chamber, it’s the dungeon for her.”

Agnes hurried to Anne, grasping her by the hand. “Come, m’lady. Come with me.”

Tears stung Anne’s eyes as her glance moved to Niall, pale and silent in his bed. He was helpless now, at the mercy of others—and someone meant to see him dead. He needed her, and she was now denied access to him. But who’d protect him, if not her?

“Come, m’lady,” Agnes pleaded, hysteria now in her voice. “It isn’t the time to defy them. Please, please, come with me.”

She was right, Anne thought. It wasn’t the time to defy or fight them. But the time would come. She wasn’t beaten yet.

Anne exhaled an acquiescent breath. “Aye, Agnes. It’ll be as ye ask. I must obey our tanist.”

But only for a time, she silently added as she followed the old maidservant from the room. *The battle isn’t over; it’s only begun. At last the enemy, whoever he be, has shown his hand.*

Agnes ushered Caitlin into Anne’s bedchamber and shut the door. The girl hurried to the window seat. Anne motioned for her to sit beside her.

“We must keep our voices low,” she hastened to explain. “There may be spies. If we talk quietly, we’re far enough from my doors that none should hear. And what I speak of must be known to none or it might cost Niall his life."

"Tell me what ye want of me," Caitlin whispered, a determined light burning in her eyes. "I won't let my brother die."

Anne took the girl's hand. "Someone poisons Niall with a drug stolen from my storage chest. There's no antidote. Only time will clear the drug from his body. In the meanwhile, we must make sure he is given no more."

"And how will we do that?"

"Ye must watch the preparation of his meals, bring them up yerself, and feed him. Ye mustn't allow the physician to give him any medicines. And ye must stay with Niall as much as possible, sleep in his room. Trade off with Agnes when ye must, but don't ever leave him alone. It's the only way to protect him."

Caitlin's smooth brow wrinkled in a frown. "But who am I to watch? Who's trying to poison my brother?"

Anne sighed. "I'm not certain. Mayhap old Murdoch, mayhap Malcolm or Duncan."

"Nay, not Uncle Duncan!" Caitlin exclaimed in horror. "Nay, it could never be him. He loves Niall and me like a father."

Anne shot her a wry glance and continued on. "Or mayhap a man outside the castle, manipulating someone within to do his bidding, even one of the servants, mayhap. I don't know, Caitlin. It's the most frightening part of all. I don't know whom to trust, whom to suspect." She shook her head in despair. "And I'm helpless, save to ask others to do my bidding. Niall needs me, yet I cannot go to him. Help me, Caitlin," Anne cried, her voice breaking. "If ye don't, I don't know what I'll do!"

"Fear not, sister. I won't fail ye or my brother."

Anne marveled at Caitlin's sudden surge of strength and maturity. Och, but it was so good to have another to bear a bit of the burden, to help where she wasn't allowed to go.

She lifted her head. "Ye mustn't reveal our plan to anyone. And that includes Duncan. If the traitor guesses, he'll find a way to stop ye. We must get Niall strong enough to know his own mind again. Then he'll have the power to refuse to eat or drink what isn't safe. Do ye understand?"

Caitlin nodded. "Aye, I understand."

Anne gave the girl a gentle push. "Then go and see to yer brother. And, Caitlin," she added, as the girl rose to leave.

"Aye?"

"When Niall rouses enough to understand, will ye tell him I'm near, that I love him?"

Caitlin smiled. "Aye, Anne. I'll say it over and over, for it'll give my brother the will to live."

"My thanks." Anne turned back to gaze out the window, her hands clenched, knuckle-white, in her lap.

✦

"I couldn't see her, m'lady," Agnes admitted regretfully late the next day. "I'm sorry."

Anne sighed. "Do ye know if they've yet begun the torture? Och, if only Niall recovers before they begin! Then he can save Ena."

Agnes averted her gaze, apparently finding sudden interest in putting away some fresh linens Anne had been folding. "The guard wouldn't say."

"Look at me, Agnes," her mistress commanded, knowing there was more here than her maid cared to reveal. "Tell me true. Have they tortured Ena?"

A look of misery in her eyes, the old woman nodded. "Aye, m'lady."

"How does she fare?" Anne asked through a suddenly constricted throat.

"She hasn't confessed, but the guard says it won't be long now."

"Och, no!" Anne breathed. "What am I to do? Duncan won't allow me down there to see her and refuses to stop that madman preacher. They'll kill her!"

"It'd be a blessing. If she died before they could extract a confession . . ."

Anne's eyes widened in horror. "How can ye say such a thing? Ena's but a kind old woman. She has never harmed a soul!"

"Aye, m'lady. That I well know. But if she confesses and names ye witch, Malcolm will turn on ye like a blood-crazed hound. Ye'll be tried and burnt before the Campbell has a chance to recover."

"He grows a little better with each passing hour. Ye and Caitlin do yer job well."

"But he still falls in and out of a deep sleep," Agnes stated grimly. "He's confused and weak as a newborn kit. And it won't be much longer before Ena breaks."

"Then we must seek help!" With resolute strides, Anne walked to her small writing desk and pulled out parchment and quill. She scribbled a quick note then sealed it. Anne motioned her maid-servant over. "Find some man whom ye can trust to deliver this. It *must* reach Iain Campbell at Balloch Castle, and quickly. If the man hurries, Iain can be here in two days' time, mayhap less."

Agnes dubiously accepted the missive. "Will he come, m'lady? There's no love lost of late between him and the Campbell."

"I know that, Agnes. He may not come for Niall, but he'll come for me."

"And isn't that a dangerous game ye play? What if the Campbell mistakes yer motives?"

"That's a chance I'll take," Anne replied. "I'm desperate and must call whatever friends I have to my aid. If Niall turns from me because of that, there's naught I can do. He said he trusted me. The time has come to put that trust to the test." She smiled sadly. "Now go, Agnes. Find yer man and send him on his way. In the meanwhile, I must go to Duncan and buy time for us all."

Agnes's eyes narrowed in suspicion. "What do ye mean to do?"

"I won't let Ena suffer a moment more for me. I pulled her into this tangled web when I asked her help in healing Niall. It's time I took responsibility for it all."

“What are ye going to tell Duncan?”

“That I asked for Ena’s help, and she only did what I asked. It’s the only way to save her.”

“Nay, m’lady! Ye’ll condemn yerself on the spot. They’ll burn ye, and no mistake.”

Anne swallowed a panicked sob. “Aye, that I know. More reason to send for Iain forthwith. We’ve little time to spare.”

17

Duncan stared up at her from the library desk. "What did ye say?"

Though her heart was hammering, Anne calmly repeated her words. "Ena's innocent. If there be fault, it's mine. She only helped because I requested it."

"And what did ye request?"

She knew what he was hoping she'd say. But, though determined to rescue Ena no matter the price, Anne wouldn't easily give him what he wanted. "Why to save Niall, of course. What else would there be? Ena and I use our skills for good, not evil."

"White or black magic, it's all the same. It's still witchcraft."

"There was no witchcraft. It was only natural healing."

Duncan leaned forward. "One of ye is a witch. Which one is it, m'lady?"

Anne knew he wanted it to be her. For some reason, he needed her out of the way, had seen her as a threat from the start. But why?

Ena was old, near the end of her life, while Anne was young with many years ahead of her. She loved Niall, had the hope of a joyous, fruitful relationship with him. By all that was logical, Ena should be the one sacrificed.

But Anne couldn't do it. Like her Lord and Savior, if need be, she'd lay down her life for a friend. And there was still hope Iain would arrive in time to save them both, but only if Anne bought that time by diverting Malcolm's witch madness to her.

She graced Duncan with a look of cool disdain. "Ena's innocent. It's I who's called the Witch of Glenstrae."

An eager light flared in Duncan's deep blue eyes. "Then ye admit it? Admit ye're a witch?"

"I'm called the Witch of Glenstrae," she repeated with exaggerated patience.

"And ye'll admit this before witnesses?"

"It's true. It's nothing I'd willingly seek out, but nonetheless, it's what I'm called."

Duncan rose from his chair and hurried to the door. "Fetch the preacher and a clerk," he ordered the guard standing outside. "Make it quick. We've a confession to witness!"

Anne walked to the open window. She gazed out upon the heath and bracken-strewn hills surrounding Loch Awe. In the sunset, the light glinted off the lake like molten gold. The swans, sailing upon it in graceful elegance, were wreathed in a luminous brilliance. Overhead, a goshawk soared in the deepening twilight, its faint, raucous cry piercing the summer silence.

It was all so beautiful, she thought with a bittersweet pang, and she might've just forfeited the right ever to see it again. *Och, Niall,* she silently cried. *What will ye think if I die before ye recover? Will ye hate me for leaving ye, or curse me for my weakness? If only I could see ye one last time, kiss ye, hold ye in my arms! I'd whisper in yer ear, though ye heard me not, that I love ye and tried hard to fight. So verra, verra hard . . . to the bitter end.*

Like the jaws of a trap closing about her, Malcolm, with an ominous-looking black leather case, hurried in. He was followed by a nervous little clerk. After a moment of whispered consultation between the preacher and Duncan, Malcolm's mouth twisted in a triumphant smile. He directed the clerk to take his seat at the desk, then motioned to Anne.

"Come here, woman. By yer own admission, yer fate's sealed. Cooperate with us, and we'll spare ye the torture."

"How kind," Anne muttered under her breath as she gathered

her skirts and came to stand before them. She eyed the preacher calmly. "And how may I help ye?"

"Don't play games with me, wench," Malcolm snarled. He jerked her to him. "Repeat yer confession, word for word as ye spoke it to our tanist. That's all I want from ye."

"Let her go, Malcolm!" Duncan snapped. "Until her confession's duly transcribed and signed, she's still lady of this house. Then ye can do with her as ye wish."

"All I want is her tried and burned."

"As do I," the tanist soothed. "As do I. But the letter of the law must be followed or the Campbell will have our heads if, and when, he recovers." Duncan motioned to Anne. "Sit, lady."

She shook her head. "Nay, I prefer to stand and face my tormentors eye to eye."

He shrugged. "Have it yer way. Transcribe all that's said from now on," Duncan instructed the clerk. He turned back to Anne. "Ye've admitted ye're the Witch of Glenstrae. Is that true?"

Her heart gave a jump and hung in her throat. *Dear Lord, here it comes!* She schooled her features into an impassive mask, refusing them the satisfaction of seeing her fear. "Aye, that's what I'm called."

"Did ye get that? Did ye write that down?" Malcolm glanced over at the clerk, who was scribbling furiously.

The man looked up and nodded.

Duncan scowled at Malcolm then turned again to Anne. "As a witch, what crimes have ye committed?"

Anne stared at him, momentarily taken aback. "What? Must I now confess crimes to satisfy ye? Wasn't my admission enough?"

"We must know it all!" Malcolm snarled. "Did ye poison the Campbell, father and son?"

She shook her head, refusing ever to be party to that accusation. "Nay. Never!"

"She lies!" the preacher cried. "Write it down," he ordered the clerk. "She'll confess to it soon enough."

"Nay." Anne moved to stay the clerk's hand. "Write that on the confession, and I'll never sign it. I won't hurt Niall with falsehoods such as that."

An evil grin twisted Malcolm's face. "Ye'll not speak so bravely after I show ye the contents of my case." He lifted the black bag onto the desk. "Shall I show it to her?" he asked Duncan.

The tanist eyed Anne. "Nay, not yet. The alleged poisoning isn't important. There are other crimes." Duncan leaned forward. "Did ye put a curse upon our cattle? Give them the murrain?"

"Nay."

His mouth tightened in irritation. "Did ye bring a stillborn bairn back to life with yer witch's powers?"

Fiona's child, Anne thought achingly. How long ago that day now seemed. It had changed her life, brought her to this moment. But in the same token, it had also brought her to Niall.

"I don't know if the babe was truly dead," she forced herself to reply, "but I breathed into her mouth, and she moved and cried. I used no witch's powers, only the breath in my body."

"So ye *did* bring a bairn back to life," Duncan persisted.

Anne sighed. "Mayhap I did. What does it matter?"

Duncan turned to the clerk. "Note she brought a stillborn back to life." He riveted his cold blue gaze upon her. "And will ye not admit to bespelling Niall Campbell? To winning his heart and soul?"

The tanist leaned close, a strange light in his eyes. "Tell us how ye did it, how ye lured him to yer bed."

Nausea welled in Anne. She had done no such thing, but she wouldn't have her and Niall's feelings for each other dissected on parchment for all to read. It was too much!

"What goes on between a man and woman is a private thing." Anne glared at him with all the righteous indignation she possessed. "Ye're his uncle, his family. How can ye do this to him?"

A murderous look flared in Duncan's eyes. "I do this to protect him against ye, lady. My nephew doesn't know his mind anymore and is hardly fit to rule the clan. When it comes to ye, he has turned against his own family. Do ye deny it?"

It was so unfair, how he twisted everything, Anne thought miserably. But, for Niall's sake, if nothing else, she'd fight him every step of the way. "And *I* say, mayhap his family has turned against him, each one for personal reasons, all selfish and unworthy."

Duncan's fist slammed on the desk. "Curse ye, woman! My patience with ye is at an end!" He glanced at Malcolm. "Show the witch yer bag. Mayhap that'll still the sharpness of her tongue. And if not," he sneered, turning the full force of his contemptuous gaze back to her, "mayhap she'll need a wee taste of the instruments."

Malcolm shot her a sly smile. With the utmost care and deliberation, he undid the latches and released the belts of the case. Then, one by one, he laid out each piece of cold, black metal upon the desk.

Anne tried not to look, but her gaze froze in horror at the magnitude of man's imagination when it came to torture. How could anyone endure for long under their gruesome application? Was Ena even still alive?

Anger swelled in her. "Ye're a madman, the devil himself, to inflict willingly such pain upon another human being! And ye call yerself a man of God! Why, ye're lower than the least of all the creatures ye claim to serve!"

Malcolm slapped her across the face. Anne recoiled, then instinctively lurched forward before something the Lord had once said filled her mind. If her words couldn't move the preacher, perhaps her actions could. She dragged in a shaky breath, then slowly offered him her other cheek.

Malcolm's eyes widened. He purpled in rage and lifted his hand to strike her again.

Duncan pulled Anne back. "Enough, Malcolm. Ye border on being played the fool. And ye, madam," he snarled in her ear as she struggled to free herself, "I'd advise not to press yer luck. I'd be sorely saddened to have ye led out of here in chains, though Malcolm would no doubt like that."

Duncan was right. They'd do what they wanted with her. Her only recourse was to buy time. No one but Iain could help her now.

"Aye," she replied. "Just keep that man away from me."

"Ye've seen enough, I'll warrant," Duncan whispered soothingly. "Ye'll sign the confession now, won't ye?"

Exhaustion flooded Anne in a sudden, mind-wearying wave. Och, what was the use? There was naught else she could do, not now at any rate. Better to give them what they wanted and bide her time, lulling them into an illusion of victory. But she wouldn't ever admit to betraying Niall.

"Let me see the confession."

Duncan released her and handed over the parchment. Anne scanned the words, noting the only crimes transcribed were her admission to being the Witch of Glenstrae and that she had brought Fiona's babe back to life. The irony of it sickened her. A name and the saving of a life might be all it took to condemn her to the stake.

Anne signed the document. "There." She handed the parchment back with a disdainful flourish. "Is that enough to win Ena's freedom?"

Malcolm chuckled snidely.

Anne whirled around. "What, pray tell, is so amusing?"

His eyes gleamed with a crazed light. "Foolish woman. Old Ena was never our true quarry."

Anne's gaze swung to the tanist. A triumphant smile glimmered on his lips. She should've known. A sickening, trapped feeling coiled in the pit of her stomach. She should've seen it coming.

"But why? What have I ever done to ye?"

"It's quite simple, really. Yer growing influence over my nephew stood in the way of our plans for the takeover of MacGregor lands." Duncan's smile turned pitying. "Innocent victim though ye be, I couldn't allow that to happen."

“So ye’ll die, witch,” Malcolm interjected gleefully, moving to Duncan’s side. “Die, burned at the stake.”

As Anne stared at the two men standing together like some evil, impregnable wall, horror slithered down her spine. How could she hope to prevail against men such as these? They were too crafty, too powerful, and far too cruel for any one person to defeat. She had been lost from the start.

Despair filled her. Her legs wobbled, barely able to support her. Anne clutched at the table. *Dear Lord, why have Ye delivered me up to them? Indeed, they have us all within their power—Niall, Ena, myself—and any other who ever dares go against them. By fair means or foul, they’ll see us all dead.*

The realization triggered something in Anne, stirring back to life that tiny ember of faith and trust in God that her despair had nearly extinguished. The Lord hadn’t deserted her. He’d yet lead her through this, if only she clung fast to Him.

“Ye’ll never win!” she cried. “Though ye burn my body, ye’ll not break me. My spirit will only come back to fight ye anew, joining with all the others who’ll rise to the cause until ye’re defeated at last. Ye don’t do the Lord’s work, and never have. Ye’re wrong—wrong to the marrow of yer bones—and even death won’t still the voices against ye!”

Anne paced the confines of her small cell, struggling yet again against the renewed panic clamoring beneath her thin veneer of self-control. Indeed, there was little in the dimly lit room of sweating stone and heavy, moldy air to distract her from it. Her gaze scanned the cell—the dank, dirty straw covering the floor, the filthy pallet in the corner, the oily torch sputtering erratically near the thick oaken door.

Her trial had been held the day after the signing of her confession. It had been anticlimactic. Her signature on the parchment had already judged and condemned her. The law, however, required she be given the opportunity to recant. Anne briefly considered it.

In the end, she stood by her confession, for it was the only truth in the whole sordid mess. Though she passionately defended herself, demanding to know why the charges were grounds for witchcraft, her judges refused to listen. Recant was all they said. When Anne refused, irreverently calling them narrow-minded oafs with whey for brains, they sentenced her to death at the stake in the village commons at noon the next day. Anne was tempted to ask why they didn't just drag her out then and there, and see the deed done.

But as she stalked the wet, black hole that was her final dwelling place, Anne realized why they had given her this last night on earth. They knew she'd not sleep. They knew the torments that would assail her, the fear, the sense of helplessness, the utter loneliness. And they wanted it for her. It was all part of her punishment.

Och, if only I could speak to someone, Anne thought in despair. *Agnes . . . Caitlin . . . Iain.* But the two women had been forbidden to see her, and Iain, it now seemed, might not make it to Kilchurn in time.

Well, at least Ena had been spared. There was comfort in that. She *had* saved Ena. And Iain, once he arrived, would take matters in hand. Her friends—and Niall, if he survived the foxglove—would at least be safe.

But there was no hope left for her.

Once more the wild fear coiled within her. Anne quickly changed the course of her thoughts. The Lord Jesus was with her, and would be to the end. She only hoped she had the courage to persevere, to hold to her faith and never, ever, let despair steal her God from her.

"But only if Ye're with me, Lord," she whispered. "I can't do this—no one could—alone. Stay with me, Lord, and help me keep the faith."

She *must* maintain control. It was all the power she had left over her life. She'd not go to her death groveling and in tears. Niall, whether he lived or died, deserved better than that.

Niall . . . Anne turned the beloved name over and over in her mind, hearing it in a voice without words. Och, how she loved him! Was he better? Were Agnes and Caitlin protecting him from the traitor, the poisoning? If so, he'd regain his senses soon.

Not soon enough to save her, but soon enough to resume the fight against the traitor and flush him out once and for all. Anne only hoped they'd spare him the news of her death until he was stronger. She didn't want anything to impede his recovery. It wouldn't help her anyway. There seemed nothing—leastwise on this earth—that could help her now.

The sound of footsteps, of two people, echoed in the hollow tunnel of stone that was the corridor. Hope spiraled within her. Were they allowing her a visitor? Was it Iain?

An iron key clanked. The lock turned, and the heavy door swung open. Anne took a hesitant step forward.

It was only Nelly, her head lowered and oddly canted to the left, bearing a tray that held a small covered pot and a spoon. Without looking up at Anne, the serving maid walked across the room and placed the tray on the floor next to her pallet. It was the only logical spot; there was nowhere else to sit.

Despite Nelly's seething animosity toward her in the past, Anne forced herself to walk toward her. The dark-haired maid was the first person allowed in since she had been so unceremoniously deposited here after the trial. Even a word or two about how Niall was doing would be heaven to Anne.

"Nelly." She hesitantly touched the other woman's arm.

The maid kept her back turned. "Aye?" she muttered in a low, sullen voice. "What do ye want?"

Anne swallowed hard. "Please, Nelly. How's Niall? Is he better? I only want to know how he fares . . ."

"He fares well enough." Nelly gestured toward the tray. "Ye won't like yer supper. It's nettle soup, flavored only with lard and gristle. The preacher insisted we make it for ye."

"It doesn't matter." Anne sighed. "A royal feast wouldn't tempt me tonight. But thank ye for yer consideration."

"How can ye be so calm, so kind, when ye're to burn on the morrow?" Nelly whirled to face her.

Anne gasped. A blackened eye and large, purpling bruise marred the left side of the serving maid's face.

"Nelly! Who did this to ye?"

The woman jerked back, terror widening her eyes. "N-no one," she stammered. "It was . . . it was an accident. I fell down some steps and struck my face."

"Nay, lass." Compassion filled Anne. "It isn't that kind of injury. Ye forget I'm a healer. I know the signs of a beating when I see them. And I ask ye again. Who did this?"

The serving maid's past mistrust and hostility crumbled in the face of Anne's gentle concern. She buried her face in her hands. "Och, what have I done? I've nearly killed the Campbell and will soon have yer soul on my conscience as well. And all to gain the gratitude of a man who seeks to steal the chieftainship." She gave a bitter laugh. "Yet this is how he thanks me."

"Who is he?" Anne kept her voice low so the guard waiting outside wouldn't hear. "Why did he beat ye?"

Nelly raised her tear-streaked face. "Why? Because I failed to slip more foxglove into the Campbell's food, of course. But Caitlin wouldn't let anyone near it. Besides, once I found out Sir Niall was near death because of me, I lost heart for the task. Though he wouldn't take me as mistress, he never failed to treat me kindly."

A dark, angry expression twisted her swollen features. "Not like *him*, who only meant to use me, beating me half to death when I only once failed him. Och, how I hate him!"

Rising excitement rippled down Anne's spine. Her pulse accelerated wildly. The traitor! Nelly was in league with the traitor! Her grip tightened on the serving maid's arm. "Who is he, Nelly? Tell me his name!"

"H-his name?" Nelly repeated, her anger gone as quickly as it had come. Sudden realization of what she had revealed dawned in her eyes. With a quick movement, the maid wrenched free from Anne's grasp. "Nay," she said, her eyes glazing over in panic. "I cannot tell ye that. He'd kill me for certain."

"Nelly, please!" As the other woman backed away, Anne's hands lifted in supplication. "Tell me his name. Niall will protect ye."

"No one can prevail against him. No one. He's too clever, too powerful." Nelly stumbled into the cell door.

Anne stood there trembling. "Please, Nelly!"

With one last, frantic glance, the serving maid turned and fled. Anne darted across the room after her and slammed into the unyielding bulk of the guard. Cold, implacable eyes stared down at her. He shoved her back into the cell with enough force to make her fall. Anne struck the dirt floor with a painful jolt. She sat there for a long moment, staring up at him.

"Ye won't escape yer just punishment, witch. Leastwise, not while I'm on duty," the burly man snarled. "And not another word out of ye this eve or I'll be forced to take the lash to ye."

Anne scooted away and, after a moment more, he backed from the cell, slamming and locking the door behind him. His hurried footsteps pounded down the corridor. A moment later, heavy silence descended upon the dungeon.

A heavy silence shattered only by the gut-wrenching sobs of the dungeon's solitary prisoner.

They came for Anne an hour before midday, binding her hands behind her. The guards, clansmen she had met many times in the two months since she had come to Kilchurn, couldn't quite meet her calm, steady gaze. Gently, almost respectfully, they led her from the dungeon and through the keep.

‡ ‡

Outside was blindingly bright, especially after the cell's dimness. Anne squinted in the sunlight until her eyes readjusted, grateful for the heat that eased the cold ache in her bones. The cart that would take her to the village commons waited in the outer bailey. Duncan and Malcolm were already mounted, the tanist in tartan trews, the preacher in blue serge and plain black bonnet.

Anne climbed into the wooden conveyance and glanced back at the keep. High in a stone-cut window, she saw the pale, strained faces of Agnes and Caitlin. She tossed her head in defiance and smiled up at them. The driver flicked his whip over the pony's back, and the cart lurched forward.

It was a glorious, ripe summer's day, birds soaring overhead, a freshened breeze rustling the trees. Anne took it all in, knowing the beloved sights would be her last; she drew on them for sustenance, for courage to face what lay ahead. She thought of God, of Glenstrae and Castle Gregor, of those carefree days of her girlhood.

She harked back to the eve she had first met Niall, of her anger at him—and her hatred. Everything, after the last few anguished days, seemed like another lifetime. Even her words to Niall, barely a week past, when she had stood there in the forest beside her ravaged herb garden.

"I'd sooner have a few months in yer arms, even if it killed me, than a lifetime without ye."

She had spoken those words to ease his fears of childbirth, but they had been prophetic in another, more horrible way. The truth of them hadn't dimmed, though. She loved him and was glad, so very glad, for the time they'd had. If only he'd remember those words, find the same comfort they now gave her.

A crowd had gathered in the commons. They were strangely quiet, shuffling uncomfortably, wearing almost shamefaced expressions.

Anne's gaze swept over them. A soft smile touched her lips. They were good, kindhearted, hardworking folk. Without the Lord to guide them, they couldn't help their weaknesses and superstitions.

In a sense, they were as much victims of the ignorance and manipulations of their leaders as she was.

Och, dear Lord, Anne uttered a fervent little prayer, *would that Niall recover to lead them again. He alone can give them the guidance, the wisdom they so sorely need.*

The cart rolled to a halt. Only then did Anne notice the stake, its base piled high with bundles of fagots. For an instant her courage fled. Then the guards lifted her down. With a proud tilt of her chin, when her feet touched ground Anne shrugged away their hands. She strode to the stake.

A narrow path had been cleared through the piles of fagots, and a small step placed at the base of the stake. She climbed it, then turned. The guards moved beside her, tying her in place and crisscrossing the ropes across her chest. Anne's breath began to come in ragged little gasps. She fought to steady herself.

The fagots were moved to fill the path before her. A guard, holding a flaming torch, stepped forward. Anne swallowed hard against the lump rising in her throat. With only the greatest of efforts did she still the sudden tremors that wracked her body. She saw Duncan look to Malcolm and nod.

The preacher stepped forward and unrolled a parchment with a slow, practiced hand. He paused to scan the crowd, waiting until he had their full attention. Then he read Anne's confession, carefully enunciating each and every word. Next came the scroll bearing her sentence.

Anne wondered when Malcolm's droning would end. At last the preacher rerolled the second parchment. He lifted his gaze to meet hers, and she glared at him with a withering scorn. His triumphant gleam faded.

"Vile puppet, inhuman creature!" Anne cried, her voice carrying to the furthest reaches of the crowd. This was her last chance to fight back against the cruel practice, and fight she would. "How dare ye call yerself a holy man and still condone such an atrocity? An atrocity condemned by the chief himself, who refuses to allow burnings on Campbell lands."

"The w-will of God and the church is reason enough for yer death," Malcolm sputtered. "How dare ye question such a holy edict? Yer defiance of church law in itself confirms yer heretical origins!"

Anne laughed, her head held high. "And since when is it heretical to love God, to save life, to ease the suffering of others? Answer me that, Preacher."

"That issue has been dealt with!"

"Yet never fairly resolved," she stubbornly countered.

"Aye," a rough male voice, unsteady in its hesitation, rumbled from the back of the crowd. "Since when has the easing of pain and misery been grounds for witchcraft? Answer the lass, Preacher."

"Her witch's powers gave her the healing skills." Malcolm raised a scroll above his head. "Her signed confession attests to that."

"And how long did ye torture the lass to get that out of her?" another clansman demanded.

"Aye, how long, Preacher?" yet another shouted.

"Answer them, Malcolm," Anne prodded softly, as the wide-eyed preacher glanced about him. "Tell them about Ena as well."

Malcolm stared at Anne, frozen by the relentless gaze she held him in. His mouth moved, but no words issued forth.

Duncan noted his hesitation, the growing look of fear on his face. The crowd began to mutter uneasily, move about. Though many looked willing to see her burn, there were others . . .

The moment must be seized. Now, before the people's resolve broke. Duncan signaled the guard holding the torch. "Light the fires. Burn the witch."

The man threw the flaming brand on the fagots directly before Anne. The torch fell into the bundles of dry kindling. With a puff of smoke, the wood burst into flame.

"Nay!" Anne screamed. "It's wrong what ye do! It's evil!"

Even as she spoke, the heat rose to a painful, smothering intensity. The fumes engulfed her. She gagged, then choked.

It was too late. It was over. Anne bit back a shuddering sob. She closed her eyes as desolation overwhelmed her once and for all. *Och, Lord, forgive them all,* she prayed, her thoughts turning one last time to her Savior. *And help Niall.*

Niall . . .

Och, Niall, my heart's true love, she silently cried. *I tried. Truly I did. Forgive me . . .*

18

His apprehension rising, Iain took the steps of the keep with long, quick strides. It was too quiet in Kilchurn. That, more than anything else, worried him.

The Great Hall was empty save for the cook, Maudie, who was descending the stairs from the sleeping chambers. She carried a covered tray. Iain stalked toward her. The woman jumped when he touched her arm.

"M'lord!" she gasped, raising tear-reddened eyes. "I-I didn't hear yer approach."

"I'd wager not, Maudie." Iain grinned at her. "Ye were sniffling so loudly, ye wouldn't have heard a band of reivers galloping through the hall. Pray, what has upset ye so?"

"Don't ye know, m'lord?" She sighed. "Nay, I suppose not. Ye've been gone from Kilchurn since the Campbell's illness and Lady Anne's trial."

Iain gripped Maudie's arm. "Trial? They sent Anne to trial? When?"

"Yesterday, m'lord. And she was condemned a witch."

"By mountain and sea!" Iain snarled. "Where is she now? In the dungeon?"

The cook's eyes filled anew with tears. "Nay, m'lord. They took her but a half hour ago to the village commons to burn her at the stake."

"What?" The incredulous shout reverberated in the silent hall. "And where's Niall to let this happen?"

"Upstairs in his bedchamber." The woman sobbed. "He's too weak to go to her aid. M-m'lord's been so verra, verra ill."

"I don't care how ill he is! If he's conscious enough to speak but a few coherent words, he's going with me to the village!"

He wheeled about and ran across the hall, taking the steps to the bedchambers two at a time. Panic churned within him, and he was hard pressed to hold it at bay. Anne was even now at the village commons. Without Niall's presence as clan chief to halt the burning, there was no way to save her.

Niall blinked in the late-morning sun. He felt rested, stronger . . . and hungry. His glance swept the room, finally alighting upon a rounded feminine figure bent over the hearth stirring a pot. He smiled.

"Annie?" He croaked out the name, startled at the hoarseness of his voice. "Is that ye, lass?"

The woman at the hearth straightened and turned, her ebony hair tumbling about her shoulders. It was Caitlin. Her eyes widened at the sight of her brother, struggling to raise himself in bed.

"Niall?" she cried. "Och, thank the Lord! Ye're better. Ye've finally left yer stupor!"

She ran to the open door separating his and Anne's bedchambers. "Agnes! Agnes, come quickly! It's Niall! He's awake at last."

Agnes hurried into the room. The old maidservant eyed him closely, then turned to Caitlin, drawing her aside. Niall frowned but, try as he might, he couldn't catch a word of what the two women were saying.

"What are we going to do, Agnes?" Caitlin demanded anxiously. "The first word out of his mouth was Anne's name. How are we to tell him that, even now, she's probably burning at the stake? The news will surely set him back, if not kill him on the spot."

"Och, if only I knew." Agnes sighed. "I suppose we—"

"How much longer will ye two women be?" Niall grumbled from his bed. "While ye talk, I hear my stomach groaning for want of food." He glanced hopefully at the hearth. "What's in that pot? Some soup, mayhap?"

Agnes inhaled a shaky breath, squared her shoulders, and nodded. "Aye, m'lord. A moment more and I'll dish ye up a bowl of hearty beef broth."

She turned to Caitlin. "Let him eat first. He'll need the strength to bear what we have to tell him."

The girl nodded. Gathering her skirts, the old woman bustled to the fireplace. She soon had a spoon and steaming bowl of soup laid out on a small tray. She gestured impatiently at Caitlin, who stood rooted to the spot where Agnes had left her.

"Come along, lass. Pull up a chair at yer brother's bedside and feed him his soup."

"I can feed myself." Niall reached for the tray that Agnes brought. "Ye'd think I was helpless as a babe to need such coddling."

Agnes surrendered the tray to Niall and shoved Caitlin down in the chair the girl brought over. "Sit with him, nonetheless. He'll soon tire."

It took only a few spoonfuls. Niall leaned back against the pillows but stayed his sister's hand when she reached for the spoon to feed him. "Nay, lass," he said. "Give me but a moment's rest. If it takes the rest of the day, I *will* feed myself this entire bowl."

The rest of the day lasted about another five minutes. When he found himself exasperatingly wearied by the attempt to lift another two spoonfuls to his mouth, Niall grabbed the bowl and downed its entire contents. That effort drained him of his remaining strength. He fell back, pale and damp-faced. A triumphant smile, however, twisted his full, firm mouth.

"And, sure, ye'll be one scoundrel of a patient," Agnes muttered under her breath, "and no mistake."

"I heard that, Agnes," Niall said, his eyes still closed. "Except for the voice, ye sound just like my Annie."

Caitlin shot her an anguished look just as the door to the bedchamber slammed open, and Iain entered. "Curse ye, Niall Campbell! While ye loll about at yer leisure, Anne soon burns at the stake! Get out of that bed before I drag ye out. Ye're coming with me to halt her execution, or I swear I'll kill ye!"

Niall jerked up in bed. "What are ye talking about?" His narrowed glance swung to encompass Agnes and his sister. "What's Iain talking about?" he demanded in a dangerously low voice. "Where's Anne?"

Caitlin blanched, her mouth moving wordlessly. Agnes, however, took the matter firmly in hand.

"It's as he says, m'lord. While ye were ill, yer tanist and the Reformed preacher forced yer lady to confess to witchcraft. She was tried yesterday. Even now, she's about to burn."

Niall swung his legs out of bed. "And when were ye to tell me? After her funeral?"

A wave of dizziness washed over him. He sucked in a steadying breath. With a superhuman effort, Niall fought it off then glanced back at the women. "Get out of here. Bring some men to help me down to the stables and have my stallion saddled. Iain," Niall said, summoning him over, "help me dress and be quick about it. There's not much time, and I've little strength to spare."

The next few minutes were filled with a flurry of activity. Two sturdy clansmen carried Niall down the stairs and from the keep, then helped him mount his horse. He swayed precariously for a moment; then righted himself. Iain swung up onto his own mount.

"Are ye sure ye can stay astride?" the younger man asked, a dubious look in his blue eyes. "Mayhap it'd be better to ride behind one of the men."

"Nay," Niall muttered, his face white, his lips clenched. "I must appear strong and sure when I arrive there. And I will, if it's my last act on this earth."

He signaled his horse. The animal sprang forward, across the cobblestoned bailey and out the main gate. Iain stared after him for a second, then urged his mount on. Niall's black stallion was fast, the finest piece of horseflesh in all of Campbell lands, and Iain was soon left behind.

Niall didn't know when he lost Iain and wouldn't have cared. All that mattered was that he reached Anne before it was too late. If he didn't . . . well, he'd kill Malcolm for sure and most likely Duncan too.

Malcolm was witch-crazed, obsessed with his single-minded persecution of any he suspected of the black magic. He'd never burn another person on Campbell lands, though. He'd likely not live long enough after today. And Duncan as clan tanist, acting in Niall's stead while he was ill, could've well prevented Anne's burning—*if* he had wished to. Why hadn't he?

The answer was too painful to consider, especially now when he needed all his strength to face what lay ahead. *Help me, Lord,* he thought in his rising desperation, turning to the only source of aid he had left. *I know I've been angry at Ye, turned my back on Ye, but in my heart of hearts I've always known Ye were there. Give me the strength now that I need. And don't let my Annie die. She's always been Yer loyal friend. If a life must be lost this day, let it be mine rather than Anne's. It's my pride and selfishness, after all, that's brought her to this. She's innocent, Lord. Innocent.*

With that, Niall urged his horse to its utmost limits, and they soon topped the hill leading to the village. From his vantage as they galloped down the other side, he could make out a large crowd gathered around the stake with smoke pouring from the fagots piled at its base.

Rage, white-hot and searing, surged through him. Strength, far beyond the capabilities of his weakened flesh, filled him. Blood pumped to his hardened muscles. His lungs heaved for air.

✢ ✢

The wild, fierce battle lust to fight and protect what he loved was Niall's only consideration. Raising a fist high over his head, he thundered into the village with the harsh Campbell battle cry on his lips.

"Cruachan!"

The people scattered before him. Niall slid to a halt at the base of the stake. A ring of fire and smoke encircled Anne. He could barely see her.

He leaped from his stallion and ran, flinging the flaming wood aside with his bare hands. With a few quick slashes from his dirk, Niall freed Anne.

She fell into his arms. With a strangled sob, Niall gathered her to him and quickly carried her from the fire.

Iain was at Niall's side in an instant more, his sword drawn. Together, the two men faced the crowd.

"Is she alive?" Iain asked without taking his eyes off the restless, churning mass of people.

"I don't know," Niall replied, his own gaze never wavering as he watched Malcolm and Duncan stride toward them. "I pray to God she is, or yer father and our cousin die this day."

"And ye, too, Niall Campbell," his companion shot at him through clenched teeth. "I warned ye about this verra—"

Anne moaned then coughed, moving restlessly in Niall's arms. Her eyes fluttered open. "N-Niall?"

He glanced down at her. "Aye, lass. It's me. Now hush. Save yer strength."

She sighed and again lost consciousness. The preacher and tanist halted before them.

"Ye've defied not only the laws of God, but of man," Malcolm screamed, ensuring that all assembled heard him, "when ye freed the witch from her just fate! Put her back, I say! Let the burning be finished!"

Niall took a menacing step forward. "Get out of my way, ye blackhearted fiend! If ye utter one more word, I'll cut out yer foul tongue, then burn *ye* at the stake!"

The man blanched. "And what crimes have I committed?" He gestured toward Anne. "She, on the other hand, has confessed, been tried, and sentenced. It's the law that she die."

"It's true, nephew."

Niall turned to face his uncle. "And what were her crimes? Were they so horrible ye couldn't have waited until I recovered?"

"She's bewitched ye! Only her burning would free ye of her spell. It was best not to wait."

Niall glared back at Duncan. "Tell me her crimes! Now!"

Duncan's gaze skittered briefly to that of Malcolm. "She admitted to being the Witch of Glenstrae and that she had brought a dead babe back to life."

For the longest moment Niall stared at his uncle, incredulity rendering him speechless. "And for that ye had her condemned?" he finally cried. "Ye're a fool, Duncan Campbell! Get out of my way! I'll deal with ye later."

As Niall turned to go, a big, burly villager stepped forward to block his way. Niall's gaze lifted to meet that of the taller man. "Will ye prevent me from leaving with my lady, Fergus?" he asked, his calm voice belying the coiled tension of his body. Beside him, Iain lifted his sword.

The peasant vehemently shook his head. "Nay, m'lord. Far from it. But ye look near to collapse yerself, and I'd offer my strong back to carry yer lady to yer horse."

Niall and Iain exchanged glances.

"I thank ye for yer loyalty, Fergus," Niall finally said. "And yer courage."

"It isn't courage, m'lord. It's good Scot's sense after what yer lady said. To heal others isn't an act of sorcery. And ye *had* condemned burnings on Campbell lands."

Niall smiled. "Aye, that I had." He stepped forward to lay Anne in the big Highlander's arms. "I'd be honored if ye'd aid me with m'lady."

Fergus's weathered face broke into a grin. "Thank ye, m'lord."

With that, he turned on his heel and faced the crowd massed before them. "Get on with ye!" he bellowed. "The day's entertainment's done. The Campbell's recovered and come for his lady. Do any of ye dispute his right to do so?"

"Nay, Fergus," a woman cried.

"Nor I, either!" Angus, the stable man, stepped forward. "The lass healed my wee Davie's hand. She's no more a witch than any woman here."

"Then out of my way!" Fergus roared as he plowed forward.

The people parted before him. Niall and Iain followed. Once Niall was remounted, Fergus carefully handed Anne's limp form to him. Iain gained his own horse's back. Without a backward glance, they rode from the village.

Behind them, Malcolm's enraged cries suddenly shattered the quiet. "Ye're bewitched, that ye are!" the preacher shrieked. "Ye've defied the law and must be punished! Ye're not fit, Niall Campbell, to be clan chief!"

By the time they returned to Kilchurn, Niall was past exhaustion. It was all he could do to hand Anne down to Iain without dropping her, and he did fall himself when he dismounted. Two clansmen were there to catch him and carry him up to his bedchamber. Iain followed behind with Anne.

The men lay Niall down on his bed. When Iain made a move to carry Anne to her room, Niall halted him. "Nay." He motioned his cousin back. "Bring her here. She'll lie by me. I don't want Anne out of my sight until I know she's recovered from this."

Iain scowled but obeyed. He laid her on the far side of the bed and was quickly pushed aside by Agnes.

"Caitlin, see to yer brother's needs," the old woman ordered.

While Caitlin hurried to Niall and began tugging his smoke-stained shirt loose from his trews, Agnes rolled Anne onto her side. She began unfastening her scorched dress then paused, as if suddenly aware of her audience. Agnes raised her eyes to scan Iain and the two clansmen.

"Out with ye, lads. It's woman's work now. We've no need of yer prying eyes."

"I want to stay," Iain protested, "until I know she's truly recovered."

"Ye heard Agnes," Niall growled from the bed. "As soon as Anne's settled and wakes, I'll send for ye."

Iain eyed him with frank suspicion. "I've yer oath on that?"

Niall shot him a thunderous glower. "Aye. Now get out."

The three men departed, and Agnes returned to her undressing of Anne. Though Anne's face and hands were smoke-blackened, a thorough inspection of her body, once she lay clad only in her shift, proved the fire hadn't touched her.

Niall fell back with a sigh of weary relief. *If one hair on her head had been harmed,* he thought with a blinding flash of anger, *I'd have risen from my bed at this verra moment and gone after Malcolm.* But God had answered his prayers and performed a miracle. A miracle not only in saving Anne's life, Niall realized as a deep sense of gratitude filled him, but a miracle in his own soul too. He would never forget, never turn his face from the Lord again.

As he watched with loving eyes, Agnes gently bathed Anne's arms and face, then dressed her in a snowy white nightgown. Just as the old woman finished tucking the comforter around her, Anne moaned.

Niall levered himself to one elbow and took her hand. "Annie?" he whispered, his voice rough with concern. "Can ye hear me? Open yer eyes, lass."

Her fragile, blue-veined lids lifted. Silver eyes gazed up at him. For a moment she stared at Niall in confusion, then recognition flared. Color bloomed in her pale face. She smiled, a soft, tender movement of her delicately curved mouth.

"Och, Niall," Anne breathed. "Ye're alive. I was so afraid for ye, yet could do naught." Her glance moved to encompass Caitlin and Agnes. "Thank ye, my friends, for doing what I couldn't. Ye've brought him back to me. I owe ye a debt I can never hope to repay."

Niall's glance followed hers. A dark brow arched in irony. "Mayhap they succeeded in saving my life, but they've yet to explain why they almost let ye die without telling me."

A small frown marred the smooth expanse of Anne's brow. She turned back to him. "There was naught they could do, my love. Duncan and Malcolm saw to that. And their first loyalty, as well it should be, was to ye. I made them promise to protect ye."

"Mayhap," Niall admitted, not sounding at all convinced. "Well, no matter. We can speak of it later. For now, I wish to know what happened to ye."

"And I need to tend yer hands, brother," Caitlin interjected, firmly taking a red, blistered palm in hers.

"Och, Niall," Anne murmured. She sat up and took the hand he had held in hers, turning it over. "How did this happen? Ye've burned yerself!"

He glanced from one woman to the other and grinned roguishly. "It's naught. I but singed them a bit getting through the fire. But if such action warrants this kind of attention, I'll be certain to take every opportunity that presents itself in the future."

Anne glanced up at Agnes. "Make a nettle tea and quick. It's too late to prevent the blistering, but compresses soaked in the tea will ease the pain and promote healing."

"Aye, m'lady," the maidservant said and hurried from the room.

"Caitlin." Anne turned to the girl. "Gather clean bandages and a bowl to soak Niall's hands in."

Caitlin nodded and sprang up, running off to find someone to help her with the task.

"Now, lass," Niall began warningly, "I don't think—"

"Hush, my love." Anne laid a gentle finger to his lips. "It's past time to worry what yer people think. I've already been condemned a witch. All our attempts to protect me by hiding my healer's skills have been for naught. I won't hide them again."

"I suppose ye're right." He sighed. "But I'll tell ye true, Annie. Though I believe my people are finally warming to ye, I don't know if we'll ever win over Malcolm. Or Duncan, either, for that matter." He shook his head. "By all that's holy, I don't understand what Duncan was about. But I intend to find out. And soon. *Verra* soon!"

She smiled, more glad than she cared to admit that Niall was finally beginning to see his uncle for the man he truly was. "Time enough for that later, my love. First, let me see to yer healing. It's all that matters to me."

He pulled her to him, careful to keep his burnt palms off her. "And all that matters to me is how to keep ye safe." His expression darkened, and a pained regret smoldered in his eyes. "Do ye know how I felt when I heard ye were to be burned? I was terrified I wouldn't make it in time, that I'd find ye dead, all black and blistered, just like I found Hugh's Dora the day they burnt her. I swear I don't know what I would've done if they'd killed ye."

Niall lowered his head to rest upon her shoulder. "Even now, I remember that awful fear, that sickening, helpless feeling in my gut. I even prayed to God, I did, to save ye."

"And He heard ye, didn't He? Ye must never forget that, or ever stop thanking Him for answering yer prayers."

"I won't, lass. I promise." He dragged in a shuddering breath. His voice broke. "Och, Annie, I don't know what I would've done without ye."

"My love, my love," she crooned, stroking his head. "It's all right. I'm safe. I won't leave ye."

He was silent for a long moment. "But mayhap ye should, lass." Niall looked up, his eyes glittering with tears. "I should send ye away."

A chill silence engulfed Anne and, from deep within it, her heart hammered in pain and fear. Pain, that it should finally come to this.

Fear, that in the doing, it might eventually sever the bonds between them. She clamped her eyes shut and fiercely shook her head.

"Nay," she moaned. "Don't ask it of me, not now, not when I've just gotten ye back. Must we speak of it? Mayhap in time, when our heads and hearts are clearer, our strength returned, but not now."

"Ye're right," he whispered hoarsely. "Time enough in a day or so, when things have had a chance to calm. But not now. I'll know, however," he continued, his voice taking on an ominous edge, "what happened to ye since I became ill. I must have the facts, and I don't want ye protecting anyone. Do ye understand me, lass?"

Anne nodded then inhaled a steadying breath. "When Ena came to help me when ye turned ill, they threw her in the dungeon . . ."

By the time she was finished with her tale, Niall was white with barely repressed fury. Anne reached out to him. "Och, Niall," she said, choking on a sob, "how can there be such evil in the world?"

"The evil that only a narrow-minded, misguided group of men in the name of religion can foster," he snarled, taking her in his arms. "A group that long ago lost sight of God's message of love and tolerance." Niall hesitated, dreading the answer even as he needed to ask it. "Did they torture ye, lass?"

"Nay, though they threatened it when I refused to admit to all the lies spread about me. In the end, Duncan was satisfied with the meager confession I signed."

"Aye." Niall laughed bitterly. "That poorest of excuses for a confession. What I still can't fathom is the depth of my uncle's animosity toward ye, to condemn ye on such feeble grounds. Malcolm, I can well understand. In his own way, he's as crazed as Hugh."

"Do ye think all of this is mayhap tied with the traitor? It'd seem—" Anne leaned back from him, excitement threading her voice. "Nelly!" she cried. "When she brought me my supper last eve, she spoke of a traitor, of working for him. She was the one who put the foxglove in yer food at the traitor's behest. Och, Niall, find Nelly and get the truth from her! She knows who the traitor is!"

Caitlin walked in at that moment, a bowl and some bandages in her hands. Niall struggled to a sitting position. "Get Iain in here! Hurry, lass. Now!"

The startled girl rushed back from the room. An instant later Iain, who must have been waiting close by, entered, Caitlin on his heels.

He headed straight for Anne and knelt beside her, taking her hand in his. "Are ye all right, lady?" he asked, his voice taut with emotion. "I came as soon as I received yer message, but still I feared—"

With a supreme effort, Niall shoved his surge of jealousy aside. For the moment at least, there were more pressing matters. "Enough, Iain! Go and fetch Nelly. I must speak with her posthaste!"

"And what's so important about Nelly," Iain demanded, "that I can't have the moment ye promised to talk with Anne?"

When Anne made a move to speak, Niall shot her a warning glance. He turned back to Iain. "Why I want Nelly doesn't concern ye." He forced his voice to calm. "Suffice it to say, it's of great import. Will ye fetch her?"

The blond man rose and rendered him a stiff bow. "Aye, m'lord. Ye're still chief. I must obey." He glanced at Caitlin. "Come with me, lass. I may need yer help."

Iain stalked from the room. Caitlin shot Niall a puzzled glance then once more hurried out. Anne watched the pair leave, noting the rigid set of Iain's shoulders and proud lift of his head.

She sighed. "Was it necessary to be so harsh with him? Iain has been a loyal friend. If not for his aid, would ye have succeeded in yer rescue of me?"

"Nay," Niall admitted, "and I'll see to his reward in due time. But I still daren't trust him. He threatened to kill me again today if ye died."

"And isn't that but the heated emotions of youth? He's concerned for me, Niall. That, and naught more."

"Why did ye send for him?"

She gave a wry laugh. "Isn't that evident? With ye as ill as ye were, there was no one powerful enough in Kilchurn to stop Duncan and Malcolm. Iain was our only hope."

"Of late he seems more able to care for ye than I," Niall muttered. "Mayhap ye'd be better off with him."

Anne smiled. "Do ye realize how like the jealous lover ye sound? Truly, *are* ye jealous?"

A pair of penetrating eyes leveled on her. "It's hard not to be when yer affection for Iain's so apparent."

"And can't a woman have a man as friend?"

"More than friendship burns in Iain's heart for ye!"

She returned his hard stare. "I do naught to foster that."

Niall sighed. "I know, Annie. But love isn't the most logical of emotions. Leastwise, not when it comes to me."

A piercing sweetness flooded Anne. "Are ye saying then, that ye love me, Niall Campbell?" She propped herself on an elbow.

His brow crinkled in puzzlement. "Of course. Surely ye knew?"

Anne fell back upon the bed, her eyes rolling in exasperation. "And how, pray tell, was I to know? Ye've never spoken the words, and I'm no seer. Och, ye're the most thick-skulled dolt of a man I've ever had the misfortune to know!"

He grinned roguishly and slid close to her. His long fingers stroked her cheek. "I must be rising in yer estimation," he said, his voice low and husky. "I'm no longer pigheaded now, only thick-skulled."

Her eyes filled with tears. "Don't mock me, Niall. It's too important."

His lips lowered to brush the sweet curve of her mouth. "Aye," he whispered. "It *is* too important. Ye're everything to me. I love ye, Annie lass, with all my heart."

As if searching for confirmation of his words, for a long moment her moisture-bright eyes scanned his face. Then the tears spilled over. Her lips moved to his. "Och, Niall," she cried. "My love!"

She kissed him hungrily. Beneath her fingers, she felt his chest muscles leap reflexively, then draw taut and hard.

‡ ‡

With a groan, Niall drew her to him, his mouth slanting fiercely back and forth over Anne's. She came to vibrant life in his arms, everything intensified by the terror of the past days. A thick, sensual haze engulfed her.

Niall seemed equally out of control. Seemingly insensitive to the pain, his burned hand moved, slid down her arm.

At his touch, Anne regained her senses. Any minute now, Iain and Caitlin would be returning with Nelly, not to mention there was the equally imminent arrival of Agnes. "N-Niall," she gasped, wrenching her mouth from his. "We must stop. Iain will be here—"

As if the words had conjured him, the young Highlander flung open the door and stalked in. His face was pale, his mouth grim. And he was alone.

With an exasperated sigh, Niall rolled away from Anne and sat up against the pillows. "I send ye on a simple errand to bring me a serving maid, and ye come back empty-handed. Why did ye bother to return without Nelly?"

Iain halted before Niall. His gaze was intense yet tinged with a strange horror. "Och, I found her all right," he rasped. "But she was dead."

"What?" Every muscle in Niall's body went rigid. "What did ye say?"

"Nelly's dead, her neck broken," Iain said. "I can't be certain when it happened, but from the stiffness of her body . . ." He paused to shoot Anne an apologetic glance. "I'd say it was late last night. Do ye realize the strength it'd take," he continued with a brutal frankness, "to break a woman's neck with yer bare hands? It requires a verra powerful man and, most likely even then, a madness would have to be upon him."

Iain eyed Niall with a cold, unwavering look. "Ye, m'lord, have a verra serious problem."

19

Anne gave a small cry and buried her face in her hands. "Och, nay! Poor Nelly. She came to me last night, and I saw the bruises on her face. She said he'd beaten her, but I never thought he'd kill her!" She lifted tear-filled eyes to Niall. "What are we to do?"

"Ye speak as if ye know who Nelly's murderer is," Iain cut in. "Who is he, Anne? And why did he kill her?"

"Iain—" she began.

"Nay, lass." Niall held her in the iron grip of his dark gaze. "She doesn't know, and neither do I," he said, turning to his cousin. "We were about to find that out from Nelly."

"But ye and she both know *why* Nelly was killed, don't ye?" Iain persisted. "And, somehow, Anne's welfare is tied in with it."

Niall clamped down on an angry retort. "The welfare of the entire clan's tied in with it. But, for the time being, I don't wish to speak further of this. Leave us."

The blond man faltered in the silence that engulfed them, a bewildered expression on his face. "The welfare of the clan? What are ye talking about? What's going on?"

Niall's rugged features tightened in anger. "Leave us, Iain!"

Anne laid a hand on Niall's arm, a silent entreaty in her eyes. She glanced up at Iain. "Do as he says, Iain. Please leave us."

His stormy countenance swung from Anne to Niall, then back.

Iain bowed low to her. "As ye wish, m'lady." He shot Niall one last, furious glare and left the room.

Niall rounded on her. "Ye'd no right to interfere. What's between us is ours to settle. Don't ever—"

"Ye're no longer so certain Iain's yer traitor, are ye?"

He paused, then sighed. "After all that's transpired in the past few days, nay, lass, I'm not. Leastwise, I'm not so certain he's alone in this. Malcolm, or even Duncan, may have a hand in the treachery as well."

"Or even be the ones solely responsible for it." Anne frowned in thoughtful consideration. "And what of Hugh? He may also be helping from the outside."

"Aye, there's Hugh to consider as well." Niall's fist pounded the bed beside him. "The suspicions are eating me alive! Not only has the traitor or a henchman tried to kill me several times, but he's now murdering others within my own castle. And I no longer even have the certainty of knowing who it is!"

"Iain wasn't even here in time to kill Nelly."

"Aye," Niall agreed, "if he was ever at Balloch to begin with. Though I begin to have second thoughts regarding Iain, I still cannot discount all the possibilities." He shifted to a more comfortable position. "Think about it, Anne. That day I sent him away, I was shot with the quarrel. Iain could've still been here, fired the crossbow from the forest. And he could have remained here, using Nelly to poison me, and then when she began to have second thoughts, killed her.

"Nay," he said, "Iain's fortuitous arrival to rescue ye may have been as well planned as everything else he did. One thing *is* a certainty. He never meant to let ye die. He wants ye for himself. But he may have needed to make it look like he'd just come from Balloch, to divert suspicion from himself when Nelly's body was found."

"A clever plan, indeed," Anne agreed softly. "Yet if Iain isn't the traitor, how much more clever is the real one to divert suspicion so skillfully to others? Don't blind yerself because of yer unreasoning jealousy. Think ye on that, Niall Campbell."

Perhaps it was his utter weariness, or the stress of the past few hours, but at her words something snapped in Niall. "And mayhap I wouldn't be so unreasonably jealous," he growled, grasping her arm, "if ye weren't so constantly and ardently defending him! Think ye on that, lady."

It was too much, after all Iain had done for them. Anne was barely able to contain the stinging retort that rose to her lips. Then reason filled her. They were both at the limits of their endurance. This wasn't the time to push the matter further.

Agnes bustled in with the nettle tea. Anne glanced at her and forced a smile. "The Campbell's ready for his hands to be tended. Do ye know what needs to be done?"

A small frown wrinkled Agnes's brow as, for the first time, she seemed to note the sudden tension in the room. "Aye, m'lady."

Gently, Anne pried Niall's fingers loose from her arm. "Good. I'll leave ye to his care. I've a need for some private time, as I'm certain," she added meaningfully, "does the Campbell himself."

With Niall's wrathful gaze burning into her, Anne rose and headed for her room.

◆

Anne slipped from her bedchamber and quietly, ever so carefully, closed the door. It was well past midnight. Kilchurn was shrouded in silence and sleep. Even the guard stationed outside her door since her return from the stake was snoring soundly.

For the span of an inhaled breath Anne hesitated, her courage deserting her. The decision to seek out Iain in his bedchamber had been supremely difficult. The consequences if Niall found her there were terrifying. Not only had she given him her word she'd not meet privately with Iain anymore and was now about to break that word, risking Niall's anger and the loss of his love, but she also endangered Iain's life as well.

In the end, however, it was all for Niall anyway, whether he ever understood or accepted it. Though the common people seemed finally to be warming to her, little had changed in Kilchurn in the past week since her rescue. If anything, thanks to Duncan and Malcolm, the situation was worsening. It was time to take matters into her own hands.

With that resolve to bolster her, Anne gathered her skirts and quietly made her way down the hall. Someone, and Anne was convinced it was either Malcolm or Duncan, had notified the queen of Niall's flagrant disregard for the law. Even now, a royal representative was on his way from Edinburgh to judge the facts and report back to Queen Mary. Niall risked losing his chieftainship, if not his life, should the findings go against him. And, until a royal judgment had been made, Niall's hands were tied when it came to Malcolm and Duncan.

In the meantime he was besieged with local officials and various Campbell lairds. All protested the course of recent events, already magnified beyond reason by rumor and speculation. Though Niall had managed to turn aside most accusations and dispel many of the false tales, sending the majority of his lairds back home satisfied with the true facts, the grumblings and unhappiness continued. Anne could see it in the faces of some of the castle servants, many of the clansmen, and, most especially, in Duncan's eyes.

His animosity had evolved into outright hatred, a hatred he made little attempt to hide. Even Caitlin, who spent many hours with Anne each day filling her in on the current state of affairs, was distressed by her uncle's unbridled rancor. The girl would pour out her heart to Anne, hurt, unable to understand what was happening.

Before her very eyes, Anne saw the Campbells being split into factions, one turned against the other. And all, it seemed, because of her. Though she was innocent of cause, it mattered not. It was tearing Niall apart.

He had avoided her ever since they argued that day. Though he was still angry over her defense of Iain, she refused to ignore his continued unfairness toward the younger man. It broke her heart to be yet another source of pain and problem to Niall, but what was she to do? Accept a wrong being perpetrated upon an innocent man? Watch Niall make a monumental error in judgment and not stand up to him over it?

She couldn't do that. To ignore a wrong went against everything Anne was and believed in. And she'd never betray her principles, not even for love.

Yet love, in the end, was what was leading her down the darkened corridors toward the room of a man whom she had promised Niall she'd not speak to, much less visit alone. But what choice was there? Anne well knew Niall's stubborn pride. He'd fight until he was overcome and destroyed. And that destruction now seemed imminent if something wasn't done soon.

She would leave Niall, go back to her people. For some reason, Duncan had made her the focal point of all the dissension. For some reason, he seemed to fear her because of her growing relationship with Niall. In her absence, she hoped at least that particular conflict would die. Niall's jealousy would also end, and he'd be able to separate Iain's desire for her from the possibility his motivations were that of a traitor.

Without those additional issues to distract him, Niall could at last turn all his efforts to discovering the real traitor, to strengthening his precarious position as Campbell chief. Perhaps he might finally even give Duncan's possible involvement greater scrutiny. It certainly seemed that he was beginning to do so. And perhaps the witch fever Malcolm continued to stir would also calm. Indeed, what would anyone care about a witch who was no longer among them?

Thanks to Caitlin inadvertently revealing its location one day, Iain's room was easy to find. It was a lucky thing she had. Anne dared not ask anyone about it or Niall would've known soon thereafter. Iain was the only one she could trust not to go to Niall. Iain, though his ultimate motives might differ, would help.

She reached his room. Before she could lose any more of her courage, Anne tried the latch. Though she hated sneaking in to wake Iain, it was better than risking possible notice by tarrying in the hall and knocking at the door. Blessedly, the latch opened. Anne slipped inside.

For a moment she stood there, searching out the bed in the dimly lit chamber. A sudden thought assailed her. What if Iain weren't alone and had taken some serving maid to his bed? Anne hesitated then decided to move closer before she woke him. If he had a companion, she'd leave as quietly as she had come.

Only one body lay in the bed. Anne touched Iain's bare shoulder. He flipped over and grabbed her arm. Before she could cry out, she was wrenched up against him, a dirk's blade pressed to her throat.

"Who sent ye," Iain rasped in her ear, "and what do ye want?"

Anne froze, the knife too dangerously close to dare struggle. "It—it's me, Iain," she whispered. "Anne."

"Anne?" The blade lowered, and he turned her face to his. "By mountain and sea, Anne," he groaned. "What are ye doing here? If Niall finds us . . ."

"I know, Iain." She shoved herself to a sitting position. "I wouldn't have come if I didn't need yer help. I don't know what else to do."

He levered himself up and resheathed his dirk. The comforter fell away, the flickering firelight revealing a muscled expanse of broad, lightly haired chest and taut abdomen. She flushed and averted her gaze.

Iain saw her embarrassed movement and smiled. "Would ye like me to dress?"

Anne jerked her glance back to him. "Nay. There's no time. What I have to say, I must say quickly and leave. It's too dangerous for me to linger."

"What do ye want from me, lass?"

A lump rose in her throat, but she forced her words past it. "I want to leave Niall and go back to my people. Will ye help me do that, Iain?"

"Why, Anne? Why do ye want to leave Niall?"

"Because I'm a danger to him, even to the possible loss of his life. He won't willingly let me go, so I must do it for him."

"I could take ye to Balloch Castle," he offered softly. "I would protect ye from him."

Anne shook her head. "Nay, Iain. It'd only make matters worse. I'll hurt Niall enough in the leaving. I won't hurt him in that way, too. I ask only that ye make arrangements for an escort for me back to Castle Gregor."

"I can do that." He frowned. "It'll be difficult getting ye out of Kilchurn unnoticed, though. Niall has ye watched at all times now, for fear of further harm befalling ye. How did ye manage to slip from bed without him waking?"

She lowered her head. "We've always slept apart."

"Aye." He gave a harsh laugh. "Most likely a result of fighting about me."

"That isn't why, but it doesn't really matter. I can't stand by and watch Niall go to his destruction. Will ye help me or not?"

Iain nodded. "Aye, ye know I will, lass. I'll send ye a message when the arrangements are made. Be ready. It could well come at a moment's notice." He paused. "The difficult part is still how to get ye out of Kilchurn."

"It isn't a problem. I know a way. Just tell me where we'll meet, and I'll be there. And, Iain," she said, touching his arm, "ye're not to go with me. Niall mustn't suspect ye're involved in this."

"And do ye think I care what he thinks? Besides, he already knows my feelings on the matter."

"But he won't be sure ye were involved if ye're here and I'm gone. I'll leave him a letter, making it appear I managed it all myself. That I sent word to my father and it was MacGregors who were waiting to take me away. Ye've only to find men who can keep our secret. Can ye do that?"

Iain leaned back and nodded. "Aye. I know a few, enough to get ye safely home."

Anne rose from the bed. "Good. I must go now, Iain."

He stayed her with a light touch on her arm. "Anne."

She glanced down at him lying there, a golden-haired young warrior. "Aye?"

"In time, may I come to visit ye?"

"Ye're my friend, Iain. Ye'll always be my friend."

His blue eyes darkened. "And Niall will always be yer love? Is that it?"

She gave a sad little nod. "Aye."

From a shadowed doorway, he watched Anne leave Iain's room. What good fortune that he had come upon her, just as she was sneaking into the lad's bedchamber.

Something was afoot, and no mistake. They'd both require some close watching in the next day or two. One way or another, though, their clandestine meeting this night would serve him well. One way or another, he'd turn it to his own advantage.

Niall strode into his bedchamber and flung himself into one of the hearth chairs. Ah, but he was weary! The day had begun badly as it was, and the arrival of the queen's envoy had only made it worse. After the initial flurry of preparing accommodations and seeing to his needs, it had been necessary to spend long hours with the man, addressing all the charges brought against him. Not surprisingly, Malcolm had been his accuser.

He thought the inquiry had gone well, that the royal envoy had been satisfied with his answers. The final decision, however, rested in the hands of the queen. It was all that prevented him from banishing Malcolm from Campbell lands. Niall smiled grimly. For a time more he must be patient, but once he had received official absolution of the crimes brought against him. . .

If everything went as he hoped, in but a matter of days Niall would be free of at least one of the thorns in his side. Just one of many, he reminded himself, but it was still progress of a sort.

The arrival of the last of his warriors sent out on the secret mission had only added to the day's stress. None had returned with any useful information. There seemed to be no true disloyalty among his lairds. Normally, that would've been the best of news, but not now. Now, he desperately wanted to find the traitor outside Kilchurn.

Hugh remained somewhere in the mountains near Ben Cruachan. His cousin ran with a group of outlaws who appeared content with periodic cattle raids upon nearby crofts. In time, Niall would see to their capture. But not now. Now, it was enough Hugh stayed far from Kilchurn and made no overt attempts against him.

If only he could catch the traitor in a false move. Even Duncan was now kept at arm's length, after a heated argument over his ruthless persecution of Anne. Though the tanist claimed he was borne along on the tide of law and religion in condemning Anne—and regretted it deeply—Niall found the act hard to forgive. His uncle's actions had heightened his suspicions about the man's true motives, motives that might well include treachery. For all practical purposes, Niall was now alienated from every close male member of his family.

Aye, he mused glumly, *and alienated from Anne as well.* The continuing dilemma of her loyalty to Iain, over what Niall saw as her expected commitment to him, ate at him. Now, more than ever, he wanted her, needed her love.

Her stubborn devotion to his cousin, however, was more than Niall could bear. He knew he was being an irrational, jealous fool, knew his feelings were clouding his judgment, but why couldn't she understand and be there for him when he needed her most? Aye, needed her most of all while he fought through this quagmire of doubts and suspicions.

He knew it was his pride that, in the end, kept him from her. He was the one at fault, not her. Yet it seemed his pride was sometimes all he had left these days.

His mouth quirked wryly. Perhaps he put far too much store in his pride, if it kept him from the woman he loved. It had kept him once from God as well, when his anger and pain at losing his first Anne had driven him from obedience to a Creator who could allow such a tragedy to occur. In the doing, he had let his life become bereft of God and the peace and joy he had once had. Would he let his foolish pride now also drive away Anne?

Niall rose from his chair, his long, lithe strides carrying him across the bedchamber and down the corridor in a matter of seconds. Before he lost courage, he must speak with Anne. Before his pride once again seized hold, he must humble himself, beg her forgiveness.

She wasn't, however, in her bedchamber. Niall frowned. Where could she be? It was nearly time for the supper meal. Mayhap she was already below, awaiting him in the Great Hall.

He turned to leave when a bit of parchment on the table just inside her bedchamber door caught his eye. His name, in Anne's feathery scrawl, was written upon a small scroll sealed with red wax. As he picked up the letter and broke it open, uneasiness coiled within him. How strange that Anne would choose such a manner to communicate with him.

Niall, twice before I begged ye to let me return to my people. I ask ye no longer. His eyes narrowed to glittering slits. *Even now I am on my way home, my clansmen having come for me. It's over between us. I beseech ye, don't follow. It's better I'm gone from yer life.*

The letter was signed simply "Anne." Niall groaned and threw back his head, his eyes clenched in pain. The parchment crumpled in his fist.

How could she do this to him? How could she be so cruel, so hard-hearted? It wasn't like her . . .

His eyes snapped open. Nay, it wasn't like Anne at all. Someone had surely said something to frighten her or convince her she was saving him by sacrificing their love. A fury smoldering within, Niall pondered all possibilities—and alighted on the most obvious culprit.

Iain. It had to be Iain. Who else would she listen to? And who else but Iain desperately wanted her to leave?

With a harsh cry, Niall stormed from the room. He paused only long enough to send the guard to gather more men, ordering him to bring them to Iain's bedchamber. Then Niall strode off.

For a brief moment he considered going back for his sword, then decided his dirk would be more than adequate. He wouldn't give his cousin opportunity to attack. He'd strike first to win the advantage.

He paused outside Iain's bedchamber to withdraw his dirk, then walked in without knocking. Iain was sitting by the fire, a book in his hands. Seemingly not at all surprised at Niall's arrival, Iain calmly closed the volume and laid it aside. His gaze when he looked up at Niall was cool, unperturbed.

Niall's temper exploded. He advanced on Iain. Grabbing the front of his shirt, he pulled his cousin to his feet and pressed the dirk to his throat. Iain tensed but said nothing.

Niall pushed the knife a little deeper. Blood welled at the blade's tip, trickling down Iain's neck and chest to stain his shirt. He still didn't move.

"How long?" Niall demanded hoarsely. "How long ago did she leave?" He pulled the dirk back a little.

"Two hours," came the terse reply.

Niall cursed. "Why did ye do it? Why couldn't ye leave Anne and me be? Ye've finally gone too far, cousin. Now ye haven't even Annie's influence to protect ye!"

"Do ye think I care?" Iain snarled in reply. "Anne's safe now. From Malcolm, my father, and most of all, from ye. She was in more danger from ye than from them, for ye professed to care for her, to protect her, and didn't. Yer selfish needs blinded ye to her danger, and always will. I'm glad I helped her escape and naught, *naught* ye can do to me will change that!"

Something inside Niall shattered, severing his emotions from all rational control. *Kill him!* a voice screamed inside his head. *Kill him! End his life once and for all! End at least one of yer problems with one clean thrust of yer blade. Then Anne can come back and all will be well . . .*

The sound of the guards rushing into the room wrenched Niall from his violent thoughts. His rage-clouded vision cleared. Once again he saw before him his cousin, a man who refused to lift a hand to defend himself. To ram the dirk home now would be murder. No matter what Iain might ultimately be—a traitor, a murderer—Niall was neither.

He removed the blade from Iain's throat and shoved him back into his chair. "Ye won't escape yer well-deserved punishment. It's only delayed until I return with Anne." Niall motioned to the guards, secretly pleased by the spark of anger that flared in Iain's eyes at his mention of bringing back Anne. "Take my cousin down to the dungeon and clamp him in chains," he ordered his men. "I'll deal with him later."

Iain leaped to his feet. If not for the drawn swords instantly pointed at him, he would've attacked Niall. As it was, his powerfully muscled form trembled with barely suppressed rage as he permitted himself to be bound.

He'd not allow the guards to lead him away, however, without firing some parting words. "Ye've also gone too far, *cousin*!" Iain cried. "This won't set well with the clan. Beware yer followers, for ye may soon have none to lead!"

All the doubts about Iain flooded Niall with renewed force. He gave a harsh laugh. "Spoken like a true traitor." He signaled the guards. "His presence sickens me. Remove him from my sight!"

✦

Their band had gotten a late start. Before departing Campbell lands, Anne had paid Ena one last visit. The old healer was well, recovered from her terrifying stay in Kilchurn's dungeons. Their farewell had been tearful, for neither knew if they'd ever see each other again.

Now, the day was edging toward twilight. Anne's gaze moved to the setting sun. They had been on the road two hours and had at least another two more before reaching Castle Gregor. It would be well into the night before she arrived home.

Anne glanced at the men riding with her. There were four of them, all "broken men" from other clans who had pledged their loyalty to Iain in return for the protection of the Campbell name. As one of Niall's under chieftains, Iain possessed considerable power and resources of his own. Yet Anne couldn't help but worry about him. When pushed far enough, Niall could have a fearsome temper. And Iain would never back down.

With a small shudder, she shoved the anxiety aside. There was naught more she could do to ease the rivalry between them, save leave them both. That in itself might be all that was needed. She hoped, she prayed, that it would be so.

Once again, Anne glanced toward the mountains. Amid a wild landscape, Ben Cruachan towered over the land. Its lower slopes were heavily wooded, thinning as the elevation rose to bare and lumpy crags, the summit split into two cones. The mountain exerted a vital, powerful influence over Campbell lands—bold, proud, compelling. So much, she realized with a bittersweet pang, like the dark man she was leaving behind.

She loved Niall, would always love him. But Anne wasn't certain there could ever be a life for them together. Mayhap in time things might settle down, tempers and unreasoning fears might fade. But that could also be a long while from now.

Niall was a virile, lusty man in his prime. He could well tire of waiting and take another wife. Their handfasting only bound them for a year, less than ten months more. And Anne knew how badly Niall desired an heir.

Tears, maddeningly frequent of late, filled her eyes. There was nothing else she could do. If she must give him up to save him, so be it. Her love could do no less. It was enough that he lived. It had to be.

Up ahead, the cry of a sparrow hawk rent the silent evening. From behind them came an answering cry. Her companions exchanged troubled glances, reining in their mounts. Unease spiraled through Anne. There was something not quite right . . .

The thunder of horses pounding over the hills bordering the road filled the air, mingling with harsh shouts and battle cries. Iain's men closed in around her, drawing their swords. Then, in a clash of horseflesh and metal, the attackers, twenty strong, were upon them.

Screams of pain as blades cut into living flesh, squeals of terrified horses, rose to engulf Anne in a horrifying cacophony. Her companions fought bravely to protect her, taking down an impressive number of the enemy before finally falling to the overwhelming odds. Almost before it had begun, the battle was over.

Anne sat there on her horse, alone amid the carnage, her traveling gown splattered with blood. She swung her gaze around the band of men encircling her. From the plaids they wore, they were Campbells, but not ones she recognized. What did they want from her? Indeed, who were they?

The sound of another rider drawing up behind her sent a premonitory prickle through Anne. There was a malevolence emanating from him so tangible, it was almost as if he had run his finger down her spine. She stiffened, dreading the confrontation to come. Slowly, she turned in her saddle.

"So, we meet again, witch." Hugh Campbell chuckled. "And once more ye're totally at my mercy." He motioned to Anne. "Bind her. We must be off. It's too dangerous to linger so near Kilchurn."

She unsheathed her bodice knife. "Kill me now, Hugh. I'll not go with ye. Let me die with these brave lads and be done with it."

"And spare ye the torment I've planned for ye this night?" He grinned, his glance skimming her slender form. "I think not. I've a taste to know yer witch's charms before I kill ye. Ye're a special lass to have enchanted a man such as Niall Campbell. I'll know the reason why." He backed his mount away. "Take her."

Four burly warriors closed in on Anne. She slashed out as the nearest one grabbed for her, leaving a deep gash in his arm. He cursed and drew back, clutching the wound.

Another arm snaked about her waist, nearly unseating her. Anne wheeled, her dagger arcing toward her newest attacker. She had meant only a glancing cut, but the man leaned forward at the last moment. The blade went deep into the outlaw's gut.

With a strangled cry, he loosened her and toppled from his mount, her dagger still embedded in his belly. Anne stared down at him, horrified at what she had done. The momentary distraction was all the advantage the others needed.

One grabbed her by the hair, dragging her off her horse. Another two leaped down to pin her roughly to the ground, wrenching her arms behind her to bind them tightly. In the next instant, she was jerked back to her feet.

Hugh rode up. "Ye'll pay for that, wench! I don't sell the lives of my men cheaply. When I'm done with ye, each and every one will have ye in turn. Then I'll slowly, but ever so thoroughly, choke yer life away."

"Never!" she cried. "Never, do ye hear me! I'll kill myself before I let that happen!"

A cruel smile touched his lips. "And when will ye have that opportunity, devil's handmaiden? We'll guard that precious life of yers with our own. Until, of course, we're done with ye. Come, let us be gone!" Hugh cried.

Turning his horse, he galloped off over the hills, headed toward Ben Cruachan. Anne was lifted into the arms of a nearby man, her mount left standing where it was. In a flurry of hoofbeats and choking dust, the outlaw band headed out after its leader.

She glanced over her shoulder. Behind her twelve bodies, all dressed in Campbell plaids, were sprawled bloody and lifeless on the ground. And nearby, heedless of the slaughter, her horse moved to graze upon a succulent patch of grass.

✦

Niall, accompanied by one of his warriors, raced his horse down the road. He had kept up the frantic pace for well over an hour. From the spacing of the hoof prints in the dirt ahead, he knew he should soon overtake Anne's much slower party. Though there were four men with her to their two, if the need arose, he felt confident they could physically overpower them. He only hoped it wouldn't come to that. He dreaded endangering Anne in a fight.

As they crested the next hill, an unnatural stillness lay upon the scene that greeted them. Bodies were scattered on the ground. In the deepening twilight, the distance made it difficult to make out form or gender. With his heart in his throat, Niall urged his stallion on, checking his speed only when he reached the bodies.

His horse skidded to a halt. Niall was off its back in an instant. He ran from one corpse to the next, quickly ascertaining Anne wasn't among them. Relief surged through him. He began to examine the bodies more closely. Four he recognized as Iain's men. The other eight he knew as men he had banished as outlaws. In the belly of one, Niall found Anne's dagger.

"Ye little wildcat," he whispered in admiration. He withdrew the knife and wiped its blood-stained blade clean on the grass. "Keep fighting them, Annie. I'm coming."

Niall slipped her dagger into his belt and swung onto his horse, readjusting the claymore hanging at his back. His clansman quirked a questioning brow.

"Their track leads toward Ben Cruachan," Niall said. "Return to Kilchurn and bring a party of forty men back on this trail. I'm riding on."

"But they're a large group, m'lord," his warrior protested. "At least ten or more men. Even ye cannot take on that many alone."

"If luck's with me," Niall muttered grimly, "I won't have to. But I don't know who has the Lady Anne, so I can't be certain what sort of danger she's in. I must go on. Now off with ye," he commanded, "and don't waste an extra moment in returning. I'll need yer help soon enough, one way or another."

"Aye, m'lord." The man reined his horse about and galloped back in the direction of Kilchurn.

Niall watched as he disappeared over the hill, then urged his own mount onward. Two hours' time would be lost before his men arrived again at this spot. And, from the looks of things here, the outlaws had at least a half-hour lead. Time was against him. Time and the unknown enemy who now had Anne.

Anne paced the confines of the small tower room, anxiously casting about for any means of escape. The narrow slit of window precluded its use. The room's single door was bolted from the outside. At the base of the winding stairs was a guard, with the rest of Hugh's men camped outside.

She ground her teeth in frustration. So many obstacles to overcome, each one nearly impassible in its own right. And so little time left before Hugh came for her.

They had ridden up into the mountains for well over an hour before arriving at the ancient stone tower. The repairs inside, however, were of a more recent nature. Anne wondered if this was the boyhood haunt of Niall, Iain, and Hugh. It would explain Hugh's use of it now to carry out his depraved revenge against her.

Anne halted at the door, a sudden thought assailing her. How had Hugh learned of her journey back to Castle Gregor? She knew Iain would've never betrayed her, and the preparations had all been made in secret. Had someone seen them leave and sent a message to Hugh? Or had some spy overheard Iain as he made the arrangements?

In the end, it didn't matter. She was now the prisoner of a madman.

Iain had said there was a madman in Kilchurn, that day he had discovered Nelly's body. Was Hugh that madman? He hated Niall. Had *he* mayhap been manipulating Nelly from the outside to do his will?

✝ ✝

Fear roiled through Anne. Niall was in terrible danger, and there was nothing she could do to warn him. Nothing indeed, she realized with a sudden surge of impotent anger. Nothing . . . but die at the hands of a witch-crazed traitor.

She sagged against the door. What had she ever done to deserve this? How had she sinned, to escape one horrible death only to fall prey to an even more gruesome one?

The burning at least would've been quick, if excruciatingly painful. But to be ravished by Hugh and all of his men before being murdered was an even more fearsome fate. At the stake, Anne still had her dignity, but even that would be stripped from her before this eve was done. Och, but she hated being so helpless, so . . .

The sound of someone climbing the stone staircase echoed hollowly in the tower. Anne lunged back from the door. Once more she scanned the room for a sign of a weapon, for hope of escape. There was none. Save for a threadbare bed, the chamber was empty.

The door unlocked with a metallic clank and swung open to reveal Hugh standing there. Anne held her ground, refusing to cower before him. Defiance flashed in her eyes.

Hugh momentarily faltered. Then the old madness crept into his eyes. "Yer spells will serve ye poorly this eve, witch!" He held up a small bag hanging from his neck. "I've an amulet to protect me." Hugh waggled the sack before her eyes and laughed.

He shut and locked the door, then dangled the key from his finger as he faced her. "Do ye want this, lassie? Well, come and take it." He slid it beneath the belt that bound his trews.

As Hugh advanced, Anne backed away until she stood beside the bed. She inhaled a steadying breath. She must confront him, must get the key. If that required touching him, letting him get close to her, then she would. She'd do whatever it took to get that key. He'd quickly discover she was no fearful maid.

Her hand moved toward him, toward the belt. A strange, excited light gleamed in his eyes. He captured her hand and twisted it roughly behind her, then grabbed her other arm and pulled it behind her as well.

"Did ye think ye'd get the key so easily, my beauteous little witch?"

His head lowered to hers. His hot breath wafted across her face. Anne fought back a surge of nausea. Hugh's body moved closer, pressing into hers.

She froze. Everything that was in her screamed to get away from him, but she forced herself to stand totally still. If she fought too hard, she'd never have a chance at the key. And the key was everything—her one hope of freedom.

Hugh chuckled, a cold edge of irony in his voice. "Ye're just like all the others. Ye'll sell yer soul to get what ye want. Only this time, the devil's in league with me. It's all part of our plan. Yer death will begin the feud anew. Niall will finally fall."

His mouth descended, grinding brutally, painfully, over hers. At the same time, he levered himself against her, forcing Anne off balance. An icy, awful fear shot through her. She fought to maintain her footing, but the effort was to no avail. With a choking cry, Anne fell onto the bed, Hugh atop her.

20

For a long while, Niall watched the tower, studying the movements of the men outside, gauging where the guards were and where Anne was likely being held. The room at the top of the winding stone staircase was the most probable spot, the only means of escape back down those stairs. Even if he managed to reach her, they could well end up trapped in that tower room if the men outside were alerted.

Whoever had brought Anne here had planned well against any rescue. The realization filled Niall with rage. As far as he knew, only two other kinsmen besides himself knew of this old tower. Hugh, Iain, and he had spent many a summer's day here, repairing the crumbling structure. It had been a labor of love for three idealistic lads steeped in tales of the glorious deeds of brave Campbell ancestors.

But idealistic no more, Niall thought with a bitter pang. Time and cruel experience had soured those high aspirations. Soured them all, for each in his own way.

Hugh had gone mad with his unrequited ambitions and the searing betrayal and loss of his beloved Dora. Iain, at the very least, coveted Anne. And he . . . he had become so weighted with cares and responsibilities, and eaten by suspicions, that he dared trust no one.

Niall's mouth twisted at the grim irony. Two men dreamed of power and would likely stoop to anything to get it. And the other, who possessed that power, was slowly being destroyed in the battle to protect it.

Tonight, however, one of them would seal his fate. Niall would soon have his proof. Whoever's followers these were, one of them could surely be persuaded to reveal the traitor, either by money or torture. All he had to do was wait. His own men would soon arrive, and then the renegades would be easily overcome.

Niall crept forward to gain a better view. At the back of the building, covered by thickly overgrown ivy, was another door. He prayed its entrance, hidden from sight in a darkly shadowed corner beneath the stairs, had yet to be discovered.

It could serve him well when the time came. If orders had been given to kill Anne in the event of an attack, Niall could quickly gain access and fight off any guards stationed inside. Her abductor hadn't thought of everything, he wagered.

He settled behind the bracken and low shrubs growing close to the far side of the tower. By his calculations, his men were still an hour's ride away. He shifted to adjust his huge claymore more comfortably against his back and eased down to rest on his elbows.

Niall gazed up at the blackened sky for a time, a sky scattered with twinkling bits of light. How close the stars seemed here in the mountains. One could almost reach out and touch them.

Once more the remorse surged through him. He and his two cousins had lain outside just like this so many summer nights ago, watching the star-studded sky, speaking of their dreams, of kinship and honor. They had been so close then, vowing to stand beside each other in battle and life, swearing to eternal loyalty. What had happened?

A cry from high in the tower drifted to Niall's ears. He heard the men outside chuckle then settle back around the fire to talk in low, amused voices. Niall rose to a crouched position behind the shrubs.

It was Anne's voice, and the sound had been one of fear. He dared not wait a moment longer. Even if he'd have to take on the outlaws without his men, he had to go to her. Anne was in danger.

With swift, stealthy strides, Niall made his way to the ivy-covered doorway. He slashed away the obstructing leaves with his dirk, then grasped the door latch. At first it wouldn't move, age and rust binding it stiffly, but Niall's determined strength finally worked the corroded metal free. He shoved open the door.

The metal hinges creaked in the stone-muffled interior. Niall froze. Footsteps moved toward him. He slipped in, his dirk clenched in his fist.

The man's hand swung to his sword when he saw the open door, but Niall was upon him before he had a chance to shout an alarm. Two quick thrusts of his dirk, and Niall had disposed of the guard. He dragged the body into the shadowed corner and cautiously crept into the main room.

The guard seemed to be the only one on watch in the tower. Niall slipped up the narrow, winding staircase. From overhead came the sounds of a struggle, another muted feminine cry. His blood stirred hotly. Someone was harming his woman. That person would die.

He reached the door and pulled down upon the latch. It was locked from the inside. He tried the door with his shoulder, slamming into it with increasingly harder blows. The thick oak stood firm. Frustrated rage exploded within him.

Niall pounded on the unyielding wood. "Anne, open the door!" he cried in a low voice. "It's Niall, lass. Open the door. Let me in!"

He heard the sound of a slap and another strangled cry. Niall went mad. He threw himself against the door again and again, heedless of the men now pouring into the tower below.

Hugh's hands roamed over Anne, tugging at her clothes, while the weight of his body pressed down, pinning her to the bed. In rising panic, she struggled against him, flinging her head from side to side to evade his hard, wet mouth. A large hand captured her face, squeezing it viciously.

Anne fought down the surge of renewed nausea, willing her mind to remain clear. *Bide yer time, Annie girl,* she inwardly cried out against her rising fear and disgust. *Yer chance will come.*

From somewhere, she heard a strange thudding sound. She wrenched her attention from Hugh and found the source of the new noise. It was coming from the door. Someone was pounding on it!

She heard a voice, calling her name. Niall's voice! Anne grabbed for the key, tugging it free. Hugh yelped in outrage and reared back. With one hand he grasped Anne's wrist, capturing the hand that held the key. With his other, he slapped her hard across the face.

Anne gave a strangled cry. From somewhere deep within her, an instinctual feminine reflex responded. Her knee jerked up. Hugh screamed in agony and fell away.

She leaped from the bed and ran across the room, the key clenched in her fist. Fingers jerky with desperation, Anne unlocked the door and began to pull it open. A hand tangled in her hair then wrenched her backward. She lost her balance, stumbled, and fell.

Niall burst into the room. He paused to take in Anne and Hugh, then slammed the door shut and locked it. He shoved the key beneath his belt.

Hugh released Anne and backed away. Niall advanced, pulling Anne to her feet. He noted her tousled hair and the reddened imprint of Hugh's hand on her cheek. "Has he harmed ye in any other way?" he demanded softly, touching the swollen side of her face.

"Nay," she whispered.

Niall turned to Hugh. Behind them, shouts rose and pounding on the door began. Niall smiled grimly. "Ye'll die before they get to ye," he snarled at his cousin. "I won't spare yer life a second time."

"Or I yers!"

With panther quickness Hugh sprang, grabbing for the dirk Niall held in his hand. The two men grappled wildly. Hugh's foot went out to entwine about Niall's lower leg. The movement was so swift, so unexpected, that it toppled Niall.

Both men fell heavily to the floor. Niall's head struck hard. For an instant he saw stars. It was enough opportunity for Hugh. He twisted the dirk in Niall's grasp until it was pointing toward Niall's chest. Then, with all his considerable strength, he threw himself down upon Niall.

Anne screamed a warning. With all the power in his hard-muscled body, Niall managed to twist the dirk upward. Hugh fell, impaled on the blade.

For a stunned moment Niall lay there, then gently shoved his cousin off him. He sat up, cradling Hugh in his arms. Anne came to kneel beside him.

The dirk protruded from the middle of Hugh's chest. Even as they watched, the injured man turned ashen. Blood bubbled from his lips. Niall held him close, forgetting all past animosity, remembering only the boyhood friend. In the background, the hammering on the door worsened, as if it were now being battered by some kind of log.

"Why, Hugh?" Niall groaned. "Why did ye do this?"

"W-why?" Hugh whispered, his eyes already beginning to glaze. "Because I should have been chief, not ye. But no m-matter. Ye've won naught. The devil himself . . . is yet to be dealt wi—"

With a gurgle, Hugh's voice faded. His eyes rolled back in his head.

A large log shattered the door, splintering its way halfway through the wood. Anne glanced from it to Niall. He seemed oblivious to the danger.

"Niall!" She shook him by the shoulder. "Hugh's dead. Let him go. His men are almost upon us!"

He lifted tormented eyes. "What?" His gaze moved to the rapidly disintegrating door. With a savage curse, Niall bolted to his feet and reached for his claymore. He grabbed Anne, shoving her toward the nearest corner.

"I'll try to fight them back out of the room and down the stairs!" he shouted above the rising din. "Stay close behind me. If there's a chance for ye to get out of the tower, run and don't look back. My men are on their way."

"I won't leave ye!"

"Ye will!" He moved into a fighting stance, his two hands gripped about his sword. "I command it!"

Though Anne's lips tightened in a mutinous line, she knew it wasn't the time to argue. What Niall needed from her now was help, not hindrance. With a sickening crash, the door gave way.

The outlaws spilled into the room. They formed a half circle before Niall, two men deep. Slowly, they moved forward. Niall was forced to back into the corner to keep any from slipping behind him.

"Surrender while ye can," he growled. "Even now, my men draw near."

"Surrender?" a large, burly man at the forefront echoed. "To what? We've naught to lose but our lives. Ye took all else away when ye named us outlaws. And I, for one, want a taste of yer blood before I die!"

He sprang at Niall with a fierce cry, and the others surged forward behind him. Niall met them with the solid length of his claymore, cutting down the burly leader in a few quick strokes. The rest fell back to a more respectful distance, eyeing Niall's sword.

He took advantage of their hesitation. He advanced. Slowly, doggedly, he battled his way across the room, forcing the pack of men out the door and down the stairs. Anne followed.

For a considerable time Niall fought with effortless strength. Eventually, though, the weight and length of his giant sword, as well as the cramped confines of the staircase that hampered its full effectiveness, began to wear him down. His movements slowed. His reactions became sluggish. More and more frequently, the outlaws were able to leave their mark upon him.

‡ ‡

Though he only fought one or two men at a time, as he backed them all down the steep, narrow stairway, Niall began to bleed from several minor wounds. His chest heaved with the strain of his exertions. The sweat rolled down his face and soaked the shirt to his back.

Hiding behind him, Anne sought desperately for some way to help. He couldn't go on much longer before someone caught him in a false move and delivered a disabling if not fatal blow. She needed a weapon.

Gingerly, Anne climbed over the next man Niall cut down, then bent to pry his fingers from his sword. It was a short sword, similar to the ones with which she had been trained. Feeling more useful now, Anne followed Niall down the stairs.

Time lost its meaning as Niall hacked his way to the first floor. His arms felt like lead weights. Every blow he parried now vibrated excruciatingly up his arms. He knew he couldn't fight much longer. Though three men lay dead or dying behind him, four more fought or waited to fight him still.

The tower's doorway loomed like some gateway to heaven. Still, he knew he dared not leave the confines of the tower. To do so would allow his attackers opportunity to come at him from all sides. If he could just hold them at the doorway . . .

A movement at the door caught his eye. In an instant slowed in time, Niall saw a crossbow lifted to a shoulder—and aimed directly at his heart. With a hoarse cry, Niall lunged aside, shoving Anne along with him. The quarrel flew by, missing him by a hairsbreadth.

The outlaw nearest Niall took advantage of his opponent's lowered guard. He sprang forward, his blade slashing into Niall's sword arm. Niall tried to recover, to raise his claymore to parry the second thrust, but his badly wounded arm was unequal to the task. His attacker's sword drove home, this time into Niall's thigh.

He sank to his knees, his weapon clattering to the floor. The man stepped forward. His sword lifted to deliver the killing blow.

✣✣

"Cruachan!" Anne screamed and leaped in front of Niall. With all her strength, she thrust her sword into the outlaw's belly.

He halted, his arm frozen in its arcing descent. The man looked down stupidly. Then, with a choking cry, he fell.

From down the hill, an answering Campbell battle cry rose from the darkness. The remaining men hesitated, then turned and fled. The pounding of hoofbeats grew louder. Shouts, mingled with screams, filled the air.

Anne ran to the doorway. A familiar face rode by. She sagged in relief. It was over.

Turning, she went back to where Niall lay bleeding on the floor.

✦

It took several hours before Niall was strong enough to travel after the cauterization of his deep arm and thigh wounds. He still insisted, however, on returning to Kilchurn on his own horse, Anne clasped securely before him.

"Why did ye leave?" he whispered into the fragrant tumble of her hair after a time of silent riding down the road. "Do ye know what it did to me, to have ye desert me in my greatest hour of need?"

Anne glanced back at him, her cheek grazing his lips. "I left to save ye from further danger, danger that was mounting against ye because of me. I couldn't stand by and watch ye fall, knowing I was the cause." She choked back a little sob. "And, even after the events of this night, how has aught changed? Now Hugh's death will be added to yer wrongs, for once again I was at fault."

"Nay," Niall replied gruffly. "Hugh was but a pawn manipulated, I'd wager, by the traitor. Ye heard him say I still had the devil himself to deal with. The traitor must have used Hugh to further his foul means, just as he did Nelly. But no more. We took several of the outlaws prisoner. I'll get the truth from them now." He chuckled grimly. "And I've Iain just where I want him as well.

When I discovered he was involved in helping ye leave, I threw him in the dungeon."

"But it wasn't Iain's fault," Anne said. "I went to him, begged him to help me. He never had any intent of abducting—"

"Who else but Iain knew of yer leaving Kilchurn? And who else wanted ye for himself?"

"Nay, ye're wrong," she countered stubbornly. "Think about it, Niall. If it was truly Iain's plot to steal me away for himself, he'd have never involved Hugh. Iain knew of Hugh's hatred for me. Yet he stayed behind at Kilchurn. Nay, Iain wouldn't have taken me this way."

"Yer words have merit." Niall sighed. "But if so, who *was* behind the scenes, playing Hugh in such a blackhearted way? The traitor—"

Anne twisted in his arms to glare back at him. "Ye're wrong, Niall Campbell, if ye still think it's Iain!"

A wry grin twisted his lips. "Ever the loyal friend, eh, Annie? Well, we'll find out soon enough now. Until then, I must consider all possibilities. Even Iain."

"And I say I'm no fool! I can look into a man's heart and see what's truly there. How else would I have put up with a pigheaded dolt like ye for so long?"

His big chest rumbled with a chuckle. "A pigheaded dolt, am I? So, we're back to that again? Fine gratitude, indeed, for saving yer life."

Anne smiled and slipped her arm about Niall's waist. "Aye, m'lord. It's why I love ye, I suppose."

"And I love ye, lass." His expression grew solemn. "When this is over and settled, I want to take ye as wife. Will ye have me as husband?"

She stared up at him, not quite believing her ears. "Ye wish to wed me?"

"Aye."

Anne laid her head back upon his chest, snuggling against him.

"I'd like that, verra much indeed." She gave a small, pensive sigh. "If only the traitor would let that be . . ."

The darkness hid the tense, anxious look that passed across Niall's rugged features. "Aye, my love. But that fight, I fear, has yet to be won."

✦

"So, he persists in flaunting the MacGregor wench before us," Duncan growled. "No matter. With this last, foolish effort, the Campbell has sealed his fate."

"Aye, that he has," Malcolm snarled beside him. "And this time he won't win."

Iain glanced at the two men, then back down from the castle parapets to the party of riders drawing up before the closed gates. It was dawn, and the first faint rays of light were just filtering over the distant horizon.

He had been free of the dungeon, thanks to his father, from the moment a force of Niall's men had ridden out to reinforce their leader in his rescue of Anne. And, in those hours since, the Campbell tanist and his half brother had worked to convince him that Niall Campbell was no longer fit to rule the clan.

It had been a relatively simple task. Iain's anger and disgust at Niall's judgments of late, most particularly when they dealt with Anne, had finally come to a head when his cousin had confronted him in his bedchamber. He didn't understand the man anymore, much less respect him. And Iain could never follow someone he didn't respect.

"He isn't fit to lead our clan," his father said. "Surely ye can see it now? His power has gone to his head. He's crazed with it. Why else would he turn first against Hugh, then ye, accusing ye both of treason? It's a surprise he even named me tanist, as close in the family as I am to him. I can only surmise he chose me because I'm old and no threat to him, as ye and Hugh's youth are."

"Hugh's mad, Father," Iain replied. "I can well understand why Niall banished him. He tried to kill Anne."

As he should've banished ye and Malcolm, too, Iain silently added. *For that, more than anything else, I fault Niall. For not avenging the insult to Anne for yer attempt to burn her at the stake. For his willingness to subject her yet again to repeated danger. Once more, though, I see that I must take matters into my own hands. As I will, just as soon as Niall's removed from power.*

"Aye, mayhap ye're right about Hugh, but I still don't understand why he turned against ye," his father intruded just then into Iain's thoughts. "Niall's mad, I tell ye. As mad as Hugh, in his own way. For the clan's sake, if naught else, we must unseat him before he drags us all down to destruction."

Iain grimly nodded his assent. There was far too much awry of late, but whether it stemmed solely from Niall's strange behavior, or additionally from another source, wasn't the issue just now.

Still, as he watched Niall's party halt before Kilchurn's gate, a niggling question again eased to the forefront of his mind. How had the outlaws known of Anne's departure and eventual destination, to be waiting for them on the road? He had told no one.

✦

"Ho, guard!" Niall reined in his stallion just shy of the drawbridge. "Open the gates!"

Duncan leaned forward between the crenellated wall. "Nay, nephew, that cannot be! Or leastwise not until ye renounce yer right to the chieftainship. Ye're no longer fit to be the Campbell!"

Niall's grip tightened around Anne. "Curse him," he muttered. "What's Duncan's game?"

Anne's glance swung to where the three men waited. "I don't know, but Malcolm and Iain stand with him. Surely Iain isn't party to this."

"Ye think not? Mayhap there has been more than one traitor all along—and they're my uncle and two remaining cousins."

"Och, Niall! What will ye do?"

"I've no choice. I cannot reenter my own castle now unless they send out a champion to fight me."

She gripped his arm. "Nay, ye can't! Ye're injured. Ye've ridden all night without sleep. The man would kill ye!"

He shot her a roguish grin. "Have ye so little faith in my warrior's abilities? Did I not, with only a wee bit of aid from ye, hold off seven men until help arrived? The stakes are different now, but just as high. I can do it again. I have to."

Niall turned back to the parapets. "I claim right to do battle for the chieftainship!" he shouted in clear, ringing tones. "Send out yer champion!"

✦

Iain exchanged a glance with his father. "Ye misjudged Niall, if ye thought he'd give up easily."

Duncan shrugged. "Did I? By the looks of him, he's tired and sorely wounded. Killing him won't be such a difficult task for a man such as ye. Go down, Iain. In the condition he's in, ye're his match and more. Once Niall's dead, I'll name ye my tanist. And ye can have his woman in the bargain."

His son's gaze narrowed. "I thought ye hated Anne and believed her a witch. Why would ye now offer her to me?"

"Aye, brother," Malcolm heatedly interjected. "That wasn't part of the—"

"She's no more a witch than ye or I," Duncan replied, raising a hand to silence the preacher, "but I dared not disobey the law. However, since the royal envoy already confided to me there was no case against the lady, I've little problem now with giving her to Iain."

He turned to his son. "Ye do want her, don't ye, lad?"

Iain stared down from the parapets, his eyes seeking out Anne possessively clasped in Niall's arms. "Aye, I want her," he admitted softly. "But she loves Niall and would never have me the way I want her. Nay," Iain finished, his deep voice raw with emotion, "I'll fight

Niall for her safety and for the clan. But not to have Anne. If I kill him, she'll never be friend to me again."

"It's for the best, at any rate." Duncan gripped his son's arm. "Have a care how ye fight Niall. Work to tire him and wait for yer opening. Give no quarter for he'll give none, not for a cause such as this. One mistake and, wounded as he is, he could well kill ye."

Iain jerked away. "Ye needn't lecture me on battle techniques. I'm well aware of Niall's prowess with the claymore. I know the fight could go either way."

"Go then," his father said, "and don't fail me."

As Iain strode away, he heard his father bellow down to Niall that his champion would soon meet him. His long strides carried him to his bedchamber, where he quickly girded himself with his own claymore, while keeping a firm rein on his emotions. There was no time left for doubts. No time to ponder the turn of events that had led to this moment—a battle to the death with his cousin and boyhood friend. Yet as strong a hold as Iain kept on his feelings, he couldn't help but wonder if something outside them all hadn't driven them to this sad course of events.

It was an uneasy, sickening feeling, but it crept back to haunt him again and again as he strode through the castle to the outer gate. He, Hugh, Niall, and Anne. All driven, all manipulated, but why? And by whom?

Kilchurn's gates swung open. Iain walked through, claymore in hand. At the sight of him, Niall cursed softly. Anne gave a small cry.

She grabbed his arm. "Nay, Niall. Not Iain. I beg ye. Don't fight Iain!"

He swung to face her, his eyes blazing pits of fire. "By mountain and sea, woman! I didn't choose to fight him. He decided that! Accept it, once and for all. He's the traitor. And accept the fact ye must finally choose between us!"

Niall advanced toward Iain. "Ye've dreamt of this day, this verra moment, for a long while now." He raised his sword before him. "Come, cousin. Let us do battle, and I'll show ye the fate of traitors!"

Iain glared back at him. "I'm not a traitor! Yer own arrogance has brought ye to this day!"

"Then let my arrogance win it for me!" Niall declared, swinging his sword.

His opponent moved quickly to parry the blow. The metallic clang of weapons meeting, the grunts of two men straining with all their might to overcome the other, filled the air. Back and forth they thrust and hacked as the minutes ticked by with lumbering slowness.

Sweat beaded Niall's brow. His recent wounds tore open to brightly stain his bandages, and he soon began to tire. Iain worked him around the battle area, quickly settling into a defensive posture in an effort to conserve his own strength while draining Niall of his.

Niall's hard-driving offense required more power and effort, but Anne knew it was the only tactic he dared use. He must overcome Iain before his strength was exhausted, ebbing away as inexorably as the blood now streaming from his wounds. It was a dangerous ploy, yet the only one he dared use.

The gamble paid off. Iain, once more inching back from a particularly vicious onslaught, stumbled over a rock jutting from the ground at an odd angle. He lost his balance. Niall took quick advantage and slammed into him.

Iain fell, his weapon still clenched in his hand. As he hit the ground, Niall lifted his sword to deliver the fatal blow. "Die, ye craven coward! Die the traitor's death ye've earned!"

"Nay!" Anne screamed, and flung herself onto Niall's sword arm. "Don't do this. I beg ye!"

Disbelief twisted his features. "Ye'd beg for his life, knowing he meant to kill me? Get out of my way, Anne! I won't have ye shame me by begging for him before all."

"And would ye rather live with the shame of knowing ye killed an innocent man?"

"What would ye have me do? Allow him to fight me again? Who would ye rather sacrifice? Iain or me?"

"He isn't a traitor!"

Something hardened in Niall. "And if ye're wrong, I could well die. Do ye wish to take that chance? Choose, and choose now, Anne."

"I don't want either of ye to die!" she cried. "I love ye, Niall. Ye're everything to me. But I can't condemn an innocent man to death because of that love. I can't; I won't choose."

He stared at her, his eyes gone suddenly bleak. "Then I'll choose for ye." Niall sighed, the sound weary and defeated. "I only hope ye can live with that decision."

He stepped back, motioning for Iain to rise. "Come, cousin." He lowered his sword to his side. "Anne claims ye're no traitor. Prove the truth of it to her—and me."

The younger man climbed to his feet, his blue eyes narrowed in suspicion. He lifted his sword to Niall's chest. Niall didn't move.

Confusion furrowed Iain's brow. He glanced at Anne.

Fear, stark and vivid, glittered in her eyes. "Iain, please. I trusted ye. I've always been yer friend. Don't do it."

He turned back to Niall, his sword falling to the ground. "I can no more hurt her by killing ye," he whispered thickly, "than ye can by killing me."

The claymore was resheathed in the scabbard hanging at his back. "And Anne's right. I'm no traitor!"

"Then who?" Niall rasped. "Who *is* the traitor?"

"Kill him!" Duncan roared from his perch high on the walls. "It's past time for the misfortunes of our family to be righted, for the chieftainship to pass into our hands. Kill him, Iain, and the chieftainship will finally be ours!"

Three pairs of eyes turned to gaze up at the Campbell tanist, the truth of Duncan's treachery filling each with horror. And, all the while, the man raved down at them.

"Kill him!" he screamed. "None will follow him anymore, not with that MacGregor witch at his side! I've seen to that. We've got MacGregor lands. We've weakened them with the feud I've stirred all these years. We can soon have it all. Don't fail me like Hugh and Nelly did. Ye're my son, Iain. Ye'll be chief someday. Kill the arrogant fool. Be done with it!"

Iain shook his head. "Nay, Father!" he shouted back. "Ye're the one who has failed us all. Ye've shamed our family with yer treachery. I'll have no part of it!"

"Then die, as will the witch and her consort!" A crossbow appeared in Duncan's hands.

"Get down, Iain!" Niall cried, pulling Anne behind him.

The crossbow glinted in the early morning sun, aimed straight at the Campbell chief. Something flashed. With a cry, Iain flung himself in front of Niall. A quarrel sunk deep into his chest.

He fell. Anne screamed and fought to go to him. Niall held her firmly behind him.

High on the parapets, swords gleamed as clansmen rushed to halt the tanist, slashing up and down until blood streamed from their razor-sharp blades. Duncan's voice rose, screeching in agony, then faded with a strangled cry.

"Kill him! Kill him! Kill hi—"

21

Anne watched Iain being carried off to his bedchamber, then turned to Niall. "It's past time I look at yer wounds. After yer battle, they're sure to need tending."

"Shouldn't ye see to Iain first?" he asked. "He's hurt worse than I, and the physician may need help removing the quarrel."

She arched a quizzical brow. "I didn't think ye'd want me near him."

He studied her for a moment in thoughtful silence. "I was wrong about him."

"Tell Iain that, not me," Anne shot back, a ripple of anger in her voice.

Niall sighed. "I will, have no fear. But I wanted ye to know too. I've been wrong about so much these past few months. I trusted no one, not even ye at times."

"I know."

Anne forced the tension to ease. It wasn't Niall she was angry with, not really. They were all on edge after the violence of the past night and today's confrontation outside the castle. But what if he were also saying he had erred in his feelings for her? It was foolish to ask, but she needed to know.

Her eyes lowered. "And were ye also wrong in loving me?"

Niall lifted her chin. "Nay, never that, lass." A fierce tenderness smoldered in his eyes. "Never that." He hesitated. "Would ye like to go to Iain? See to his proper tending?"

She smiled and nodded. "Aye, for a wee bit of time, if ye will. The quarrel missed any vital organs, but I'd like to see Iain's wound properly cleansed and dressed so it won't fester."

Niall motioned her forward. "Then go, lass. I'll be here when ye return."

Love flared in her eyes. Then, gathering her skirts, Anne hurried off.

Murdoch had just finished removing the quarrel from Iain's chest. Anne found her friend in bed, pale and pain-wracked, his eyes clamped shut. She knelt and took his clenched hand in hers. Gently, she pried open his long, strong fingers, then moistened a cloth and wiped his sweat-damp brow.

Iain's lids fluttered open. Eyes, as blue as Loch Awe on a summer's day, gazed up at her. "Ye shouldn't see me like this."

"And what do I see," she countered softly, "but a verra braw man? It was wonderful what ye did for Niall, putting yerself between him and the crossbow."

He smiled wanly. "I couldn't betray yer trust. Ye've never failed to champion me, even in the darkest moments." Iain's mouth twitched in self-disgust. "Even when I unwittingly failed ye and sent ye into a greater danger than Niall ever did."

She put a gentle finger to his lips. "Hush, Iain. Save yer strength. It's of no import anymore. Let us tend yer wound."

"Nay, a moment more, lass." Iain caught her hand. "Let me say what I must. Only then will it be truly over."

"Then tell me."

He dragged in a steadying breath. "I should've guessed it was my father who was behind all of this. Long have I known he coveted the chieftainship. I just never thought him capable of such cold-hearted murder and treachery." Iain shook his head in disbelief. "Och, what a fool I was!"

"Don't blame yerself, my friend. He fooled us all. He'd had years to plot and plan, from the beginning of the feud until now. And he was such a clever man. He knew how to turn the weaknesses of others to his own gain." Anne stroked Iain's cheek. "But he'd no power over strength. Our friendship saw us through."

"Aye," Iain agreed gruffly. "Our friendship and the love between ye and Niall. I only hope to find such a love some day." He grinned wryly. "One that's equally returned, of course."

Anne laughed. "And are ye trying to tell me, Iain Campbell, that no lass has ever fallen in love with ye? Why, ye're one of the handsomest Highlanders I've ever set eyes on."

His grin faded to a sad wistfulness. "There's never been a lass like ye, Anne MacGregor."

"But there will, Iain," she whispered fervently, moved by the tenderness of his gaze. "One who's my match, and more. One who's truly worthy of a man as braw and good as ye. Now, not another word," she said, rising to her feet. "It's time to see to yer injury. I can't tarry here all day. Niall's wounds need tending too."

A dark blond brow quirked in surprise. "He let ye come to me first?"

"He *sent* me to ye."

"I hope we can someday be friends again." Iain sighed. "We were once, ye know. The best of friends."

"And ye will again. But I think the course of yer friendship will depend more upon ye than Niall."

"Och, and how so?"

"Niall's a proud man. He'll feel awkward around ye for a time, imagine he's not worthy of yer acceptance or forgiveness."

Iain's expression darkened. "As well he should. He was unreasonable and arrogant."

"Aye." Anne nodded. "But he also knew, from the day my clan captured him, that a traitor was involved. Right or wrong, he suspected it was ye. So, he couldn't verra well confide in ye, and yer attentions to me were so easily misinterpreted in light of those suspicions. Niall thought ye were using me in some way to further yer plotting."

Iain frowned in thought. "It explains many things." He met her gaze. "I'll talk with him. In time, we'll work out the problems between us."

"Good. I grow weary, ye know, of being the peacemaker between ye." Anne paused to signal Murdoch. "Come now; let's see to Iain's wound."

The old physician nodded and shuffled over.

◆

It was a glorious late July day. Sparrow hawks and golden eagles soared overhead, their hoarse screams rending the deep summer silence. The purple-pink heather was just beginning to bloom on the hills. Fragrant lavender, growing along the sides of the road, perfumed the air with its delicate scent.

As their party rode along, Anne's gaze swept the familiar landscape. The scene stirred a memory of that day, now nearly three months past, when she had ridden the opposite way toward Campbell lands. Then she had been handfasted to a man she despised, her life in a shambles.

Now she was going home to MacGregor land, if home could ever again be anywhere Niall wasn't. She glanced at him. His attention was momentarily diverted as he spoke with Iain, who rode beside him. Anne's eyes softened with love.

He had been so busy in the past month since Hugh's and Duncan's deaths. The queen had accepted the royal envoy's findings. All charges against Niall had been dropped.

Once Hugh's and Duncan's funerals were over and the two men properly buried, Niall had lost no time in banishing Malcolm from Campbell lands. The preacher had been escorted away, unrepentant to the end, raving about witchcraft and Anne's guilt.

In the long days Niall and Iain both spent recuperating from their wounds, Anne had begun Caitlin's lessons in the healing art. The ebony-haired girl was an apt pupil, showing a real talent for the craft. Slowly, as she gained confidence and enthusiasm for her new skill, her love-struck preoccupation with Rory MacArthur eased.

In the time not spent with Anne learning to mix the various concoctions and potions, Caitlin talked with her brother. Anne couldn't help but laugh at Niall's surprise at the depth of his sister's maturity. She had chided him, telling him he'd have known Caitlin better if he had cared to take the time.

He had laughed and pulled her into his arms, admitting that, once again, she was right.

There was much, indeed, to be thankful for in the past days, including Niall's surprising offer to take her to Castle Gregor for a short visit. Anne knew it had been a great sacrifice on his part, to spare the time for what was essentially a frivolous journey. She was grateful and loved him even more because of it. There remained but one small doubt to nibble away at what would've been her complete happiness.

Since the night he had rescued her from Hugh's evil clutches and asked her to be his wife, Niall had never again mentioned marrying her. Anne wondered about that. After much thought, she could only find one reason for his reticence on the subject. Niall regretted the offer.

She knew she should be patient and trust that Niall would again broach the subject when the time was right. She wasn't one to nag, and would never force him to wed because of a prior offer likely made in haste. Niall would come to her willingly or not at all.

Perhaps she was foolish to doubt Niall's devotion to her. He treated her, as he had for a long while now, with all the heartfelt abandon of a man in love. If only, Anne sighed, as she redirected her attention to the road ahead, he would seal that love with the final commitment of marriage vows.

As they neared the village of Glenstrae, a large crowd of peasants began to line the road. Anne turned a questioning gaze to Niall.

He grinned back. "Yer people, m'lady. Turned out to welcome ye home."

A suspicious half smile curled the corner of her mouth. "Another of yer surprises, m'lord? I wonder what else that devious mind has in store for me this day?"

"Ye'll have to wait and see, won't ye?" he drawled in reply. Niall glanced at Iain. "What say ye, tanist? Will she like what I have in store for her?"

Iain chuckled. "I don't know. She was none too pleased the last time we were here. Ye may find, cousin, ye've more trouble on yer hands than ye bargained for."

"Whatever are ye two men talking about?" Anne demanded in exasperation. "I don't like being left out of this conversation, much less yer plans."

Niall smiled. "Have patience, my love. In due time, all will be revealed."

She opened her mouth to tell him exactly what she thought of his suggestion, when a woman with a child in her arms ran forward from the crowd. It was Fiona.

"Her name's Annie," the young peasant said, lifting a fat, healthy infant up to Anne.

She took the baby in her arms and cuddled it to her. "Isn't she beautiful?" Anne asked, glancing over at Niall.

Tenderness flared in his eyes. "Aye, lass, that she is."

Anne flushed and quickly handed the baby back to its mother. "Come to the castle soon, and we'll spend more time with the bairn. I've a wish to know my namesake better."

"Aye, m'lady," Fiona agreed happily. "Why, this verra eve I'll be there for ye. The whole village is—"

"Come along, Anne." Niall took hold of her horse's reins, urging her on. "Time enough to visit later. Yer father awaits."

Anne glanced in momentary confusion from Fiona to Niall, then nudged her mount to catch up with Niall's. "What was she talking about? Exactly what is the whole village up to?"

He shrugged. "Mayhap yer father has something special planned. We'll find out soon enough."

"Aye, I suppose we will," Anne muttered, still bewildered.

Their arrival in Castle Gregor was a joyous affair. After the usual greetings, Anne found herself bustled upstairs to her old bedchamber by Agnes and Anne's two married sisters. While all happily gossiped, her clothes were unpacked and belongings put away. Then Mary, Anne's youngest sister, brought out a gown of shimmering ivory silk. Its neckline was a simple, rounded scoop edged with the finest lace, the sleeves long and snug, the dress fitted in bosom and waist before flaring gently to the floor.

"It was Mither's," Mary offered, her voice choked with memories. "We'd like ye to wear it today, in honor of an end to the feud and the joining of our clans."

"Och, but it's too beautiful for a simple feast," Anne said.

"But ye'll wear it, nonetheless." Agnes stepped forward and began unfastening Anne's traveling gown. "Ye won't begin yer visit here by hurting feelings. Yer sisters wish for ye to wear it, and wear it ye shall."

Anne protested no more. She allowed herself to be undressed and bathed before donning the beautiful gown. The MacGregor tartan was then draped over her shoulder and fastened with the clan brooch. Her hair was brushed until it gleamed and fastened away from her face in a simple, feminine fashion, allowing the thick mass of russet curls to tumble about her shoulders and down her back.

Finally, as the sun slid behind the mountains, Agnes stepped back to admire their handiwork. "Ye're so beautiful, m'lady," she whispered.

Anne smiled at her loyal maidservant. "Only because ye've made me look so."

A firm knock sounded at the door. Anne's sisters were suddenly in a flutter. She cocked a quizzical brow and hurried to open the door.

Niall stood there, grinning back at her. He was dressed in his belted plaid, a snowy-white shirt beneath, a blue bonnet bearing the three eagle feathers denoting his rank as clan chief perched rakishly atop his ebony hair. He looked the picture of a Highland warrior, full of barely restrained power and masculine vitality. *A fine, braw Highland warrior,* Anne thought with a surge of pride, *and mine.*

Niall offered his arm. "Come, m'lady."

She eyed him warily. "What are ye about? It's a half hour before the feasting begins."

"We go to see yer father. We've a few things unfinished to discuss."

Anne placed her hand on his arm. "As ye wish, m'lord."

Alastair MacGregor, dressed as well in full Highland regalia, awaited them in his chambers. His eyes softened when he saw Anne. He walked to her and placed his hands on her shoulders.

"Ye look so like yer sainted mither in that dress. I'm proud of ye, lassie." His glance momentarily strayed to Niall. "Have ye found happiness with the Campbell?" Alastair's piercing gaze returned to her. "Did I do well in giving ye to him?"

Anne looked to Niall. A soft smile curved her lips. In spite of it all, in spite of the lingering doubts she had about the depth of Niall's commitment, she was content. She loved him with all her heart, and would stay with him for the full length of their handfasting. After that . . . well, it was still a time away and, God willing, mayhap by then even that last little misgiving would finally be eased.

She turned back to her father. "Aye, I'm happy with him. Ye did well, Father."

"Good. Then I grant him his request." He faced Niall. "Ye may take my Annie as wife."

"Wife?" Anne's grip tightened on Niall's arm. "Ye want me as wife?"

"Didn't I already ask ye that? Why would I have changed my mind?"

She flushed, not quite able to meet his gaze. "I . . . Ye never spoke of it since. I wasn't sure . . ."

"There were preparations to be made, and I wanted to surprise ye." Niall took her chin and lifted her gaze to meet his. "I thought ye'd like being wed here, where it all began with our handfasting."

"Here? When?"

"Today, my love. In but a few moments more."

"Och, Niall!" A lump formed in her throat.

"But first, I've a small wedding gift for ye." He motioned for her to follow him to her father's huge desk, then unrolled a large parchment scroll.

She frowned. "What's this?"

"The grant deeding MacGregor lands to Clan Campbell. I wish to give them back as my wedding gift."

Hot tears flooded Anne's eyes and spilled down her cheeks. "Thank ye," she whispered.

Niall rerolled it, then handed it to the MacGregor for safekeeping. He once more offered her his arm. "It's time for a wedding, m'lady."

Anne smiled up at him, all the love in her heart shining in that single glance. "Aye, m'lord."

With Alastair following, he led her from her father's chambers and down the long, stone corridors to her clan's Great Hall. They paused at the head of the stairs to gaze down on a room lavishly decorated with pine and heather, ribbons of crimson, green, and white interwoven among the branches. In the deepening twilight, hundreds of candles illuminated the huge chamber, casting a soft glow upon all the faces gazing up at them.

Iain was there, good friend and true, smiling his encouragement. Caitlin, Agnes, and Anne's sisters stood around him, tears of joy in their eyes. And, in the mass of people, Anne saw Fiona and Donald with little Annie proudly cradled in her father's arms. At that moment the babe gurgled loudly.

Niall chuckled. "That's a bonny babe ye helped birth, lassie. May ours someday be as lively and healthy."

A small, mischievous giggle escaped Anne.

Tawny brown eyes shifted back to her. "And, pray, what's so amusing?"

She tossed her head. "Och, naught, m'lord, save that babes can be verra noisy and demanding. And, with parents such as we—a rumored witch and a wolf, no less—ye may well come to rue those braw words."

"Well," Niall remarked with feigned casualness, "the wolf part doesn't overly concern me, and as for my wife being thought a witch . . . well, I've always said a spirited filly, if gentled well, is of greater value than some plodding nag."

Anne scowled in mock outrage. "And there ye go again, Niall Campbell, comparing me to a horse!"

He threw back his head and gave a shout of laughter. Then, to the accompaniment of the wailing bagpipes and arm in arm with the man she loved, Anne MacGregor, Child of the Mist, went down to her wedding.

Dear Readers,

Well, I hope you enjoyed *Child of the Mist*, the first book in the These Highland Hills series. As always, I put Anne and Niall through some tough times, but, as always, their love for and faith in the Lord—and their love for each other—pulled them through. I'm considering doing Iain's story next. Let me know what you think about that idea. The second book in this series (I'm still tossing around several titles) will be coming next spring. Watch my website for updates on that release.

There's more exciting news as well, as you will gather when you read the excerpt that follows this letter. Beginning this summer, I'll be releasing another series entitled Guardians of Gadiel. This one's a fantasy series along the lines of Lord of the Rings. The first book, currently entitled *Giver of Roses* (due in stores August 2005), is the tale of a good man called to a higher, more heroic destiny, a woman whose life inexorably entwines with his, and a land teetering on the brink of unremitting evil. Only a holy quest can save them all, but the journey demands a courage—and love—the like of which transcends life itself.

For those of you who've never read a fantasy, I think you might be pleasantly surprised. I love fantasies because they are a wonderful kind of storytelling that offers a unique way of dealing with today's concerns. In a distant time and place, one can frequently see things with a clearer perspective. Consider these thoughts from Frederick Buechner in "The Gospel as Fairy Tale," from *The Chris-*

✝ ✝

tian Imagination: The Practice of Faith in Literature and Writing, edited by Leland Ryken, which, for me, epitomize the appeal of fantasy fiction:

> What gives them their real power and meaning is the world they evoke. It is a world of magic and mystery, of deep darkness and flickering starlight. It is a world where terrible things happen and wonderful things too. It is a world where goodness is pitted against evil, love against hate, order against chaos, in a great struggle where often it is hard to be sure who belongs to which side because appearances are endlessly deceptive. Yet for all its confusion and wildness, it is a world where the battle goes ultimately to the good, who live happily ever after, and where in the long run everybody, good and evil alike, becomes known by his true name.

I had so much fun creating this world, its peoples, cultures, history, flora and fauna, and language. In the end, though, as are all my books, *Giver of Roses* is a tale of the only story worth telling—the story of sin and redemption. The story of God's great and merciful love. The story of people, with all their hopes, dreams, joys, sorrows, losses, and human failings, struggling to live with courage, honor, and decency, saved, in the end, by the redeeming power of love.

A more extensive excerpt of *Giver of Roses* and all my other previously published books are available on my website at www.kathleenmorgan.com. And I'm always happy to hear from readers. To be included on a mailing list for updates on future books, email me through my website.

Blessings,

Kathleen Morgan

February 2005

Giver of Roses

Vartan Karayan, crown prince of the besieged city of Astara, has been challenged to a fight to the death by Ladon, the reputably invincible minion of the dark lord of the underworld. In this scene, Danae, one of Vartan's servants, contemplates the battle to be played out the next day, and what she fears will be its tragic outcome.

"He fills your thoughts more than ever, doesn't he?" A voice softly intruded on Danae's pensive musings. "But indeed, he fills all our thoughts, today, this most tragic of days."

Hot blood flooding her cheeks, Danae jerked around to find Vartan's younger sister, Zagiri, standing beside the fountain. The water's soft music, she realized, must have muted the sound of the other woman's approach. Danae rose to her feet.

"I—I don't know what you're talking about," she stammered, a response she instantly knew sounded stupid and false. Still, it took a moment under Zagiri's steady, compassionate gaze before she finally relented. "Well, aye, I suppose I am thinking of Vartan. It's just so cruel, so unfair . . ." Her eyes began to sting, and Danae flushed all the more. "I'm sorry," she mumbled, glancing down to hide the tears. "It's just that . . . just that he's always been so good to me . . ."

"I know. I understand . . . more than you might realize."

Slender and of medium height like Danae, thirty-year-old Zagiri had a pleasant face, smooth, pink cheeks, and a gentle mouth.

She wore her wavy, dark brown hair cut short and was always garbed, despite her regal status, in a rather shapeless, hooded, long brown robe. Considered cursed with a strange sort of madness—she mouthed prophecies that never made sense—the middle child of the royal siblings had always treated Danae kindly, in time even becoming her spiritual mentor.

She gestured to the bench Danae had just vacated. "Let's sit. We've things to speak of. Important things, like how only you can now aid my brother."

Danae all but fell back onto the bench. "Aid Vartan? How?"

Zagiri walked over and took a seat beside her. "How else," she asked, her voice low and melodious, "but to teach him of Athan and His precious Son, Eisa? Then, though Vartan may die, he'll live."

Of course, Danae thought. To accept the All-Knowing, the Creator, into one's heart was to gain immortality in the Afterlife. And, according to Zagiri, Vartan was not and never had been one of the Faithful.

"I would do that, and gladly," she said, "but what could I say, as unschooled as I still am in the ways of Athan, when all your efforts have failed? Especially now, when there's so little time left?"

"We're all instruments in Athan's hands. Some He uses for one task, and some are meant for others. You're called to aid my brother in the hard times to come. I must mouth prophecies no one of House Karayan or the city of Astara believes."

"Well, I believe them!"

Zagiri smiled. "But then, you aren't of House Karayan or of Astara, are you?"

Danae grinned. "Nay, I'm not."

"Yet, since you do believe, I've one last prophecy to share with you." She paused, closed her eyes for a moment, then turned the full force of her striking sea-blue gaze—eyes Danae had long ago noted were the same shade as her oldest brother's—on her. "It's not of my making, mind you, but it's past time you know of whom this prophecy speaks."

"And what exactly is this prophecy?"

“Listen closely, dear friend,” Zagiri said, drawing even nearer and dropping her voice. “I dare not utter it too loudly in these troubled times, for fear some unholy creature might overhear and seek to put an end to it before it can be fulfilled.”

“Is that possible?” Danae asked, frowning in puzzlement. “To prevent some divinely inspired future event?”

“Unfortunately, aye, if the instruments are unwilling or choose the wrong path.” She smiled sadly. “It’s the one variable in the Divine plan. Our right—one of Athan’s greatest and most loving gifts—to refuse Him.”

Zagiri took Danae’s hand. “Now, listen . . . and hear with the ears of your heart.”

Desperate times
Death and destruction.
The Guardian returns,
Blind to his destiny.

Evil breaks free,
A land lost in shadows.
The Guardian returns,
From ruin to rebirth.

All praise to the Son
Whose marks he now carries.
The Guardian returns,
His hands filled with roses.

“It comes from the Song of the Ancients,” Vartan’s sister, after a brief pause, explained. “This Prophecy of prophecies.”

Along with The Covenant of Athan, the Song of the Ancients was one of the Faithfuls’ two most sacred books. Danae’s mouth quirked. “It must be well into that holy tome, then, for I’ve yet to study it. But what do those verses mean? What are the marks this Guardian carries? And what does this person hope to do with but a handful of roses?”

“I’ve yet to discern the true significance of the marks,” Zagiri replied, “though I have my suspicions. The Guardian, however, is meant to save Gadiel. And the blue rose has always been the sacred flower of the land, symbolic of truth, unity, and a pure, loving heart. Those who go in peace must always carry blue roses. But, over the centuries as the old Alliance fell by the wayside, and distrust and feuding grew more and more prevalent in the land, so the blue rose of Gadiel began to disappear. Now, there are few to be found anywhere.”

She had seen the blue flower encircled by a golden crown emblazoned on the white silk banners flying from various positions around the city but had never thought to ask about its significance. Now, Danae knew, understood. It was the flag of Gadiel, and the royal city of Astara had the singular honor, above all cities, to display it. There was yet one unanswered question, though.

“Why do you tell me this? Why now, when most likely I’ll be rejoined with my father and people on the morrow? What will it matter, when I’ll soon put Astara and Gadiel far behind me and return to my former life?”

“Will you, Danae? Return to your former life, I mean?” Zagiri averted her gaze, a faraway look in her eyes. “What if Athan asks you to do differently? Will you, too, refuse Him?”

“After all you’ve taught me of Athan, and how I’ve come to love Him and His Son, you know I couldn’t.” Even the consideration made her heart ache. “But what could He possibly want from me, leastwise in regards to Astara and Gadiel? I’m no hero, and certainly not the one of whom the Prophecy speaks.”

A sudden thought assailed her, and with it came a rising sense of presentiment. “Who does the Prophecy speak of, Zagiri? The one who brings the roses, who saves the land?”

A soft, enigmatic smile touched the other woman’s lips. “The giver of roses.”

“The giver of roses?”

“Aye. Vartan, of course. Didn’t you know? In the ancient tongue, his name means ‘giver of roses.’”

Kathleen Morgan has authored numerous novels for the general market and now focuses her writing on inspirational books. She has won many awards for her romance writing, including the 2002 Rose Award for Best Inspirational Romance. She lives in Colorado Springs, Colorado.

Other books by Kathleen Morgan

Brides of Culdee Creek Series

Daughter of Joy
Woman of Grace
Lady of Light
Child of Promise

Culdee Creek Christmas

All Good Gifts
The Christkindl's Gift